THE SUN ROAD

A Woman of Viking Age Iceland
seeks Love, Land and Luck

A novel by Afiena Kamminga

Produced by:

FriesenPress

Suite 300 – 852 Fort Street
Victoria, BC, Canada V8W 1H8

www.friesenpress.com

Distributed to the trade by The Ingram Book Company

In tenth century Iceland a young woman, Thora Thorvinnsdottir, orphaned at age fifteen, is out of a home and close to destitute. She decides to make the most of what she has left, assets she can count on her fingers and toes — a small flock of sheep, a splendid horse, majestic dog, a young slave of many skills, and a proud awareness of who she is, a well-born woman free to make her own decisions. Goaded by her misfortune Thora strives to fill in the gaps in the weaving pattern of her life, by using weft threads of her own choice to intertwine with the warp threads arranged by the Norns, those fickle-minded maidens of fate. Set on a road of self-determination unusual for her times and place in a gender-biased world, Thora sails west to the new frontier named Greenland, hoping to acquire another farm of her own. In Greenland she agrees to a marriage ill-conceived to begin with, and ill-fated in the end.

In her search for a proper place in the world she joins her husband's timber-seeking expedition across the western sea to an unexplored land rumoured to be the source of driftwood littering Greenland beaches. The land is indeed there, waiting for them, and it holds more than vast forests of prime timber. They encounter novel forms of life — plants, animals and people unknown even to the most traveled Norseman among them. The maiden Norns, living up to their whimsical reputation, grant Thora a chance to achieve the first major goal she set for herself, in a way she never imagined.

ABOUT THIS STORY

The fictional events in this novel are set around 985-988 AD, some time before the documented journeys by Norsemen to North America. Those historical journeys believed to have taken place around the year 1000 AD, are described in two sagas from Iceland, *The Saga of Greenlanders (Graenlendinga S)*, and the *Saga of Erik the Red (Eirik Rauda S)*.

Most Norse saga tales and chronicles are based on oral records of events in pre-Christian times. In the early Middle-Ages, Christian scholars preserved the old tales and chronicles of northern Europe in written form. Prominent among them were Icelandic writers, Ari Thorgilsson and Snorri Sturluson, who produced a vast body of work known as the Icelandic Sagas. Most of these stories are written in terse, straightforward prose, unlike medieval literature from other parts of Europe which is often written in verse.

For more flavour of the people and times in this novel I have placed at the chapter heads short saga quotations (after the English translations published on the Gutenberg Internet site.)

FOR MY MOTHER

WHO SHOWED ME THE JOY OF LIVING MULTIPLE LIVES
ONE NOVEL AT THE TIME

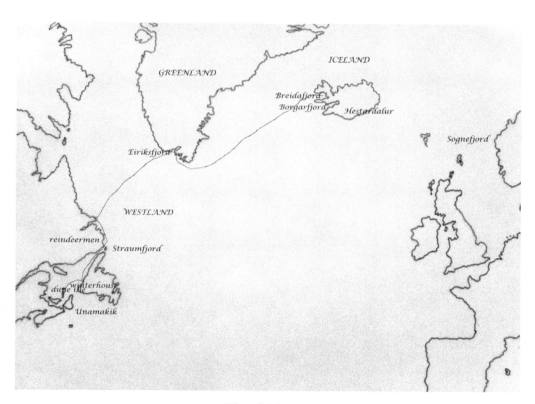

Thora's Voyage

LIST OF NAMES AND WORDS

Achren, young Irish woman slave, Ivar's bed-woman

Aegir's Pride, *knorr* skippered to Westland by Sigurd Halldurson

Agni, maid of Thora's mother, Rannveig

Akka, old woman slave born in Lappland

Arvak, younger mare

Asta Sigurdsdottir from Reykholt, widow of Asbjorn Steinson, Ulf's new bride

Atli, Icelandic *karl* sailing to Westland, brother to Hrut

Auzur, see Mord

berserkr, bear shirt, frenzied warrior

Bjarni Herjolfson, first Norse seafarer to catch sight of Westland

Brattalid, Eirik Rauda's anchoring site and homestead in Eiriksfjord, Greenland

Eidyll, house *thrall*

Eirik Rauda, master of Brattalid.

Elkimu, captured native Westlander

Father's brother Sveinar, Uncle Sveinar

Fluga, older mare

geirfugl, spearbill, giant auk, 'northern penguin', now extinct

Geysir, the 'original' geyser in Iceland

Grim, see Skeggi

Gunnhild Gormsdottir, Ulf's wife

godi, Icelandic official, priestly in early days, later secular, seeing to the proper observation of rules and ceremony

grindehval, pilot whale

Groa, woman slave, Ragnar's bedwoman

Halla, old woman slave borrowed from Thjodhild, knowledgeable about healing

Halldis, infant daughter of Gunnhild and Ulf

Hauk, son of Thurid and Sveinar

Helga Ulfsdottir, daughter of Ulf and Gunnhild

Helgi Thorlakson, Thurid's son by her first husband

Herjolf and Gunnar, brothers from Borgarfjord, Thorvinn's creditors

Holmgard, Novgorod

Hrut, Icelandic *karl* sailing to Westland, brother to Atli

Ivar Ulfson, son of Ulf and Gunnhild

jarl, earl

Khagan, Khazar-bred herd protection dog

knorr, Norse freightship

Maelstrom Tamer, Ulf's ship carrying settlers to
Greenland/later, skippered by Ivar, to Westland

Magni Aslaksdottir, Helgi's bride to be

Miklagard, Constantinople

Mord, (and Auzur) Ragnar's nephews sailing with Ivar

Narfi, son of Thorvinn's bedwoman, Gudfinna

naust ship-house

Nifel Hel, Place of torture in the afterlife

Odi and Ottar, two brothers sailing with Maelstrom Tamer

Papar, Christian priests and monks

Ragnar Asbjornson, 'Bearbladder' Norwegian, old friend of Thorvinn's

Rannveig Asgrimsdottir, Thora's mother

rjupa, ptarmigan

Rus, Swedes and other Scandinavians active
along the Dnjepr and Volga rivers

Sandurness farm, homestead of Ulf and Gunnhild in Greenland

Sigrid Sigurdsdottir, sister of Asta

Sigurd Halldurson of Breidafjord, owner/skipper
of Aegir's Pride, also journeying to Westland

Skeggi (and Grim), Greenlanders, *karls* of Ulf, sailing with Ivar

Skjald, skald, old-Scandinavian bard

Sol, Sun, who drives her gold chariot across the sky every
day — daughter of Mundilfore, keeper of the World Mill

Surf Leaper, *knorr* skippered by Thorvinn

Thing/Althing, periodic meeting of free farmers in Iceland
to make laws and pass judgments, held in each district under
leadership of Law Speakers, prominent men esteemed for their
legal knowledge. The *Althing* for the entire nation was held
annually in Thingvellir, a natural stage near Reykjavik.

Thjodhild, Eirik Rauda's wife

Thora Thorvinnsdottir, protagonist

Thorgerd Hauksdottir, Thurid's mother

Thorvinn Haraldson, Thora's father

Thrand Leidolfson, Ragnar's Norwegian trading partner

Thurid Herjolfsdottir, wife of Sveinar

Toki, (Driftwood T) retired *thrall* crofter at Gronsetur

Ulf Thorsteinson, owner/skipper of Maelstrom
Tamer sailing to Greenland

Unna, house maid of Gunnhild

wadmal, coarse woolen homespun

warp, (in weaving) threads running lengthwise, crossed by the weft or woof

weft, (also, *woof*) the yarns carried by the shuttle
back and forth across the warp

There is an ash named Yggdrasil
sprinkled with sparkling water
The fountain of dew which blankets the dales
Ever green, arching over the well of Urd
Three maids filled with wisdom approach
From their dwelling below the tree
The first one is Urd, the second, Verdandi
And Skuld is the third
Laws they make, life they grant
To the children of men, their destiny ...
POETIC EDDA, VOLUSPA

ICELAND

In the days of Harald Harfagri (Fairhair) Iceland was settled from Norway ...at that
time..... to the reckoning of Teitr, my foster father, a person I
consider most wise, son of Bishop Isleif, ...and Thurid, daughter of
Snorri the chieftain who
was very wise and reliable....it was eight hundred and seventy winters
after the birth of Christ

ISLENDINGABOK

ONE

I knew the sons of Fitiung when they had sheep in their folds
They carry the beggar's staff now
Fortune changes in the twinkle of an eye
No friend is more fickle than wealth

EDDA, EYVIND'S SKALDASPILLER

Furious barking erupted outside. Thora dropped the cloth she had been holding to the light allowed in through the half open door. The sound of the dogs faded into the distance. The maids tried to peer out the doorway from their looms, crowded together to capture the daylight.

Thora, at fifteen winters the youngest woman on the farm, struggled to remain in charge. She frowned disapproval at her maids and waved them back to their weaving.

"I'll see to the cause of this commotion," she said. "There's no need for you to idle."

Since early summer when her father, Thorvinn, left her in charge of Hestardalur Farm, she had cultivated a snappy tone with the maids and farmhands – to good effect. The women kept working the looms, walking to and fro threading the shuttle and stealing a glance outside each time they paused to beat up the weft.

Thora squeezed past the looms, stooped under the low timbered doorway and straightened up shivering in the blustery fall wind outside. With her back to the house wall of stacked rocks and turf, she scanned the treeless hillsides, feeling anxious. Her father's absence had left her with a responsibility almost too heavy to bear. The sheep, she saw with relief, were grazing peacefully scattered across the land, not bunched together, heads up in alarm.

She looked to the farm lads out by the corrals, narrowing her eyes to follow their gaze to the rocky ridge that towered behind the farm, less than three arrow shots away. Dark shapes, a dozen or more, stood high on the ridge. She counted seven riders on fidgeting horses looking down at the valley. All of a sudden they barreled along the steep trail down to the farm, followed by free running spare horses which veered away from the path to skid straight downhill to the lush grazing below.

Thora held her breath. Who were these men? Few raiders would be bold enough to approach a large farm in clear daylight. Then again, some might do the unexpected.

At the bottom of the hill the strangers pulled up their mounts. At least they had the good manners to wait for an invitation before entering the grounds.

Thora turned to her trusted house *thrall*, Eidyll, a fleet-footed young Briton.

"Go quickly and find out their names and the purpose of their visit."

She waited, willing herself to look calm and composed. The *thrall* made his way back to the farm after a short talk, which seemed friendly enough.

"They are Gunnar Snorrisson, the 'Cross-eyed,' and his brother, Herjolf, with some neighbours and *karls*." Eidyll reported. "They have come to settle a business matter resulting from a deal they made with your father before he left for Greenland."

Thora sighed with relief. Gunnar and Herjolf were friends of her father, respected landowners and traders from the Borgarfjord district some two or three days travel from Hestardalur.

"Ask them to come to the house."

"You," she called to the maids huddled by the doorway, "bring out two benches and a table and place them against the house wall — in the sunshine, mind you."

Seated at the table, Thora spread her shift and kirtle across the bench to appear less slender and young. If only she could have had time to cover her curly brown hair in the manner of a mature married woman, the kind of woman these men would expect to find in charge of the farm.

The dogs, some of them limping, drifted into the yard ahead of the riders who walked their mounts slowly toward the corrals. Up close, Thora recognized two of the older men as Gunnar and Herjolf. They walked to the house leaving their *karls* by the corrals to relieve the saddle horses of their tack. Two others, men she had never seen before, followed the brothers.

"Welcome to Hestardalur," she said. "I am Thora Thorvinnsdottir. My father left me in charge of the farm when he went away. Friends of his are most welcome. Won't you sit down for a rest and refreshments?"

She turned to Gudrun, the eldest maid.

"Bring us fresh *skyr* from yesterday's barrel."

The men leaned their spears and shields against the house wall before they sat down to savour the drink of thick milk left to sour overnight.

"It is rare to be treated to *skyr* as mild and creamy as this," Gunnar said, licking the foam from his lips. "Best thing in the world to help weary travelers back on their feet."

He grinned at his brother.

"One knows a good housewife by the *skyr* she makes."

Thora caught sight of Herjolf frowning at his brother. *I'm imagining things*, she told herself.

Between sips, the brothers introduced themselves and their two neighbours, fellow sea-traders of good reputation. They passed on greetings and news of friends and acquaintances up their way before falling silent and holding out their mugs for refills.

One of the neighbours took a long look at the grasslands surrounding them.

"Your mother's father, Old Asgrim Egilson, chose wisely to settle his family in this place," he said to Thora. "Well-watered land with low hills on both sides protected from the worst weather..."

He gazed at the outbuildings.

"Your elders, seems to me, put a good deal of thought into the arrangement of buildings and corrals, placing the animal byres not too close to the house, and yet close enough for easy winter care."

He turned to Herjolf. "Well laid out, wouldn't you say?"

Herjolf nodded agreement.

"A first rate location you have here...much of the property appears to be fertile bottomland."

Thora smiled; she was proud of her home and farm blessed with well-watered grassland near Gullfoss gorge with its twin waterfalls.

"You have taken good care of your father's property, Thora Thorvinnsdottir," said Gunnar, a heavy set man with a middle-age bulge. He squinted at her with pale eyes. She shifted uneasily under his restless, cross-eyed glance.

"You're a credit to your father."

Thora lowered her head keeping her silence. *Only fools and ravens speak without need.*

Gunnar raised his bushy eyebrows. "You are aware I suppose that Thorvinn's Greenland voyage to Eiriksfjord has ended in disaster."

Thora's eyes widened.

"It remains to be seen, I thought."

Word had come by mid-summer from the fledgling Greenland settlement that her father and his ship full of merchandise hadn't arrived there. Since then she had heard no other news of him, good or bad. Still, it had happened before like this. Her father and plenty others seafarers like him, when faced with bad weather or other set-backs, often returned late from a summer's journey just as the winter was about to set in, or even as late as next spring. She saw no reason yet to give up hope for his safe return.

"We know nothing of the ship's fate and that of her skipper and crew," she said.

Gunnar continued to stare at her in silence.

Herjolf spoke up.

"Well, elder brother," he said, "I'll lend you the use of my tongue."

He leaned his elbows on the table and captured her gaze.

"We have come with bad tidings I fear. Men from Isafjord sent word to us with unsettling news. They found wreckage of a freight ship scattered along the shore, a ship the same size and type as Surf Leaper, the *knorr* your father set out with for Greenland. Washed up on the same stretch of coast, the folks of Isafjord found the drowned bodies of two men known to have sailed out with your father."

He leaned closer.

"No survivors were found and no cargo washed up on the beach. It can be assumed that Surf Leaper went down with all of her crew and cargo."

Thora stared at them with unseeing eyes, her ears resounding with Herjolf's ominous words. Inside her a numb, heavy feeling spread like a hefty wet bearskin smothering part of her pain, sorrow, and disbelief. She struggled to respond, seeking for words that would hide her despair from these self-assured men. The questions whirling about in her head went unspoken. *How could this be?* She had clung to the belief that her father's ship was merely blown off course, that he would return safely, though late, from an eventful journey, loaded with Greenland goods, furs, hides, tusks, young falcons and perhaps a bear cub or two. Her father was a survivor. Now, without warning, the Borgarfjord brothers had shattered her dream, snuffed out the embers of hope she kept glowing all through the summer.

She squirmed under Gunnar's mis-aligned stare.

Herjolf continued, pointing to his neighbours across the table.

"These men were witness to the agreement we made with your father. We were to provide him with a ship, cargo and crew to undertake the voyage to Greenland selling timber and iron in the new settlement of Eirik the Red. Your father, my brother and I, each agreed to a third share in the outcome. Since the ship as well as the goods and most of the crew were provided by us, your father put up security for his part."

Gunnar turned to his brother opening his mouth to interrupt, but Herjolf waved him aside.

"To come to the point — your father pledged Hestardalur farm and all that goes with it, land, livestock and *thralls*, as security in case he failed to return."

He leaned his back against the house wall.

"The sailing season is at its end. Thorvinn hasn't returned and his ship was found wrecked at Isafjord."

He pointed a thick finger at her.

"We intend to come back here, Thora Thorvinsdottir, before the first snow to take possession of what's rightfully ours."

Thora stared at the driftwood table top, oblivious of the unsightly knots in the boards which at other times caused her no end of aggravation. She fought to hold back the sobs trying to claw up inside her throat.

The men rose to their feet. Thora raised her hand, and they sat down again. Words were springing to her mind at last, one by one. She struggled, her voice sounding strained, the voice of a stranger.

"It is... good of you... to let me know... how things stand... My father will be pleased with... your conduct, should he return... before the snow."

She took a deep breath and went on more smoothly, "You've made a long journey... I suggest you rest before you ride home."

The men waved her offer aside. They rose as one, took their spears and shields from the house wall, thanked her for the kind reception and headed for their horses. Thora, ready to follow her guests to bid them farewell, paused to snap at the maids leaning against the doorway.

"Wrap those braids over your big insolent ears and clear off the table!"

All summer long she had struggled to appear strong and uncompromising, leaving no question that she, the master's young daughter and nobody else, was left in charge of both the farm and the household. Now, striding out to catch up with her visitors, she thought she could feel the maids' stares stinging her back. Never mind. Proper custom demanded she walk these men to their horses. And she, Hestardalur's mistress, would not be found lacking in manners.

She caught up with Gunnar lingering beside the corral and ignoring the others, already mounted and ready to round up the spare horses and drive them back up the ridge. The heavy-set man adjusted the tack on his horse, glancing sideways at her. Thora waited. He sent her a horse-toothed grin and turned to his mount; like a young man he used his spear to vault into the saddle.

The dapple grey mare, at pains to follow her friends, was jigging back and forth. Thora frowned at the rough way the man jerked his horse in the mouth with the thin iron bit. He bent down from the high-cantled saddle.

"Be assured," he said in a low voice, "that my brother and I intend to respect proper procedure. If you desire, we'll postpone our taking possession of the land and property until the spring after the first *Thing* gathering...you may wish to present your case for arbitration. In the absence of your father or anyone else to speak for you, you have of course the right to address the Lawspeakers on your own behalf."

Once more he struggled unsuccessfully to focus both eyes on her face.

"You're your own mistress now, I understand, with no elder relative to arrange your marriage. It must have been fated that I buried my wife before last winter. If you wish to consider a wealthy man for a husband, I suggest you send word to me."

He dug his spurs into his horse and the mare bounded up the slope.

Slowly, stiffly, Thora turned around. She had no clear image in mind of the man she would wish for her husband one day. Except that he must have hands which knew to be gentle with a child or a horse, or a woman, a man with a straight, steady gaze, and a waist narrow enough for a woman to wrap her arms around.

TWO

_____

_____

*...was heard that there had been a change of faith
in Norway....and many said.... casting off the old
faith was a strange and wicked thing to do.*

NJAL's SAGA

_____

_____

Thora pulled her woolen cloak tight against the cold wind
rising from the gorge. She turned to look back at the farm of
Hestardalur. Soon the first winterstorms would blow in from
the coast. In late winter the low-slung house with its heavy sod-roof
would be partially buried in snow; when she was a child in her fifth
winter, a party of lost travelers had mistaken the snow-covered roof for
a hillock and tried to make their reluctant horses climb up and over.
Her eyes filled with tears. Whatever the coming winter would bring to
this farm, it was no longer any concern of hers. By now the farm's new
masters would have left Borgarfjord and be well on their way to take
possession. *Before the first snows,* the younger brother had said.

It was time to pack up and wait at the house for the two *karls* sent by Father's brother Sveinar, to escort her to her new home. At first she had wished to wait for the Thing session, and contest the brothers' claim on Thorvinn's farm; later it dawned on her that to wait would be a waste of time, cruel postponement of the day she must say farewell to both her cherished home and much of her pride. None of the Lawspeakers expected to attend at the upcoming Thing was an associate of Thorvinn Haraldson, a man born and raised outside Iceland while three of the Speakers had close ties with the Snorrison brothers. She could only trust one Lawman to be on her side – Roald, her mother's foster brother; he was likely to speak out in her favour, but his lone voice stood no chance of refuting the brothers' claim against Thorvinn. There could be no doubt about the outcome.

She as well as anyone else regarded to be of no use to the new masters of Hestardalur, would be cast out. Unless... *If you wish to consider a wealthy man for a husband, I suggest you send word to me.*

She tried to think of something that might speak in his favour, to make up for the unfeeling way in which Gunnar had reined his anxious mare and whipped her uphill. Did she feel attracted to him in any way? He was a strong man not entirely without appeal, well-built with a powerful torso and limbs corded with muscle though rather thick-set and lacking the well-defined waist of youth.

Her thoughts turned to her mother, Rannveig Asgrimsdottir, whose nearness in spite of her death seven summers ago, she thought she could feel at times when she needed advice, a presence unreachable, untouchable, a mere glimpse caught at the edge of her vision. She tried to face the presence, but Rannveig's hazy shape remained turned away, unresponsive to the pleas of her daughter. Perhaps Rannveig felt she had fulfilled her maternal duties while alive by listing for her daughter a set of basic guidelines to live by, including all the advice on marriage she was supposed to need. *If a girl is to make up her mind over a proposed marriage, she needs to ask herself three questions; first of all, do I want to bear this man's children? Second, will he be a good provider? Third, does he have a proper farm for his wife to run while he's away, a farm rich enough to supply the household's needs without hardship until he returns?*

Clearly, her mother had heeded the advice, which she in turn would have received from her own mother. Rannveig, daughter of a prosperous sheep farmer in Iceland, had married Thorvinn Haraldson, a young Norwegian with plenty of charm and good looks, and a firstborn son, heir to his father's property in Norway by the Sognefjord. Thorvinn took his bride away from Iceland overseas to his farm by the fjord, a splendid property with sizable landholdings; until fate turned against them in the shape of a powerful enemy forcing them to flee the country, to Iceland, to make their home at Hestardalur, Rannveig's ancestral farm which she, the only suriving child of her parents, stood to inherit.

Thora unfolded her arms, letting the wind catch her cloak. Slowly she walked back to the farm and into the yard, feeling every depression, every rock and every tuft of weeds touched by the thin soles of her indoor shoes, and storing the memories away. She saturated her eyes with the familiar shapes enhanced in the low winter sunlight, the shapes of walls and rails enclosing buildings and corrals. All this she locked into a corner of her mind, a place where her spirit could enter whenever she wished.

She thought of Gunnar, of the way he gazed at her from the saddle before he spun his horse around. *Do I want to bear this man's children?* She stood motionless, recalling the drifting gaze of his eyes, pale and bulging like sheep's eyes — did she want to bear children cursed with the gaze of a ram?

No, she did not. It was better to take the untried road toward an uncertain future.

*   *   *   *   *

Hemmed in by towering cliffs the waters of the Whale Fjord, deprived of sunshine for another month, appeared before her like a black watery gate to the underworld. A persistent wind chilled the land and everywhere she looked, grass and herbs were late to green. Would the meadows of Hestardalur, Thora wondered, also be late this spring to turn green? Not that it mattered any more.

She climbed to the highest point of the cliff to head some errant ewes back to safety. It felt good to be out in the hills with a flock of non-judgmental sheep for company. Still, it was by no means easy to commit all day to the care of livestock belonging, for the most part, to another woman. Only a small number, no more than a dozen ewes, she owned herself and these were easy to spot, even without catching sight of their ear notches – her own Hestardalur sheep were larger and meatier, with thicker wool, and, yes, brainier, than Thurid's lot. These prime ewes were a farewell gift from Gunnar, the cross-eyed Borgarfjord brother who had taken a liking to her.

The bulk of this flock belonged to Thurid, mistress of Gronsetur Farm, wife of Fathers brother Sveinar. Thora shrugged. It was preferable in any case to wander the hills with another woman's sheep, instead of spending her days in another woman's home and be told to do household chores, this and that all day long and after all else was done, there would be weaving, always more weaving to do. Shepherding on the other hand allowed her to roam outside, leaving it to Thurid's maids to wear out their shoes walking hither and tither all day by their looms.

Thora skipped from one rock to the next in pursuit of the venturesome ewes; she moved easily in her short tunic and men's leggings, careful to keep her feet dry. No need to get her sheepskin foot-wraps soaked by stepping in a patch of coarse, gritty spring-snow lingering between boulders.

Just before the stray ewes reached the top of the highest cliff, she caught up and shooed them back, cursing their stubborn sheepishness.

"Kshshah, kshshah, you lot! You're dumber than trolls."

A sudden wind rose off the water hurling up icy gusts which cut through the worn under-arm spots in her tunic. She looked in dismay at the sheep trundling downhill, in no hurry to reach the hollow below and find refuge from the chilling wind; and yet, half of them were already plucked of their winter wool! They ought to be shivering.

She stood for a moment catching her breath, scanning the grassy hollow below where the blaze-faced mare kept to herself grazing a little away from the sheep among tussocks of brown winter grass and melting snowdrifts. Thurid's black sheepdog, Svart, followed the horse for a chance to sneak up on rodents cowering between the tussocks, or perhaps catch an early nesting bird stirred up by the horse. Thora regarded Thurid's old dog with a scowl. *Some useless old sheep dog you are. What kind of sheepdog can't be bothered to keep those brainless ewes from wandering up the cliffs and quite likely fall to their death?*

There might be some truth to Thurid's story of how sheep came about. The gods, Thurid said, created sheep as an afterthought. They gave all other beasts their proper shape and mind before granting them breath... all except sheep, the last beast to be created. The gods had no more cunning left to give them. And so they collected fragments of mind-matter lying scattered around the spent body of the giant Hymir, and they parceled those out between the first pair of sheep.

According to Thurid, the gods thought of this as a joke, wagering between themselves whether or not the ill-equipped wool-bearing beasts could survive and multiply.

And, Thurid liked to add, *the gods are still arguing over the outcome.*

Argue? Thora laughed aloud. *Hah! What's there to argue? Everyone knows sheep wouldn'tt stay alive any time on their own, without a shepherd and his dogs to keep them out of trouble.*

She called to the old sheepdog.

"Svart, you lazy beast, get ye'r old bones up here and chase those ewes down to the others. Go, go, get!"

Surely the mistress of Gronsetur Farm could have spared her a younger dog to herd Gronsetur's precious flock. Or did she think Thora's tall white dog would take to herding?

Gunnar had granted her besides a few sheep, ownership of the large long-legged guardian dog, Khagan, The white Khazar dog had been bred and raised in a faraway land to live peaceably among the livestock he guarded, never to chase them. Raised on the wolf-infested grass plains of his native land beyond Sweden the Cold, Khagan had proved his mettle in Iceland, a land without wolves, by keeping his flock safe from rustlers and marauding foxes out to snatch newborn lambs.

Thora's glance drifted to Fluga, the mare Gunnar had also allowed her to keep. And when he insisted she also take a slave with her, one of her own choice, she decided on her house-*thrall*, Eidyll, a young lad of many skills.

Already on the first day of her arrival at Gronsetur, Thurid had openly questioned her husband's decision to take in his brother's orphaned daughter. *For how long you think I can stand to look at that girl with her insolent eyes of light piercing grey, cold and clear like chunks of freshwater ice?*

Sveinar's ready response had left a lasting warm feeling inside Thora's heart. *She'll stay here for as long as it takes to find her a proper husband... in any case, my niece did not come here altogether destitute. She may not be eager to take on a good deal of women's work around the house, but I hear she's a good worker with livestock and in the dairy shed. Besides, her thrall, young as he is, knows how to do ironwork. I say we got us a good deal, and you ought to stop complaining.*

Thora followed the ewes down to the sheltered hollow to make sure they joined the other sheep nibbling on sedges along the rivulet. She sat down beside her saddle bags, fishing for a chunk of ryebread. The barley-coloured mare looked up and nickered, tossing her head and swirling her thick flaxen mane which glowed like gold thread in the late afternoon sunshine.

"What makes you think I owe you a treat?" Thora grumbled. "There's plenty of grass here for a horse to fill up... perhaps you're starved for decent company...'s that it? Tired of this bleating brainless lot...Listen, here's a bit of good news.Your horse friends are supposed to come back home today."

Thora smiled to herself. She had better go home early. Father's brother Sveinar was expected back from his five day visit to the market in Reykjavik. There would be news and stories to tell and purchases passed around for all to see. Sveinar was a shrewd trader, and farm products tended to fetch good prices in early spring – the season of want on many farms.

Eyes narrowed, she searched for the guardian dog – her eyesight these days seemed less keen than it used to. There he was, Khagan, sprawled across a tall flat-topped rock like a fleece blanket left to dry in the wind. She smiled to herself. Rustlers with eyesight no better than hers, might take the white dog for a blanket, or a patch of spring-snow – to their peril.

Thora called the mare over to feed her a crust of black bread. She mounted and whistled the dogs to begin the trek home, leaving it to the black sheepdog to keep the ewes moving on behind the horse. Cheered by the thought of seeing her uncle tonight, she quickened the pace, humming to herself and the flaxen-maned mare.

Dark-haired Sveinar, two years younger than his russet-haired brother, Thorvinn, reminded her in many ways of her father; the Haraldson brothers shared similar looks and even sounded like one another when laughing or talking. Loyal to his older brother, Sveinar had followed Thorvinn in exile to Iceland. There he married a widow, Thurid Herjolfsdottir, and settled down on his wife's farm, Gronsetur. Sveinar lacked the restless enterprise that drove his brother, Thorvinn, on annual ventures overseas in the pursuit of wealth. On Gronsetur farm the family's wealth owed as much to Sveinar's skills at marketing his wife's farm products, as it did to Thurid's skills turning milk and wool from her flock into first rate cheeses and cloth.

Thora sighed. Why could Thorvinn not be more like his brother? Her father had never been satisfied with only the profits from trading his famous horses. Each spring he sailed away to trade and raid in distant lands, leaving his wife in charge of the farm. Already as a young lad back in Norway he took to sea with his father, Harald, going a-viking to the south-lands together — to Frankland, Friesland, and the isles of Britons, Angles and Irish. Later in Iceland, he continued his ways, heading south like his father, or at other times heading east by river and lake to Sweden the Cold; Khagan, her prize dog, was among the treasures Thorvinn took home from the land of the Rus three summers ago.

Thora looked fondly at the tall white dog jogging ahead of the horse, plumed tail curled across his back; she cherished this gift from her father almost as much as the first gift he gave her, a horse of her own, a filly of the very best breeding. That was seven summers ago when Fluga was a weanling; Thorvinn granted the cream-coloured foal to his young daughter on condition that she take care of the horse herself. With his help she learned to gentle the filly and bring her under saddle when the time came. Thora rated the horse and the dog among her most prized possessions, together with Eidyll, the slave Thorvinn purchased four summers ago from a Danish slave trader in Hedeby. These gifts were all she had left of her father now.

Thora wiped her eyes with her muddy sleeve. She took a deep breath and pushed aside the memory of his teasing grin which so drastically altered the sternness of her father's features.

She halted the horse briefly on top of the last hill down, marveling at the unfolding vieuw. From up here, the large farm below in the valley appeared insignificant. The longhouse, corrals and outbuildings seemed no more than specks, pitiful tokens of human endeavour, meaningless rubble in a world of black cinder-stone spilled long ago from the earth's fiery furnaces.

Thora nudged the horse downhill. Halfway down the slope, the farmstead was revealed as a substantial place inexplicably thriving among barren rock, a sprawling arrangement of human-made features in a valley of grey and black lava-stone where fleeting cloud shadows carried on never-ending battles.

They forded the stream at the valley bottom, and here the reason for the farm's prosperity became clear. A wide ribbon of green wound its way along the stream, well-watered grassland with stretches of lush grass running up the hillsides like green tongues licking the bare, rocky cliffs above. The ridge loomed high, outlined in black against the darkening sky, a jagged, gigantic troll spine. The valley was wide, letting in plenty of sunshine in spring, summer and fall. Already the marshy banks nearest to the stream were lush with spring grass and even the steep, rock-strewn slopes above showed patches of green in the hollows between scattered boulders – these consisted of alder bushes and crouching, wind-tortured birch cautiously probing the early spring air with hesitant leaves.

Gronsetur came into full vieuw stretched out before her – a size-able farm, well-maintained, no less prosperous than Hestardalur and arranged with similar care.

They reached the other side of the shallow ford; Thora waited for the last sheep to wade through before nudging the mare for more speed to catch up with Khagan.

"Surely, you're not too old to keep up with a dog!"

Khagan, relieved of his guard duties now that the flock moved in one bunch encircled by the black sheepdog, was loping ahead, eager to receive his evening meal at the farm. The sinking sun was about to dip behind the ridge and Thora poked the horse on. She needed daylight to milk the ewes without risking a spill. Ewe's milk, coming only in small quantities and taking much time to collect, was rich and highly valued by Thurid for her specialty cheese. There was never much to spare after setting aside what was needed for the lambs, and Thurid Herjolfsdottir demanded that every spare drop be made into cheese — Gronsetur's famous sheep's cheese, aged for two winters, was without par in the district.

Thora turned around in the saddle resting her hand on the mare's swinging quarters.

"Heya, Svart!" she yelled at the sheep dog, "bring up the laggards or we'll be caught out after troll time."

The mare broke into a speedy *toelt*, clattering along in the quick-footed running walk she was bred and raised to perform.

"Shhh, now you're going too fast... slow down, girl," Thora laughed. "At this pace you're getting the ewes all worn out!"

Fluga raised her head and called – a drawn out squeal intended to be heard by horses far away. The mare turned her head to the low hills behind the farm and swiveled her ears, straining to catch a response.

"Come on you lot," Thora urged the sheep, lingering in a patch of fresh spring grass. "Cut out your nibbling and keep moving, or I'll have this sorry old bag of dog bones nipping your hocks so they bleed."

It was dark when Thora completed her chores. She had taken her time, disappointed to find that Father's brother hadn't come home yet. Fluga paced back and forth along the fence in the next pen, ears perked, calling out to the hills every time she rounded the far corner.

Thora watched her. *They won't be long now; the mare hears them coming.*

She had milked the ewes and the few goats and let the lambs into the sheep pen to nuzzle tufts of moldering hay together with their mothers. The white dog was crouched in a corner making short work of his meal — cooked barley in sour milk. Thora took his empty feed bowl of soapstone and put it aside to rinse. She scrutinized the dog, broad-skulled with long limbs and a light-boned frame, every rib defined. He had lost weight again. Khagan had always been lean. Now he was emaciated.

The large white dog looked outlandish, a stranger among the native Icelandic farmdogs, which were sturdy, short-limbed and born to herd.

Thora, watching her dog rise and stretch, bit her lips. *Any day now, and I'll be able to hear those bones rattle. This dog cannot subsist on the skimpy fare Thurid allots to her farm dogs.*

She clenched her fists. How much longer could she go on like this, living the life of a poor relative kept under another woman's thumb and surrounded by people who seemd to wish her ill. She had tried to explain to Thurid about her tall, rangy dog, reminded her that he came from the sea of grass beyond the forests of Sweden the Cold, and that his kind needed more nourishment than a regular dog.

"You're free to share your own meals with your dog," Thurid said with a shrug.

"Oh, but I do," Thora argued, "or rather, I would, if I found enough left over to eat by the time I come into the house at night."

Tonight though, there would be plenty to eat after dark in celebration of Sveinar's homecoming, and enough left to carry some off for the dog.

"I'll be back to bring you a feast," she said to Khagan. "And here's something else for you to enjoy right now."

She lifted the lid from a pail half full of fresh milk and filled Khagan's soapstone bowl to the rim. If Thurid complained about milk missing, she would simply tell her that a dog who kept sheep rustlers away from the flock day after day, needed to be fed well to keep up his strength and fighting spirit. Lately, Gronsetur's *karls* had seen wanderers stalking sheep in the hills. They tried to go after them they said, but the strangers disappeared like smoke over the ridge. And yet, all of this time with the white dog watching over them, not a single lamb was spirited away.

Sveinar and the four *karls* with him arrived home after dark with a train of twelve heavily loaded packhorses. Thora helped to relieve the horses of their burdens and turn them loose in the corral. She stayed, raising her torch to watch them rolling and rubbing their sweaty faces in the dirt, before they jumped to their feet to mob the livestock *thralls* darting between them with arms full of hay.

Alerted by noises from a small pen on the other side of the corral fence, Thora raised her torch high; she stared in awe at the black horse revealed in the uncertain light. A truly magnificent stud colt! The lads had turned the new horse, four winters old at most, loose in a pen by himself; he paced back and forth along the tall driftwood fence working up a lather. She found it hard to make out details of the moving dark shape wrapped in dancing shadows. He looked to be solid black without markings other than a star on his forehead. Though shaggy with winter hair, he seemed to be lean with legs of more than average length and a distinctive, chiseled head. Thora smiled. The colt was lithe and quick on his feet, sure to become a remarkable stallion, possibly of the same Vestmann stock that gave Fluga and the other horses bred by her father their edge.

She tore herself away from the new colt and went to the hall, squeezing in through the half open door, picking her way between Svart and other elderly dogs sprawled inside the doorway. She passed by seven winters old Hauk, the son of Sveinar and Thurid. The boy was down on his knees stoking the fire, adding more peat to the first of the hearths and pulling back from the leaping flames each time the door opened to let more people in.

Seated on a low stool in the back of the house by the second fire was Thurid's old mother, Thorgerd Hauksdottir, stirring a pot of stew; she brushed a lank strand of grey hair from her sweaty face and glowered at the careless young *karls* who left the door wide open; one, too young to grow a beard, turned around with a sheepish grin and pulled the door shut.

Last to come inside were the field *thralls* drawn by the thick smell of stewed goose.

The master and his family were seated on the wooden platform close to the second hearth. From the high seat which was sheltered by its own roof, Sveinar scanned the crowd with benevolent blue eyes, nodding to some, and frowning at others. Ruddy-faced, still wearing travel-stained trousers of brown homespun, he looked out of place between the stacked furs and feather-stuffed blankets his wife propped up around him.

Thora worked her way along the fire trench toward the second hearth between two dozen hungry men and women seated on stools and benches. She grabbed a three-legged stool and put it down near the wall, well away from Thurid though close enough to the master's seat to hear Sveinar speak. At least she didn't have to be wary of Helgi tonight, *Helgi the lout.* Thurid's adult son by her first husband had left five days ago to woe a wealthy girl in the next district; if all went well, he wasn't expected to be back for a while. Maybe he would find this girl, Magni, much to his liking, *and maybe he'll no longer try to catch my eye by making lewd gestures.*

She turned to look at the two women besides the high seat, old Thorgerd shriveled with age, and her daughter, Thurid, a squarely built woman with a determined jaw. Thurid sent her husband's niece a chill stare and Thora responded in kind. Neither woman would blink until a noisy dog fight erupted at the door, silenced by a few well-placed kicks. Thurid whisper-spoke to her nearly deaf mother, loud enough for Thora to catch some of it, "...impudent girl... getting on she is too...sixteen... hard to marry off by now..."

She pretended not to hear the whispers; instead she gazed at her uncle. How much longer would Sveinar keep the household waiting? When was he going to share the news brought back from the market? She had already seen him swallowing three helpings of stew; now he was tackling his fourth. How much stewed goose could one man put away? She had to admit, there was never a shortage of food in Thurid's household – unless, on most days, for those who came late.

Thurid prided herself on generously feeding her housefolk, free or bonded; the daughter of a Norwegian who grew wealthy in the Lapland trade before he settled in Iceland, Thurid adhered to her mother's advice. *The surest way for a woman to increase her family's fortune is to be known as one who feeds her household and guests with generosity,* Thorgerd liked to stress to all who would hear.

Still, tonight most people swallowed the rich stew in haste and declined a second helping; they shuffled their feet and clamoured for Sveinar to begin telling them of his journey.

At last the master put down his bowl and spoon, looked around and cleared his throat.

"You who are gathered here to listen to news of our journey," he said, "tell me something. Do you want to hear the good news first, or rather that which gives cause for concern?"

"Let's hear the bad tidings first," somebody yelled.

Sveinar raised his eyebrows.

"This may be good news or bad, depending on one's judgment... word goes around that men have been sent to Iceland by the Dane king, Harald Gormson Bluetooth, with instructions to attend the next Althing meeting. Now, as everyone knows, the Dane king claims to rule Norway, though many folk over there insist they answer only to Hakon Sigurdson. They're fooling themselves because Jarl Hakon, it's no secret, must answer in turn to the Dane king."

Some men and women chuckled. When all were silent, Sveinar continued.

"These men the king sent to Iceland are servants of White Christ and their mission is to bring the Christ teachings to us all. As if there's any need. The same newfangled ideas were brought up from the South some years ago by Thorvaldur Farfarer! And he at least was one of us, well-liked and respected, an upstanding man from Stora Gilja!"

Sveinar paused, sipping a fresh mug of foaming *skyr* – *better than the wife's beer*, he was fond of saying.

Thurid reached over to pour water on his hands and make sure he washed the froth from his beard.

Sveinar ran his tongue along his lips; he glanced at the frowning faces lit by the glow of the fires.

"Well now, family, friends and servants of this household. Do you think this good news or bad? Come now, speak up."

Thora scanned the faces close to her. Most people stared into their empty bowls. A few looked to the rafters as if they expected to see roof-dwelling ghosts sneaking a peek at them. It would be hard to find anyone in this household prepared to speak out on matters of the spirit. The Christ faith was a tender issue all over Iceland. The topic had spawned disagreement for years, causing squabbles and full-blown feuds, pitting kin against kin and friend against friend.

She caught sight of Eidyll squatting near the doorway; he seemed to be carving something out of a goose bone, a flute perhaps. Flute playing was another one of her *thrall's* talents.

Eidyll interrupted what he was doing to fetch more peat for Hauk to add to the fire. Thora tried to read the *thrall's* face, but Eidyll didn't appear to have heard Sveinar's question. Like most Britons, Eidyll was a follower of White Christ though he and others of his ilk rarely discussed their beliefs. Christian slaves and most of their fellows whether or not they adhered to the new creed, hoped that the new faith would take root in Iceland and free them from bondage. White Christ and his servants, people said, disagreed with the notion that there were two kinds of people in the world, bonded slaves on the one hand, free men and women on the other. A good number of free folk for their part argued against the new religion which, in their eyes, was a ploy to weaken the people of Iceland and take away their right to rule themselves. *They mean to turn us into mewling bear cubs*, was Sveinar's way of putting it.

Thora closed her eyes listening to the murmured talk. Some people seemed to think that Sveinar was, secretly, in favour of Christian ways after all.

"He hasn't made sacrifice to a single *Asa-god* since last winter," a red-faced *karl* said to others near him.

"And the same goes for Thurid," a frizzy-haired maid said in a half-whisper. "I've heard her say that it might be a good thing if White Christ came to change a few things in Iceland. The new faith might make our men change their ways, she said."

Thora nodded to herself. Thurid's favourite rant was familiar to all. *It's high time someone tells our men to stay home in the summer. Let them help with everyday farmwork instead of getting themselves killed in faraway places or taking their wives' farm products to market in return for good silver which they then gamble away at the horse fights, or use to purchase a new fighting stallion after which they come home empty-handed.*

Sveinar grinned at the circle of faces obscured by the blanket of smoke caught under the roof.

"Well then," he said, "I venture to speak my own mind in the matter. I see no reason to open my house to men sent from Norway or Denmark to enslave us, free-born Iceland folk, and make us pay taxes to some high and mighty king living in some overseas land."

He rested his head in his hands, waiting for people to gather closer around the dying fire. When everyone had settled in a warm spot, he continued.

"Many people are readying ships to sail with Red Eirik Thorvaldson to his new settlement overseas; that place as you know used to be called Gunnbjorn's land, until he gave it a new fancy name...'Greenland.' I doubt it could be all that green, judging from the piles of white bear-skins he took home to trade, and walrus tusks, and narwhale teeth; everyone knows those kinds of treasures aren't found in lands that have lush green pastures."

He wiped his brow.

"Red Eirik, you will recall, was exiled from Iceland three years ago on account of slayings he committed. Seems he returned last summer with a ship full of furs and ivory, and sold the lot for enough silver to pay the man-price owed to the families of the slain. Now he says, when the ice goes out, he intends to return to this Greenland of his and settle there for good. He invites others to come and settle there too, promising free land to all who will join him."

A stir of excitement rippled through the audience. Thora, warm and sleepy after a big helping of stew, jolted upright.

"Red Eirik," Sveinar went on, "claims that his new land is rich with promise, virgin grassland which has never been grazed, sea and rivers teeming with fish, and plenty of birds and wild meat to hunt. And, he says, he'll grant no favours to followers of Christ; he'll suffer no royal tax collectors to set foot in his green land."

Sveinar fell silent. He picked up a piece of fresh cheese, swallowed it and burped, flicking the white crumbs from his beard.

Thora scraped her empty bowl clean of goose grease; she reached for the kettle to rinse out the bowl, feeling her cheeks aflush with excitement. *Land granted for free.* What if she went to Eirik's new land to eke out a new homestead for herself? Then again, a woman venturing out alone without family or fortune might not be the kind of settler Eirik had in mind.

Sveinar talked on, listing the trades he made.

"I swapped a quarter of Thurid's sheep for a splendid four year old stud horse, barely gentled...I sold the cheeses and most of the cloth for two saddle bags filled with silver pieces; the remaining sheep, most of them wethers and dry ewes, I exchanged for a pile of Moorish coins. I didn't let go of Thurid's best milking ewes till I found a good trade in exchange, a flock of fine ewes brought down all the way from the north shore. They carry exceptional fleece, thicker and finer than the wool of our sheep — as close to eider down as sheep's fleece can possibly be."

Thurid slammed her empty bowl on the arm rest of her seat.

"But will they give any surplus milk for my cheeses? And why have we not seen these fabulous sheep filing into our yard to be safely penned in for the night?"

"Because," said Sveinar, scowling, "I didn't want a bunch of disagreeable sheep to slow me down. I decided to go straight home instead of chasing this way and that after obstinate ewes trying to break away and head for their old grazing grounds. There's no need to worry."

"Of course there's every reason to worry over a flock of valuable sheep left to find their own way," Thurid scoffed. "Are you out of your mind?"

"Woman, don't call me a fool," Sveinar huffed. "What do you take me for? I arranged with the seller to leave our new flock at the hot springs – he's passing by there on his way home. Those ewes will be happy enough for a while at the springs next to the crossroads, grazing on early grass in the warm spots. We can fetch them any day we choose."

"Hah!" said Thurid, returning her husband's scowl. "I suggest you and your lads take fast horses first thing in the morning, and bring those ewes home safely. You're assuming a good deal about the honesty of a trader, and besides, what of the outlaws? Everyone knows that travelers on their way home from market love to pause at the crossroads for a warm soak in the springs; there'll be clothes and belongings scattered all over the place drawing runaway *thralls,* outlaws and sundry rascals out of their hiding caves as surely as a dead sheep draws the foxes out of their dens. Only a fool abandons a flock of prize ewes at the hot springs!"

THREE

Starkad had a good chestnut horse, which people thought couldn't be matched in a fight....' we are told that thou hast a good horse, and we wish to challenge thee to a horse fight.'

NJAL's SAGA

Dressed in a homespun shift and kirtle — the only set of indoor clothes in her possession these days — Thora went out at sunrise before anyone else stirred in the house. Yesterday her uncle and two *karls* had left for the hot springs; now that the master — always first to get up — was away, there would be no maids stirring early to light the fire at daybreak and cook gruel for Sveinar's breakfast. For once she would be able to enjoy a walk outside in the real world before Thurid called her over to spend the rest of her day at the house.

A brisk walk in the hills would give her strength to face a long day at the farm.

Late last night before bed, Thurid said to her, "We need all the women on this farm to prepare food and beer for Helgi's upcoming wedding, and that includes you. I'll arrange for a pair of young lads to go out with the sheep and the dogs tomorrow," Thurid added. "You need no longer be spending your days on the fells taking care of the flock."

Thora paused at the horse-pen looking at Eidyll who waited in the yard for Tjalling, a Friesian *thrall* and Gronsetur's herdsman, to lead the new horse out of the pen. Thora envied her *thrall*. If only she could trade places with him right now and pass the day gentling Sveinar's black colt herself, ordering Eidyll to help in her place with the wedding preparations.

How foolish of her to boast to her uncle of Eidyll's horse handling skills. *My thrall is good at dealing with horses…*she told Sveinar on the day they arrived at Gronsetur. *Christian monks in his homeland, he tells me, hired him as a groom and caretaker on horse buying ventures to Ireland.* What had possessed her to tell her uncle? It was quite enough for him to know that Eidyll, in his own land a blacksmith's apprentice, knew how to forge iron. If she'd never mentioned his horse handling skills, Sveinar might have chosen her instead of her *thrall* to bring his new colt under saddle.

Can I borrow your lad to turn my black colt into a saddle horse? Sveinar asked her last night. *I'll be leaving at dawn to fetch the sheep at the springs, and I want someone to work with the horse while I'm away.*

What choice did she have?

I'll be glad to lend him to you. She almost bit off her tongue with the effort to hide from her uncle how much she longed to be put in charge of his horse. Now there was no more chance of that. Thurid demanded she help with the womens work, and she was in no position to refuse.

She lingered at the horse pen; Tjalling had a hard time controlling the fidgety colt. Surtur – as Sveinar had named him after the fire giant of old lore – would barely stand still long enough for Eidyll to swing up on his back. Once he was securely mounted, the other *thrall* let go of the bridle; the horse planted his feet ignoring Eidyll's nudge to move off.

"Never mind," Eidyll said to Tjalling. "He doesn't seem to know anything yet. By this evening we should with some luck, have him gentled well enough to stand for mounting and move away from the leg, before the master returns."

26

He sat quietly, waiting for the horse's next move.

Thora saw a subtle shift in the black colt, a softening of the back-muscles. Again the rider nudged him, and the colt took a tentative step, and another; next he bolted for the hills, kicking, twisting and spiraling though failing to unseat his rider.

Thora had to admit, not many riders she knew could have stayed on.

She watched horse and rider flying as one along the grassy stretch of valley land. Surtur… an appropriate name for a horse with a coat as luminous black as the glassy shards found on the slopes of fire-mountains.

Thora raised her hand to shade her eyes against the rising sun; she marveled at the black phantom horse bearing its rider across the bronze-coloured folds of berry patches cloaking the uplands. Away over the hills they skimmed on swift hooves barely touching the earth. Thora turned around, resigned to go back to the house.

If only Sveinar had known that she, his brother's daughter, had gentled the annual crop of Hestadalur horses all by herself for the last three summers. She had loved those long summer days away from the domestic grind, standing in the gentling pen with the sun warming her face or her back, guiding a young horse in a circle around her, or nudging it through its first steps under saddle. Nothing compared with the thrill of riding a green horse in the hills, connecting with its body and mind, blowing across wind-flattened grass like terns skimming the waves, raced by gulls riding the wind above her head. And here she was, headed for home and a long day making cheese or malting barley.

Thora felt for her necklace, aware she could no longer feel the weight of the amber beads. Her mother's precious necklace – did it snap? The double strand of twined silk supposed to hold the polished transparent beads securely, was gone. She felt under her kirtle, probed above her woven waist belt and breathed relief; her fingers touched a cluster of beads. She fished for the pieces and counted the beads, twenty four in all, not one missing thanks to her mother's foresight. Meticulous Rannveig had strung the necklace with her own hands, taking great care to tie little silk knots after each bead.

One by one, Thora held up the beads against the sky, delighted to see the rosy light of dawn turning each into a golden tear drop touched by pink. She blinked away tears; the necklace became hers on that life-changing morning when she was eight winters old and Agni, her mother's old maid, called her to Rannveig's bedside. *Your mother is dying. She wants to see you.*

Agni had pushed her toward the bed holding her firmly when Thora tried to step back, afraid of the strange woman in the bed, with a newborn infant swaddled beside her, a woman pretending to be her mother; but she was not fooled; this wasn't the mother she knew. Her mother was Rannveig Asgrimsdottir, a woman known for her lovely face and remarkable eyes — a delicate colour of grey with a silver shine, clear like water flowing over pebbles; the woman in the bed stared up to her with dull-black eyes like soot-covered buttons, much too large for her leathery shrunken face.

Another push from behind and Agni whispered into her ear, *Stay still, and reach out your hand.*

In a flash Thora knew that it must be her mother after all, because of the necklace. Too weak to lift her head, Rannveig took her daughter's hand and closed it around the amber necklace, the treasure she valued more than any other possession; Thora gathered her courage and looked into her mother's unearthly, bottomless eyes and in there was an unspoken message, *These beads, my dear child, are for you to remember me by.*

Thora sighed. How different her life would be today if her mother and newborn brother had lived. Thorvinn might have been less reckless in his raiding and trading ventures. With a wife and a son as well as a daughter, waiting at home, he might have thought twice before he put up the farm for security and exposed his family to the risk of losing their home.

She grimaced at the sky. A good thing proud Rannveig was unable now to see her daughter subjected to another woman's demands.

Hoof beats behind her back told her that Eidyll, or his horse, had decided to head home.

She resisted turning around; instead she quickened her pace, pleading in whispers with the god Njord, "Listen, you lord of the winds lashing these hills — and you other gods, you might as well hear me too.

How can it be right that a well-born free woman is made to serve as a house maid, forced to watch her bonded *thrall* bathing in glory on the back of the finest young stallion in Iceland?"

She straightened her shoulders, determined to see that Eidyll wouldn't much longer be showing off horse handling skills. Next time Father's brother Sveinar went to market, she would ask him to take her *thrall* to town and exchange him for a good mare or two. Her mood brightened. With two good mares to her name, she would have a chance to get back on her feet again. Sveinar would surely allow her to breed her mares to his new prize stallion, a first step in building her own herd of horses that matched her father's famous stock in speed and fighting valour. Next she must think of a way to acquire some land of her own, in Iceland or...in Greenland ...and not any old land either; it took out-standing grassland to raise the exceptional horses she had in mind.

The hoofbeats behind her came closer. Thora strode on, aware that Eidyll, to judge by the hoofbeats, pulled the horse to a walk at a respect-ful distance behind her. She pushed her hair away from her ears to listen to some unsettling noise which came drifting up from the farm in the valley; there were shouts, and screams, and thin wailing sounds. What was happening? She began to run down the slope, followed by the clip-clopping horse.

Cousin Hauk came rushing up the trail.

"Come quickly, Thora Thorvinnsdottir!" the boy cried, brushing tawny hair from his tear-streaked face. "Tack up your mare and ride out to the springs ... something terrible has happened to Father!"

Side by side they sped down the last hill. Hauk, between gulps of air, explained, "Thorolf came home on foot with terrible news. Father had an accident at the springs...overcome by vapours...foul breath from ...underworld... horses all dead... not one left alive to bring Father home..."

He grabbed Thora's shoulders and pulled her to a halt.

"All of our horses except for your mare... are turned out on the fells...! Mother said... tell Thora to take her mare ... hasten to the springs!"

They splashed across the ford and hurried through the low meadow into the yard.

Eidyll passed them by on the horse. He jumped off, turning to Thora to wait for orders.

"Find a saddle for the colt," Thora yelled, "and get my mare tacked up while I change into clothes fit for riding. You and I ride out to the springs."

She dashed into the house for her old riding clothes, the shepherd's tunic and greasy leggings.

After a long mad gallop up and down steep slopes slick with meltwater and a last flat-out run through bare cinder fields, Thora and Eidyll reached the springs before noon; not far from the bubbling hot pot they found Sveinar's crumpled body, face turned to the sky, glassy blue eyes bulging, a stiffened fist holding the plaited horsehair rein of Bleika, his favourite dun-coloured mare who lay dead by his side, mouth agape. All around them the ground was gouged out by thrashing limbs — death hadn't come easy to man nor beast. Scattered nearby were dead sheep and other dead horses, and a brown and white sheep dog.

Thora fell to her knees, arms wrapped around her head to stifle her sobs. Slumped over at Sveinar's feet was Ulfar, the young *karl* assigned by Thorolf to keep watch over their master while he went to get help at the farm. The lad, a Christian convert, mumbled prayers to White Christ in a language which only priests of the new faith could understand. Thora reached out to touch her uncle's cheek, recoiling from the cold flesh, hard, unforgiving like granite.

It took all of her determination to speak without sobbing.

"How did this happen?"

Ulfar's response came in whispers.

"We were rounding up sheep... when we saw something wrong by the springs... horses close to the water were staggering... sheep too... Sveinar yelled at us to drive our flock away from the springs. I'll see to the horses, he shouted...running to his precious Bleika right by the steaming spring."

Ulfar shivered. He hugged his shoulders and lowered his chin to his chest.

Hey!" Thora shook him.

"And nobody thought to rush over and drag him away? Once out of the fumes he could have recovered, but you two, you left him to die!"

Ulfar jumped up.

"No!" he shouted. "It didn't happen like that! We drove the sheep a distance away like he told us, and then we looked back...and Sveinar was on the ground with the horse on top of him. Thorolf hollered at me to stay with the sheep while he ran back toward the master. Halfway down, his knees buckled...he started coughing...he turned, staggered back to me and fell to the ground...he kept on going, at a crawl. I ran over and helped him up, dragged him farther away from the fumes...he was gasping, but he was alive."

The young *karl* wiped tears from his beardless face.

"There was nothing more we could do. We sat and waited. Later, we drove some sheep ahead of us to the springs and found that earth's evil breath had lifted. We went to the master, rolled the horse off his chest and saw the master was dead."

He looked up.

"We did all we could to revive him, Thora Thorvinnsdottir...but he wouldn't breathe. You must believe me."

Thora remained silent. Perhaps the fumes had killed Sveinar, or perhaps it was the weight of the horse on his chest. That would have made for an easier death, better than to be gasping for air with his lungs burned to cinders by the vapours escaping from Nifel-hel.

She ran her hand over Sveinar's thick, dark curls streaked silver around the ears. The earth had turned against Sveinar Haraldson as the sea had turned against his brother, Thorvinn. Disaster could happen anywhere, anytime, to those whose luck ran out.

Thora rose to her feet, fighting to keep her tears down; in her short time on his farm, she had grown fond of her uncle, a man both strong and gentle like his brother; but Sveinar, unlike restless, unpredictable Thorvinn, had been fond of farm life, reluctant to leave his home and family. And he had been good to her, a loyal uncle taking in his orphaned niece against the objections of his outspoken wife who felt entitled to rule with an iron hand on the farm she inherited from her father.

"Thank you for everything," she whispered to the dead man. Though at a loss where to go next, she was convinced that her time at Gronsetur was over; without Sveinar's help and protection, she could no longer hope for a decent future here.

She turned to Ulfar.

"Lift him up on the mare and rest him across her back. And you," she said to Eidyll, "you must ride ahead on the colt and let Thurid know we are bringing Sveinar home to be buried."

To Ulfar she said, "Hold on to his legs. I'll lead the mare at a slow walk. You are to make sure that he doesn't slide off."

Thurid received them in dignified silence – crying and sobbing wasn't her way. She merely shook her head, wondering aloud why Sveinar had been so reckless to tempt his fate without good cause.

"To think that he risked his life trying to salvage a horse beyond help already, by all accounts...any fool knows to keep away from a hot-spot when livestock drop dead all over the place."

FOUR

The stallion was black, large and powerful, and of proven fighting spirit.

LAXDAELA SAGA

After Sveinar's sudden death Thurid decided to postpone her son's wedding. She ordered all hands on the farm to help instead with the burial preparations.

"We can't spare any lads to stay with the sheep," she said to Thora. "I want you to bring the flock to the hills in the morning and leave them there with only the guard dog to watch over them. You return to the house and help to prepare food and drink – we can expect many guests to attend Sveinar's burial."

On her way home after bringing the sheep out to pasture, Thora picked up a horn rope someone had lost in the mud. She entered the cow byre to place the rope back on one of the pegs, turned to leave, and found herself face to face with Helgi barring her exit. He grabbed her arms trying to push her down into the moldy hay, Thora boilt with fury – assaulting her, his cousin by custom if not by blood! She broke away, whirled around and kicked his shins hard before stepping back, a raised knee aimed for his crotch.

"You move, and I'll crush your tools. Try growing 'em back!"

He stepped away, a foolish grin on his face.

"What's the matter with you, cousin? Can't you take a joke?"

"Can I have a word with you?"

Thora, stacking finished cheeses on the storage shelf, turned to see Thorgerd supported by her stout walking stick limping toward her. The old woman nodded approvingly at the rows of cheeses freshly wiped with salt.

"You can leave the rest for now," she said. "Why don't you go out and see if the lads have finished slaughtering the hogs? Take someone else along to put up the meat for curing."

Inga, the youngest maid, volunteered.

"I'll go with you, if you'll teach me to make blood pudding."

The men had killed five young boars and placed the carcasses gutted and split across the stone wall of the livestock pen. Thora and Inga went to work with saws, hatchets and knives. The hogs, farrowed only last fall, carried little fat after the long winter. One of the lads helped to carry choice cuts uphill to the smoke-house. The rest of the meat Thora decided to ground up and mix with mutton fat to make sausage. The men had collected the blood of the slaughtered pigs in big tubs and left them inside the cookshed to be made into blood pudding.

As long as Sveinar's corpse lay unburied, no fires could be lit in the house in case his ghost returned to take residence in his former home en render the place uninhabitable for the living. All cooking had to take place in the open air, or in the summer cook-shed to be safe from rain.

Thora and Inga poured the pig blood into an iron pot and added chunks of mutton fat. They lowered the pot inside a larger cauldron half filled with water suspended over the fire, and kept stirring while it was heating. Soon as the mixture came to a boil they added salt and dried juniper berries and continued to stir waiting for the blood to coagulate. The air was thick with whirling steam and the girls, gasping for air, decided to take turns stepping outside the cook shed.

When it was her turn, Thora filled her lungs eagerly with the crisp spring air. The nauseating smell of warm blood inside the shed brought back a memory she would prefer to banish from her mind – it dwelled inside her head in a rarely entered corner, the memory of a stench more loathsome than this, a thick cloud of putrefied air which, after the death of her mother and newborn brother, had turned the house and the yard at Hestardalur unfit for the living.

It was mid-summer when they died and there was no snow or frozen soil left to store the bodies. Thorvinn consulted a seeress to find the proper auspicious time for burial. When the seeress walked into the hall Thora crawled under her father's high seat and remained hidden, hardly daring to breathe; the seeress was a frightening sight to behold, gaunt and haggard, flat breasts covered with rattling necklaces made of dog and boar teeth, mysterious bone pieces and smelly strips of uncured animal hide.

The moon was close to half, the night Rannveig and her newborn died; the seeress insisted that Thorvinn postpone the burial till the full moon. Within two days the stench drove everyone to despair and after two more days, Thorvinn ordered the corpses burned. At the appropriate burial time, he had the charred remains collected and placed in a proper grave.

Thora took another deep breath to savour the fresh air before returning to the steaming pot. *Why am I doing this to myself? Why am I still here?*

Ever since Sveinar mentioned Eirik Rauda's call for folks to settle in his fabled Greenland, she had played with the thought of answering the call; a chance to leave servitude and bad fortune behind, once and for all.

Any prospects she might have had at Gronsetur to marry a man with land and fortune had surely melted away after the death of her uncle. *It is foolish of a young woman,* her mother used to say, *to hold out for a man with good looks, strength and daring, if that's all he has to account for himself."*

Thora's lips tightened to a wry smile. Her mother had hardly needed to follow the advice commonly given to girls, that they marry a husband with a farm of his own. In the absence of a brother, Rannveig, the eldest of three sisters and the only one to survive beyond childhood, stood to inherit the farm of Hestardalur. After she and Thorvinn were forced to abandon their home in Norway and move to Iceland, they reclaimed Rannveig's property from her mother's cousin left in charge after the death of her parents. Had it not been for Thorvinn's ill-fated trading gamble, Thora would have inherited her mother's ancestral farm after the death of her father. Now, with no claim to a farm of her own, she had no chance to marry a prominent man — unless she agreed to marry old Gunnar.

But what if she went to Greenland? Eirik's call for settlers seemed to offer a rare chance for a woman to acquire a farm of her own other than by inheritance. How much longer was she going to stay here, ordered about by a snooty woman and on top of it all, putting up with Thurid's lout of a son?

I cannot leave before Sveinar's remains are buried.

It was proper and right that she pay her last respects to her father's loyal brother, who had followed their little family to exile in Iceland and later welcomed his brother's orphaned daughter to his home against his wife's wishes.

Most folks on this farm would be happy enough to see her go and rather sooner than later. Though Helgi, the new master of Gronsetur, would need to find someone else to torment, he would be pleased enough to see the departure of his stepfather's poor niece, and the relinquishing of her claims to support.

Helgi. Angered, she stirred with ever more vigour until hot liquid splashed over the edge.

"Hey, look what you're doing!" Inga yelped, brushing the splashes from her arms.

"I didn't mean to!" Thora said miserably. She touched her fingertip to the scald spots on Inga's arm. "How bad is it? Let me get you some mutton fat to put on it."

Inga shook her head. "It's not that bad. What were you thinking of?"

She rested her paddle, waiting.

Thora gave a dismissive shrug.

"Not thinking at all, I'm afraid. I'm not cut out for boring work like this."

Young Inga was still a child, almost. No point in telling the girl that Thurid's ill will had been weighing her down since the day she arrived at this farm. No point either to explain that without the protective shield of Sveinar's loyal kindness, she did not expect to have a future here

She took up the stirring paddle.

"Did you know?" she said casually, "that Thurid wants me to give up shepherding for good? I'm supposed to stay here and take care of women's chores, make butter and cheese all summer and spend the winters spinning and weaving from one bedtime to another."

Inga smiled. "You'll see it's not so bad to stay home instead of roaming the hills with a bunch of sheep. When it turns cold, you may find the indoors more to your liking."

Thora stirred briskly in the mass of blood and fat now thickening fast. Did people truly expect her to settle for a summertime life spent in the dairy shed, followed by long winters inside the house, barely able to breathe, staring at her loom all day by the flickering light of a peat fire or a smoking, sputtering wick? They must be mad.

She resolved to leave right after the burial, before Helgi's wedding. Things would only get worse after Helgi's bride moved in. The last thing she needed was another woman to order her about! Thurid seemed to regard Magni Aslaksdottir, Helgi's bride, as a great catch. Well-born to begin with, the bride was reputed to have exceptional beauty and property to match.

For the benefit of all ears Thurid had repeatedly listed the assets coming to the household as part of Magni's dowry — *no less than two smallholder-places near the fjord and a rare patch of crop-field in a hot-spot where the soil never freezes.*

Thora and Inga ladled the steaming mass of blood and fat into wooden forms and set them on shelves to cool. *The trolls fetch Helgi Thorlakson! What kind of man soon to be wedded, would exercise his manhood at the expense of a woman who wants no dealings with him?*

Helgi had laughed it off; *a joke,* he had called the cowshed encounter. Sure. Magni Aslaksdottir wouldn't think it a joke if she happened upon her newly wed husband in a dark corner pawing his cousin; they would, needless to say, blame her, Thora, for leading a young married man astray. Just as well that she made up her mind – better to leave of her own free will than be chased away in disgrace.

*   *   *   *   *

"Come over here, girl – we have another load for you to take up."

Thora carried her yoke with empty pails past milkmaids and hobbled cows to the back of the milking pen and waited for Thurid and Thorgerd to refill the pair of leather pails with foaming milk. Thurid called Inga down from the dairy shed to hook the pails to Thora's yoke. Thora straightened up and moved off with her load at a shuffling jog to the dairy shed halfway up the hill.

Inga ran ahead to the dairy shed to stuff more hay into the large driftwood box used to curdle the milk. Together they poured the foaming liquid still warm from the cows, into an iron pot scrubbed clean with fine sand, added a handful of curds from an earlier batch and left the pot, lid closed, inside the hay-filled box to separate.

"I'm afraid we've no milk to spare to make *skyr* for tomorrow," Inga said, rolling her eyes. Every last drop of milk was claimed by Thurid these days to make still more cheeses to add to the mountains of cheese she intended to serve at the burial meal.

Thora hooked two forms with pressed cheese curds to her yoke and left the shed to climb to the smoke shed on top of the hill, pausing when Thurid stepped in her way.

"We need to have a word, you and I."

Thora frowned. Thurid had spoken softly, almost kindly, which made her ill at ease.

"It's time we come to an understanding about your future," Thurid said, her voice pinched after her march uphill to the dairy shed.

"It isn't right I feel for a well-born young woman to play maid on the farm of relatives. You deserve to run a homestead of your own."

Thora waited, filled with suspicion. Thurid had never considered her husband's niece to be her responsibility, a girl who, she argued, *refuses all help to find her a husband.* Why all of a sudden would her uncle's wife be so concerned for her?

"We, Mother, I and Helgi, have given some thought to your future," Thurid went on, her face somewhat softened by a tight smile.

"We think it's high time to settle your marriage and, as it happens, we found a suitable husband for you right here at Gronsetur. Driftwood Toki came to mind. What do you think?"

Speechless, Thora lowered the cheese forms to the ground and let the yoke slide from her shoulders.

Old Toki? They must be joking!

How could they even suggest that she consider a feeble old man for a husband, a shriveled old *thrall* whom her uncle had freed out of pity? She knew the old former slave well enough from his regular visits to the farm. A familiar figure trudging the path to the milking shed with a small pail, hoping for hand-outs when the goats at his croftstead had gone dry once again. Years ago, an accident had shattered his knee and left him crippled, unfit for most labour. Sveinar granted him a piece of uphill land with a small goat byre, and Toki had built a tiny loft under the roof which he used for a living space.

"Toki's croftstead could easily support the needs of two people and a child or two," Thurid resumed with an encouraging nod. "Many folks will be gathered here shortly for Sveinar's burial – no better occasion than that to announce your betrothal."

She pointed to the forms with pressed cheese.

"Why don't you put those up in the smokehouse and think about it? I'll wait in the yard for your answer."

Abruptly, Thurid turned around and went back to the milking shed leaving Thora bristling.

Had Thurid gone mad?

She plonked the cheeses on the water-soaked wicker racks in the smokehouse, rubbed salt on them, added fresh peat to the smouldering pile at the bottom and took the empty cheese forms outside with her, slamming the door shut.

Thurid waited in the yard below.

"Well?"

She held Thora's gaze with eyes like black dots.

Thora stared back. *How round her eyes are, round and black like crow-berries and just as unappealing.*

Thurid squeezed out another smile.

"We'll give you a dowry of course... some nice *wadmal* I thought, to make a new set of clothes for you both. I could let you have old Svart as well. You'll need a savvy old sheepdog to keep your sheep up there in the hills by themselves, away from our flock down here."

Thurid's suggestions, Thora decided, were too absurd to merit her anger. She burst out laughing.

"No," she said after catching her breath. "It's not at all what I had in mind for myself."

Thurid frowned.

"Don't play games with me, girl," she said sharply. "Don't be greedy."

She waved her arms in a magnanimous gesture.

"We could spare you another goat besides the two Toki has up there already. A younger one — and you could bring her down here every second year to be bred at no charge."

Thora shook her head, struggling to keep a straight face. What could possibly make Thurid believe any well-born girl would consider sharing a wretched shack with Driftwood Toki, let alone bearing his children? And she, a girl who, had she wished, could have married Gunnar Snorrisson, the most respected trader around Borgarfjord!

"I have no intention right now to marry anyone," Thora said. "And, Thurid Herjolfsdottir, there's no need for you to worry about my future. Neither I nor my *thrall* or my animals I assure you, will be a burden to Gronsetur Farm any longer."

Thurid looked puzzled.

"Well," she said with a shrug, "you would do well to think again...a girl in your situation can't be choosy. Let me know when you're decided. I'll be in the dairy shed."

Thora abandoned the yoke and stalked off straight into the house to pack her things. Now that Thurid had forced her hand she might as well leave for the coast right away, today. Perhaps it was for the better. She would have plenty of time to make her way overland to Borgarfjord, the southern gathering point for settlers wishing to sail with Eirik to Greenland; those gathered at Borgarfjord would later sail north to Breidafjord and meet up with Eirik and settlers from the North shore, before setting out together for Greenland.

No doubt her sudden departure would stir up much talk and scandalized whispering. *That ungrateful girl…* they would say. *She couldn't be bothered to attend her father's brother's funeral, can you believe that?… and after all that he did for her.*

Older women would shake their heads. *No good could come of a widowed man bringing up his daughter as if she were a son,* they would all agree. *Rumour goes that Thorvinn Haraldson taught his girl to hunt and roam the hills … only served to make her wilful…. no one in charge to teach her women's skills … at Hestardalur, they say, the maids took pretty much care of all weaving…what to expect of a young girl, unsupervised…not knowing enough to supervise others.*

Well, never mind. Thora laughed aloud. She wouldn't be here to listen to the talk.

She tied the straps of her twin saddle bags and carried them outside — one bag filled with travel food selected from the pantry shelf, the other with assorted belongings from the chest under her bed. They were welcome to keep some of her things, mere trinkets, as well as the unwieldy chest she had brought from home; she would need a lightweight sea chest instead, able to cope with salt spray.

She found Eidyll in the smithy repairing a hay fork.

"Never mind that now," Thora said, taking the fork from him. "We're leaving here, for good. Get the mare tacked up and ride out to round up my ewes and bring them here, those that are mine, remember to make sure of their ear notches. I will not be accused of stealing Thurid's sheep."

She went back to the house, laughing again. Thurid was welcome to keep her goat, her rickety old sheepdog and poor old Toki.

She stuffed her remaining posessions, clothes, footwear and a sleeping bag, in twin willow pack baskets and struggled with the heavy load across the muddy yard to the horse pen.

"Hey," Thurid cried out behind her. "Going somewhere?"

Thora swung around, coming face to face with Thurid and her mother.

Old Thorgerd raised her eyebrows.

"You're not leaving us?" She sounded genuinely surprised.

"Yes I am," Thora said. "I'm leaving this farm for good."

Thurid's face flushed with anger.

"Without telling us?" she cried. "And before you've paid your respect to your dead uncle by seeing him to the grave?"

Thora stared at Thurid's quivering cheeks.

Why so upset? Of course! People would think that Thurid and Helgi, now the sole masters of Gronsetur Farm, were too greedy to wait for Sveinar's burial before sending his poor niece away. All who came to the burial would be scandalized.

Thora shrugged.

"I've been here too long," she said simply, almost pleasantly; she took a firm grip on the basket handles and prepared to continue her way.

Thurid's cheeks darkened to crimson and Thorgerd put a hand on her daughter's arm.

"There, there now," the older woman said. "Surely we can think of a fitting gift for Sveinar's niece, now that she is leaving. It wouldn't be right to let her go without a reward for her dutiful sheep tending. Not a single ewe was lost, remember, while she was in charge of the flock."

"Thanks to the white dog," Thurid said with a snort.

Thorgerd called out to Helgi who sat by the house wall with visiting neighbours.

"Helgi Thorlakson! Thora Thorvinnsdottir is leaving us, for good. How much do you think we owe her for her services?"

Helgi came across the yard. "Leaving? What do you mean?"

He halted facing Thora; his glance lingered on her breast and hips.

Thora swallowed her anger. No point in making a scene.

"Well," said Helgi in a voice loud enough to be heard by the lads repairing the fence around the horse-pen.

"If you truly must leave us, dear cousin, name the farewell gift you desire. Name any possession of ours that can be carried away."

A cluster of maids on their way home from the stream, set their waterpails down to listen.

"We will not be found small-minded," said Helgi, underlining his words with grand gestures. "No one shall say that we of Gronsetur lack generosity."

He raised both arms, repeating, "Anything you care to carry, dear cousin, name it and it will be yours."

"I have all that I need," Thora said stiffly. "Why should I make my good mare carry more weight than needed?"

She tugged on her baskets, eager to head for the horse-pen.

Old Thorgerd called out, "Think again, girl. You need not burden your horse with more weight. Not if you choose a gift that carries itself on four feet!"

She tugged her daughter's sleeve.

"Thurid here will agree I think that you ought to have the black horse you seem to value so. What would you say if she gave you the colt which her husband saw fit to pay for with a load of homespun and some of her best ewes?"

Thora took a step backwards. *Give away Sveinar's prize horse? They must be teasing!*

Thurid appeared just as stunned, but recovered quickly. She nudged Helgi.

"Go and call the household together to bid farewell to your cousin. We want every maid, free or bonded, every *karl*, and *thrall* to attend your farewell speech on the occasion of Thora's leaving."

Helgi went off to round up all the folk he could find. Men, women and children drifted over from the byres and pens, and others were called in from the home fields. More than two dozen people of all ages gathered in a half circle around Helgi, eager to hear the words of Gronsetur's new master.

Helgi spoke well. He thanked Thora for her work in the hills and in the dairy shed. Next he praised the black colt, his farewell gift to her; he recited the horse's impeccable breeding and physical attributes, leaving out nothing that might help to impress on people the uncommon generosity of granting so splendid a gift to a poor relative.

Thora suppressed a chuckle. *A colt so unruly, that Thurid believes no other than Eidyll, the thrall who will be leaving with me, is able to ride the black stud or manage him profitably at the horse fights. Without the help of my thrall, she thinks the horse will be of no use to anyone here.*

She glanced at Gronsetur's mistress who seemed to be watching and listening closely to the crowd's response. Thurid turned to her mother and talked loudly into her left ear, less deaf than the other.

"There is no sign, Mother, of your good sense going dim with the years."

Thorgerd's soft-spoken response was lost in the wind.

The small crowd dispersed slowly. Thora caught the looks of satisfaction passing between mother and son. Helgi had indeed spoken well in front of all, including the slaves. Gronsetur's slaves would report the event to their fellows arriving soon with their masters to be at Sveinar's burial. Word would travel quickly of the lavish farewell gift Gronsetur's new master did grant to his stepfather's poor relative; a feat of generosity that would go far in serving Helgi's reputation as a promising leader in the district.

FIVE

Hrut said, I think it be best that Hauskuld and I name witnesses, and that Hallgerda speaks out to betroth herself, if the Lawman thinks it right and lawful? It is right and lawful, Thorarin said.

NJAL'S SAGA

The high-tailed mare carried her rider on swift hooves that seemed to sprout feelers, across rocks, bogs and lava fields. Thora, nudging the horse to more speed, settled back humming fragments of wedding songs. Here she was, riding into a future of her own choosing, breathing the freedom of mountains, moors and boulder-strewn river plains under the crisp sky of early summer; best of all, she was free to revel in joyful wedding songs without having to attend the wedding of Helgi and Magni, nor her own to seal a preposterous marriage to Driftwood Toki.

Eidyl on the black colt beside her raised his bird-bone flute to his lips, almost dropping the instrument when his horse threw a fit at the shrill tones ripping by its ears. Eidyll persisted, and the colt settled, moving along with the mare in stride with the music.

For now it was easy enough to find their way. They were still travelling past familiar farmsteads with friendly neighbours who allowed them to graze their small flock of sheep on good pasture. Toward evening they found a place to stay the night; a shallow grassy ravine thick with birch, plenty to graze and browse for the horses. Eidyll made camp and Thora, after stringing her bow, went looking for something to eat. Yesterday they ate the last of their rations of cooked goose and early this morning they swallowed the last of the cold barley porridge they had taken along.

She glanced over her shoulder at the tiny camp and noticed that Eidyll was watching her. She gave him a stare until he lowered his head and continued to gather kindling.

Thora fitted a bird-arrow to her bow and urged the dog, "Off with you, Khagan! Find us some *rjupa* to eat!"

She set out at a slow walk scanning the ground and taking pleasure in running her fingers along the smooth double curve of her bow. Her bow, rare to begin with in Iceland, might be the only one of its kind in Greenland. The recurved bow was built by Khazar craftsmen on the eastern plains; it was both shorter and lighter than the self bows used by most men, which were harder to handle for a woman. *These bows*, her father said when he presented it to her four winters ago upon his return from his journey, *are intended for use on horseback at a full gallop*.

That same fall, back from his journey to Sweden the Cold, Thorvinn gave her the tall white dog as well. *His name is Khagan*, he said, *meaning 'Jarl', in the Khazar language.*

Thora slowed her step paying close attention to the rocky ground. It took a good eye at the best of times to hunt *rjupa*. This time of year the ground dwelling birds were cloaked in mottled brown and grey. Huddled among rocks and lichens, ptarmigan were hard to spot for a human hunter, and even a dog would be hard presssed to find any, for the birds gave off little scent.

There! Khagan flushed a bird right in front of his feet, leapt up after it...and caught it! No arrow needed for this one.

"Prrr, give it up! Go find another."

She gave him a pat and fingered the plump bird, chuckling at the thought of the addle-brained Khazar who – pickled in Swedish ale maybe – traded away such a matchless dog.

*　　*　　*　　*　　*

They traveled at a leisurely pace following he main drover trail at some distance and pausing often to allow the sheep time to graze, taking care not to move too far away from the main route northwest. Neither of them was familiar with these parts and it would be easy to lose their way. Thora wore her shepherding clothes with a man's leather skull cap pulled over her hair and ears, pretending to be just another farm lad from Gronsetur farm.

"Should we meet someone who wants to know who we are," she said to Eidyll, "I'll pretend I'm unable to speak; you must tell them we are on our way from Gronsetur Farm with a small flock of sheep to sell to the settlers gathering at Borgarfjord."

It wouldn't do for a well-born woman to be found traveling without armed company, an invitation to robbers and outlaws to seize her and demand a ransom for her release.

After eight days of slow uneventful travel, they arrived with their sheep at Borgarfjord. Thora pulled to a halt halfway down the last slope, awed by the sight of so many ships and people and livestock.

All along the shores on both sides of the fjord were camps of prospective settlers, anchored ships and small boats hauled ashore.

Thora removed her cap, releasing her hair for the first time in days, happy to be among decent folk, free to speak and be herself without fear of outlaws.

Everywhere among the scattered boulders were people camped with their livestock. Late arrivals had no other choice than to make camp right on top of the sheep tracks gouging the land, muddied by many hooves churning up remnants of melting snow in places shaded by boulders. Family groups moved about collecting rocks for marking the boundaries of their camps, clusters of shelters built of driftwood and turf roofed with sheets of oiled leather. Others simply unrolled their leather sleeping bags under the sky.

Not all of those gathered here, intended to sail on to Breidafjord to join Eirik and other settlers taking part in the Greenland venture. Many came to offer trade and services to the land-seekers, and others for no other reason than the chance to watch so many ships setting out all at once.

Thora left Eidyll with the horses and sheep in a narrow space between scattered rocks, a space too small for a family group and their livestock to set up camp.

"You'll need to stack up some more rocks to keep the ewes from roaming," Thora told Eidyll before she left to stroll along the shore path lined with market stalls, booths of stacked stone and turf with drift-wood rafters covered with sail cloth. Women traded wool cloth, home-spun *wadmal* dyed black or brown or left in natural shades of white, peat brown and gravel grey. Men and women hawked linens brought in from foreign lands by seafaring friends or relatives.

Thora lingered in front of a stall where a young woman sold fine Friesian woolens dyed bright blue and red, brought from Denmark by her husband she said. Thora admired the beautiful cloth before moving on; next she paused by the stall of an older woman hawking bundles of dried herbs.

The vendor sized her up.

"At your stage of life," she said, "no woman ought to be without this."

She rummaged in a dirty cloth bag and brought out a handful of small squares, dried peat by the looks of them.

"These herbs are used as a potion. I give you twenty of them for ten half pieces of silver – no woman should be without."

Thora took one of the lumps in her hand; it felt dry and crumbly, almost as light as a raven's feather.

"What is it for?"

"As I said, it's a women's potion. You nip off a pinch, crumble it in boiling water and let it steep to make a tea. Wait till it's cool and drink all at once."

"Why? What does it do?" Thora asked, ready to walk on.

The woman pressed her finger against the side of her nose.

"Listen carefully. After you drink the potion you may go ahead and lie with any man you desire, making sport to your heart's delight. Afterwards you make a fresh batch of tea and drink it to make double sure that you haven't conceived. Life ought to be fun for a woman, free of worry ... like a man's, right?"

Thora pursed her lips. Did she look gullible enough to pay good silver for mere chunks of peat? In any case, she had no silver to spare. First she needed to trade her sheep for enough silver to buy passage and necessities for the journey. Besides, she didn't expect to, nor wish to, lie with a man in the near future.

She handed the merchandise back to the woman and sniffed the crumbs remaining in the palm of her hand: as she thought — *genuine peat*. With so many things waiting to be purchased, it would be foolish to take a chance on questionable herbs.

Thora paused at the sellers of leatherwork to sort through the horse tack and saddlery, belts and shoes, boots, leggings and tie-straps. Agitated vendors ran back and forth shooing children away who tried to bounce on the saddles displayed for sale. Thora counted the few silver coins, wholes and halves, in her pouch before she used half a coin to purchase a bundle of rawhide lashing and a long rope of braided horse hair. She ran her hand over a sturdy pack-saddle but decided the price was too high. She had no idea until she had sold her sheep, how much silver she would have left to spend on things other than the sea passage.

The noise in this place was unnerving. Harried traders jogged by driving bleating flocks of sheep ahead of them, aided by dogs yapping and nipping the sheep sending tufts of wool flying. After a while Thora noticed the same flocks moving back and forth, changing hands many times. Cows and heifers lumbered by, bellowing after friends and herd-mates sold and driven away. Above the general din came the piercing squeals of anxious horses separated from friends, calling, listening for a response and calling again.

Not many horses were here to be traded. Most came from farms in the district, loaded with goods offered for sale to the settlers. Staked or hobbled beside sleds and pack baskets, the horses stood waiting for their owners to wrap up the trading and begin the trek home.

Farmers living nearby came with summer-sleds piled high with cut grass, fresh or cured, for the livestock. Others brought pails, barrels and baskets of food for the voyagers. Thora ignored the fresh cheese and eggs on offer. She needed food that could keep — aged cheese and cured meats, fowl or fish, air or smoke-dried. A few vendors sold barley grain in small bags for outrageous prices, too costly to use for bread or beer making. They hoped to find settlers in dire need of seed grain. After the long winter, grain was in short supply and most farmers held on to what they had, afraid to run short at seeding time.

Thora asked around to get a feel for the going livestock prices. Fat ewes such as hers, prime breeding stock to take to Greenland, were in short supply; quality ewes were selling at premium prices to settlers who could afford to bring some choice animals to Greenland to build up new flocks. The majority of sheep offered for sale had arrived in bad shape, underweight, stressed after long marching journeys without enough time to graze, pushed on by owners who feared they might arrive at the coast too late after the ships departed. Those preparing to settle in Greenland were also selling off second rate livestock against any price; only those able to pay for the shipment of a small number of sheep, shopped around for promising ewes like those offered by Thora for sale. Her small flock ought to fetch six or more silver pieces a head.

First, Thora decided before trading her sheep away, she needed to find a skipper willing to take her, and Eidyll, the dog and the horses to Greenland, for a fee she could afford. She made her way slowly along the shore looking at the ships and talking to the skippers in their shore booths. Many vessels were owned by men with large families, filled to capacity with the owner, his wife, children and other kin, *karls*, maids bonded and free, and male slaves as well. Only a handful of skippers would take paying passengers.

Thora settled on a seasoned shipmaster from Akranes, 'Bowlegs' Ulf Thorsteinson. He agreed to keep a space for her in his *knorr*, Maelstrom Tamer, and asked how many others would travel with her.

"I can take a few more people ...no livestock."

"I need passage for two, myself and my lad," Thora said. "I'm selling my sheep, but I will not part with my dog or my two horses. I need tie-space for them and a corner to store hay and four barrels of water, enough for ten days. My lad will take care of watering, feeding and mucking out."

"It's going to cost you," Ulf warned. "I'll charge you full passenger fare for that oversized dog, and for each horse you pay the rate of three sheep."

"I'll think about it," Thora said walking away.

Could she afford to lose this chance to board a ship for Greenland? Unlike many others gathered here to depart, she had no home to return to. She tried to imagine what her mother would tell her to do. Rannveig would be ill-pleased with her plans to leave Iceland instead of finding a way to regain possession of Hestardalur – *How, by marrying Gunnar?*

She must make up her own mind.

Thora sat down on a lichen-encrusted rock resting her head in her hands. What other choice did she have than to pay the fare Ulf was asking? She couldn't miss out on the chance to go to Greenland and get her hands on some land. Once she had her own homestead, everything else in her life would fall into place. Any woman with a farm to her name could hope to marry a man of some consequence, a man with the connections and means to secure a proper station in life for his family.

Thora returned to where she had left Eidyll in charge of the flock; the place was in turmoil. Eidyll was panting with exhaustion, yelling and jogging circles around the sheep which for their part seemed determined to escape from this place of mud; Eidyll's long drover whip kept lashing out at the savvy ewes which tried to scramble over the low wall of stacked rocks in search of grass.

"I can't keep them in here much longer ... Thora ... Thorvinnsdottir," Eidyll blurted out. "These ornery ewes won't stay around unless... you purchase some fodder, right away."

"That won't be necessary," Thora said, grinning. "Hang in there; I'll be back with a buyer."

She marched off, fingering the amber necklace she wore hidden under her tunic. If she didn't receive enough silver for her sheep, she might have to sell this, her most valuable possession. If she did, would her mother whose presence she felt so strongly these days, be angry? Surely Rannveig would know that her daughter wouldn't sell the treasured necklace on a whim but only as a last resort. She looked up to the sky. *Isn't it time that you, Mother, decided to trust my judgment?*

They might soon be parting company anyway, if it was true what some people said, that spirits and ghosts were unable to cross the sea. Thora took a deep breath, disturbed by the thought that from here on decisions she made at the turning points in her life, would be hers alone. There would be no one to help her decide which path to take, no one to ask for advice, not even her mother's ghost, if there was truth in what people said.

I'll have no one to blame but myself if things should turn out badly.

SIX

So they set out on their voyage and as they made their
way across the sea, they were attacked by vikings intent on
robbing them and carry away everything they desired...

CORMAC'S SAGA

Thora strolled by the vendors' booths one more time keeping her hand firmly around her purse with silver pieces. She found she had plenty left after all else was paid for.

At a clothes seller's booth she examined woolen garments and settled on a Friesian-made cloak of fine wool, dyed red with non-fading madder root — a garment fit for a well-bred woman to wear on the day she married a man of her own choice, a man of means whom she liked well enough.

She returned to the herb woman's booth determined to take a chance after all on the peaty lumps – in case she met a good looking man she thought irresistible, though unsuitable for a husband. If the potion worked as the vendor promised, it could make her life as the woman said, *free of worry – like a man's.*

After a lengthy negotiation, Thora slid five half coins into the woman's palm one by one; the vendor scratched each bit of silver with a dirt-rimmed fingernail before putting them on her scales to make sure they weren't filed down. Thora tried not to wince. She had haggled the woman down to five half coins for thirty lumps of mystery herb, still too high a price if it turned out she had bought thirty worthless lumps of crumbly brown peat; then again, if these were indeed herbs holding the powers claimed for them, she couldn't consider herself cheated. Many women would pay a good deal more for such herbs, if effective, and she might be able to sell some to other women in Greenland.

*   *   *   *   *

People came from far to see the ships, ten of them all told, setting out of Borgarfjord headed north to meet with Eirik and the others at Breidafjord, where they would set out together for Greenland hoping their numbers would protect them against lurking sea rovers; few vikings would dare single out and attack a freight vessel sailing in the company of so many others. In any case, most men going a-viking preferred to operate in southern waters for richer pickings; then again, news of a fleet of plodding freight ships loaded with settlers and their belongings, might draw a few roving longships north.

One ship after another pushed away under oar, carried to sea on the outgoing tide; people onboard were milling around, waving to those who stayed behind. As soon as the vessels reached deep water, the skippers ordered the square sails raised and the ships rode the waves like eider ducks or giant geese with wings half-raised.

Most ships were seagoing *knorr*, broad-chested open cargo vessels, clinker-built with overlapping strakes and able to hold some thirty people and a dozen heads of livestock crowded mid-ships. They were carefully crafted to hug the water, moving back and forth with the wash of the sea instead of fighting the waves, thanks to the lashings that linked the boards below water level instead of the iron rivets holding the hull together above the waterline.

They anchored briefly at Breidafjord waiting for the other settlers to break up camp, board ship and push off. At first, in the fjord, all twenty-five ships traveled closely together, close enough for people to shout back and forth exchanging news and banter.

Chaos ruled aboard the ships; flustered mothers tried to corral their young children chasing about with the yapping sheepdogs, overturning baskets with panicked chickens and ducks, boxes with frantic ferrets and the odd basket with a hissing cat inside.

The *knorr* of Bowlegs Ulf carried almost two dozen people, adults and children, with their belongings and livestock and one large white dog — taking up as much space, Ulf grumbled when he caught sight of Khagan, as two regular herding dogs or one man.

He had charged Thora accordingly, and she decided not to argue. The skipper had charged her regular horse fare for both horses although they, too, were larger than others of their kind.

She leaned back against her sea-chest rubbing the smooth beads of her necklace between her cold fingers to warm them; she held them up to warm her heart by these glowing drops of sunshine forever trapped. Warm and almost ready to sleep, Thora sighed with relief. Her ewes had fetched top prices, enough to purchase food and other necessities for the journey as well as the light weight sea-chest now supporting her back. It was large, allowing plenty of room for her clothes, horse tack and travel food; yet, the chest was surprisingly light, crafted of willow-branches and covered with oiled horse-hide and a lid of stretched sealskin.

The gentle rocking of the ship made everyone drowsy. Thora slumped down for comfort against the chest, padded with a blanket and firmly lashed against the ship's port side. Sleepily, she ran her fingers over the belt pouch around her waist. Inside was the linen-wrapped package of mystery herbs she purchased. *Keep in the dark and well wrapped*, the herb-vendor had said. *The herbs will lose power if exposed to air and light.*

*   *   *   *   *

Off the point of Hellisandur Eirik signalled the other skippers to gather, roping their ships together to form a gigantic bobbing raft; Eirik's *knorr* in the middle remained visible to all because of the high-rising bow crowned with a carved horse head painted in garish colours.

Thora listened to Eirik shouting out the sailing directions to Greenland before they each went their way. From this point onward, the ships were likely to move out of touch and sight, depending on wind, water and the sailing abilities of each vessel.

They entered the open sea sailing on a northeastern breeze still in close proximity of one another until, in the low light of the summer evening, they lost sight of some ships and others became reduced to tiny specks on the horizon.

On board of Maelstrom Tamer people settled into a routine of talking, eating, sleeping, waking up and repeating it all again.

Ulf ordered the younger men to take turns as lookouts strapped to the top of the mast to keep an eye out for seaborne raiders.

Thora shifted and stretched her limbs, stiff from leaning against the side of the ship. It wasn't her nature to talk without need, and so she kept to herself, eating and sleeping, addressing the doubts that plagued her mind. What if Thorvinn were still alive, delayed longer than anyone could have thought? What if he came home the next spring after spending a second winter in some faraway place? Would she receive word of his return to Iceland? It could take more than one summer for news from Iceland to travel to Greenland.

Thora shivered; seated with most other passengers in the *knorr's* open mid-ship section, she was splashed continuously by waves jumping over the sides. The ship seemed bow-heavy, digging into the seas rather than snaking through, giving with the surface as it was built to do. Some mid-ships passengers glared at the skipper's wife and family huddled behind the bow under a spray-cover of walrus-hide between bulging bags and hefty chests the size of a large calf.

Ulf ordered some of his family's weighty chests moved to aft; the move did improve the *knorr's* balance, though some water still splashed in now and then, and Thora resigned herself to the prospect of being soaked till the end of the journey. She felt dizzy looking at the restless water gurgling around the ship, and she closed her eyes trying to imagine Eirik's Greenland — a gigantic *joekull,* some said, a solid ice glacier ringed with habitable land along the coasts.

Half asleep she listened to the talk around her, opening her eyes when a young woman loudly declared, "In his speech at the last Thing gathering, Eirik assured us the new land is as good as Iceland used to be at the time of the first settlers; Iceland is now without trees they say because the livestock keeps eating everything down, and people used to burn trees and bushes for firewood and more pasture. Eirik promised us plenty of trees and untouched pastureland in Greenland."

It had better be so, for all our sakes. Thora looked to the dark-haired young woman with the piping voice who just spoke. She, according to the gossip on board, was married without a dowry to the curly-haired young man asleep beside her, a freed slave with nothing to his name.

"I wouldn't take Eirik's word for it!" argued an older man. "I've seen it, and I say this Greenland isn't nearly as good as Iceland was in the old days."

Thora, keeping her eyes closed, remembered this man with the rasping voice – an old sea farer from Norway who had sailed with Eirik on the first Greenland venture.

"There are no trees of a useful size in Eirik's new land," the old man continued. "There are none that are large and straight enough for boat building. I saw nothing but tangles of creeping willow and birch, same as in Iceland today after a hundred and more winters of settlement."

What if the man told the truth? Years ago Thora heard a discussion between her father and a visiting horse buyer. Thorvinn had questioned the potential of the rumoured new land — 'Gunnbjorn's Land' they called it then — and the visitor said, *I've heard it's a poor place for timber.* No wonder her father had hoped to make a fortune sailing timber and other goods over to Greenland.

She drummed with her fingers on the oiled hide of the chest. Would the journey to the new land bring her better luck than it had brought Thorvinn? *After all he did to secure his luck.*

On the day of departure for Greenland, Thorvinn had, once the ship was out in the fjord and still under oar, sacrificed a young bull to Njord, ruler of waves and wind. Thora, standing on the shore after waving fare-well, watched the ship towing the black yearling bull out to deep water. From her place on the shore she could hear the bull grunting and see the white of its eyes; it put up a spirited fight but had to give in to the towline around its rump dragging it out to the choppy water of open sea where Thorvinn ordered the lads to push the beast under with oars; it took a long time to drown the young bull, strong and vigorous — a worthy sacrifice. After the waters closed over it for good, Thorvinn lost no time to raise the sail and begin the journey while his luck was fresh.

Thora pursed her lips. Whatever good the sacrifice might have done for that day, it seemed that her father's luck had run out before the end of the journey. Perhaps Njord wasn't impressed with a bull only one winter old, though well grown.

She straightened up hoping that Ulf's luck and that of his ship and all who sailed in her, would last till they reached their destination.

*　　*　　*　　*　　*　　*

After three days of sailing the settlers grew bored and quite a few young men and women turned loud and unruly. Mothers with small children yelled at them to tone down, or their children would never fall asleep. As long as the fair wind held, Ulf had no use for strong arms to push oars and squabbles erupted among the idle young men.

Ivar, the skipper's son, seemed to have the loudest mouth of all. About twenty winters old, Ivar Ulfson was well-built, handsome and bold with a touch of menace; blond-haired, he had thick darkbrown eyebrows sheltering his brooding eyes, which shifted colour between slate and blueish grey, depending on the light.

Inspite of his good looks, boastful Ivar held little appeal for her and Thora kept her eyes firmly closed; she sensed he was staring at her from his favourite place leaned against the mast.

Colts and young men have much in common – unruly and bothersome unless dead tired.

Nothing, short of several days and nights of continuous rowing and relentless bailing, would quiet these lads down. For now, the waves and the favourable wind remained as they were, briskly pushing the ship along without aid from the oars. Half asleep, Thora listened to the wind strumming the rigging with sounds like a home-made harp plunked by a child playing at being a *skjald*.

She felt the body of the *knorr* moving with the water as if the ship was alive, her lower hull of lashed planking giving back and forth with the waves. She imagined being on the back of a horse roaming the hills, free to go where she wished instead of riding the waves cooped up with two dozen others in a hollow sea steed made of planks, steered by a single hand determining the course for her and everyone else. *Truly, sailing the seas is a wretched way to travel.* And yet, many a seafaring man, home after a long sailing journey, could be found wandering the shore casting restless glances at the fjord. If asked, he would say that it was time for him and his friends to return to the sea, to the freedom found there.

How could anyone think of seafaring as a way to gain freedom? To her, no place felt less free than the cramped space allotted to those aboard a seagoing *knorr*. Thurid's rants, as repetitive as they were, did on occasion make sense. *Men,* Thurid used to say, *are all too eager to answer the call of the sea, to escape from the demands made on them by their womenfolk. Men prefer to sail off to glory leaving it to the women at home with their maids and slaves, to deal with the grind of daily life.*

Thora glanced to the horses dozing side by side mid-ships, eyes closed and heads hanging low. Every so often one dropped suddenly to its knees, jolted awake and straightened up re-locking its knee-joints. She sighed. A ship at sea was no place for a horse, or a horse woman.

During the night the wind died down and the *knorr* drifted about becalmed. For a while the sail flapped listlessly, touched by occasional whiffs of air, like sighs escaping the chest of some god or goddess asleep on the surface of the sea. Soon there was no more movement at all, only dead air clinging to the limp sail which drooped from the yard like a giant single leaf attached to a tree that had only two limbs stiffly stretched sideways.

Most of the ship's passengers were farmers rather than seafaring folk by inclination; abandoned by the wind, they were quick to loose heart.

"We'll run out of things to eat and then we'll have to kill our live-stock," a woman with four small children declared to no one in particular. "And then we might as well die. We cannot survive in the new land without breeding animals to start new flocks."

Ulf frowned at her.

"Silence your tongue, woman, if you cannot talk sense."

He called a dozen men to the oars.

* * * * *

On the first windless day Eidyll played the new flute he had fashioned of goose-bone before boarding ship, and for a while his merry tunes cheered people up. Men and women tapped their feet and children clapped their hands. Later though, people grew annoyed; they reminded themselves and each other of all the things they were worried about, and soon they took to pelting the flute playing *thrall* with mutton bones and fish skins, until he put away his flute.

As soon as he did, the wind returned – this time from the South and people, cheered by the breeze, smiled at the *thrall*.

"Njord must've been pleased by the music," some said.

"He relented and sent us fresh wind for our sail."

Still, Ulf pointed out that this wind was pushing them north against the current which had earlier combined with the northeast wind to carry them southwest to their destination. He overruled objections, ordered the sail reefed and the oars manned again; progress by rowing was painfully slow; Maelstrom Tamer was a freightship, unable to reach good speed under oar. In the absence of a favourable wind, the power of her six pairs of oars was barely able to keep the vessel on course in the relentless battle against sideways drift.

Toward evening the breeze once more dwindled to nothing and people slept fitfully in the half light of she short summer night.

Unable to sleep after too many days of forced rest, Thora sat up to stretch. Most of the others were asleep or pretended to be. Only Eidyll, after mucking out around the livestock, seemed widely awake, bent over a piece of leather, scratching lines in it.

"What are you doing? Show me," Thora demanded.

Eidyll handed her the sheet. She turned it around twice, examining it from every angle.

"So that's what your Christian writing looks like. I know runes... that is to say, I know not the magic that's in them according to some; but I know to write and read rune signs ... still, I cannot make sense of these squiggles."

She turned the sheet right side up.

"These can't be too hard to learn, seems to me – no harder to learn than runes. Tell me, why are these signs shaped in curves, rounded and looped? Wouldn't they be harder than rune signs to chisel into wood and stone?"

"They aren't meant to be scratched or cut into wood or stone," Eidyll explained.

"They're supposed to be drawn on vellum with a quill dipped in black."

Thora handed the sheet back.

"Read to me what you wrote."

He read aloud, "Anno Domini 985 may the Lord deliver us safely to Greater Ireland."

She stared at him, a skeptical look in her ice-grey eyes.

"Greater Ireland...what kind of place is that? Surely, we're headed for Greenland!"

With reluctance, Eidyll told of the tales he had heard in the towns of his Briton homeland, and later on his travels with a party of horse buying monks to Ireland across the sea channel.

"It is said there were holy Christian fathers living in Iceland before Norsemen settled there. These monks sailed away from Iceland when the Norse settlers came, and they're believed to have settled in another land which the Irish call, Greater Ireland. Perhaps, I thought, this could be Greenland, and there might still be holy men living there."

Thora burst into laughter.

"You're a foolish lad to believe in silly rumours," she said. "Anyone with a grain of sense would know such stories for what they are, tall tales."

She pointed to the sea.

"Look at those black, icy waters. Now think again and imagine a bunch of chicken-hearted priests devoted to White Christ, men clad in shifts as if they were women! How could any of them fight their way through the domain of Njord to the freezing edge of the world? You say those holy men of yours left Ireland a long time ago, and no one has seen or heard of them since. That's no surprise. If such men ever did sail out of Ireland this far northwest and beyond, they would have perished long ago."

Eidyll kept silent, rolling up the calf skin.

"Now," Thora said, pointing to his tattered sleeping bag.

"I suggest you go to sleep now as long as the sea remains calm and allows you to sleep without turning green in the face. You told me you were sick all the way at sea when my father brought you from Hedeby to Iceland."

She unrolled her own sleeping bag and slipped inside, lodging herself in the corner against her sea-chest and the side of the ship, a fist clenched around the horsehair dog leash.

*   *   *   *   *   *   *   *   *   *

GREENLAND

There was a man from Breidafjord, Eirik Raudi, who journeyed from here to take land in a place he named Eiriksfjord. He gave a name to the entire land, calling it Greenland, and he said people would be more eager to go there because the land had a good name

ISLENDINGABOK

SEVEN

———————————————————
———————————————

*Three great waves broke over their ship...Flosi said they must
be near land, for this must be a ground swell...and they barely
knew where they were before they were tossed ashore in the dark
of night, and the men were saved, but the ship all smashed to
pieces and they could not save their belongings...then they sought
a hiding place and covered themselves with moss and rested.*

NJAL'S SAGA

———————————————————
———————————————

In the perpetual twilight of the summer night the people aboard
Maelstrom Tamer, by now all asleep, were jolted awake. Around and
below them the ship lunged and bucked like a horse gone out of its
mind. Children whimpered in fright pulling blankets over their heads.
The ship tossed and turned on a tumultuous sea of black water touched
by silver flashes like fish scales in the pale light of the low, distant sun as
if all the sea had turned into a writhing, hissing, finned monster aroused
from the deep. Maelstrom Tamer didn't seem to live up to her name;

those clinging to her hull expected the ship to slide any time from the monster's bucking spine to a watery doom.

Thora struggled to make sense of the turmoil. It seemed only a heartbeat ago that she went to sleep in the clinging, lifeless air. Strangely, she didn't feel or hear any wind. Where did they come from, these fearsome mountains of heaving water which caused the ship to throw such tantrums? Others, just as bewildered, asked the same question.

"It's the maelstrom!" an old woman wailed. "We're doomed!"

Thora gasped. Could it really be so? Were they caught in the mid-sea maelstrom of seafarer lore, the wicked funnel of churning water said to be the roaring cauldron of Hvergelmer which boils on the sea floor underneath the World Mill? Around her men and women called on the gods for mercy and others begged White Christ to save them.

Timbers creaked and waves reached up along the spray-soaked sail dragging it down to one side of the ship's hull, resisting the crew's frantic efforts to haul it onboard. At last they succeeded to pull it in, struggling with the heavy soaked *wadmal* in their effort to roll it and store it away from the people who crawled about, hollering to locate family and friends. Most tried holding on to the sides of the bucking ship or to roped-down packs, and all prayed for deliverance to whoever they thought would hear them.

The sea fell into violent spasms sending terrified children tumbling about in the belly of the ship, in danger of being kicked or trampled by the panicked livestock scrambling to stay on their feet. Bellowing cows were down on their knees entangled in rope, with bawling calves underneath them struggling to get back up, knocked down again on top of each other, amongst and on top of bleating sheep.

After the men had folded the sodden sail tight and secured it with lashings of walrus-hide, the ship became easier to manage and Ulf ordered the oars manned.

"And see to it that we're keeping the bow headed into the seas."

The flexible hull resumed a steady course through the turbulence, and the waves now came at regular intervals allowing the *knorr* to slide down the back of one and rise with the next.

Everyone was breathing relief, when suddenly out of nowhere glassy green towers of water rose up all around them, leaving the ship floundered at the bottom of a watery trough without a chance to rise.

Thora happened to look aft just as the sea, without a sound, heaved up behind the stern; she shouted a warning, tied the dog leash around her waist and threw herself on top of her roped down sea-chest grasping the handle with both fists – as long as the lashings would hold the chest to the ship and as long as the ship stayed right side up, the sea would not get the better of her. *Was this how Thorvinn met his end?* An image crept into her mind, of Thorvinn, both of his hands clawed around the steering oar, stubbornly trusting his luck and the strength of his boldly named ship, Surf Leaper — until the boards shattered below and around him.

She shook her head firmly to chase out the wretched image.

The walls of water rose no further, as if by magic remaining suspended around and over the *knorr* before cresting slowly, then faster, to crash on top of the ship unleashing its fury — glassy green water was everywhere, gurgling, tracing criss-crossing patterns of foam, sending people and animals afloat.

Another wave reared up; terrified people, wide-eyed, scarcely breathing, braced themselves. Thora blinked her eyes against the sting of saltwater. The ship, more than half full of water slopping back and forth, heaved slowly like a harpooned whale nearing death.

Thora caught sight of Gunnhild Grimsdottir, the skipper's wife, swept away from her place in the bow and halted by the mast; she seemed dazed, holding on to the mast with one arm. Another wave crested; it came down on one side of the ship and splashed out over the opposite side; the powerful pull of the outgoing water lifted Gunnhild clear off her feet and threatened to wash her overboard.

"No, hold on!" Thora yelled. She kept one hand clutching the handle of her chest and reached out with the other grasping the woman's ankle, straining to hold on, gritting her teeth.

In another moment of quiet, Thora let go and Gunnhild crawled back to the mast, wrapped both arms around it just before another mountain of water smashed down. Thora let go of the chest handle and crawled toward the horses dragging the white dog by the rope around her waist.

Gunnhild yelled, "Where are you going, girl! Come over here and stay put, hold on to the mast!"

Another wave crashed down inside the ship lifting Thora off her feet and carrying her off like flotsam. She groped for something to hold, something firm; panic made way for an eerie calm. *This is my last moment alive in this world…the sea is claiming me as it has claimed my father.*

The wash of outgoing water carried her across and over the shipboard, a last chance to hold on and be saved; she reached for the board with arms and legs and managed to hook her left knee around the edge of the shipboard struggling against the water's pull that threatened to dislodge her; she reached out her arms, failing to find any hold, and she felt her leg slipping; a painful jerk at her waist took her breath away; she was thrown clear back inside the ship up to her neck in water.

Thora opened her eyes, blinking at Gunnhild who hovered over her with a broad smile.

"Good thing I was there to give a hand to your dog who was trying his very best to pull you back inside the ship."

The skipper's wife let go of the dog leash; she picked up a broken cow rope, linked herself and Thora at the waist and secured the other end to the mast in time before the next wave hit, and another, each one less powerful than the one before.

People breathed more easily; they looked about searching for those dear to them.

Thora untied the cow rope.

"I owe you, Gunnhild Grimsdottir," she said in a hoarse voice.

"And I owe you," Gunnhild croaked in response, dropping the rope.

Thora watched the skipper's wife making her way back to the bow, up to her hips in water, and bend over to look under the bow cover; Gunnhild straightened up, waving her arms in a panic, adding her frenzied calls to those of many others.

"Helga, Helga! Where are you? Has anyone seen my daughter?"

"Here, mother, I'm here!"

A blonde girl, appearing unharmed though shaken, slipped from under the stern cover and staggered to the bow of the ship.

"I was washed down to the stern..." She fell into her mother's arms.

Gunnhild turned her face to the low sun, calling across the water, "Thank you, White Christ! Thank you for saving my girl!"

*   *   *   *   *

Ulf passed around wooden bailing scoops to the crew and others unpacked household pails and buckets to help emptying the ship of seawater. The waves were still running high and bailing turned into a lengthy and arduous task in the chill, wet air. When they had scooped out the last of the rank smelling water, men and women threw down their scoops and faced each other in silence, exhausted and frowning as if they found it hard to believe they were still able to breathe – and that all of them were still here. Incredibly, no one, neither adult nor child, was lost aboard Maelstrom Tamer, though many were bruised and bloodied from minor wounds.

Two cows aborted their calves, and a young bull stumbled about with a broken foreleg. The owners thought highly of the bull, purchased for good silver to start their new herd, and they tried to save it by hog-tying the bawling yearling so it couldn't get up and further damage the injured limb.

"If only we could get our beast ashore in good time, find some drift-wood and brace the leg," they said, "that bull just might live to breed our heifers on their first heat."

There were more injured livestock and a few had been lost. Ivar Ulfson's chestnut mare had pulled a tendon, and two ewes and a young sheepdog had been washed overboard.

Toward mid-day a steady breeze lifted people's spirits. The waves had settled into a pattern at last, gently lifting and lowering the ship. Ulf ordered four lads to untie a yearling heifer, the smallest of Gunnhild's cows, and offer it to the gods to thank them.

Gunnhild, said to have followed the teachings of White Christ since last summer, looked away, her face rigid with disapproval.

The scrawny heifer put up a spirited struggle; she kicked a lad in the face before they succeeded at last to push her overboard and hold her down long enough to drown.

No more of this strange, windless mayhem occurred in the following days, nor did any storms come upon them. Many believed they owed their good fortune to Ulf's decision to sacrifice, though the Christians among them argued the Christian god had saved them all.

Thora remarked to Gunnhild, "I can hardly believe that Maelstrom Tamer stayed together to keep us all from being sucked into the maelstrom. Ulf named his ship well."

It was re-assuring to think that gods and Norns after all were smiling on her, for now at least. Both of her horses emerged from the mishap without major injury thanks to Eidyll, who stayed right with them throughout the ordeal. Amazingly, the dutiful *thrall* suffered no broken bones from his efforts to hang on to the panicked horses, though he did receive some cuts and a few nasty looking bruises on arms and legs.

Thora finished inspecting the horses; she gave them each a reassuring pat and a playful tug on brine-soaked ears before turning to Eidyll.

"You're a sore sight to behold. Let's take care of those bruises."

She tore and old linen shift to strips and beamed him a rare smile.

"'tWas brave of you to stay with the horses," she said, pointing to the side of the ship.

"Now you must be brave and give those cuts a salty rinse."

Eidyll took his time dipping arms and legs in the gentle green swells, now harmless with playful bubbles and streaks of white foam. Thora bandaged the cuts with the practiced hands of one who has tended countless scrapes on the legs of horses — not too slack, nor too tight. She pulled the last knot snug and sent the *thrall* another smile.

Eidyll blinked his eyes.

"Is something wrong with your eyes?" Thora asked.

"Uhm, no, nothing," Eidyll mumbled. "It's just that you, Thora Thorvinnsdottir... seem so pleased."

Thora squeezed his arm below the bandaged elbow.
"Yes…you did very well I think."

EIGHT

_____

_____

There are many islands in the ocean, and Greenland is not the least of
them, located in the ocean across from the mountains of Sweden.....

To there it is five to seven days sailing they say from the coast of
Norway, the same as sailing to Iceland. The region gets its name
because the people there are greenish from the salt water. They
live the same way as the Icelanders do, except they are fiercer
and inclined to making pirate attacks on seafarers. There are
reports that Christianity has winged its way to them lately.

ADAM OF BREMEN

_____

_____

They scanned the horizon for a long time searching in vain for any other ships, finding nothing but empty water and sky. Thora listened to the talk between Ulf and the crew. All experienced seafarers agreed that the strange turbulence had come upon them from the Southeast and pushed them a good distance northwest.

Ulf decided, "We'll go due south for a while to make up for lost distance before resuming our southwest course."

The sky remained overcast, and Ulf needed his sunstone to find the way. Thora asked to be allowed a peek through the crystal; the sun today was invisible, and yet the crystal showed two rays of bright light.

"Look at the point where they cross," Ulf said. "That's where the sun is."

Those not needed on stand-by, fell asleep, rocked by the long slow swells. Families huddled close to combat the chill from drenched clothing and soaked bedding which invaded flesh to the bone.

The next day at dawn they met with jagged ice rafts followed by taller chunks, some the size of a farmhouse. The ice was soiled with gravelly dust and marked with blue cracks as if carved by a giant's chisel. Uneasy whispers traveled from bow to stern and back. A tall, ginger-haired settler from Borgarfjord rose to his feet, gazing at Ulf with accusing eyes.

"Now, what will be next?" he shouted. "Are we to be crushed by ice monsters next time the sea rears up?"

He stared at the faces around him and added, "I say, shouldn't the skipper before setting sail have made sacrifice for the sake of us all? He took our good silver to get us to Greenland. Hah! Did anyone see him spend some of our silver to buy a steer and offer a worthy feast to the gods?"

People shook their heads; some asked their neighbours if they had seen Ulf making sacrifice before setting sail. Nobody could say they had.

"His wife wouldn't allow it," the red-haired farmer jeered. "Everyone knows she has of late thrown in her fate with White Christ. No wonder the gods feel free to toy with us, calling up waves from the Netherworld to frighten us, and now, what have we here? Chunks of ice that could crush the ship and all who sail in her, in our sleep....what, I wonder, will the gods be thinking of next?"

Ulf at the steering board threw him a glance of contempt.

"By the great dragon, Nidhog," he growled, "would you folks stop whimpering? The heifer we offered up to Njord after the turmoil ought to be plenty payment to keep us safe for the rest of the journey."

He ordered a change of course and hung on tight to the steering board, picking his way through the floating ice.

"We must be closing in on southern Greenland," he assured the others. "It can't be long now before we see the first landmarks."

He ordered Ivar to remove the carved troll head with gaping fangs from its perch on the bow.

"Take down the carving and put it well out of sight underneath the bow cover...we don't want to offend the spirits of this land, if any are watching out and happen to see us approaching their shores. Afterwards it's your turn to climb the mast and look out for landmarks...we had better not sail past Eiriks fjord."

It fell to sharp-sighted Odi to bear the news all were waiting for. Soon after he took his turn in the mast strapped to the yard, he gave a loud cry, "Birds! I see scores of sea birds out there flying low over the water!"

Before long they could all see the coast, craggy, forbidding. Ulf kept out to sea without losing sight of the land.

"I reckon Eirik's anchoring place is still half a day's sailing from here."

By late afternoon they turned into shore and headed up a narrow fjord marked by conical piles of rocks stacked on the headlands to each side. Everyone tried to climb on top of the bow-cover, crowding and pushing, stretching tall, losing their balance and sliding off the slippery, wiggly wet walrus hide, only to clamber back up again.

Thora, craning her neck to scan the new land, felt disappointed – the shore looked much the same as the one they had left, one vast stretch of skerries which required all of the skipper's navigational skills winding his way safely between black outcrops covered in mats of rockweed that lifted and sank with the waves like mermaids' locks.

Ulf called, "Get ready to drop the sail and man the oars."

Thora slipped from the bow cover to calm the horses; they stood with heads high, ears pricked and nostrils flaring to catch the scents and sounds reaching them from the land. The cattle were also excited, up on their feet, all except the injured bull which thrashed around, desperate to get up; the cows, slimy muzzles held high to test the air, rotated their shaggy ears this way and that trying to make out unfamiliar sounds coming from the land. Only the sheep stayed calm except for the flick of an ear now and then.

A loud-voiced argument erupted between Ivar Ulfson who stood by the mast to help roll up the sail, and two of his father's *karls* waiting to take up their oars.

"Oh no, make no mistake!" Odi shouted.

"We," he pointed to his brother, Ottar, "were promised good land, all of us, not just the men who're here with their families."

"Don't count on it," Ivar said with a shrug.

"You'll see!" Odi argued. "Ottar and I intend to take land side by side, so we can work it together. We'll build ourselves a house and then another one, and then we'll find us each a wife and start our own families."

Ivar sent them a mocking grin.

"Red Eirik won't grant land to just any single young man wanting to settle and farm," he scoffed. "He wouldn't give out any land to a pair like you two, with nothing to call your own and up to your ears in debt to my family."

He grinned again.

"Or do I need to remind you two? My father took care of your passage for free and now he's entitled to your help building our new farm. He'll never agree to the two of you striking out on your own before you've paid what you owe."

"And who's to settle affairs in this place between folks who cannot agree?" Ottar asked with a sly smile. "See if we both don't have a farm and wives of our own before you do."

Thora took a long look at the brothers, mousy Odi and burly, pock marked Ottar.

It'll take more than average good luck for the two of you to find yourselves wives in a place like this with few women and many more men.

Ottar took a step forward and pushed his chin into Ivar's face.

"Well? Who'll be here then to settle our disputes? We all know there's no such thing in this land as a *Thing*. There isn't a single appointed Lawspeaker in the green land!"

Thora frowned. She had to agree with the obstinate lad. The absence of a *Thing* in Eirik's new land to settle differences, had worried her from the day she decided to take a chance on Eirik's promises. With no *Thing* to decide people's disputes, any quarrel over land could quickly lead to violence. Then again, with so much coast, water and wilderness unclaimed by anyone, not even by Eirik, everyone would be free to hunt and fish where they wished for survival; without flocks of sheep to sustain them through winter, they would all need to rely on wild meat.

She leaned against her mare reveling in the thought she would once again be able to run her own farm without having another woman to answer to. A small, disquieting voice poked a hole in her daydream. A farm – she knew this as well as anyone — was more than a piece of land. The largest parcel of good grazing land was of no use without livestock to graze it... and with only two pairs of hands to put up hay, she and Eidyll might not be able to gather enough winter forage even for just the two horses. The winters in Greenland were long people said, longer than in Iceland.

She thought of the linen grain sack tucked away in her sea-chest. It was pitifully small, considering it held all the seed grain she had procured in exchange for one of her ewes, but she would have enough next spring to seed a field large enough to supply their needs for the winter that followed. Still, without a plow and other proper tools, how was she going to prepare and plant even a small field of barley next spring? True, Eidyll was a fair hand at basic smithing, but to carry out ironwork, he needed iron; without it, no smith could fashion and repair farming tools... there wouldn't likely be any for sale here, not after her father failed to deliver his shipload of iron to Greenland.

She ran her fingers through the mare's stringy manes.

"Don't worry," she whispered. "I'll find a way to feed you and your mate through the winter, whatever it takes."

She had to; without the mare and the stallion to carry on the line of Hestardalur horses, her vision of building a prosperous horse farm of her own would prove short-lived, nothing more than a fading dream, extinguished before the end of their first winter.

She chided herself. *No, my dream will not die; I will not allow it; I will think of a way.*

Ulf's ship wasn't the first nor the last to arrive at Eirik's farmstead; for five more days battered ships made their way up the fjord to unload exhausted, thirsty and hungry people and animals at Brattalid and all were made to feel welcome at Eirik's fledgling farm; the greening grass lifted the spirits of people and livestock, and Eirik's *thralls* rushed off and on with food and drink for new arrivals. After the fourteenth ship had anchored, they waited anxiously for six more days until all hope for the others had faded. Of the twenty-five ships which had set out with Eirik from Iceland, only fourteen completed the journey to Brattalid. The others were now presumed lost, wrecked with no one to witness and no one to rescue those who might for a while have clung to pieces of flotsam.

Some of the lost ships had carried people from the Whale Fjord, and Thora had known a number of women and men who sailed in them. Their names and faces kept coming up in her mind. They had cherished hopes similar to hers. Why had their luck run out, and hers had not?

Some of the perished families, before departure, had sacrificed fat oxen or sheep on the shore, while she hadn't made sacrifice to any god. Yet here she was, alive, with all that she owned, her *thrall*, her horses and her dog, all of them safe and uninjured after the harrowing voyage.

Perhaps she and the others aboard Maelstrom Tamer owed their good fortune to the personal luck of their skipper; Ulf's apparent good fortune had been enough to protect everyone who sailed with him. Or perhaps her mother's ghost had traveled along, hovering above the ship, protecting her daughter and everyone with her... perhaps there was no truth in people's belief that only mortals could travel overseas.

Thora heaved a sigh; now, with her feet back on dry land, much would depend on some good luck of her own.

This had better be a good land, for it exacts a high price from people.

NINE

---

*People say things have been cast to the tide when someone
gets rid of possessions and receives nothing in return.*

LAXDAELA SAGA

Six days after the last ship arrived, Eirik announced it was time to
consider the mourning for lost friends done and over with. He
sent out his *thralls* among the settlers' booths clustered along the
shore, inviting everyone to gather at his farm house, one winter old and
freshly roofed over with another layer of green sod.

Thora kept to the back of the crowd catching only glimpses of Jarl
Eirik, a short, rather slight man with a big voice and a large reputation,
standing in front of the side entry to his house demanding silence.

"I've decided to put on a roasting feast today with plenty for all to
eat, and barrels brimming with beer to lift our spirits."

People cheered and shouted approval.

The feasting went on and on with people falling asleep, waking up and feasting some more, or tumbling down between the childen, all of them by now firmly asleep. Thora looked to the cookfires, barely visible under the light summer night sky, though the aroma of roasting mutton pointed the way. She closed her eyes for she couldn't eat another morsel.

"Thora, wake up, time to present yourself to Eirik."

Gunnhild was kneeling beside her, shaking her arm.

"Come quickly! Eirik is out by the main fire assigning land to the larger families right now; soon it'll be Ulf's turn together with other men who have small families, and after that he says there'll be plenty land to give out to young, single people who wish to make a claim. Get yourself over there! You've slept enough, I say."

Ulf spent a long time talking with Eirik before he returned to his family, a happy smile on his face.

"We're the first family to be assigned land on the other side of the fjord," Ulf told them, "and he says we can take as much of the bottom land as we're able to work, and also take our first choice of upland for pasture. I'll row across right now in the small boat to make my choice, and I'll take Ivar with me to help putting up the first of our bound-ary rocks."

Gunnhild embraced him.

"You're a shrewd man, my husband, and I know you'll make good choices but don't forget we need besides well watered land for barley fields and good grazing, a source of fresh water close to the house site to ease women's work."

She turned to Thora, pushing her in the direction of Eirik's circle.

"Your turn; next he'll give out land to young people without a family. Go on...no, wait, you want me to come with you?"

"If you wish," Thora said casually, trying to hide her sense of relief. Eirik the Red, though short and of slighter build than she expected, had an intimidating bearing, a commanding voice and a frightening way of laughing, not merely raucous like that of her father and most other men, no, Eirik's laughter was more like thunder claps in the sky, akin to the laughter of Thor.

Thora halted just outside Eirk's circle by the fire.

"Wait here for me," she said to Gunnhild, squeezing her hand. "It looks more appropriate if I go up there alone."

The circle around Eirik opened to let her through. Ottar and Odi had just finished talking with the master of Brattalid. Both had satisfied smiles on their faces. *Eirik did after all grant them land to strike out on their own, despite Ivar's claims about debts owed by these lads to Ulf and his family.*

She stepped forward to present herself. Eirik squinted at her with a look of annoyance as if displeased by the sight of this young woman so tall, he needed to tilt his head back to face her.

"Greetings, Jarl Eirik." she said. "I am Thora Thorvinnsdottir from Hestardalur by Gullfoss, and I have come here to claim land for a farm."

Eirik frowned.

"Who else is with you?" he asked.

"I came with my slave and two horses, a mare and a stallion, prime breeding stock."

"You have no father or husband here?"

"My father perished last summer on his way to Greenland with a shipload of timber and iron.

Eirik nodded slowly.

"I heard…Thorvinn Haraldson, a man followed by bad luck."

He shrugged, giving her another dark frown.

"Well, Thora Thorvinnsdottir, if you insist. You can take some of the upland above Ulf Thorsteinson's claim, next to the brothers, Ottar and Odi; you may choose any land they have no mind of taking. And… *did the man smile in his beard?* Perhaps you could come to an, uhm, understanding with one of them, join your lands together to mutual advantage so to speak."

Thora flushed a deep red, trying not to hear the snickering around her.

Lost for words she stared at the smug face, scarred and ruddy above the solid neck torque of twisted gold gleaming in the low sunlight. She couldn't bring herself to thank him for what was, to her mind as well as to most bystanders no doubt, an allotment designed to belittle her; *have I come all that way for this?* She deserved better surely.

Thora squeezed her hands to fists, struggling to keep the tears she felt rising where they belonged, away from her eyes.

Eirik said, "I bear you no ill will, Thora Thorvinnsdottir, but a woman alone cannot build a farm unless she has a man to rely on; I have granted you land right beside that of two free-born young men who are both unattached. I believe I can do no more for you."

Thora turned on her heels and walked off without a polite word of leaving, let alone words of thanks.

Behind her Eirik bellowed a fit of good-humoured laughter.

Thora stood with Gunnhild on a low knoll surveying the stream-valley land which Eirik had granted to Ulf's family. The family's holdings included the bottomland as far as they could see, as well as the hilly slopes to the East terminating in a row of stony outcrops where Thora's rocky upland allotment began.

The two women looked into the stream valley to the nearly completed house of rock and sod built by the family not far from the fjord. It looked substantial, though hardly large enough to house all of the members belonging to Ulf and Gunnhild's household. Thora stole a glance behind her halfway up the slope where Eidyll was stacking sod for a dwelling the size of a summer sheep shelter. The spot she had chosen was well away from the building site of the brothers further down the fjord; Ottar and Odi — showing reluctance to live close to Ulf's farmstead — were building their hovel across two more ridges, out of sight for Ulf's homestead as well as her own.

"Come," Gunnhild said, leading the way to the top of the outcrops. "Let's have a good look at your land."

Gunnhild shook her head gazing across the scraggly stone-pocked grassland bearing a few struggling bushes in places where a little soil was trapped between the rocks.

Thora was silent, nursing her anger over the way Eirik had treated her.

Gunnhild pointed inland to a white shimmer in the sky, said to be the reflection of a distant *joekull*, a vast icefield rumoured to blanket the land away from the coast — how far the ice stretched, nobody knew.

"It'll be no good," Gunnhild said, "if you try to raise horses let alone sheep on these uplands, right in the path of the icy breath that blows down from the *joekull* it seems even in summer."

"I know."

Thora tried to swallow her disappointment. In this land without a *Thing* or properly appointed Lawspeakers, she had nowhere to turn for redress. Eirik, self-appointed *jarl* of his so-called green land, could do with the land as he pleased, giving out whichever grants to whomever he saw fit.

She forced herself to a smile for Gunnhild's sake, determined to nourish her friendship with this woman, her closest neighbor and the only ally she felt she could trust.

"With so little grass for grazing," she said with a forced smile, "I hope my horses lose no time honing their browsing skills. They had better develop a taste for willow brush."

"Mmm," Gunnhild considered. "Unless...."

She took a deep breath.

"Unless you and the two of us, Ulf and myself, could come to an agreement. I have discussed the situation with Ulf and we agreed to make you an offer."

She paused again, searching Thora's face.

Thora broke into a smile.

"How can I decide if you don't tell me what you're proposing?"

"Alright then, but promise me you'll not be offended. You were very brave to come here on your own with only one slave, and I know you possess a proud spirit, as proud as that black colt of yours. Still, here's something you may want to think about."

"Then tell me," Thora urged. "Don't keep me guessing."

"What if you and your slave became members of our household for the time being? It would benefit us all. Our household is short of hands to build up a proper farmstead and the necessary sheds and byres all at once; it will take many hands to collect fuel, make hay and ready the crop land, and do it all in one summer. The same goes for you, on your own with only one *thrall*. You're likely to end up overwhelmed by all you need to accomplish before winter sets in. We, on the other hand, have been allotted plenty good grassland to carry our own livestock as well as your horses, and more bottom land than we need to grow enough barley to make beer and bread for us all. Think about it."

A slow smile softened Thora's face. The Norns seemed to favour her after all, handing her not only this woman's friendship but also providing her with an opportunity she hadn't thought of. Though her hopes for good land in Greenland had not been rewarded, here she was offered a chance after all to turn her luck around.

Who can fathom the minds of the fickle maidens of fate?

She embraced Gunnhild and gave her a long hug.

"I'd be a fool not to accept...thank you. You will not regret this. I'm a hard worker, you'll see, and my *thrall* is skilled in many crafts.

*   *   *   *   *

At mid-morning Thora took a break from wandering the hillsides with the small flock of sheep. Today life seemed easy enough in the new land on a bright, smiling morning when it was a pleasure to roam the grassy slopes below the rocky outcrops that separated Ulf's holdings from her own land. Still, here she was, once again minding another woman's sheep. Little had changed for all her hardship of journeying to Greenland. Only this time she needn't deal with the likes of Thurid Herjolfsdottir and her son, although... Thora frowned at the thought of Gunnhild's son, Ivar. He might prove to be a worse pain than Helgi had been.

A good thing she had a fine *thrall* to contribute to Ulf and Gunnhild's household, or she would've felt indebted to the family who had taken her in and treated her with such kindness. Eidyll had worked hard, cutting and hauling building sod. Yesterday, on her way to the sheep pen, she passed him unloading pack baskets filled with sod and some turf to dry for fuel. She paused to ask if he had learned any more about the holy *papar* reputed to live in this land. Eidyll shook his head, a look of dejection on his face.

"I talked to the maids of Eirik's spouse, Thjodhild," he said. "Some of them are followers of the faith, as is the lady Thjodhild herself. Still, none of them has heard of monks living anywhere on the coast where people can be expected to live. And they say that nobody, not even *papar* favoured by the lord Christ, would be able to live in the freezing uplands."

"Well there you have it," Thora said. "It is as I thought; this land isn't the Greater Ireland of which you were dreaming. Like it or not, to persist with your quest you would need to take another journey to some other new land overseas, into the forests of the Varns perhaps beyond the western horizon... I doubt the warrior Varns would lower their swords and step aside to let you pass, just the one of you, let alone an entire party of holy men from Ireland dressed like women."

She laughed at his scowl and went on to saddle her mare.

Gunnhild announced she was with child once again. She had known before they set sail, though she hadn't wished to speak of it until their safe arrival in Greenland.

"I thought it not something to talk of till after our journey," she said to Thora one morning when they sat together in the sunshine carding old wool.

"Why ever wouldn't you?" Thora asked, removing a handful of wool from the spiked card.

Gunnhild explained.

"I lost two children before term and I believe it happened because I was cursed by a maid I expelled for stealing from our household. When I found I was expecting again, I thought it better to move off to Greenland first — in case the curse still held power — before I told anyone. Now, in this new land, I feel safe. They say a curse cannot follow its target across any sea."

Thora nodded. There was no need to upset this good woman, of course. *But surely Gunnhild must know there are other things than a curse which can keep a woman from birthing a healthy child.* Gunnhild hadn't born a live child since she had her daughter, Helga, now twelve winters old.

One early evening the men were still out and the maids were putting out trenchers for the evening stew. Gunnhild and Thora had a quiet moment together warming their feet in the afterglow of the cook fire. Suddenly, Gunnhild smiled. She placed her hand on her mid-riff.

"I feel something moving," she whispered. "How good it feels to bear life again. I nearly gave up, but now I dare hope there might still be others following this one – a good thing too, especially now that we're here."

She stared into the fading glow at their feet.

"It takes many sons and daughters," the older woman resumed, "to prosper in a land as empty as this... and own blood's always best, even if children take a painful long time to grow to a useful age... Still, family's preferable to hired hands let alone slaves."

Thora remained silent. *Preferable also to someone like me, neither one nor the other, slave nor hired maid.*

Not that she had reason to complain. Gunnhild treated her like a foster daughter rather than a maid. Every day Thora prayed to the gods that they grant Gunnhild Grimsdottir delivery of a healthy child.

Thora was on her knees before the fire place at dawn trying to encourage the faint glow that lingered in the coals to flare up. Gunnhild was kneeling beside her with her arms on a bench whispering her morning prayers to the Christian god. Thora caught some of the words, a plea that the mother of Christ grant her a safe delivery in due time, not too early — and that the child be blessed with good health.

Later that day, alone with the sheep under a gloomy sky, Thora repeated Gunnhild's plea, addressing it to Freya, goddess of fertility and childbirth. Surely, in this remote and harsh land, White Christ and his gentle virgin mother were ill-equipped to compete with the Norse gods. Gunnhild kept in her clothes chest a painted picture of the Christian god's mother. A few days ago she showed Thora the picture of Mary, the mother of Christ, a frail looking woman with soft, drooping features and a look of suffering in her large, calf-like eyes. Since the day she set eyes on the painting, Thora nursed strong doubts regarding the powers of this woman and her tiny boy child. It didn't make sense to expect any help from someone like that. *How could this mother and her infant son from the sun-scorched Saracen lands in the South, have powers here in a far corner of the North? How could they, unaccustomed to snow and ice, be of any help to people who must battle the cold? I'll have to talk to Gunnhild to make sure she doesn't rely too much on the new faith she embraced.*

Gunnhild, to Thora's surprise, agreed to offer up a newborn lamb to Freya in the spring.

"You're right," she said. "I'll need all the help I can get…every one of the children I lost before term took some of my strength away. It's time I tried changing my luck by whatever it takes, new ways or old ones, to secure the blessing of any powers, whichever they may be, that are ruling this land."

One cold and windy morning Thora hurried home from the fells to save a newborn lamb she had found abandoned. She wrapped it in a sheep-skin from her bed and placed it, chilled and close to death, beside the fire. About to walk to the high seat and leave the house through the side entry, she paused to listen; a loud argument had erupted at the high seat where Gunnhild and Ulf were taking a rest, and her name came up as part of the argument.

"Really," Gunnhild insisted, "we have only a small flock of sheep to watch over and we could easily find someone else to go out with them, some young lad not strong enough to be any good at digging peat. I don't see why Thora Thorvinnsdottir needs to spend her days out in the hills watching her dog watching our sheep!"

After a pause, Gunnhild went on, "Oh, I can guess what you're about to say, what about sheep rustlers? Just think! With so few people in all of Greenland, how could anyone hope to dispose of a stolen sheep and not be found out?"

"Out here we have no reason to worry over sheep rustlers," Ulf agreed. "Still, we're no longer in Iceland and this land presents other threats to our livestock. Ivar saw tracks of ice-bears out by the shore yesterday, and Eidyll thought he heard wolves howling in the hills."

"I'm sure the white dog could take care of them," Gunnhild said.

Ulf remained skeptical.

"It isn't only the sheep which need to be protected," he said. "Our barley's growing well and must be kept safe from ravenous sheep; it takes both a shepherd and a hard working sheepdog to keep even this small a flock away from the crop land. The white dog is an excellent guard, but he's no herder dog and we do need someone out there to make sure the sheep go only where they're supposed to go."

Thora could no longer leave without revealing she had heard their argument. She returned quietly to the fire place in the other end of the house and kneeled beside the lamb, rubbing its belly and massaging the limp, half-frozen ears.

Gunnhild raised her voice.

"Why husband, I only wish for someone to stay home with me and be company, is that too much to ask? I want to have someone around I can talk with."

Thora heard Ulf scramble to his feet.

"I say, by the trolls and black elves hiding in the sea caves below the cliffs! Woman, what is the matter with you? You have your daughter as well as two maids to talk with all day. What more do you want?"

Gunnhild persisted.

"Helga's still a child, and I have no other woman with me in the house except the two bonded maids. I need a freeborn woman to keep me company, someone with whom I can talk about things that concern me."

The next day Gunnhild asked Thora to stay home with her. Thora, though briefly inclined to refuse, decided she liked Gunnhild well enough to give up her solitary vigils on the fells for a while. She wrapped her arms around the older woman.

"Yes, I'll be keeping you company in the house, Gunnhild Gormsdottir, until after the birth of your child."

Gunnhild's face brightened with joy.

"I'll tell Ulf to spare a young lad to stay with the sheep, and it had better be a fleet-footed lad. Even with the help of a herder dog, it'll be hard work to keep the woolies away from the barley patch now that the kernels are setting."

Thora found it easier than expected to settle into the home routine, for she enjoyed Gunnhild's company. Steady-tempered and kind, the older woman seemed ready to listen any time and give thoughtful advice when asked for, or not. Amused, Thora tried to follow Gunnhild's well-intended instructions. Her new foster mother seemed to think Thora's upbringing left much to be desired and that her sewing and embroidering skills in particular could do with improvement.

"This scarf," Gunnhild said one dark morning, unfolding a square cloth of cream-coloured silk, "would look nice don't you think, embroidered with flowers in the style favoured by women in Frankland? Feel free to choose some coloured silk yarn from my sewing box and I'll show you some of my special stitches."

Another time Gunnhild threw up her hands declaring, "I can tell you were raised by a man…now that isn't all bad, mind you," she hastened to add, "not at all. I see that you know as much about horses and other livestock as any man does. And you know more about hunting and the use of small boats than any other woman I know. Your father is also to be commended for making sure that you learned to read and write runes and make verse, as befits a well-born woman or man."

She breathed a sigh.

"Still, there are some things you don't seem to know, things which a properly brought up girl needs to be aware of."

"And what might they be?" Thora asked, seated in the open doorway struggling with the fine blue embroidery silk and having a hard time keeping her stitches even.

"Let's hear it, Foster mother. Tell me what else I should learn, so we can get started and have it over with quickly."

Gunnhild pulled up a stool; she counted off on her fingers.

"A proper young woman should learn to think before speaking, something you generally do, I admit; she also should practice moving sedately and with style, which you generally don't do; she should use proper wording when addressing older relatives and visitors, which is hard for you to practice since you have no relatives here and we get so few visitors; she should dress with care, matching the colours of her shift and kirtle, and she must wear her hair done up in a respectable manner. If you like, I can show you how to make the best of that thick, unruly hair of yours."

Slowly, Thora shook her head.

"Don't trouble yourself, Gunnhild Gormsdottir," she said. "I have no desire to learn how to be a fancy woman and I do not think there is any need to be fancy, not in this remote place."

Gunnhild reached out, running her fingers through Thora's golden-brown curls braided at the ears which left the remainder free to cascade down her back.

"Then allow me at least to properly braid your hair. You're an attractive young woman, or could be – fine facial features, a high forehead, shapely nose and grey eyes so wide and clear... some time ago you showed me a silver mirror that used to belong to your mother. I never see you using it. Do you not care how you look?"

"Of course I do," Thora said, frowning. "Do you not notice how hard I try to look dignified, wearing women's clothes around the house day in day out? It is quite the change I should think from my worn shepherd's outfit."

She fingered the silver brooches holding the shoulder straps to her kirtle.

"These also used to be my mother's."

"She was a lady of good taste," Gunnhild said softly.

Thora put the embroidery work down. She went to her chest and gathered up all of Rannveig's jewelry.

"Will you help me decide what to wear with these clothes?"

She showed Gunnhild the necklace of amber beads.

"This was my mother's favourite piece."

Gunnhild slid the beads through her hands, marveling.

"They feel so warm, just the way they look, chunks of trapped sunlight."

Thora nodded.

"My mother gave the necklace to me shortly before she died. The other pieces of jewelry I don't really consider my own. She didn't give them to me, but my father did, after her death."

One by one she arranged her mother's precious things on her bed: the winged brooch of embossed Friesian silver, two Danish made arm rings of twisted silver, a gold wristlet from Ireland, a handful of silver finger rings and a pair of gold ones from Frankland, one plain, one set with carnelians.

"I don't wear these because it wouldn't feel right. They should've been buried with my mother's ashes."

"Oh no, you are wrong." Gunnhild said firmly.

"I think your mother wanted you to have these. You told me she fell suddenly ill after delivering a son... seems she had no time to give these to you, and your father was right to pass them on, carrying out your mother's wishes no doubt... Wear her jewelry, Thora Rannveigsdottir, if for no other reason than to pour new life into your mother's treasured things."

Thora looked up in surprise.

"I never thought of it in that way."

It was now late summer and the winds seemed to blow colder each day. Gunnhild traced her finger along the gaps between the crooked driftwood boards used to line the sod walls.

"It feels as if all of this dank sod provides more chill air than any of us care to breathe," she said to Thora. "I'll show you a way to cut down on the drafts; we'll make wall hangings to cover the worst gaps."

"I would very much like to learn how to make a nice rug to hang on the wall," Thora said. "Still, without a large flock of sheep, how can we find enough wool?"

Gunnhild sent her a proud smile.

"I made sure to bring plenty wool from Iceland to have some to spare for rugs. We'll spin it to yarn and dye it in bright colours for wall hangings which can brighten our spirits after the daylight abandons the world once again. I know of some runes supposed to bring luck, and we could weave those in with the rest of the pattern. We'll need to call on all of the luck that may be drifting about here looking for a place to settle, even if it involves a little heathen magic."

She ordered every woman in the household to put other things aside until they had completed the rugs, three large wall hangings that covered the draftiest sections of the long side-walls.

Eirik's wife, Thjodhild, a skilled healer and midwife, came over one day to discuss the birthing arrangements.

"I promise to come right away when you need me," she said to Gunnhild. "It's unfortunate your time will come at the very end of winter...not a good time to travel; the fjord will be impassable, covered with stacked drift-ice frozen solid; we'll have to take the long route over-land around the bottom of the fjord; just send a lad to me with a spare horse, not bearing a saddle mind you — I prefer to use my own."

She turned to Thora.

"And you," she said. "I'll call on you to assist me. The girl, Helga, is too young to be of use, and I have my doubts regarding the maids you have here, untidy they seem to me."

"I will do my best to help you," Thora said, "though my experience with matters of birth is limited to foaling mares and other livestock. I was eight winters old when my brother was born," she explained, "and the grown-ups ordered me to stay outside."

Thjodhild left and Thora sat quietly for a while.

TEN

...a dun mare with a dark stripe down her back...I call her Keingala. She is very knowing about the weather, and aware that rain is coming. ....when very cold weather set in with snow, making grazing difficult...Keingala always chose the windiest places, never coming down the meadow in time to get home before nightfall. Grettir desired to play a trick upon Keingala to pay her out for her wandering.

GRETTIR's SAGA

Daylight dwindled and the nights grew longer. They had gleaned enough hay from the patches of good grassland to keep the breeding animals fed through the winter, and it was time to harvest the barley.

Ulf took daily inventory of the number of grain bags the horses packed in from the thrashing site. He shook his head.

"I can't think why our grain yield turns out so poorly on this virgin land — daylight time seems to be no shorter than in Iceland. After we set aside what is needed for seed, there will be little left to keep us all fed through the winter."

"It's because of the cold breath of the ice up there," Gunnhild said, pointing north to the white shimmering skyline.

Ulf and Ivar explored along the coast in both directions for places to hunt seal and geese; without spare livestock to slaughter, they would need to depend on wild meat, fowl, and fish to see them through.

After the harvest, Ulf put his men to building a *naust* near the gravel beach by the fjord to house the ship. Next he and Ivar with three young *karls* set out to hunt seals, leaving Gunnhild and Thora in charge of the slaves and maids he had ordered to build storage sheds and livestock shelters during his absence.

First they built a sod-roofed shed large enough to house both milking cows, and four low walls with a half roof at one end, to shelter the sheep. The horses, hardiest of livestock, were expected to stay outside and forage on their own. Only during bad winter storms would they be penned for shelter between a natural rock face and a wall of stacked fieldstone. Thora directed the slaves to build a roofed hayshed against the back of the horse pen to store what little winter fodder they could spare for them.

The *thralls* became apprehensive.

"The house is too small for us all," said one of the maids. "There's no time to add more living space to this cramped little hall; where are we, bonded folk, to spend the winter?"

"We cannot afford the time to build more," said Gunnhild. "We need all hands for putting up peat and bedding turf and to gather enough driftwood to cook meals and heat the hall this winter. You, young maids and field *thralls*, will have to move in with the cows for the winter. The beasts will keep you warm right enough."

"And cows need fodder to stoke their fires," Thora added. "Near the ship house I noticed a patch of good grass still standing, ready to be cut; so there, off you go."

Gunnhild had named the new homestead 'Sandurness,' after the sandy delta nearby. The small house, though easy to heat, was too crowded for comfort with much of the space against the back wall taken up with supplies, sacks of stored grain, bundles of smoked meat and fish, and bags filled with dried berries.

Helga and Thora shared a sleep platform; three older housemaids permitted to winter inside the house, slept in one bed, and Ulf's six *karls* shared two beds between them. The master's high seat though modest in size, stood out as a place of splendor with its four carved poles painted red and green. But more than anything else, Gunnhild's wall hangings turned the humble makeshift hall into a cosy winter dwelling.

It was quiet around the house with most of the men going off fishing and hunting. Thora and other young women went out daily to pick the last wild berries and lay them out to dry in sunshine and wind.

Ulf ordered two of his *karls* skilled in woodwork to build two boats, a small one with two oars and a larger one with four; it would take all of the remaining timber he had brought on the ship.

Ivar announced he had no mind to learn carpentry skills.

"I'll go after the last of the waterfowl before they've all left."

Later that day on the way home from the cowshed, Thora and Helga passed by the big rowboat which the men had just finished riveting. They paused to admire the work.

"It has the shape of a porpoise," Helga observed, "with a nose somewhat pointed to cut through water, yet rounded enough for the current to wash around."

The woodworker, a freed Saxon named Widulf, agreed.

"Oh yes, she's a good boat...and ought to be...'t took a mountain of driftwood to heat the strakes for proper shaping."

Alerted by approaching hoofbeats Thora looked to the path that ran by the marshy shore of the fjord. Ivar and his chestnut mare followed by a packhorse came pacing toward them at a furious clip.

Widulf slipped away.

Helga, beaming a smile at her brother, poked Thora in the ribs; she pointed to the load on the packhorse.

"We'll have a hearty stew tonight."

Ivar appeared splattered with mud up to his chin, clip-clopping into the yard on his flaxen-maned mare tailed by his father's grey mare loaded with geese carcasses. He called out to Helga in high spirits.

"Run, little sister, run to the house and ask Mother if she wants all of these birds done up for the smoke shed, or some kept at the house for the stewpot tonight!"

He brushed an unruly mop of wavy blond hair from his eyes and waited for Helga to move out of earshot before he fixed his gaze on Thora. She stiffened under his insolent glance creeping over her silver-embroidered belt, lingering on her breasts under the cup-shaped silver kirtle-clasps, and traveling up to her wind-blown hair.

He narrowed his eyes.

"Isn't it time, Foster sister, that you wrapped a scarf around that unruly hair and displayed some modesty? Glad to see at least you no longer wear ragged shepherd's trousers. Women's clothes suit those curves of yours a whole lot better...besides..." *Did he wink at her, the lout?*

"I'm partial to a woman who wears a shift and kirtle ...no man with sports on his mind likes to deal with a woman in troublesome trousers."

He spun his exhausted horse and rode off, roaring with laughter.

Thora scooped up a handful of rocks and pelted the quarters of the chestnut mare. Too tired to bolt, the horse took to bucking and nearly unseated her rider; though he had lost both stirrups, Ivar stayed on braced on the horse's neck, looking ridiculous. He pushed himself back in the saddle and kicked the jigging mare sideways past the walled sheep pen, ignoring the snickering field *thralls* perched on top of the wall stacking stones. Thora walked to the house with a spring in her step.

*   *   *   *

On a drizzly morning with a cold sea fog hugging the shore, Ulf, Ivar and two field *thralls* packed the large rowboat full of hunting gear and rowed through the marshy lagoon out to the fjord. At the same time Ulf had arranged for two *karls*, Ofeig and Odd, to set out overland with Ulf's grey mare and Ivar's chestnut, to meet the boat at the sealing grounds down the coast.

With half of the men gone, the household grew quiet and Gunnhild's spirits appeared to sag, her appetite dwindling to one cup of gruel a day, causing Thora to worry. *Some fresh fowl might do her good.*

"Foster mother," she ventured, "would you like me to go out for a day or so and bring you some ptarmigan, or perhaps a fat goose or two? The men won't be back for a while and it seems to me you need a taste of fresh food."

Gunnhild shrugged. She sat with her hands on a piece of embroidery which she had held in her lap all morning without looking at it.

"I'll tell Eidyll to stay in the house," Thora offered. "He can help the maids with the chores to make up for my absence."

Gunnhild gave her a tired smile.

"I'm not sure a fat-dripping fall goose would cure whatever ails me – though it wouldn't do harm I suppose. Perhaps the smell of goose in the stew pot will restore my appetite. I sure dread facing another chunk of dried cod tonight."

Thora rushed outside to tell Eidyll she would need her mare ready. She went back in the house to dress in her new set of shepherd clothes, untried, and a short cloak of white foxskin. She wrapped her bow, two bowstrings and a selection of arrows together with her short lance in a strip of horsehide, packed four sheepskins to a tight roll, kissed Gunnhild goodbye and made for the door.

"I may be gone for one or two nights and you're not to worry, you hear!" she said. "I can look after myself, and I'll take the white dog along."

Gunnhild frowned.

"Even so, you need to be very careful, my girl. Ofeig saw a white bear roaming around in the salt marsh four days ago, and who knows if there couldn't be outlaws roaming those hills."

Thora laughed.

"Really, Foster mother! In a land with so few people, no man has failed by now to find a welcoming farm where another pair of hands is welcomed, in exchange for a daily meal and a place to sleep; there's no need for any man to resort to banditry!"

She closed the half-open door and returned to Gunnhild, patting her hand.

"Do not frown, dear Gunnhild. Remember what they say — mother's frown, scar-faced child."

Thora deepened her seat and the horse responded by striding out; she turned around, cheered by the sight of the mare's silver tail fanning out on the breeze. How she had longed for this, to feel the wind playing catch and release with her thick curly hair, left to blow free without the constraint of a scarf or a hat. She looked to the great white dog trotting behind them with his nose low, almost touching Fluga's hoofprints, and she urged him on.

"Tsssh, tsssh! Come up front. I know you relish those scents of earth freshly churned up by the horse, but I need you to come up front where I can see you."

She laughed.

"Get up there! I need you to catch sight or scent of Ofeig's sea-bear before the horse does."

Khagan loped past her, tongue lolling, slant eyes squeezed to narrow slits and nose held high to taste the wind.

Thora leaned sideways to glance at the mare's face, impassive or so it seemed; horses didn't have the same means of facial expression as people and dogs to reveal their moods. Yet from the bounce in her step and her swiveling ears, there was no mistaking the mare's joy.

Thora took in the vast land, hers to explore — hills covered with wind-rippled grass, sedge and reindeer moss, rocks glowing with colourful lichens, barren gravel patches, cracks in the earth lined with the twisted limbs of creeping trees, pillows of willow and birch that clung to the earth cowered by relentless assaults of a brutal, continuous wind.

She released the mare's head and Fluga slipped into a canter, a gallop, and then an all-out run, horse and rider racing their shadow, flaxen mane and curly bronze hair streaming in the wind like spider spin in the fall.

At last it was time to touch earth again – the mare's breathing sounded strained. Thora sat back to slow the horse to a jog, and down to a long leisurely walk; she straightened her back, breathing deeply, slowly, to savour the fresh air. How could she have spent so much time lately inside the smoke-filled house taking cautious, shallow breaths of stale indoor air thick with ashes and dust and fumes from smoldering peat? After her lengthy time inside the house doing women's work, she had better enjoy the chance to roam this exciting new land to the fullest while she still could, before Gunnhild's time arrived.

She gazed from the coastal cliffs to the inland plateau on her right, gradually rising to a white icy shimmer on the horizon. The mare responded to the subtle weight shift in the saddle by veering away from the coast.

Thora laughed.

"You seem keen to head for the hills, old girl. I couldn't agree more. Our men are hunting by the sea shore and we ought to leave them to be among themselves, fishing and hunting and telling tall tales. Men need to gush off steam no less than restless *Geysir*, after a summer at home instead of going a-viking.

And I surely don't want to see any more of Ivar if I can help it. Lately he had trailed her in the way a zealous sheepdog might stalk a ewe suspected of having a mind of her own. *Except that Ivar if he should catch me has no intention to chase me back to the fold.*

A chill ran down her spine. She thought of his eyes, dull greyish blue when he looked at her, like the eyes of a cod caught more than three days ago. She slapped the mare's quarters startling her into a canter; the dog, jogging alongside, took off ahead.

"Good dog," she called out. "Find us a meal!"

It was too late in the season to find geese or ducks in the uplands. They were more likely to come across ptarmigan. She fingered her bow, delighting in its graceful curves, sinew-covered back, thin layers of laminated wood, the features which gave the bow its power and accuracy.

She recalled her father's words on the day he handed it to her. *With this, my daughter, you'll be able to down birds from a great distance and fend off foes, sheep-rustlers, marauding sea-bears, anything you find stalking our sheep.*

Happy and proud she had been, pleased that he understood her so well; how many fathers would spend good silver to bring back a prize bow for a young daughter eager to hunt?

Now, many winters later, a disturbing thought crossed her mind. Could it be that Thorvinn already expected his daughter would need a Khazar-made bow suited to a woman's limited strength? That she might need to fight off marauders attacking the farm after he and his fighting *karls* failed to return from a fateful journey? She shook her head trying to dislodge the anger which sometimes crept up inside her. *He surely had no intention to desert me and the rest of our household or trade away our home.*

The high country turned out to be empty of wildlife worth eating, though there were signs of voles everywhere and a line of foraging ravens advanced slowly through some of the colourful berry patches on the high tableland. Perhaps the birds were hunting voles up there rather than collecting the shriveled, frost-sweetened berries left on some of the plants.

Thora put her bow away. They could've had roasted vole to eat if she'd thought to bring a net. Khagan was sniffing a patch of crowberries snapping up scampering rodents left and right, swallowing them whole.

She found a drained patch of level ground near a rivulet and decided to unpack and stay for the night. The clear running stream was icy to touch — straight from the inland ice. Thora sighed. This land, unlike Iceland, seemed to hold no hot springs or streams born from the earth's fires offering comfort to weary travelers.

The mare, freed from her tack, drifted off to graze on the dry near-dormant grasses and sedges. Thora collected flat rocks as a base for her fire. With the help of some shredded peat from her saddle bag she soon had a small fire going, fuelled by willow stems and twigs. She waited a while, warming her hands and listening to the flames crackling in the still evening air before she raked the hot ashes aside to make room for the small soapstone bowl she had filled with water; she tossed in strips of dried mutton, parched barley and shredded willowbark, and searched for greens but she found nothing palatable. The mutton — from an old ewe never recovered after the sea journey — remained tough to chew no matter how long it was boiled; Thora kept chewing and when she could no longer taste any sheep flavour, she threw the bits to Khagan.

"That's all for tonight I'm afraid," she said to the dog.

"Perhaps we'll eat better tomorrow."

The fire had died and a numbing chill seeped through her fox cloak. There would be a good freeze tonight. She kicked some rocks aside to clear a level spot with thick turf, spread out her sheep skins and stretched out, taking off her low cowhide boots and placing them under her knees; with the sheepskin wrapped around legs and hips and the cloak of fox-fur pulled over her shoulders, neck and face except for a small gap to breathe, she felt comfortably warm.

"There, you lie down right there," she said to the dog, pointing to a spot behind her back. "I need you to hug my back to cut out the draft."

Unable to fall asleep, she gazed at the clear sky of darkest blue sprinkled with early evening stars; the air, though colder than she had hoped, carried a pleasing sweetness. How could this air be so different, so alive and wholly unlike its stale counterpart inside the house where people were forced to breathe the perpetual smoke mingled with dust caught under the roof rafters?

Odd to think how many people considered it dangerous to sleep out under the sky, besieged by night spirits and trolls. Thorvinn took her out one day on an overnight hunting venture when she was barely six winters old; toward nightfall she asked him about the trolls who inhabit the dark, and Thorvinn laughed her fears away.

In our old home across the sea the night is crowded with evil beings roaming the dark, but here in Iceland we needn't fear. Back home by the fjord, the land was pocked with old homesteads where people who died unready, might turn into roaming spirits, unable, or unwilling, to leave their old homes. After some time they become angry ghosts who wish to harm the living.

In the old country there are ancient trees and even older rocks where spirits dwell; gifted folk can see the ghoulish misfits that are tied to such places, trolls for example, or rarest of all, the odd giant who was born before time. But these lost and evil beings are doomed to stay put where they belong, and we need not fear them in Iceland, not at this timet before many more generations of people have lived and died in this land, leaving some of them behind to unhappily walk the earth as ghosts. For now, my girl, we needn't worry…go to sleep and trust your dreams to carry you to the stars.

Years later, Thora found that many folks in Iceland were as fearful of home-grown trolls and ghosts as people back in the old land had been. Many rated the beings born of Iceland's underground fires more evil and malicious than anything present in the old country.

Thora turned on her other side. In any case, the fire spirits of Iceland weren't likely to cross the water to Greenland and even if some of them should succeed, there were no fire mountains in Greenland for them to make their homes in.

She pulled up the fox-fur to shield her face from the bright moon-light, but it made no difference. Sleep refused to seek her out.

Here she was once again making her home in some new place, unfamiliar except for the sky which seemed to change through the moons and seasons the same way it did in Iceland. Still, the familiar patterns up there held no comfort. *The sky is too distant to be a friend.*

Why was it that each new place she moved to failed to feel like home until she left and moved to some place new? She was an angry, unhappy little girl for a long time after they moved to Iceland, the treeless, wind-blown homeland of her mother; she pined for the towering trees that sheltered her childhood home high on a ridge beside the dark fjord. She even missed the chill wind that rose from the black cove shaded all day by tall cliffs except in mid-summer when, briefly, a narrow beam of bold sunlight crept down to touch its water. Long after they arrived in Rannveig's homeland, wind-blown and lava-strewn, Thora used to dream she could smell the scent of sun-warmed spruce that spiced the air around their old home.

And look at me now, settling of my own free will in a land with even less trees than Iceland!

Then again, few places could be better for raising horses than this land with it patches of short, aromatic grasses. Over time she would learn to like it here no doubt, as she had learned to appreciate the land of her mother for its excellent grazing which enabled young horses to grow strong bones. On this land her father built up his herd by mating imported Lofoten stock to the speedy, long-legged Vestland horses sporadically found in Iceland, and his horses became widely known for excellence.

She rolled onto her other side, washed over by memories of the events which brought her to Greenland. In the summer when she was eight winters old, her world turned upside down. One day at dawn her mother gave birth to a boy, a brother instead of the little sister Thora had hoped for. She didn't care to see him or know his name, supposed to be kept a secret until the newborn would be old enough to be named, but whispered of anyway around the house – Eyulf, a name fit for a boy destined to become a man to be reckoned with.

Before the end of the day she had changed her mind and her tiny brother, helpless like a newborn dog whelp, found his way into her sister's heart. The house pulsed with joy and excitement, until Rannveig fell ill and people became quiet and hushed around the sick woman thrashing with fever. Her milk dried up, and four days later Rannveig Asgrimsdottir died in the house where she was born twenty five years ago.

Thorvinn rode off on his seal-brown stallion scouring the district for a wet nurse to save the life of his son. He came home three days later, alone. Another day went by, and the newborn's wailing weakened to whispered wheezes. The maids tried to make the child suck ewe's milk and cow's milk – any milk available — from a piece of twisted wool. The boy who one day would have been Eyulf Thorvinnson, suffered painful spasms and his sister, unable to bear the sight of his tormented little body, escaped outside waiting for her brother to follow their mother to the place of death.

A blast of cold air invaded Thora's furry cocoon prompting her to burrow deeper into the fox cloak; she lay very still relishing the softness of fur touching her cheeks. For many years she used to take the touch of fur, linen and fine foreign-made woolens for granted, until her father's luck ran out and his fortune drained away. Since that time her skin had grown accustomed to the scratchy touch of homespun.

And now she had nobody left whose luck, good or bad, she was destined to share. It was time she trusted her own luck and it had better be good for she needed good fortune and judgment to work yarns of her own chosing to good advantage into her life's weaving pattern; it would take skill, even cunning, to pass the shuttle under and over the warp threads set by the Norns, to shape her life into the pattern she wished for herself.

Thora widened her eyes, tracing the path of the fast rising moon and trying to shake off her growing sense of bad luck approaching.

*   *   *   *   *

Hunter's luck found her the next day. Khagan flushed two ptarmigans at once, and she brought them down with two bird arrows released in quick succession. They were nice birds, plump after a summer of feasting – just what Gunnhild needed. She was fastening the birds to Fluga's saddle when the dog growled a low warning and took off over the ridge.

Thora pulled the knot tight, mounted and cantered up and over the ridge; she came to an abrupt halt face to face with Ivar who stood on the narrow path holding his horse, blocking her way down the ridge.

The day, bright and carefree a moment ago, seemed suddenly darkened by a thunder cloud out of nowhere. How was it that other women found this man so attractive? Did they not see the stony cold in those pale eyes? Her eyesight, at distance perhaps not as keen as should be, served her at close proximity well enough to reveal the nastiness buried in the eyes facing her.

She pitied his poor horse, heaving with exhaustion after running up the ridge with a tall, muscular rider and carrying an assortment of traps, hunting gear, and two fat pink-footed geese.

Thora waited for him to speak.

Ivar lifted the geese tied together by the feet.

"I heard you left the house intending to hunt in the uplands. Why didn't you ask my advice? There's nothing there, except stringy ptarmigan."

He pointed his chin at the geese.

"I brought you a pair of decent fowl instead."

"Very thoughtful of you," Thora said stiffly, slinging the pink-footed pair of geese across Fluga's withers.

Ivar grasped her thigh; quick as lightning Thora spun her mare around; Ivar stumbled; he straightened back up, glowering.

Thora raised her eyebrows.

"How did you find me?"

Ivar took a deep breath.

"Mother talked to the lads we sent home with a boatload of birds. She asked them to tell me to go looking for you; didn't seem to think you should be up here all by yourself."

Thora shrugged. She pointed to the coast

"You're camped somewhere yonder I suppose."

He nodded.

"We're in a small cove below that red bluff, and Father doesn't need me right now. I told him I wouldn't be back tonight."

He reached over to tickle a goose feet.

"We've killed plenty fat birds for now. Next we'll leave for the skerries to look for seals and spearbills."

Thora narrowed her eyes against the low sun.

"No need then to spend any more time on my behalf," she said. "Thanks for the geese."

Ivar gave her a sly look. He took off his headband of shimmering sealskin, stroking the tuft of falcon feathers under its silver clasp.

"I had in mind to join you for a bit," he said pleasantly. "A lone woman riding her horse over treacherous footing could get into all sorts of trouble up there. These fells are littered with sharp rocks, hidden bogs and treacherous quick-sands. What if your horse steps into a crevice and breaks a leg…how will you get home?"

"Same as you would, or anyone else," Thora snapped.

She drew her hunting knife and ran her thumb over the sharp edge.

"I'd release my horse from its misery and make my way home on foot…You had better return to your father, Ivar Ulfson," she added, her eyes glaring.

"I wish you folks good hunting on the skerries."

She called Khagan, swiveled her mare around and cantered the way she had come, up and over, listening for sounds behind her back. Moments later she heard his horse cantering up behind her. Ivar Ulfson was too much of a hunter to give up easily.

She turned Fluga toward a stretch of flat grassland, gave the horse her head and nudged her sides.

"Go, run, my good mare, run your heart out."

Behind her the rattle of hooves faded quickly. Ivar's short-legged mare carried twice as much weight as Fluga, and the horse hadn't had long enough to recover from the previous exertion. She had no way of catching up with speedy, long-legged Fluga.

Thora ventured to look back. Rider and horse had come to a standstill, a distant dot in the landscape. She slowed her mare down to a walk, hoping Ivar's horse wasn't near death. She looked again and saw that he had dismounted; there were now two dots moving slowly side by side. Thora rode on.

The encounter had taken away her joy, robbed her of the desire to stay out any longer. She turned the horse toward home and gave her a long rein.

"There, my friend, I leave it to you to find the shortest way back where we came from."

ELEVEN

I wish an old witch that I know of,
wealthy and proud,
turned into a steed tied in the stable
and I, the rider!
I'd bit her, and bridle, and saddle,
I'd back her and drive her and tame her;

KORMAC's SAGA

Four days later the men returned home, their boats filled to the rims with more meat and fish than they could preserve before it would spoil. Now was the time to call for a feast, a first chance to celebrate their succesful effort of settling.

They roasted and boiled fresh fish by the basket full — eel from the rivermouth, flat fish speared in the coastal shallows, cod and haddock caught with long lines around the sealing skerries – as well as waterfowl, geese and all kinds of sea ducks.

Women and men laboured together after the feast to clean and preserve as much meat, fowl and fish as they could store, and Gunnhild beamed with satisfaction.

"We'll have enough food stored to last us into the summer...there'll be no need in the spring to kill any of the new lambs."

On the days they weren't needed at the farm, Thora and Helga went out to collect bundles of stunted, knee-high spruce growing here and there along the creek banks. To people raised in Iceland, unfamiliar with trees except small, wind-tortured birch, willow and alder, these resinous needle trees with evergreen branches were a novelty. Thora told of the tall spruce in her childhood home, and how people made use of the aromatic green boughs, similar to these except for size and appearance. She showed the others how to use bundles of prickly boughs to generate aromatic smoke for curing choice fish and meat cuts.

"This way we'll soon be eating better here than we ever did in Iceland!"

*   *   *   *   *

Thora woke up to a gloomy dawn. The first to stir in the house, she stepped out of bed, dressed and went outside to feed the horses penned in their shelter because of yesterday's sleet storm.

She sloshed to the hay shed around the back of the horse pen, gathered an armful of hay and tossed it over the wall to the horses. If confined for longer and left to depend on the rations the *thralls* forked out to them in the pen, the horses would surely be dead of starvation before the sun returned to green the world once again.

Thora made her way back to the house wondering if Achren, the slave girl whose duty it was to start the morning's fire in the house, would be late again coming in from her bed among the cows. Achren had overslept lately and Thora had prepared and lit the fire before anyone else stirred awake in the house.

She paused in the doorway, frowning. Once again she was left to do the early morning chores. The fire trench bi-secting the floor was as cold and unattended as when she left the house. She looked around once more — no Achren. This time she would give the girl a good talking-to, or would she?

Thora kneeled on the cold floor pursing her lips. She stirred up the ashes to find sparks to nurture into a proper fire using shredded peat, and she had a kettle of water boiling by the time a furtive, disheveled Achren slipped into the house.

Though Thora's patience with Achren was running low, she found out last night it was Ivar who caused the slave girl to neglect her duties.

In the deepest dark just before dawn, she had gone out to pay a visit to the latrine because she disliked using the piss bucket inside the house like the others did. She was seeking her way outside guided by little more than feel, until a half moon made an appearance through a gap in the clouds, wrapping the cowshed in front of her in silvery light. Warm humid air came in misty swirls through the cracks in the wall, giving the shed a ghostly appearance. Thora paused to watch until the clouds returned, once again obscuring the moon.

She heard a doorlatch lifting and she decided to wait, shivering in the icy wind. Perhaps one of the field *thralls* making his bed with the cows, decided to visit the latrine. Why though would anyone used to sleeping in cow filth, bother to go out for a piss in the cold?

Another spell of moonlight enabled her to see the door opening wide; a man stepped out, fumbling with his breeches. His purposeful stride left her no doubt here was Ivar heading back for the house.

Not that it was any concern of hers. Ivar wasn't the first nor would he be the last freeborn man to amuse himself with a slave girl. But, unlike most men, Ivar Ulfson hadn't told the other slaves asleep in the cowbarn to get lost while he made sport with one of the girls. No, Ivar wasn't like most men. *He enjoys performing in front of an audience.*

That wouldn't concern her either except for the fact that Ivar's pleasures kept Achren away from her household duties. She would ask Gunnhild to have a firm talk with her son.

Another dark wintery morning, and another storm was brewing at daybreak; Thora passed by the horse pen whistling a tune on her way to feeding the horses their morning hay. This time she was sure there would be a fire burning when she returned to the house. Gunnhild had a lengthy talk with her son yesterday, telling him to take his pleasures with Achren at another time not close to daybreak.

She approached the horse pen and hastened her steps, puzzled by the quiet. No shuffling of hooves, no nickers of anticipation, no sounds other than that of horses chewing. Had any of the slaves been out early to feed the horses against her instructions that they leave it to her? She peeked over the wall and frowned. The four horses stood neatly spaced, each munching its own pile of hay – exactly the way she herself liked to feed them, except that these piles were too large, enough for two days. Fluga lifted her head to nicker a brief greeting before turning back to her hay.

Thora frowned. At this rate there would soon be no hay left at all. Too little, or too much — what was it with *thralls* that they couldn't get anything right?

She turned to go back to the house and froze, startled by the rustle of clothes behind her. Strong arms wrapped around her, squeezing the air from her lungs and nearly crushing her ribs. A broad hand pressed down on her mouth and she heard Ivar's heavy breathing, felt his lips brushing her ear.

"I thought you would like a little help with feeding chores this morning," he whispered, "to save you some time, so we can have sport together."

He pushed her toward the hay shed, deftly turning to avoid the knee she had aimed for his groin, and giving her another hard squeeze.

"You'll enjoy the little love nest I prepared for us."

She tried to land a kick — one good, crushing kick she trusted would set her free – and tripped over her shift. Ivar lifted her off her feet and she was carried, kicking and punching, into the shed. He pushed her down on the hay and dropped on his knees beside her, looming dark against the dim morning light like an evil, shapeless troll.

"Such sweet, clean hay we have here...," he muttered, "a much better place for a freeborn woman to enjoy a bit of sport, I thought, than a rank cowshed. Only a slave girl enjoys cows and dim-witted *thrall* folk watching as she takes pleasure."

Thora almost wriggled free, and Ivar laughed, tightening his grasp.

"First I thought of the sheep pen....but then I remembered your four-legged white shadow with the ghoulish fangs lives in there. We don't want your personal werewolf to misunderstand and ruin our fun, do we?"

Shame kept Thora from hollering for help; shame prompted her to keep her voice down to a hissed whisper.

"What kind of misfit are you? One of the troll folk disguised as a man?"

"If you're a nice girl," Ivar drawled, "I'll show you how much of a man I am... the kind of man who gets tired of being ignored."

He pressed his mouth on hers.

She fought to push him off...tried to roll out from under him, but he held her arms tight, forced her mouth open and thrust his tongue inside, rubbing his scratchy beard all over the tender skin of her cheeks and nose. She gagged and bit down hard on his tongue.

"Aoww, you wicked sow!"

He pinned her arms behind her back and brought his full weight down on her.

"You haughty beggar bitch! You'll pay a price for spiting me."

She jabbed her right knee into his side and for a moment he shifted his weight; she freed her leg, raised it high and pounded the heel into his kidneys. He hollowed his back stifling a groan, raised his arm and struck her hard across the mouth. She spat out blood and fragments of tooth like bits of mutton bone in broth. He squeezed her throat till she gagged, struggling to free her windpipe and at the same time resist his knees pushing apart her legs; his fists ripped at her shift.

Thora choked; she came close to submerging in darkness before Ivar let go of her throat; she coughed up blood and chips of tooth, swallowing some and spitting some out, dimly aware that her shift no longer protected her. She tried to pretend she wasn't here any more, that the gasping came from another woman in distress; he entered her with a violent thrust and she could no longer pretend it wasn't happening; her body went into spasms, unable to cope with the deep searing pain that seemed to tear her to shreds. Unaware of time passing, a lifetime, a moment, at some point she felt he was spent and collapsed on top of her; she lay limp, her futile rage melted and drained away, hot tears running down the sides of her face, wetting her hair. Defeated, defiled, she had lost all sense of time or place.

He rolled off her and got to his feet. Wide-eyed, she watched him leaving through the half-open door into the shimmer of dawn, triumphant, fiddling with the front of his breeches in the self-satisfied way she had seen before.

He was gone. Thora curled up on her side in the hay without moving, waiting for her breathing to steady; the shuffle of horses behind the back wall and the placid sounds of their chewing seemed out of place, as if all were well with the world. She clutched an armful of hay against her chest and buried her face in the prickly sweet smelling pillow to keep from screaming, sobbing instead without sound.

If her mother were still alive, she could've run home to tell her. *No, if Mother had been alive today, nothing like this would have happened to me, a well-born girl, daughter of a woman who is mistress of a thriving farm; daughter of a father respected as a warrior and trader, a man who returns each fall from his journeys with new-found wealth and wondrous gifts for his family and friends.*

A beam of grey light crept through the crack in the door touching her feet. She pushed up on her knees and turned her face to the light.

"Mother," she whispered, "If you can hear me...I know you must be as distressed as I am. And I swear I will make this man pay in every way I can, as long as he and I will have a breath left."

For the second day in a row Thora did not get up early. She remained in bed, curled on her side, knees against her chest, her face buried in foxfur.

"This is not like you," said Gunnhild stopping by. "Are you ill?"

"I don't feel too well," Thora said. "Nothing unusual ... It'll pass when my bleeding comes through."

The next day she pushed herself out of bed late well after dawn, and surprised the others by staying indoors leaving the horse chores to the *thralls*. In the evening after the household had gathered for supper, Thora raised herself tall; she met Ivar's mocking glance from across the fire trench. He licked his lips slowly. She moved her gaze elsewhere, casually, as if her glance had only brushed by one of the old dogs permitted inside the house to warm the old bones.

She took Helga aside.

"Ask your brother to come to my sleeping platform. I have something to show him."

She pulled up a brightly burning lamp filled with fresh seal oil, walked with it to her bed platform and drove the prong into the dirt floor beside her bed; she dragged her chest from under the bed platform and rummaged its contents, ignoring Ivar behind her.

"You asked for me I'm told...finding it hard to wait for more sports, are you? Try to be patient. 't Wouldn't be seemly for us to carry on in here."

She returned his pale-eyed stare without blinking.

"As long as we're fated to live under the same roof, you and I," she said, tightening her fingers around the cloth-wrapped package retrieved from her chest, "you had better remember this. If you ever should touch me...again," her voice became a slow, articulate whisper, "I'll see that you meet with your death, an inglorious death not worthy of a warrior. And should you decide to rid the world of me first, I'll be haunting you all the days and nights of your miserable life...I'll haunt you till you jump off a cliff or use your sword on yourself to escape me."

Ivar smirked.

"What's this? Playing hard to catch of a sudden? Bit late for that, I say..."

He threw his head back and laughed, loud enough for Helga to send them an inquisitive look.

In a low voice, he added, "I like a spirited woman both before and after I have my way with her, no matter – both make for excellent sport."

"If you should touch me again," Thora repeated, stressing each word, "you'll want your poor wench, Achren, to taste every morsel of food and every sip of drink before you put any of it into your own mouth. Regardless, I will find a way to see you dead and buried without honour."

She opened her hand to reveal a pinch of the brown fibrous something she had bought from the herb woman; she rubbed the pinch between thumb and forefinger and raised her hand so Ivar could catch a whiff of its mouldy odour, *an appropriate smell for a poisonous herb.*

"Last spring at Borgarfjord before we sailed north to the meeting place, I paid good silver for this. The vendor assured me it never fails to aid a woman faced with men-problems – a sure and quick way to solve them, she said. I asked her to make rune signs over it for extra strength and lasting power."

"Women's tales," Ivar sneered.

Thora shrugged.

"I fed some of it to the sickly lamb we had this summer...you remember... the triplets born to the young brindle ewe, and one of them wouldn't suck. It took a tiny pinch, less than this, dissolved in a bit of milk, and smeared it on its nostrils... helped it right out of its misery."

He clawed at her hand but she was quick to slide the package inside her shift between her breasts. "Don't bother..." she hissed. "I've plenty more stashed away in places where you'll never think to look."

He snorted, "I know peat when I see it. You don't scare me, you spiteful sow."

Close-lipped, she watched him stomping back to the fire trench. *For all his brawn, he'll remember my words.*

Thora ignored the whispers behind her back. Nobody asked forthright why she no longer went out of the house since the morning she came home with scratches all over her face and missing a tooth. The maids preferred to make up their own stories.

"She must've run into a troll," Thora heard one of them say. "Serves her right. Always up and about before anyone else; we all know better than to be outside after troll time."

"Yes, serves her right."

"Never knew another woman like her, tramping outside in the dark," someone else said.

Achren smirked; she waited for Thora to be within earshot before piping up.

"Well, you know what they say; folks who want to be werewolves need to knock out a tooth or two first to make space for the fangs."

Thora ignored the talk, comforted by the thought that nobody had an inkling of what really happened to her.

"The colt threw a tantrum," she told Gunnhild, who demanded to know what had caused the bleeding gap in her mouth.

"And your clothing… shift all ripped up…did the horse do that too? He could've torn the hide off you like he would with another stallion."

"Oh but," Thora said to Surtur's defense, "he isn't mean-tempered; he's just a frisky colt."

The others grew used to seeing her indoors day after day weaving another wall-hanging as if her life depended on it and leaving all horse chores to the field *thralls*.

The days continued to grow shorter and people went about their chores in gloomy twilight. A profound chill took hold of the world, stifling body and spirit of both people and livestock in their overcrowded quarters. Had there ever been such cold before?

Yule came and went without feasting. They couldn't afford to slaughter fresh meat and they had no barley to spare for beer.

The acrid smell of burning peat too hastily cured, combined with the stench of unwashed people crept into clothing and hair; the shaggy hides of cooped animals wallowing in their own dung became crusted with filth and the elderly dogs seeking comfort and warmth in the house gave off rank smells before fastidious maids ordered them out. Cattle and sheep became lethargic in their dark, dank quarters, eating little of their rations, sparse as they were. Only the horses living outside continued to be bright-eyed and sure-footed.

People played endless games of *Hnefatafl* and other board games. They engaged in story telling and verse making contests. From midwinter and onward, life seemed on hold for the people of Sandurness carrying out the daily routines in perpetual half-light.

The day Ivar knocked out her tooth Thora took her mother's silver handmirror to the privacy of her bed to assess the damage. Maybe the gap wouldn't show as long as she remembered to talk without smiling.

When she was sure that no one was watching, she fingered the tender edges of her torn gums. *I'll be smiling like a five year old for the rest of my life.* If she accustomed herself to not smiling at all, people would forget she was missing a tooth and after some time they would quit making up stories.

Gunnhild though didn't forget. She sat Thora down daily to inspect the healing of her gums. "Sure you didn't run into a fork or a rake?"

Thora shook her head. "I keep telling you. The mares were right on the other side of the fence, and the colt dashed over to them, knocking me aside. Things do happen fast around horses."

She gave her practiced new smile with closed lips.

"I'm alright now. The pain is gone."

Gunnhild shook her head.

"You ought to leave handling that rogue horse of yours to the field *thralls*, or to Eidyll."

"I've learned my lesson," Thora said. "He won't catch me off guard again."

No, he won't, the rogue, I'll make sure of that.

She sent the older woman a smile, determined to keep it from Gunnhild that her son was a rogue far worse than the meanest horse.

TWELVE

...there has been talk between your father and my brother Thorarin and myself. That I might get you, Hallgerda, for my wife. You need to want this as much as they do. And so, you must say right now if such a match should be to your liking, or not.

NJAL's SAGA

Thora changed her nightly routine so she didn't need to go out of the house to visit the latrine pit. She demanded instead that the maids empty the waste-pail each time after somebody used it.

"And scour and rinse the pail thoroughly before you put it back in the house," she ordered them, paying no mind to the frowns and grumbles, nor to the names they called her behind her back, 'Sourface Snaggletooth.'

Never mind. Ivar wouldn't be able ever again to catch her out alone, and that was all that mattered. She was prepared to stay in the house until spring, taking her time to decide on a way to stay safe from him in the summer.

"After the new child is born, and as soon as travel becomes easy again in the spring," Thora said to Gunnhild, "I should like to move to Eirik's farm in Brattalid to assist the lady Thjodhild around the house as she asked me. In return, she says she'll teach me about healing and herb craft."

Gunnhild objected.

"Who can I trust to manage the livestock throughout the grazing season as well as you do? And who will entertain me with interesting tales about matters I never had a chance to become familiar with? I want to hear you talk of hunting and raising horses and falcons. I know little of such things, because men generally don't bother to discuss them with a woman; any exciting pursuits, they seem to think, had better be the domain of men only."

Thora longed to tell Gunnhild the real reasons she wanted to leave Gronsetur in the spring. It wasn't just an attempt to stay out of Ivar's way. It was mostly for the sake of Gunnhild and her newborn that she wouldn't, or shouldn't, stay at Sandurness after Gunnhild gave birth. *My presence could bring bad luck to her and the new child. Did I not bring misfortune to my mother and newborn brother?*

What other reason could there have been for their deaths than the childish curse which her eight-winter-old self had called out to the wind that morning after her brother was born? It is said that curses are apt to follow those who turn them loose. They can turn around to harm the one who let let them fly, and also harm others who are near and dear to the one who called out the curse in the first place. Could it be that this curse had followed her all the way to Greenland and caused her to be raped? If true, where would it turn to next? She uttered a long sigh. Her troubles seemed to be multiplying.

After the rape she had taken the tea purchased at Borgarfjord, twice a day for a period of five or six days and yet – two moons had passed since, and her bleeding had not returned. To the world she pretended all was as it should be with her. She counted the days and after each score she took care not to handle fresh milk in case her presumed woman's condition would cause it to go off and curdle improperly.

But why had her moon blood failed to return? Had the herb woman cheated her after all? Could it be that she was with child? She imagined the scorn of the others, pictured Gunnhild's distress over the wagging tongues rumouring that her foster daughter had dispensed favours to some low-born man...and how would she be able to defend herself against such accusations, other than by telling Gunnhild the truth about her lout of a son...*and she may not believe me...is there any mother who would?*

Without a well-born man to call father, her child would be rated as un-free, a mere *thrall*-child.

There would be no help for her if she told the truth, nor would it help if she didn't tell; either road would lead her and her child to a future of living as outcasts. There had to be a third road somewhere, an acceptable course to steer her out of this tangle. *There has to be a way out of this bind.*

*   *   *

At last the sunlight had turned around, lasting a little longer every day to soften the sea ice and break it up. Fleets of rafting ice – shiny white or dull with grit — rode the fjord out to sea, leisurely floating by like pods of white whales basking on the surface. Day after day the sun climbed a little higher and people and dogs drifted down to the sandy shore at mid-day to indulge a little leisure. Family members, maids and *karls*, everyone found an excuse to come down and relish the sunshine bounced off the water and melting snow. Even the field *thralls* clearing melting snow and mud from the livestock pens found ways to cut short their chores and take a break by the water side.

There was much talk and merry laughter, and people sang spring songs and composed new verse. Winter grievances melted and rode on the ice out to sea.

Gunnhild, in her eighth month, could no longer bend over or even sit up straight. Thora had Eidyll arrange rocks and boulders against the gravel ridge by the beach. She carried eiderdown pillows from the house to cover the rocks, and persuaded Gunnhild to come out to enjoy some sunshine. In spite of her woolen cloak and the pillows tucked in around her, Gunnhild was shivering, and Thora returned to the house to fetch the white bearskin from the high seat.

Inside she found Helga tidying up, picking up men's cloaks and tunics where they had dropped them and securing them on pegs in the wall. Together they rolled the bearskin into a tight bundle.

"I'm so glad you decided to stay with us at Sandurness till after the birth," the girl said with a shy smile. "It'll be her time soon Mother told me this morning, and I don't know enough to be of help."

"Neither do I," Thora admitted offering her half-smile. "Still, I trust it can't be that different from a foaling. Besides, the lady Thjodhild promised to help with the delivery."

She gave the girl's hands a squeeze.

"You mustn't worry so, Helga. There's no need."

"Go quickly," Helga said, handing Thora the rolled bearskin. "Don't let her catch a chill."

Thora was halfway out the doorway when Helga called her back, green eyes wide with sudden panic.

"Oh, Foster-sister, I'm afraid. What if she dies? So many women seem to die giving birth or shortly after."

Thora paused.

"Don't upset yourself. We're all here to help — I will be here, and old Unna who has born many children in her days; best of all, the lady Thjodhild promised to come at first notice. She's well versed in healing and midwifery and famous for her knowledge of herbs and potions."

She ruffled Helga's silken hair, golden blond tinged with copper.

"Why don't you when you're done here, come down and join us by the shore? You could do with some sunshine and rest to lift your spirit."

Barely able to see over the rolled bearskin she held in her arms, Thora picked her way between the rocks lining the path to the beach; she heard Ivar's voice among those drifting up from the beach. Thora hesitated, pausing to listen. No mistake. Ivar was having a talk with his mother and his voice carried far. Thora sat down to wait with her back against a sun-warmed boulder hearing every one of Ivar's words.

"Something has been on my mind, Mother, and I would like your advice. It's time for me to find a wife and start my own family, do you agree?"

Thora didn't catch Gunnhild's soft-voiced response.

She sighed, stroking the bearskin. This could turn into a lengthy conversation. What if Gunnhild were catching a cold out there on the beach? Perhaps she ought to ignore Ivar and go down with the bearskin regardless. She was about to rise when she heard Ivar's voice rising in argument.

"But Mother, surely, you're not suggesting that I marry a servant girl? Besides, I believe Thora Thorvinnsdottir has no fond feelings toward me."

Thora strained to hear Gunnhild's response.

"Ah, that I cannot ...but she has good sense...master of Sandurness... your wife... in charge..."

Thora peeked between the rocks toward the beach. Ivar stood, feet planted, towering over his mother sliding a fistful of pebbles from one hand to another, looking uncomfortable.

"Alright, Mother, I promise I'll think about it some more, since you seem to have set your heart on the girl. Meanwhile I suggest you talk to her to find out if she wouldn't kick me in the chin instead of hearing out my proposal."

He stalked off along the beach kicking stones, shells and wads of seaweed out of the way.

Thora waited not long before she went to the beach and tucked the bearskin around Gunnhild's shoulders putting an end to the shivering. Gunnhild patted a flat rock beside her flicking off a thin layer of sand.

"Sit down with me, dear," she said. "I've had a talk with Ivar. He and I have had this discussion before and it's time I share the matter with you, since it could involve your future."

"I'm listening, Foster mother."

"Ivar and his father intend to go north this spring to hunt walrus; with some luck they'll also capture young falcons and perhaps a few eaglets on the steep cliffs up there. If they gather enough ivory, oil, skins, and young birds to fill a ship, they plan to sail in the summer to Kaupang in Norway to trade, or maybe all the way south to the Dane town of Hedeby."

"Seems a good idea," Thora said, delighted to hear that Ivar would be away for the summer.

"I think so too," Gunnhild said. "But you must know that Ivar's mind is pre-occupied with other things besides trading."

Thora raised her eyebrows.

"Like most young men Ivar aspires to make his fortune quickly; once he has enough wealth to his name he hopes to find a suitable wife in Iceland, a woman of means to support his ambition to become a rich and powerful man."

"Hm," said Thora. "A wealthy woman...one who's prepared to leave Iceland and build a new life far from her family in Eirik's green land... that sort of woman I think will not be easy to find."

"Quite." Gunnhild nodded. "Quite impossible to find, I told him. Besides, I said, a woman of means in Iceland is likely to bring property to her marriage – property in Iceland. What earthly good would that do to us here in Greenland? Unless my son intends to return to Iceland for good and take care of his wife's assets...but Ivar assures me he wishes to stay settled in Greenland."

Eyebrows raised, Thora waited till Gunnhild continued.

"In that case," I said to him, "you intend to tow your wife's property to Greenland perhaps? Think about it, my son. If you marry a woman with property in Iceland that needs attending to, it'll cause you no end of hassle and grief."

Thora nodded. She had an uneasy suspicion where this might be leading.

"So," said Gunnhild, casting a meaningful glance her way, "I told him he would be better off marrying a woman already settled in Greenland, a woman who knows how to hunt and raise fledgling falcons and perhaps rear a bear cub or two till they're ready for sale, a woman who's skilled in raising livestock and bringing young horses under saddle..."

Thora jumped up, ready to protest but Gunnhild raised her hand.

"Please, hear me out. Furthermore, I said, it would make sense for you to marry a woman who owns land in Greenland, a plot right next to our own close enough to be grazed jointly with our Sandurness pastures. That would be wiser than chasing around Iceland in search of a bride I said... And yes, of course I'm thinking of you, Thora Thorvinnsdottir."

No, she can't be serious! The unspoken words whirled inside Thora's head. She clenched her teeth. *Think!* This wasn't Ivar's idea either. What was it he said? *You're not suggesting I marry a servant girl?"*

She folded her arms around her knees, squeezing her hands to keep them from shaking.

"Ivar," she said quietly, "thinks of me as a servant girl."

She left it at that, still not prepared to reveal his assault on her.

Gunnhild said gently, "I reminded Ivar that you didn't come to our household as a servant girl."

She reached out and took Thora's hand into hers.

"Ivar is a good son; he tends to listen to his mother's advice and he knows it would please me a good deal to see you, Thora Thorvinnsdottir, becoming a member of our family. He promised to think it over, and I hope you will too."

For three nights Thora was unable to sleep; she lay in bed turning this way then that, tossing things over in her mind, and on the third morning she dragged herself out of bed, her eyes heavy but her mind clear and made up. As hard as it might be, she would accept Ivar's proposal for marriage should it come. This must after all be the road laid out for her by the Norns, the third way, the one to lead her out of dishonour and ruin. Had she not wished for a way out of the disgrace that would follow her and the child she might have, whose father she couldn't name? If she became Ivar's wife, she and any child of hers would be treated with proper respect. *And I'll get the chance, sooner or later, to make him pay for what he did to me.*

THIRTEEN

_____

_____

She shall ...know the full extent of our deliberations and settle between Glum and herself whether she will have him or not; and then she cannot lay the blame on anyone else if it does not turn out well.

NJAL's SAGA

_____

_____

The horse seemed a trifle lame.

Thora stood by the wall of the horse enclosure unable to turn her eyes away from Surtur, fussing and pawing the dirt. She snapped her fingers to startle the colt into a trot and show her more clearly if something was bothering him.

"Thora!" Ivar approached with long purposeful strides.

She waited stony-faced, guessing his mission.

Ivar dispensed with the bother of playing the eager suitor.

"It would seem to make sense in this new land of few people, that we consider marriage between us. What do you say?"

Her mouth went dry at the thought of him as her husband, but she had made up her mind; grim-faced and unable to speak, she nodded consent.

Ivar seemed relieved.

"That's settled then," he said, turning around and strutting his way back to the house.

Thora pressed her hands to her burning eyes. *Is this how a man pronounced guilty of manslaughter feels, trapped between two dismal choices — agree to pay the set man-price and be impoverished, or choose to be outlawed and live in exile?*

Although innocent of any misdeed and merely cursed by misfortune, she had just sentenced herself to becoming the wife of this loathsome man, a high price to pay for avoiding shame and yet, the only way she could see to secure a proper future for herself and the child she feared she was carrying.

If she turned out to be with child, the birth would take place in late summer; she pictured herself confined to her bed having to bear the talk of Ivar and his friends drinking in celebration of Ivar Ulfson's firstborn; the new father would go about boasting among his rowdy peers who kept raising their horns for refills and slapping the back of the proud father. *Well done, lad, well done... lost no time to plow the furrow, ha ha ha!*

Thora entered the horse pen to be with her mare for a while. She straightened out the matted mane with her fingers and buried her face in the wet, sweet-smelling fur of the horse's neck; after a while her throbbing headache had vanished.

No, there would be no pleasure in marrying this man but then, pleasure wasn't what marriage was about. She could name half a dozen married men and women who resented one another and who did settle down all the same, sharing between them the running of a prosperous household and farm. There was no strict need for a husband and wife to share the same bed more often than necessary to conceive offspring. Already, mercifully, Ivar seemed to have lost interest in her. His pale, roving eyes were no longer seeking her out and even his visits with Achren seemed to be less frequent lately – any time now, and he would choose another bond-woman for his bed.

*   *   *   *   *

The news of Thora Thorvinnsdottir and Ivar Ulfson's betrothal lifted winter-weary spirits at Sandurness. Helga could hardly wait till people would be able to travel again by boat and horseback, making their way to Sandurness for the wedding.

"To think," the young girl exclaimed giving Thora a hug, "that we'll be like true sisters, you and I, and the first wedding celebrated in Greenland is to take place right here at our farm!"

Gunnhild appeared not as excited over the upcoming wedding as might be expected. Now that her time was drawing close, she seemed to have lost the strength to deal with daily affairs. When Helga or one of the maids approached her about household matters big or small, Gunnhild waved her away.

"Ask Thora." she said, adding with a faint smile. "You can ask her about anything, except matters to do with spinning or weaving; for those you had better come to me."

The settlers were dismayed to find how long it took here in the new land before winter retreated to make place for summer. The time of early thaw when mild air and sunshine had drawn them out to the beach, had been short-lived and a succession of storms brought more heavy wet snow to cover up the tawny patches of winter grass exposed by the thaw. After a sleet storm, the roof of the near-empty hay storage collapsed and they needed to dig underneath the rubble for remnants of forage, skimpy rations for sheep and cows. The horses, turned loose to fend on their own, dug through the snow to feed on last season's shrivelled brown vegetation.

Then a severe cold spell turned the sleet into ice and winter at its worst settled in once again. Ulf ordered all hands out to remove ice and uncover any vegetation found in the farmyard along the sheltering walls. He made them drag the emaciated cows and sheep out of their pens and byres and leave them to forage where they lay, unable to get to their feet, weakened by a winter in which they were starved for feed and had no way to move about. After they had their overgrown hooves trimmed to proper size and were revived by the fresh air, some found the strength to rise to their feet and stagger from one patch to the next attempting to graze.

It was early morning, with another storm brewing, when Gunnhild's pains began.

Thora helped her to bed and sat besides her holding her hand.

"I've sent Eidyll to Brattalid with my two horses to fetch Thjodhild," she said. "We must be patient. It will take time even for my horses with their long legs to get through the deep snow in the pass and make it to Eirik's place and back again with the lady Thjodhild."

She pitied the horses — breaking through the crust of ice with every step, sinking up to their knees in snow, blood running down their legs — but she kept her thoughts to herself, giving Gunnhild's hand a squeeze.

"There's no reason to worry should things with you run along faster than it takes for Thjodhild to be here. Unna knows what to do and I ... I'm a quick learner. We could have you and the new child all comfortable and asleep by the time Thjodhild makes her way to here!"

Calf-faced Unna strained her rheumy eyes for a close look at her mistress, nodding and mumbling to herself. She instructed the younger maids to take turns putting the bellows to the flames. Thora set water to heat in the large cauldron.

Gunnhild's first wave of pain began to settle; Thora went to the linen chest to take out a stack of folded clean cloth.

The door opened and Ulf, Ivar and two lads came in as well as a blast of icy wind; Gunnhild, reclined on the high seat platform, pulled the bed covers up to her chin.

"Her time has come then, has it?" said Ulf scanning the linen laid out on a bench and casting a glance at the squat shape of Unna busying herself at the fire.

"Suppose we had better get out of the way and leave things to you, women." He turned to Thora.

"Have you sent for Thjodhild?"

Thora nodded. "I sent my *thrall* with the two swift horses to Brattalid a while ago, but the storm seems to be worsening...it may be a while before they make it through."

Ulf heaved a sigh, his grey-blue eyes dark with concern. He sent the *karls* back out with torches to wait for the midwife's arrival; he and Ivar moved into the rear section of the house, set up the game board and talked for a while in hushed voices.

Unna massaged Gunnhild's belly, tight like drumskin; she told Thora to get more pillows to put under Gunnhild's back.

"She should sit up straighter, or rather"... Unna looked up to the ceiling. "We need a rope long enough to reach from the rafter down to the bed."

Thora fetched a thick rope of horsehair. She kneeled on the bed and looped one end over the rafter tying the ends together; Unna handed the knot to her mistress.

"There, for you to hold on tight."

The pain returned; Gunnhild clenched her teeth; she grasped the rope, raised herself up to a squat and strained until she fell back on the pillows.

Suppertime came and went. Maids and lads silently filed in for a ladle of yesterday's reheated gruel and some of yesterday's seal flipper stew. They ate up quickly and hurried out, back into the storm.

Toward midnight Gunnhild made a lengthy, painful effort.

"There!" Unna pointed. A tiny patch of skull had appeared, plastered with whirls of thin hair.

"At last," Unna laughed, "at last the little laggard decides to quit playing games! One more time, mistress...another deep breath and one more push!"

But Gunnhild, reclined on the pillows, failed to respond.

Unna kneaded Gunnhild's belly with her broad hands, strong stubby fingers cupped like mole claws. Thora took a clean cloth, dipped it in lukewarm water and washed the sweat from Gunnhild's face and breasts; she allowed her thoughts to roam.

How is it that women, compared to beasts, need to go through so much suffering to give birth? The gods surely were in a wrathful mood when they gave big oversized heads to the children of women to torment their mothers at birth. For cows, mares, ewes and bitches, birthing is a mere trifle by comparison.

Only once Thora witnessed a difficult foaling, a wide-shouldered colt foal that caused much hardship to the unfortunate mare. The problem was with the foals' shoulders, not with its head. Strange to think that people would need heads this huge to think their way through a life that, for most people, lasted little longer than the life of a horse. *Once again the gods have played a joke on us mortals by giving us more mind than we need; only serves to send our thoughts roaming at will, landing us in no end of trouble.*

Gunnhild sat up racked by a new wave of pain. Thora clenched her fists in her lap, unable to think of something she could do to help.

Unna took Thora's hands and compared them to her own.

"My paws are too large to go inside her. You have such slender hands. Helga, get us some *skyr* to pour over her hands."

Thora swallowed, fighting her rising panic.

Gunnhild appeared to gather up every remaining shred of strength; Thora bent over, breathing along with her, squeezing her shoulders while waiting for Helga to return with the *skyr*; with a tremendous heave, Gunnhild arched up, and the child slipped out like a wrinkled fish carried on gushing water and blood.

Unna grinned fondly at Gunnhild, collapsed on the pillows; she took the girl child and turned her upside down slapping her bottom and rewarded by hearty wailing; after a wash in warm water, the newborn was swaddled to a neat bundle and placed into her mother's arms.

Thora hurried to replace the soiled bedding and Gunnhild whispered to her new daughter till she fell asleep.

Ulf and Ivar abandoned their game to join the women by the bed. Gently, Ulf tapped his wife's cheek until she opened her eyes.

"Another girl I hear...and she seems healthy enough."

He bent over to whisper in Gunnhild's ear. She gave him a tired smile and a whispered response.

Ulf straightened up; he gazed down on his wife with a rare look of tenderness.

"A good thing we devoted prayers all winter to Freya, my idea, and I'm glad that we did. That mealy-mouthed Christ of yours can't be trusted to deal with a difficult birthing."

He turned to Helga.

"You're a big girl now; you'll help to take good care of your mother and new sister, won't you?"

Helga, a shine in her eyes, nodded eagerly.

"Thora and I, we won't leave her side," she said with a toss of her braids.

"Aw, that's enough woman's talk for a day," Ivar said. "Let's go back to our game."

The two men hurried back to the rear of the house.

Unna opened a chest for more linen. Thora sat by Gunnhild's side looking closely at her face, pale and drawn, buried in goose down pillows; Thora stroked her forehead, surprised to feel the cold of the flesh and see the change in Gunnhild's face; in less than a day her foster mother's handsome, strong features had turned narrow and pointed like the face of a mouse.

What did it mean? Was everything as it should be, or was something amiss? *Should she be sleeping at this point before passing the afterbirth?*

Mares generally stayed on their feet after foaling, awake and fully alert, pacing about to dislodge the foal sack. *How long after birthing does it take for a woman to clean out?*

She asked Unna.

"It all depends...some women are quick, others slow to pass all of it... the lady Thjodhild surely knows."

Thjodhild... still out there somewhere... caught in the storm.

Thora slumped on top of the bed unable to keep her eyes open, vaguely aware of Helga beside her fully asleep.

Unna called out.

"Wake up, everyone."

The girls bolted to their feet.

"What?"

Unna put a finger to her lips.

"Shh, listen!"

They heard no sounds other than the wind howling.

"There it is again!" Unna whispered. "Do you hear?"

Flooded with relief, Thora grabbed Helga's shoulder.

"They're here! Listen for yourself."

There it was again, a horse hollering loud and clear.

"That is Fluga's call."

Thora ran to the door, opened it a crack and stared into the darkness squeezing her eyes almost shut against the stinging snow. There was no sign of the torch bearers Ulf had sent out to show the way to the house.

Thora grabbed a torch of braided hay soaked in seal oil from the stack by the door; she touched it to the fire to set it alight and went out to make her way through the jumble of ice and snow toward the flickering torchlights by the horse pen. The two horses stood in the circle of light, flanks heaving, covered from ears to tail with frozen snow, and Eidyll stood beside the mare waiting for the mistress of Brattalid to step into his cupped hands. Thjodhild grunted, lowering her bulk from the saddle — her own unwieldy woman's saddle, equipped with a wooden shelf on the near side. Her foot missed Eidyll's hands by a hair, and she hit the snow on soft sealskin boots grabbing his shoulder.

"My joints don't take well to a long ride any more," she grumbled, shifting some of her weight to Thora's shoulder.

"Well, child, I'll never know how we made it through this freezing hell – ice and snow and raging winds strong enough to blow a horse off its feet."

She chuckled.

"I lost all sense of what's up and what's down, let alone of where we were going...perhaps your lad did too....we couldn't talk.... good thing a horse can always tell the way home.....tell me, how's she doing, the mistress Gunnhild?"

"She's doing fine I believe," Thora said, for now keeping her concerns to herself.

"She gave birth to a healthy well-made little girl."

They worked their way to the house, struggling to keep upright in the knee-deep snow.

"They're both resting," Thora went on. "She...I don't know...she's not done yet, and I wonder... it's only a hunch...but I wonder if she's not taking awfully long..."

Thjodhild, barely inside the door, threw off her sheepskin mittens without wasting time on small talk. She marched over to the bed still shaking snow from her otterskin cloak, and tapped Gunnhild's cheeks to wake her.

Thora watched as the midwife examined mother and child, feeling the pulse; she gazed into their eyes and gently pinched Gunnhild's skin. Thjodhild looked up.

"Did you say she hasn't passed the afterbirth?"

"She did not."

Thjodhild frowned. She took some herbs from the pigskin pouch around her waist and told Unna to steep them in hot water.

"And don't let them come to a boil."

After the water had turned a drab green Thjodhild asked for a piece of clean cloth, strained the hot liquid into a wooden bowl and set it to cool.

"Wait till it's lukewarm," she instructed. "Then take a small spoon and feed her half of it, slowly, little by little, wait another short while and give her the rest."

Thora took a small wooden spoon from the wall and waited for the herb mixture to cool.

Thjodhild lowered herself carefully on a sturdy stool by the bed; Helga handed her a bowl of hot stew and the midwife warmed her hands on the bowl impatiently blowing the steam aside.

"After that ride from hell I could eat a spring foal all by myself."

Thora helped Gunnhild to sit up and drink the green potion. Each time she swallowed a spoonful, Gunhild tried to go back to sleep until, suddenly, she sat up straight tensing her back.

"See?" Thjodhild said. "I told you those herbs never fail."

She rose, handing Thora her empty bowl.

"Here take this and put it away; keep yourself and the other girl out of the way as well."

She helped Gunnhild down from the bed and began walking her up and down the hall offering her own solid bulk for support.

"Go on. Put all your weight on me."

Gunnhild came to a sudden halt. Thjodhild grabbed her arms and told her to squat.

"Now, push."

A gush of blood soaked the dirt floor and with it came the blood-stained bundle they had been waiting for.

Thora brought water, and after a quick wash she settled Gunnhild back in her bed.

The midwife turned to the maids.

"Find me a sturdy hayfork."

She took her time poking the mass on the floor with the three wooden prongs, lifting and spreading the membranes beside the fire for close scrutiny. She shook her head.

"Bring a light."

Thora pulled up one of the oil lamps and stuck the iron spike in the ground beside the soiled, ragged membranes. Thjodhild's face brightened.

"Not a single shred missing as far's I can tell."

She raised the mass up on the fork and handed it to the maid.

"Take this outside and bury it well out of reach for the dogs. Put plenty of rocks on top if you can find any in this snow, or you could take some from the wall around your sheep pen... unless, of course...."

The midwife hesitated.

"Unless you folks insist on following the old ways…I hope you're not thinking of burying this under the doorstep for heathen luck, are you?"

Her dark eyebrows knitted together in a frown.

"The lady Gunnhild told me that she follows the ways of White Christ."

Thora looked at the midwife's eyes, glittering under hooded eyelids. Did she see a hint of worry there?

Thjodhild stared at Gunnhild's drawn face.

"I don't know what to say," she muttered. "She cleaned out late...it was all there, of that I made sure....but it was in bad shape... We must hope and pray that she doesn't get the fever."

She rummaged again inside her pouch for another package of herbs which she handed to Thora.

"Steep a pinch of these in hot water till the liquid turns a dark golden," she said.

"Give her two full spoons of it every morning and evening for the next two days. Afterwards, use it only when needed. It should return her energy and get her milk to flow."

She hesitated.

"Don't waste these. They're from Iceland. I've given you half of my supply and I haven't yet found any of these herbs growing in this land."

She glanced at the bed platforms along the walls.

"Now, you had better show me a place to take a nap. I'm getting too old to trek on horseback through a wicked storm, turn right around and go back home again."

Thora offered her own bed piled high with additional sheepskins taken from Helga's bed.

She stored the precious herbs in the wooden box used by Gunnhild to keep her small treasures, and she lingered over the box for a moment, running her finger over the painted green leaves and red flowers on the lid. Gunnhild was fond of colours; she liked to collect beautiful things – so like her own mother.

One by one maids and *karls* filed back into the house and headed for bed after taking a peek at the mistress and her new child. Helga went also to bed after Thora promised to keep watch by the bed side, stoking the fire from time to time; everyone else in the household had fallen asleep.

It wasn't long before Helga woke up; she left her bed.

"Let me take your place," she whispered. "You try catching some sleep now."

Thora woke up because someone was patting her cheeks. Thjodhild stood by her bedside.

"I think the storm is over...I find I'm too old to sleep any other place than in my own bed under my own quilted swan down. Tell your horse *thrall* to get the horses ready and find me something to drink and a little to eat before he takes me home."

Thora woke Eidyll in his corner bed by the door. She lit a fresh torch, handed it to him and sent him out in the dark.

Thjodhild emptied a bowl of reheated fish broth, set it down and went to take a long look at Gunnhild, soundly asleep, a faint smile on her face. The midwife pursed her lips. She pointed to Gunnhild's sunken cheeks.

"See the glow? I don't like this flush on her face."

She took another package from her pouch and pressed it into Thora's hand.

"These are herbs for purifying bad blood. If you notice a foul smell around her you give her these right away dissolved in warm water, all of it. And send your *thrall* to me on the fast mare for more. It's all we can do besides praying."

Before she stepped outside Thjodhild turned in the doorway to gaze at the sleepy faces peeking at her from under the blankets.

"I'll pray for her to White Christ," she said, "and I urge all of you housefolk to pray for her too. Pray to anyone or anything you want, but do pray as often and as long as you can. And remember, she needs to be watched closely. I do not like the way she looks...I do not like it at all."

Gunnhild's milk began to flow and the child was alert and feeding well. Still, Thora felt uneasy, mindful of Thjodhild's warning. On the third morning she lifted Gunnhild's bedcovers, and took a sudden step back wrinkling her nose at the foul odour drifting up. Immediately she sent Eidyll out to fetch more of Thjodhild's herbs.

The *thrall* returned with two small bundles of herbs and something else.

"The mistress of Brattalid told me to give you this."

He handed Thora a wooden carving half a hand high.

"It represents the mother of Christ," he explained, "and the divine child."

Intrigued, Thora examined the little sculpture carved out of birch — a slender woman in a flowing robe cradling a newborn infant in the crook of her arm. The child's face was tiny, the size and shape of a mouse ear. If it weren't for the Christ child in the carving, the fair woman might be taken for Freyja. Perhaps it would be helpful to tuck the charm under Gunnhild's pillow.

Thora stood a while holding the carving, allowing the warmth from her hands to trickle into the wood and waiting for a response until she was sure there would be none. She sensed no power, no tickle of the healing force it was supposed to hold – nothing – not even the eerie sensation of warmth returning to her hands whenever she held her mother's amber necklace.

FOURTEEN

_____

_____

Late in the summer Thorstein made ready to go to the Althing. He said to his wife, Jofrid, "You are soon going to give birth. If you have a girl, it must be left out to die, but if it is a boy, it will be brought up."... Jofrid replied, "It is most unfitting for a man of your position to talk like that and it cannot seem right to do such a scandalous thing."

"You're fully acquainted with my temper," Thorstein said. "It will not do for you or anyone else to cross me."

GUNNLAUGS SAGA ORMSTUNGU

_____

_____

Ulf had been under the impression that all was well with his wife and new daughter. Now he began to worry. Once again he made sacrifice to Freyja, but Gunnhild failed to get better. She lost her milk and the child took to crying day and night. Thora sent Eidyll to Thjodhild to ask if she knew of a nursing mother who would foster the newborn. Thjodhild told Eidyll she knew of quite a few women due to give birth later, though not until summer. She suggested raising the child on goat's milk – fresh or soured, either would do.

The little girl was no longer crying much; worn out, she lay quietly beside her mother and the soft flutter of her breathing could barely be noticed. At night in the sleep-quiet house they took the child away to keep her safe because Gunnhild spent the nights tossing, turning, and talking to the dark.

Thora and Helga took turns rocking the swaddled child and seeking to soothe the mother who wouldn't be comforted. During the day when they laid the tiny girl in her mother's arms for a nap, Gunnhild came to rest, contented until the child woke up and tried to nurse in vain; Thora sent Helga out on some errand or other to spare her the sight of her little sister's distress, the sound of her feeble cries and the sight of her tiny fists hammering at her mother's shriveled breasts.

Each day there were a few cups of goat milk squeezed out from the one skinny doe still in milk, to give the child who kept crying for more. Unna insisted they use cow's milk as well, and ewe's milk, any milk they could get their hands on, but Thora didn't give in. The painful death of her little brother had come only days after the maids began to give him cow's milk.

Unna asked Ulf to make Thora see reason.

Ulf said, "It's up to you women to decide how and if you keep trying to raise this child. I'm greatly concerned for her mother, and I want you to know that her welfare takes precedence. I will not have you fuss to excess with this newborn at the expense of caring for her mother."

Gunnhild began to see and hear things which nobody else could sense. Frightened of horrors only she was able to see, she tried to fling herself out of bed.

Eight days after giving birth Gunnhild fell quiet, her breathing reduced to short, shallow puffs. The child was crying in Helga's lap; Thora put the little girl beside her mother to calm her, but the child wouldn't be comforted; she kept up a thin, mournful whining; overcome by exhaustion, Thora and Helga both fell asleep.

Toward morning Thora startled awake. The child was no longer crying. Alarmed, Thora searched Gunnhild's face and listened, unable to hear the faintest breathing; she slid her hand under Gunnhild's breasts; the feverish heat had drained away and the skin was no longer sweaty; the flesh felt strangely firm, almost rock-hard and cold as freshly caught fish. Some time during the night Gunnhild had died.

The newborn lay in the crook of her mother's arm not moving, her limp little fists turning blue.

*   *   *   *   *

Helga sobbed and clung to her mother's body. Gently, Ulf removed his daughter from the bedside, carried her to his own bed and left her there under a pile of fox blankets before he stepped outside to announce the death.

Thora helped Unna to wash Gunnhild's body and dress her in a clean linen shift; they stood back against the wall watching the household members shuffling by in a silent farewell to the mistress of the house.

At mid-day Ulf called everone away from their daily tasks to accompany Gunnhild to her temporary resting place. The ground was still frozen too hard for the digging of a grave, and they had no fuel to spare for burning the body.

"Besides," Ulf reflected, "followers of White Christ disapprove of burning the dead, and my wife favoured new-fangled Christian ways."

For now he decided to place her body in the hay storage shed; there, in this cold, it would stay frozen and out of reach of wolves, dogs and foxes — though not for stray ice bears venturing ashore.

"I'll leave Khagan out at night to patrol the yard rather than shutting him in with the sheep," Thora said.

Even at mid-day there was no wind; the air was sullen, caught under a lead-coloured sky.

Arm in arm Thora, Helga and behind them the maids followed the men who carried Gunnhild's remains to the shed. Helga cried softly stumbling with every step. Thora forced herself to walk straight and dry-eyed in spite of the ache inside, as if someone had stabbed a knife through her heart and twisted the blade.

Ulf and Ivar carried the shrouded corpse on top of some boards to the hay shed. The livestock *thralls* kicked the snow aside ahead of them, pausing at the shed to shovel away the snow piled high against the door. They forced the door open wide enough to enter the cramped sod-walled space, one man at a time. Ulf and Ivar went inside with their burden. The others waited at the door.

The men re-emerged and Thora cast a last glance through the open doorway at Gunnhild's frail face, ghostly white above the shroud of grey homespun. She had received many kind words from this woman, and ready advice, whether asked for or not – she would always remember her foster mother as a wise, thoughtful woman.

Gunnhild's death had been peaceful in the end; she had slipped away calmly, her face resigned, not contorted in agony as Rannveig's had been; her mother's contorted body and bloated face floated to the surface in Thora's mind and she could no longer keep the tears from washing down her cheeks.

She grasped Helga's arm.

"Come, it is done. We must return to the house."

Behind them the *thralls* banged the door shut.

Thora insisted they feed the infant no other than goat's milk, though there was never enough and the child failed to thrive. Her tiny face remained wrinkled and thin like the ancient face of a dwarf.

"Maybe," Helga said, "her spirit belongs to the dwarf folk that live in the earth below our feet; maybe they tossed her out by mistake to live with us, mortals in Midgard, and maybe she is now lost to her own kind for all times."

"Perhaps," Unna agreed. "The Norns in any case have decided that she is to follow her mother."

Ulf rose from his seat by the fire, though not as usual to signal bed time. He stared into the flames talking to no one in particular giving voice to what everyone else, Thora suspected, was thinking.

"We must allow fate to have its way with this child. It is time we exposed her."

Ivar spoke up in agreement.

"It's good to see that you, Father, have come to your senses at least over this."

Thora clenched her fists struggling to keep silent. It wasn't her place to speak out. She looked sideways to Helga who sat cross-legged on her bed cradling her tiny sister; Helga's face betrayed her anxiety.

Not that anyone could be blamed for the death of a child born without luck, no more than anyone was to blame at Hestardalur for the death of Rannveig and her son, although deep down, Thora felt that her brother's death was her fault.

As soon as she learned she had a brother, Thora fled the house seeking the company of the horse herd browsing on willow and birch in the sheltered glen. For a long time she lay on a cushion of creeping birch surrounded by foraging horses; even now she could still feel the prickly twigs scratching her arms on that long ago day, arms she had wrapped around her head to shut out the world. *Now he has a son, a boy, to take hunting and riding with him instead of his daughter. All fathers prefer a son for company.*

She had jumped up waving her fists and there between the browsing horses, she had cursed her new brother aloud, asking the gods that he would never grow up. Back in the house, torn by guilt and regret, she had offered to help with the care of her mother and brother, and when the illness came she returned to the glen and recalled her curse three times. *They must live, they must live, they must live.*

After they died Thora was overcome with remorse. This time though, things were different, were they not? No longer a selfish child, she had wished nothing but good fortune to befall Gunnhild and her child. And yet, could it be she still was to blame for their death? Could it be that the curse she called into life so many years ago, took wings and had followed her even here?

Now and then she felt an eerie compulsion to cast a quick glance over her shoulder hoping to catch a glimpse of the something that seemed to be always there hovering right behind her on dark, leathery wings, rising like smoke and already dissolved before she could get a clear vieuw.

Would she always bring bad luck however unintended, to the people around her, even to those she loved the most?

Ulf it turned out couldn't bring himself to order his tiny daughter
exposed and so, against all reason, Thora was left in peace to persist with
her fight for the infant's life. She tried spoon feeding goat's milk with bits
of chewed fish stirred in. The child, though swallowing some, burped it
all up right away and every day she became more frail and lethargic.

The maids remained silent; they watched Thora's efforts without
comment except for old Unna, who muttered, "It's a fool who keeps
wielding a sword when no one's left alive on the battlefield other than
ravens, eagles and wolves."

Ulf remarked a few more times that the child must be put outside
to chill.

"The nights are still cold enough to put a quick, merciful end to the
sputtering wick of her life."

But he stopped short of giving the order, and Thora carried on with
her solitary struggle.

Ulf asked Ivar to talk sense into the woman who had betrothed
herself to become his wife, and one day Ivar took her aside for a rant.

"Give it up! You're going way beyond duty or reason — and you of
all people, not even related by blood to this child!"

Thora paid him no mind.

Ivar said to his father.

"The woman isn't capable of reason!"

Ulf said, "Then let her be. It'll come to a natural end very soon."

There was only one thing to be glad of, Unna remarked.

"Gunnhild never named the child, and so there won't be a need for
burial gifts."

"A very good thing in these circumstances," Ivar agreed.

"Our household can ill afford gifts, let alone burial sacrifices for a
child perished so soon."

Thora shrugged.

"It wouldn't matter if Gunnhild had decided on a name, because this
child isn't fated to die; she will not slip out of this mortal life any time
soon, nor will she linger about without flesh to haunt us; have no fear."

Ten days after Gunnhild's death the child, though feeble, still clutched to life. After the morning's milking Helga barged into the doorway with a pail full of foaming milk instead of the usual two cups.

"The brindle goat kidded last night," she shouted. "I told the lads to kill the kids at once, and now look at all this milk I squeezed out! We have plenty of goodness now for my sister to grow strong, and some to spare for the household besides!"

Thora embraced her foster sister, smiling broadly without a thought for her missing tooth.

"I always knew her luck would turn around!"

With each new day the little girl's life spark burned stronger inside her small frame; before long it had grown to a powerful flame, no longer easily quelled. The household rejoiced. Even the sky seemed less gloomy, and the silence in which people had carried out chores was replaced by laughter, talk and good-humoured teasing.

* * * * *

Ulf was excited and pleased over his new daughter. He turned to Helga with a teasing smile on his bearded face.

"Now, older daughter," he said. "You do understand I hope that your sister's gain is your loss....when the time comes you'll have to share with her all which I intended to set aside for your dowry..."

He gave her coppery braid a playful tug.

"I'm only one man with only one farm and only one ship... last time I looked about this green land I saw no fabled trees bearing nuts of gold or fruits of silver."

"Why can't we just do away with dowries?" Helga asked, keeping her braids out of her father's reach.

"Isn't it true that we came to this land to live our lives the way we see fit? You and Mother kept telling us over and over again. What's to stop us from making new rules for ourselves? The first new rule I want to propose is that girls be free to be married without the need for a dowry."

Ulf slapped his knees with laughter.

"I see…no more, nor less. The next thing my daughter proposes no doubt, is that young women be allowed to marry whomever they fancy without involving their elders. You're growing into a strong-minded woman, my girl! I pity the man who takes you on for a wife some day!"

He looked around the circle of farmhands and maids, his face suddenly solemn.

"Now, everyone listen. It's time to name my new daughter. Her name will be Halldis, after her maternal grandmother. It was Gunnhild's wish though she never said so aloud. She whispered it into my ear one night as she lay sleepless, and I am duty bound to respect her wish."

The weather at last turned around for good, chasing the frost away; perhaps the gods had finally grown tired of playing their cruel games with the people and livestock of Greenland.

"It is time to dig Gunnhild's grave," Ulf said.

The burial would be far from lavish, and they wouldn't perform any blood sacrifice.

"It wouldn't be proper," Ulf said, "considering that Gunnhild was no longer happy to seek favours from the old gods."

In any case, everyone knew that right now they couldn't spare any animal to slaughter and burn for the rich smoke the gods liked to savour and neither could they afford to give up valuables for burial gifts. Back in Iceland a woman of Gunnhild's status would be given some of her prize possessions to sustain her after this life, things to wear or to use for barter during the course of the afterlife journey. But this wasn't Iceland; new settlers couldn't risk parting with valuables they might need some day to trade for supplies in order to survive in this life. And besides, everyone knew that Christians didn't believe the dead needed to take anything with them. And so Ulf decided to pass on Gunnhild's fine furs and most of her jewelry to Helga and the remainder he said, would be given to Halldis some day as part of her dowry.

On the day of the burial Thora took her mother's amber necklace out of her jewelry box and sat down with it on her bed. She had to untie many of the little knots to remove her favourite bead, the one that held a small beetle captive in its golden heart. She attached the bead to a yarn of red silk she found in Gunnhild's embroidery box.

At the gravesite when it was her turn to come forward to say farewell, Thora placed the bead pendant around Gunnhild's neck. She rubbed it till it was warm and glowing like a tiny sun.

"A small gift from my mother and me to you, dear Foster mother," she whispered.

"May it warm you on your journey through the icy wastelands and help to see you safely to your place of destination, Hela — I think — or perhaps that other place, Heaven, where your White Christ is believed to dwell."

She had Thjodhild's permission to do what she wished with the carved mother and child. Now, before tucking it underneath Gunnhild's folded hands, she gave it a vigorous rub, but the wood remained as before, cold and ungiving. No wonder the Christian charm failed to heal Gunnhild's sickness; it kept its powers well-hidden, assuming it had any; still, it might be of use to the good woman's spirit while seeking to enter the Christian afterlife.

After the burial, life for the people at Sandurness resumed its daily course. Helga took care of her little sister feeding her pre-chewed food mixed with goat milk, and Halldis was turning from frail and sickly to a robust child blessed with steady growth.

Thora could no longer avoid facing her upcoming marriage. Every day she wondered about the wisdom of her decision, especially since she had reason to doubt after all that she was with child. She tried on her old shepherd's clothes for daily wear on horseback, and found that the drawstring around the waist tightened to the same knot as before. If she were with child, shouldn't her waist by now have expanded some? Unna would be able to tell her, but to ask her would set the maids gossiping. And so, with no one in whom she wished to confide, Thora kept all such questions to herself.

There was still snow left in the hills and the foraging livestock roamed close to the farmstead or down by the beach seeking early green growth. Thora supervised the maids handiwork, even the sewing involved in the making of a new sail for Ulf's ship; they spent long days laying out lengths of coarse homespun brought from Iceland, and sewing them together with strips of leather to secure the seams.

On windy days *karls* and field *thralls* liked to stay close to the house after the mid-day meal. With their backs against the lee side wall they repaired nets and harpoons for the upcoming spring hunt and fishery. The maids also liked to take their work outside for some fresh air, escaping the poor light and perennial smoke inside the house. Laughter and good cheer had returned, and the days went by fast.

"Why don't we take a mid-day break today by the beach," Thora suggested to Ulf, "to boost our housefolk's spirits and soak up some of that glorious sunshine. Afterwards it'll be easier for all to keep to our tasks."

"Yes, why not," Ulf said. "I sure wouldn't mind taking my daily nap on the beach ... as long as you see to it that folks don't linger about for too long."

Thora sat down in her favourite spot at the high-tide line on a pile of bleached driftwood. Khagan lay by her feet, head raised, watching the others talking and laughing or walking along the beach to collect crabs and periwinkles, anything juicy and big enough to be worth the effort of making a cook fire on the beach. A freshwater stream meeting up with the fjord nearby was bordered by fields of salty marsh grass favoured by the sheep. Lambs frolicked at the waterline and last winter's only surviving calf made awkward attempts to join the lambs in their spirited butting games.

Go on you lot, have a good time while you still can. Thora smiled at the frisky ram lambs destined to become roasts at her wedding feast. All too soon...She and Ivar hadn't exchanged more than ten words since they agreed to be married. Was it madness to become the wife of a man she resented so deeply, and who hated her back just as much?

Once again she listed Rannveig's requirements for a good husband. *Will he be a good provider?* With regard to Ivar, the answer would likely be 'yes'. *Do I want to bear this man's children?* Her answer would be a resounding 'no', if she still had a choice, but did she?

One day Gunnhild had called her and Helga together to pass out advice that echoed Rannveig's words of long ago. *When considering a man for a husband,* Gunnhild said, *a girl and her parents ought to ask themselves two things: can he provide all that a woman needs to keep a household going? Can he shelter, feed and protect their children and afford to raise them to their proper station in life?*

How many times did people repeat this same song, advising their daughters to marry a man regardless of mutual attraction? *Never mind,* they said. *Over the years he'll learn to like you, and you'll learn to like him well enough.*

"Not I," Thora whispered. "Not in my entire lifetime could I learn to like this man."

As if aware of her thoughts, Khagan turned his head to fix her with his golden-eyed glance.

"Both of my mothers talked as if there was nothing to this matter," she said to the dog. "Easy enough for them to say, considering that Rannveig and Gunnhild both had caring parents who made sure that only kind and reasonable men came to propose to their daughters."

The dog sighed, lowering his head on his paws.

"Look at me when I'm talking to you," Thora demanded, lifting the dog's head to make him face her.

"What's your opinion of Ivar? You don't like him much I can tell.... I trust you can keep a secret; you see, right now I need to follow through with my promise to marry this man, because as his wife I'll have a better chance to make him pay for what he did to me."

She fondled the dog's ears.

"If I hadn't promised on my mother's honour to find a way to make him pay for the outrage he did me, I would refuse to go through with this wedding. Instead I would seek for a husband a man with the nature of a Khazar dog, loyal and generous, caring and protective like you are."

She smiled and patted the dog's wet nose with her finger tips.

"Of course this man would also need to be handsome, as handsome in his own way as you are in your dog way."

Khagan sighed twice, lowered his head back on his paws and closed his eyes.

Thora folded her arms. She looked along the beach with its drifts of drab, desiccated rockweed mixed with sand. Shivers ran up her spine, fanning out across her shoulders till she trembled facing the life that awaited her by the side of a husband she hated, and who hated her right back.

She straightened up squaring her shoulders and scanning her own pitiful land allotment in the hills behind the farmhouse; there was another reason, strong and compelling, why she must marry Ivar Ulfson, the future master of Sandurness Farm. If she chose not to, if she attempted instead to survive on her own miserable upland allotment, then surely she, Ivar's poor and resented woman neighbour, would be doomed to live and be buried as a woman of no consequence; she would be subject to the whims of her neigbour, rich, powerful, and merciless, and she would have nowhere to go for recourse in this land without Thing or Lawspeakers.

FIFTEEN

Hauskuld and Hrut and their friends took up one bench and the bride-
groom another. Hallgerda sat on the crossbench acting well-behaved.

Thiostolf went about with his axe raised high and no
one seemed to notice; the wedding was a success.

On the way home she insisted she wouldn't
take care of the housekeeping.

NJAL's SAGA

...and took care of running the farm together with her husband... she
turned out to be smart and skilled at many things, quite strong-minded
too. They got along well, although they showed little mutual affection.

LAXDAELA SAGA

Thora did not wish for an elaborate wedding so soon after Gunnhild's death, and it turned out she needn't have worried. There weren't enough settlers in the area to invite as many as was the custom for a proper wedding in Iceland. Neighbours here were few and scattered far apart, and none were close relatives of either bride or groom. And so they invited all fourteen neighbours and their households — everyone within three days travel by sea or on horseback – and that was that.

They could't afford to kill any beef. Thora selected for slaughter a yearling colt and a weedy, unpromising filly in addition to the sheep she chose earlier — four wethers and two runty ewe-lambs, one of them crippled. She hoped that together they would yield enough roast meat for all, and afterwards enough stew for a few more days.

Upon their betrothal Jarl Eirik had made them a gift of grain, barley and a small bag of wheat brought up from the South and traded to Iceland more than a year ago. Eirik's generous gift on behalf of the first wedding among the new settlers boosted his reputation. People spoke exceedingly well of the master of Brattalid.

Thora put some of the barley and all of the wheat aside to be made into bread. The remaining barley she set to ferment – they would not have a wedding without beer.

In the absence of a parent or custodian to negotiate for the bride, Eirik of Brattalid stepped in on Thora's behalf. In front of witnesses Eirik listed the terms of the marriage. The bride would bring in all of the land allotted to her. In return she could claim a third share in her husband's property present and future after he inherited his father's farm, land, livestock and slaves, as well as any ships Ulf might own at that time. Personal belongings such as tools, weapons, horses and bonded personal servants brought into the household at the time of marriage, remained the property of each respective spouse.

"Be advised," Eirik said, stroking his greying red beard and stressing his words to make sure they all heard and understood, "that each spouse has a say in the disposal of property other than the personal belongings of the other."

Eirik also assumed, for lack of a *godi* in the Greenland settlement, the duty of overseeing the marriage ritual. There was no family present on Thora's side to provide the heirloom weapon needed for the ceremonial sword exchange, and so Eirik also provided a sword on her behalf to enable the proper exchange of the wedding rings which were to be be placed on its hilt.

After the colt was ritually slaughtered and its blood splattered on all, new spouses and bystanders alike, Eirik re-stated the details of the arrangement twice in front of all, and the spouses swore to be true to the marriage.

"And now," Eirik roared, "let the feasting begin!"

Late at night Thora underwent the bedding ceremony with eyes shut and teeth clenched, wiping everything to do with her husband and the required attendants out of her mind. She didn't open her eyes before the witnesses had stomped out of the house back to the feast.

Thora sat up, wrapped in her shift. She turned to face Ivar.

"If you know what's good for you, Ivar Ulfson, you lay not a finger on me again tonight or at any other time unless I allow you to for reasons of my own. If you do not respect my wish in this matter, I'll find the shortest way to becoming your widow instead of your wife."

His gaze, clouded by ale, rested briefly on her face before he turned away and, with a grunt, stretched out on the bed.

"I've no mind to lay a finger or anything else on anyone," he muttered. "Methinks I've earned a nap."

After two days the food supplies ran out; around the same time the last beer was also drunk and the event fizzled to an early end. There had been no honey available to brew the traditional wedding mead, and both spouses seemed happy enough to escape the lengthy, excessive honey-moon drinking supposed to assure fertility.

Even so, the occasion would long be remembered and talked about – the first time this many settlers in Greenland had gathered to celebrate.

Thora scanned the faces of guests taking their leave, satisfied to find that most appeared to be well-pleased. Here and there she had caught comments, mostly flattering. *See how well matched a pair they are...look at that young man's broad shoulders... still so young, and already a respectable beard!...and she, tall and striking, and proud of bearing as well; did you ever see hair more alive and lustrous? ...a pity to tuck it away wrapped in a house-wife's head-linen.*

Other comments came from people sensing there was something amiss. *Why does the bride look so severe...anyone seen her smile?*

Thora shrugged at the whispered remarks, resisting temptation to respond.

The bride's choice of groom might account for that.

The newly married couple stood by the horse corral wishing the last of their guests a safe journey home; Thora felt a sudden dull sensation below the waist and a suggestion of little fingers probing her insides — the familiar faint belly ache, almost forgotten, that used to announce her monthly bleeding.

She rushed to the outhouse built over the latrine pit not long ago for the comfort of the wedding guests. Inside, sheltered from curious eyes, she stared at the blood trickling down her legs, and tried coming to terms with the certainty that she wasn't with child. She felt a brief stab of unreasoned regret, followed by whole hearted relief as she grabbed a wad of dried moss to clean up, humming a tune. No wonder she was still comfortable wearing her breeches.

She laughed aloud, relieved of her latest worry — that she would bear a son or a daughter who grew up sharing Ivar's inclination toward cruel and wicked pleasures.

Back in the house she opened her clothes chest to find the red cloak of Friesian wool she had bought at Borgarfjord and never worn; she held the fine comforting wool against her cheek before folding it carefully and placing it in the bottom of the chest – not this time. She intended to wear this cloak on the day she married the man she desired, and one day she would do just that.

There had been much talk among the wedding guests of a recent
journey made by Bjarni Herjolfson. Bjarni was a trader from Iceland
whose elderly father, Herjolf, had sailed to Greenland at Eirik's invitation; later in the summer Bjarni sailed after his father, following navi-
gation instructions to Greenland which the old man had left for him.
Three days out of Iceland Bjarni's ship was caught in a northern gale
which blew the ship off course for several days, relentlesly pushing them
to the Southwest. Eventually one day Bjarni and his crew sighted land,
barren white-flecked cliffs, and later another land covered with trees.
As soon as the weather cleared Bjarni took his bearings and headed
for Greenland on a northeasterly course, safely landing at Herjolfsfjord
where his father had settled.

Many people made fun of him, thinking it odd that a man wouldn't
try to set foot in unknown lands he had chanced upon. Others defended
Bjarni's decision, arguing it was wise and prudent to avoid dealings
with a treacherous, unfamiliar coast, risking ship, crew and cargo for no
better reason than foolish curiosity.

Thora was excited to learn that Bjarni had seen trees growing aplenty
in this unexplored land. Even in Iceland people were forced to buy high
priced timber from Norway or beyond; in remote Greenland, traders
charged excessively for a few crooked boards. Not many Greenlanders
besides Eirik could afford imported wood to build boats and houses;
most made do with driftwood for roof rafters, and some had no other
wood available even for boat repairs.

No wonder people made fun of Bjarni Herjolfson and his timid
ways. Had he decided to explore the new land, he might have had a
valuable load of timber to deliver in Greenland and who knows what
else he might have found to turn a neat profit.

Thora smiled at her own eagerness to find out all she could about the
mysterious new land to the West. What sense was there in her dreaming
of some other new land? She had just married the man who, no matter
how loathsome, would assure her a proper position in life as mistress of
Sandurness Farm.

Thora took quickly to the daily routine befitting the wife of the master's son. Buoyed by her newfound authority she turned all of her energy to managing the household and livestock, enjoying her freedom to make decisions without needing another woman's approval.

Ulf sent the lads out to cut and haul sod needed to build a proper smokehouse. They also extended the main house, adding a porch and sleeping space near the inner door for the *thralls*.

"No *thrall* of mine," Ulf insisted, "need ever again spend the winter in a place without a warm fire."

As time went by, people wondered about their widowed master who seemed in no hurry to select a woman slave for his bed. Some also wondered about the master's son. Though newly married, Ivar kept stealing away from the bed platform he shared with his wife to join Achren in her narrow bed of eelgrass between the storage boxes. No one thought to discuss the subject in Thora's presence, until Helga breached the subject one day.

"Dear sister, I gather that you're expecting?"

"No little sister, I am not," Thora responded. "And it suits me fine to watch my husband placing his favours elsewhere."

She continued with her silk embroidery, pretending not to notice the puzzled faces around her.

How could she explain to Helga that she and Ivar tried to outdo one another in mutual disgust? Her marriage had brought her the comfort to be left alone by him; Ivar, once ready to pounce on her like a hound on a ptarmigan, seemed happy to turn his desires elsewhere. *The challenge has gone out of his game.*

Now that she had no more need herself for the tea brewed from the mysterious brown lumps, she took to slipping a few crumbles of musty herb into Achren's supper every night. It wouldn't do after all for Ivar's bedmate to conceive a child, a son perhaps. Many a man lacking a legitimate, freeborn heir was tempted to legitimize a bastard son out of some bonded bed woman he favoured. She had better not run out of the herb before she found a way to restock her supply, or learned of another powerful herb to replace it...next time she rode over to Brattalid she would ask Thjodhild if she had seen any kind of woman's herb growing in Greenland.

Early summer brought prosperity to Sandurness Farm. The flocks thrived on virgin pasture, remaining healthy and free of worms and disease on land where none of their kind had roamed before. The spring walrus hunt had gone better than expected and the lads had gathered up a dozen fledgling falcons from cliff top eyries by the coast.

Thora took time away from her other tasks to raise the young falcons, leaving Helga and the two milkmaids in charge of dairying.

With so much fish, fowl and meat cured and cheeses smoked, they had plenty to trade, enough to make a good cargo for the journey Ulf and Ivar intended to make to Norway. Still, by the time weather and wind had turned to favour departure, Ulf had changed his mind; he now wished to stay home through the summer to make sure the farm became firmly established.

"Ivar can take Maelstrom Tamer on the shorter run to Iceland instead," he said.

"It will be a suitable voyage for a young man's first attempt to command a trading vessel and be a leader of men."

Ivar jumped at the opportunity to prove his mettle. He and the lads rolled the *knorr* out of the ship-house, re-fitted her and loaded her up with supplies and trade goods. On an overcast, breezy day, Maelstrom Tamer skippered by Ivar and manned by twelve *karls*, rowed down the wind-rippled fjord out to sea.

Thora lived happy carefree days during Ivar's absence.

All too soon – it was still early summer — those tranquil days came to an end; Helga, out with a maid to gather seaweed, came rushing home from the beach.

"They're back, they're back! Maelstrom Tamer's out on the fjord headed for shore."

Thora forced herself to smile at the excited girls chattering like geese, pointing to the water.

"They're wading ashore now...and look, they're bringing visitors!"

The news of visitors spending the summer at Sandurness, spread rapidly across the district of Eiriksfjord, the way ashes spread from fire mountains. Neighbours dropped in to meet the two middle-aged women from Iceland who had traveled aboard Ivar's ship – without paying passage rumour had it, because they were here on Ulf's invitation.

The master of Sandurness, generally known for his stoic nature, outdid himself laughing, talking, and taking pains to please and entertain his guests. Ivar, interrogated by Helga, grinned and admitted he had at Ulf's request asked an elder cousin in Iceland to help him scout for a suitable marriage prospect on behalf of his widowed father.

Ulf seemed after all to be tired of being a windower.

"I feel that our farm needs a mature woman in charge," he said, "to allow this young woman," and he pointed to Thora, "to turn her attention to the bearing of children."

Ivar prided himself on having brought not one, but two suitable marriage prospects home to his father. The women, twin sisters in their forties, were well to do and well connected. One of them, Asta Sigurdsdottir, was a widow from Reykholt eager to indulge her lifelong desire to journey beyond Iceland. The other, Sigrid, had lived in her sister's household through all the twenty three years of Asta's marriage to a wealthy farmer named Asbjorn Steinson.

The sisters had welcomed Ivar's suggestion that they both come to Greenland and see how things work out with his father. If they, after spending a summer and winter at Sandurness, should fail to come to an agreement with Ulf, they would receive free passage back to Iceland in the spring.

The young skipper also prided himself on the succesful trades he made. Aside from grain and iron, he brought home a load of timber, six breeding ewes of a fine-wooled sheep strain as well as two first rate milking cows, in exchange for the bundles of walrus ivory and barrels of seal, walrus and spearbill oil he had carried to Iceland.

"A man from Hedeby gave me a pile of silver for the young falcons," he said.

"With some of the silver I bought myself a good sword made in Frankland, and also I used some to buy gifts for all."

He held up a blue cloak of finest wool. People gasped when he turned around and under the eyes of his wife, handed the cloak to his bed-woman, Achren.

Thora walked stiffly over to her.

"You would do well, girl, to put that away in a safe place. No slave in this household wears coloured clothing as long as I'm around."

Ulf seemed to get on well enough with both of the sisters. The issue of who would be married to him was resolved between the sisters themselves. Asta, experienced at marriage, would become the new wife of the master of Sandurness, and Sigrid would once again take on her sisterly share of the household tasks. They called the maids together to explain the way they intended to divide household responsibilities between them.

Asta said she would supervise the housekeeping and daily food preparation and Sigrid would take charge of milking and dairying.

"Thus we had it arranged at Asbjorn Steinson's farm, and no one fared the worse for it."

Asta smiled at Thora seated beside her on the dais.

"Won't you be happy, my dear, to have a pair of experienced old hands taking over the daily chores? You're too young to be burdened with such drudgery."

Inspite of her initial resentment, Thora had to admit life at Sandurness Farm took on a new shine with the coming of Asta and Sigrid. Asta, the widow of a wealthy man, was a woman of means. The sisters each brought with them a chest full of colourful clothes and another one filled with fine household items. For everyday wear they dressed in shifts of cream-coloured silk topped with wool kirtles in brilliant hues from fiery red to startling blue, fastened with large silver brooches. Another chest was packed with wall hangings and household utensils which – like the large copper kettle and two copper tubs — found ready use in their new household.

Asta, her face soft and plain like a freshly pressed cheese, laid her hand on Thora's arm.

"Don't be shy to take from our things anything that might be useful around here."

She reached under the dais and pulled out a wooden box painted green with red and white flowers, lifting the lid to reveal a collection of silver spoons and cups.

"Feel free to use these as your own."

Thora gave her a thin smile.

"I should think these too good for daily use."

She had never met women like these two squat, lively sisters buzzing about like bumblebees, always talking no matter what their busy hands were doing. They laughed often and heartily for no apparent reason. Within days they had gained the devotion of young Helga and met with the maids' warm approval.

Thora kept herself aside, watching, listening to the ripples of good cheer. Stripped of most responsibilities, she spent a good deal of time playing with little Halldis, abandoned in her crib by her big sister who was busy talking and laughing with her foster mothers.

Thora bent over the crib, tickling Halldis till the squirming child squealed with laughter. *Perhaps it has to be this way.*

She tucked in the little girl's blanket and went to sit down on her bed in the square sunlit patch under the roof vent to repair a tear in her shift and gather her thoughts. Perhaps it wasn't her destiny after all to settle at Sandurness after Gunnhild died; people seemed to think that at her age she wasn't capable of filling the empty place which Gunnhild had left in the household.

Thora glanced along the middle section of the house to the cluster of women sewing and spinning near the half open door; the sense of home she had found here was rapidly slipping away. Often these days her thoughts returned to the story which had so amused the wedding guests — the intriguing tale of Bjarni Herjolfson's westward journey and his sighting of unknown lands, some covered in trees, a potential source of great profits for an enterprising man, or woman.

She smiled to herself, secured the last stitch and cut the twine with Gunnhild's sewing scissors. Her mind made up, she felt the familiar glow which always warmed her inside and out after she made a life changing decision.

SIXTEEN

_____

_____

(Jarl Eirik) received him well. Bjarni told of his voyage and the
many lands he had glimpsed. And many people laughed since he had
nothing to tell of these lands and they made fun of his lack of cursiosity.
Bjarni became one of the jarl's followers and the following summer he
sailed to Greenland. By now people talked of looking for new lands.

GRAENLENDINGA SAGA

_____

_____

After the plan to sail westward took shape, no one at Sandurness
could remember who had been the first to talk of it. The
venture was sparked at some point in the minds of a few, and
from there it grew into something talked about by all from morning to
evening. It could've been Thora's insistence that the stacks of driftwood
found on the beaches of treeless Greenland had to come from the land
to the West which Bjarni had seen. Markland he called it because of the
dark stands of trees along its coast.

"The driftlogs we find on our beaches," Thora argued, "must be floating in from the forests in the unexplored land across, carried on the same current which brought Bjarni Herjolfson back to Greenland."

Ivar appeared to nurture dreams of his own about the rumoured lands beyond the western sea.

"If this unexplored Westland has people as well as timber for the taking," he said, "a single return journey could yield slaves as well as timber, plenty of each to make the fortunes of skipper and crew."

The thought caused other settlers to sit up and listen. In Greenland, slaves were as hard to come by as timber.

Ivar said, "Exotic slaves are in great demand in the sun-baked lands of the Saracens; folk in the southlands I hear will readily pay good silver for all things unusual, like novelty slaves; they could fetch even more than icebears, and for the same reason – because people enjoy owning things which makes them the envy of others."

Ulf said, "If you must go, you'll have to wait till next season because I have decided myself to take the ship to Norway after all; we'll need a shipload of timber this summer to expand the house and outbuildings in preparation for our upcoming wedding."

Asta disagreed.

"Our stocks of trade goods," she argued, "are depleted since Ivar's journey to Iceland; we had better postpone the wedding till next summer after the spring hunt. That would allow us more time to harvest and cure a fresh supply of ivory and hides, enough to buy all the iron and timber we need to turn this house into a proper, well-appointed hall. You need not go to Norway in a hurry this summer; why not have Ivar take the ship to Westland instead, and if he should find timber to make a shipload, we may not need to buy any at all."

Ulf admitted that she talked sense. They would need at least a shipload of timber for their building plans. Without a fresh supply of roofing timber, they couldn't extend the house with a small women's room in the back, something Asta insisted on – nor did they have any wood left to make a more solid roof for the dairy shed and summer kitchen, something Sigrid said needed to be done, *before the grass sets seed and all hands are needed to make hay.* They would need at least one full load of timber, and they had no goods left to trade for that much.

Thora agreed wholeheartedly with the sisters from Iceland.

"Even if we waited till after the next spring hunt, to buy timber," she said, "it would make little sense to trade away goods such as oil and feathers which we ourselves can scarcely do without, in exchange for more wood; why not sail to Westland now and trust our luck? We may find all the timber we need, free for the cutting. Bjarni reported seeing no sign of people who might have a claim on the trees he saw."

For once in agreement with his wife, Ivar added, "And if we should run into native Westlanders, we might capture and bring home some slaves to sell, adding more value to our profits."

Ulf objected, "Why risk a good ship in waters about which we know little except that the coast, according to Bjarni Herjolfson, is a treacherous one, dotted with reefs and floating ice? Besides, if we did find those trees everyone talks about, we would end up spending the winter there cutting them down, and I do not take kindly to being away that long from our farm which is still only half built."

"You don't need to be away at all," said Asta Sigurdsdottir. "I see no need for you to go voyaging to distant places; has your son not proved himself to be a shipmaster in his own right? Why not put the *knorr* under Ivar's command and let him do as he wishes? It's not too late yet to sail westward this summer and explore whatever lands there may be at the end of the world. They could spend the fall and winter cutting trees and head home the next spring with a full load. That way we'd have enough timber to add two more wings to the house and build a freshly dug, properly covered outhouse in good time to put on a grand wedding some time next summer."

Others spoke in favour of Asta's arguments and after some more urging Ulf agreed to lend Maelstrom Tamer to his son for a journey to Westland.

"Go then," he said, "go and do us all proud exploring the timberland which Bjarni Herjolfson chose to ignore."

"A wife," Thora said a few days later to Ivar, "should if at all possible go where her husband goes. I believe this household runs smoothly enough with Asta and Sigrid in charge, and little Halldis is well cared for by her big sister. Seeing as I'm no longer needed here, I've decided to come with you on the journey to Westland."

"Out of the question," he bristled. "No skipper takes his wife along on a major voyage of exploration. It's ill-advised to allow a woman to travel in a ship full of men; a few slave girls are needed, of course, on a venture like this, for general purposes and to carry out chores. Other than that, most sea farers agree that it brings bad luck if a ship has a woman onboard. Remember, almost half of the fleet sailing with us for Greenland last spring perished at sea. There were too many women aboard those hapless ships."

"More than half of us who set out from Iceland," Thora said, "made it to Greenland alive — women too."

Ivar sent her a glare.

"That may be so, but men are unwilling to sail on a ship which has women onboard, and that's what counts. There are hardly enough *karls* to spare in all of our Greenland settlements to crew a ship the size of Maelstrom Tamer for such a voyage. And if we could find enough men prepared to join our venture, a good many of those will change their mind when they learn that my wife plans to journey with us. It's out of the question. We cannot afford to lose good seafaring men on your account."

Thora didn't bother responding, confident that Ulf would see her side of the argument if she took the matter to him.

"Mmm," Ulf said after hearing her out.

"I have noticed, Thora Thorvinnsdottir, that things seem not quite well between you and the sisters from Iceland. If you were to go on this journey to Westland, it might clear the air between you and the sisters; yes, you'll have my support. I wish to have peace between the women in my household and so, you shall have your way."

Before they sailed, they needed at least one more ship joining the venture.

Ulf and Ivar went on a visit to Brattalid waiting for Sigurd and Thrand, Ulf's former trading partners; these men, one from Iceland and the other from Norway, were expected to arrive at Eirik's farm with the remainder of their cargo from Norway, half of which they had failed to sell at their first landfall in Iceland.

"I trust we can talk them into joining this venture to new unexplored lands," Ulf said. "They're not likely to pass up a chance to return to Iceland with a full load of Westland timber."

Five days later they returned in high spirits from Brattalid. Ulf's friend and longtime partner in Iceland, Sigurd Halldorson from Breidafjord, had committed his crew and ship, Aegir's Pride, to the Westland venture. Thrand Leidolfson, Sigurd's friend and partner from Norway and part-owner of Aegir's Pride, also agreed to come on the exploration journey across the waters west of Greenland. Thrand, an elderly man short-statured and pot-bellied, chuckled in his beard.

"It should be easy to find our way," he grinned. "We'll have the path of the sun to follow, laid out daily by fair Sol herself across the waters of the West Sea."

Sigurd had brought more men on his ship than he needed for crew, enough to lend some to Ivar to complement the small number of Greenlanders he had found willing to join.

"All in all we have enough men to crew a third ship on the way home," Ivar said. "If we do find as many good trees as hoped for in Westland, I intend to build my own *knorr* with the help of the shipwrights Thrand brought from Norway."

He turned to his father.

"If my luck turns out well, I might return with a trade ship of my own to add to our family's fortune."

Flushed with excitement, Thora and the two sisters made preparations for the journey, rushing about day after day. They worked together in good spirits and became better acquainted, almost friendly with one another.

SEVENTEEN

_Another island among the many found in that ocean is called
Vinland, because vines that make excellent wine grow wild there.
Unsown crops abound on that island we have learned, not from
fabulous reports, but from the trustworthy relation of the Danes.
Beyond that island, no habitable land is found in the ocean. There
every place is full of impenetrable ice and intense darkness._

ADAM OF BREMEN

Thora looked forward to spending the upcoming sea voyage
in relative comfort this time. There would be enough room
aboard Maelstrom Tamer for everyone to move about, keep
limber and sleep fully stretched out.

Five of Thrand's Norwegian company agreed to sail with Ivar in
addition to a half dozen young lads from the Greenland settlements;
these included Ottar and Odi, recruited by Ulf in exchange for the
promise to be released from their debts. Also on board were four bond-
maids and Eidyll, the only male slave.

At first Ivar refused to take Eidyll along. It was bad practice he said to have male slaves along on a dangerous venture like this.

It invites no end of trouble and treachery and escape will be the least of it."

Once again Thora turned to Ulf.

"I intend to bring my dog along to assist with our hunting," she said, "and my mare to haul logs. We'll have sheep onboard and a few goats for fresh milk and later for meat. I can think of none better than Eidyll to put in charge of the livestock chores. He's also a good hand at ironwork, an asset in many ways. We would be foolish not to take him along."

Ulf persuaded Ivar to take Eidyll on board.

"You'll need someone skilled with horses to calm that flighty mare your wife wishes to bring —that horse did panic, remember, at the first big waves we came across on our voyage to Greenland."

Thora rushed to the smithy shed to tell Eidyll.

"You had better put down those bellows and gather up some of the things you'll need for a long voyage, because you're coming with me on the journey to Westland. You'll end up a seasoned sea faring man after all."

Eidyll looked stunned, muttering, lamenting his fate; abruptly he raked aside the batch of nails he was attempting to straighten.

"Don't scatter those about," Thora smiled. "You'll have a chance to return to your anvil later. Seafaring folk are always short of nails to make ship repairs."

The men preparing to crew the ships were camped on the shore near the mouth of the fjord where the two ships lay beached at the low tide line.

For days they sorted out goods and people, ferrying luggage and supplies out to the ships. When all was ready they waited a few more days for the wind to shift north-east, bringing with it from the inland ice a blast of cold air like a frost giant's breath.

Thora wandered off to a tall bluff on the point; she looked out over the sea facing west, eyes narrowed against the low sun which traced a glittering road across the water as far as the eye could see — fair Sol in her chariot beckoning seafarers to follow her path to the unknown land where she went to sleep every night.

Thora looked into the dark water below the bluff; she fished a half dozen silver pieces from her pouch – the last she had left from the sale of her sheep – and let them splash into the sea one by one making a deal with the gods. She called out the names of Thor and Njord and Aegir, imploring them to assure a safe sea-journey, and she called on Odin and the Vana warlord, Tyr, to support them in any battles they might face. Her words flew away on the wind to be carried on the sun road, all the way to Westland perhaps.

"Other than to guide us to prime timber, Thor, I ask of you and all others dwelling in Asgard or in the depths of the West Sea, to grant me two things – that I and the others of our party may safely cross the sea and back again ...and furthermore, that I may be freed of my husband and return to Iceland some day with enough wealth to buy back my mother's farm."

She paused to examine the last Saracen coin resting in her palm, intrigued by the squiggly patterns covering the surface. With the tip of her finger she traced the elegant loops and swirls of the Moorish script – could they be runes of a kind she hadn't been taught? Could these loops and dots , like certain runes, be used to make magic?

She tilted her hand and watched the coin hitting the water with a tiny splash before sinking to the shadowy depth, and she whispered one more request, "Grant that I may find a man to my liking some day, a man whose children I wish to bear and raise."

The sacrifice had already begun when Thora returned to the camp. Ulf had supplied two wethers, full-grown though on the skinny side. The sheep were slaughtered and put on the fire to roast. The vapours of roasting mutton and burning fat rose on the thick billowing smoke, sure to mellow the sternest of gods so they might favour the mortals who put on this feast for their benefit.

Thora watched the men teasing the fire along until all fat was burnt and the meat reduced to charred remnants. They hung the blood-streaked hides on stakes exposed to the wind and spiked the sheep heads on top of the stakes trusting the gods would be pleased with their efforts.

*   *   *   *   *

They were loading the last of the sheep onto Maelstrom Tamer and the horse was next in line to go on; Thora chewed her lips watching the *karl*, Floki, marching the mare to the two narrow boards which served as a ramp. Fluga followed him a few steps on the boards before backing up and digging in her feet; she refused to take another step forward, suspicious of the thin boards which had dipped under her weight.

Floki waited, holding the leadrope tight. Thora looked around for Eidyll; why was he, the designated livestock *thrall*, not here when he was needed? Another of Ulf's *karls* approached with a rope to pass behind the horse's hocks.

Thora frowned. She waved both *karls* aside, took the leadrope and talked softly to the mare, rubbing the rigid neck and ruffling the thick blond mane till she felt the hard muscles softening.

The horse placed a forehoof back on the boards, then another. Thora waited, whispering encouragement. All of a sudden the mare gathered herself, bolted up the ramp and scrambled into the ship. Thora tied her beside the sheep to the central tether line attached to the mast.

She heaved a sigh of relief at the sight of Eidyll hurrying down the beach. *He didn't run away after all to escape the sea journey he so dreads.* Floki had removed the ramp after the horse arrived safely onboard, and Eidyll splashed out through the water hoisting himself, his bedroll and slim bundle of assorted belongings on board; he stood for a while looking back to shore, sallow-faced, like a man about to be executed.

*   *   *   *   *

Thora claimed her seat near the bow cover, close enough to seek shelter underneath it when needed — the privilege of a skipper's wife; she indulged in the comfort that came with her new status, so unlike the other time on the crowded ship to Greenland when she traveled as a common settler. On this journey there was plenty of room aboard ship for everyone, and there would still be more space after some of the sheep were slaughtered at landfalls, leaving on board only a handful of sheep and the goats.

From her place by the spray cover Thora was able to keep a close eye on the drinking water and food supplies stored in the bow: smoked fish and mutton, cheese, flatbread, and a barrel of precious beer. They had made an early cut of nutritious hay for the journey, and Thora told Eidyll to sort the fodder and feed the best to the horse.

She looked closely at the four bond-women aboard the ship. Two of them of advanced middle age were on loan from Brattalid, sorry looking women worn with work and serving men's needs in their better days. The other two were young, shapely and in good spirits, giddy with eagerness to go on this venture. Achren and Groa – the youngest at fourteen winters — came both from Sandurness Farm. Achren, it was understood by all, came not only along as a maid but also as Ivar's bedwoman. The two Brattalid women, Akka and Halla, were all-round farm maids growing a bit slow with age. Halla had been loaned for the journey by Eirik's wife, Thjodhild, because she knew healing plants.

There were five women slaves present on Aegir's Pride — three young girls and two older women, all brought from Iceland by Sigurd.

Throughout the first day they sailed on a calm sea under a sunny sky pushed along by a following wind. Thora sat slumped against the side of the ship, shifting for comfort now and then; perhaps she should have brought along her sealskin-covered saddle that had served her so well for support during the journey to Greenland.

She let her gaze wander over the faces of the others, pausing at Eidyll who looked out across the placid, glimmering waters with apprehension in his eyes. *No need for you to worry my lad, so far.* Njord and Aegir seemed to be in a mellow mood, taking a nap perhaps. At least for today her landlubber *thrall* wasn't tormented by heaving seas.

The crew shouted challenges to those in the other ship which sailed ahead of them; they egged Ivar on to give chase and overtake Aegir's Pride. It wasn't long before Maelstrom Tamer passed the ship from

Iceland; they kept the lead until Ivar, unwisely, granted his crew a round of beer; distracted, the men failed to keep the sail tight and properly angled, and Aegir's Pride overtook them and, favoured by her lighter load – people only, no livestock – stayed ahead.

The rivalry and banter died down. Weary of the long summer day, people slumped down in what little shade they could find except for a handful of young men absorbed in dice games, and for the two slave girls near the bow, staring into the rushing water and seeming to relish their first long day of leisure.

Thora gazed at the girls from under her eyelids. *How foolish men are to take young bond-women on a demanding venture like ours, for no better reason than to please themselves now and then.* It would be all these girls proved to be good for if she, the skipper's wife, didn't make sure they carried out their fair share of the work; it would take hard work, and plenty of it, to get established in Westland before the winter.

Thora's frown deepened. There would be much strenuous work to come, and only Eidyll to help the women with chores that required the strength of a man. She herself would need Eidyll's help with milking and dairying chores, leaving him little time to assist the women slaves. She couldn't rely on bond-maids to help her with the dairying; that kind of work required more skill and diligence than such girls were capable of, and there was no quicker way to spread death and disease than by foul-handling people's food — a risk they could ill afford on this haz-ardous journey. *Never let young maids out of your sight,* Thurid used to argue, *if you must have slaves working around food at all.*

Achren and Groa had moved to the stern, having a merry time laughing and joking with the young steersman.

Ivar sat midships leaning against his bed-roll, asleep after handing the steering oar to his *karl,* Gorm. Thora frowned at Gorm and the girls. The steersman kept looking, as Ivar did earlier, at the girls rather than the faraway cloud formations he was supposed to keep in sight, to stay roughly on course between celestial bearings.

She looked to the face of her sleeping husband – handsome, except for the cruel twist of his mouth. *Achren's welcome to him.* Perhaps it was a mistake for her and Ivar to voyage together, forced to spend an entire winter face to face in close quarters; unless the new land offered spaces as vast as the hills and fjords in Greenland for some breathing space when needed, the coming winter might be hard to endure.

Thora gazed at the bubbly wake trailing the ship. *At some point, my husband, our ways shall part...though not if I can help it, before you've paid me your dues.*

She leaned back against the bulky roll of her leather sleeping sack and closed her eyes, withdrawing to a world of mere sound, smell and touch. Perhaps it wasn't so hard to see after all, why men liked to travel the sea. This far from land there were few distractions — no voices of living things except for those in the ship, no seabirds calling, nothing that could serve as a reminder of regular concerns of farm and family, a rare chance to reflect on matters other than the daily grind of life at home.

By late afternoon the wind grew stronger and the *knorr* groaned with effort, straining to resist the push of water and wind, trying to flex with the waves as a whale flexes its sinuous bulk. The air was clear and invigourating; it carried the smell of seal tar and fresh hay wetted by salt spray, and of livestock dung. Soon the air would become odorous and molding hay would be the least of it. On the earlier voyage from Iceland they traveled for the longest time in a thickening stench of excrement and vomit mingled with stale animal waste. On this journey the day would come, inescapably, when some piece of rotting fish sickened people who ate of it, and some would be unable to keep over the side when relieving themselves, and if the sickness kept spreading, there wouldn't be any voyagers left with enough energy to empty used waste buckets.

Still, for the time being it appeared the gods did accept the sheep Ulf had sacrificed on the shore in exchange for a safe voyage to Westland, at least for some of the way; with luck the gods would continue to favour them, sending more gentle swells their way. And if the sun continued her daily appearances no matter how briefly to light the spark inside Ivar's sunstone for guidance, they might, like Bjarni, catch sight of Westland's barren white-flecked cliffs in only eight days.

A shadow touched Thora's face – she opened her eyes. Ragnar, a burly Norwegian in his fifties who had come to Greenland with Thrand and Sigurd loomed over her.

"I hear your name is Thora Thorvinnsdottir."

His voice was deep and rumbling like rocks sliding down a mountain.

"May I ask which Thorvinn is the lucky man claiming you for his daughter?"

EIGHTEEN

The snowcrested surges caress us
And sweep us away with their kisses

KORMAC'S SAGA

efore they set sail, Thora had met with the tall, bear-like Norwegian and wondered why he chose to sail with Ivar, rather than stay with his friends on Sigurd's ship. His voice and his name, Ragnar Asbjornson 'Bear Bladder,' stirred vague memories though she couldn't determine where and when, or even if, they had met before.

She patted the sea chest beside her.

"Won't you take a seat?"

"I was wondering," he said, setting his bulk down beside her, "if your sire by chance is the Thorvinn I used to know."

"I'm the daughter of Thorvinn Haraldson of Hestardalur," Thora said. "My father and mother came to Iceland from Norway. The thought crossed my mind that I may have seen you before. Did you happen to visit our farm, Hestardalur, to buy horses?

"Horses ...no, I bought no horses there."

After a long silence he resumed, "Your mother's name was Rannveig, I think...Rannveig Asgrimsdottir from Iceland who married the Norwegian, Thorvinn Haraldson, and settled on his property not far from the Sognefjord...you were born there."

"I..." Thora hesitated. "Yes, I...I was a little girl when we all moved to Iceland, and Father's brother, Sveinar, came too; we sailed to Iceland and went to live at Hestardalur, my mother's ancestral farm."

She looked at him uncertainly.

"I was only a child then, not old enough perhaps to remember you among the men who came to our farm in the years that followed to have dealings with my father."

Ragnar's grizzled face split in a bearish grin.

"I should've recognized you soon's as I set eyes on you when we arrived at Sandurness fjord; you have your mother's hair, thick and curly...only hers was a darker colour, as dark as a narrow fjord hugged by tall clifs... yours now...yours is the colour of oak leaves in winter."

She laughed.

"If you say so; it's been so long since I last saw and oak tree in winter or in any season at all."

Ragnar shook his head searching her face with pale blue eyes half hidden by shaggy brows.

"Rannveig's daughter, well, well...an attractive young woman... as could be expected. Even your eyes," he told her, "are like your mother's, wide, luminous grey...when I bade your family farewell by the fjord the day of their exile, I thought I would never again come across a pair of eyes like hers."

"But surely you must've visited us later in Iceland, or I couldn't have these memories of you, no matter how vague."

He shrugged.

"Once I did visit your farm in Iceland, and over the years your father and I continued to meet every spring in the Daneland to set out on some summer venture or other. We grew up together and came of age together, and we also sailed out together trading and raiding, the usual ...those were good days..."

Thora's eyes widened.

"Were you with my father in Sweden the Cold?"

"A number of times," Ragnar said. "For three summers we journeyed downriver from Holmgard in Sweden the Cold, to distant Miklagard — 'Constantinopolis' in the speech of its people. The imperial city is a wondrous place I can tell you, straddling a narrow sound between two seas. On our third visit I was appointed officer in the imperial guard and so I decided not to go home in the fall with your father and the rest of our company; I stayed there all winter and the following summer and then another winter."

Thora gave him a half smile.

"I hear life in the imperial city is easy, blessed with sunshine and wealth...what made you return to the North?"

Ragnar looked up to the body of feathery cloud running the length of the sky before meeting with the sea.

"I felt sick for the land of my birth," he said at last. "I saved my pay and the profits I had made from trading, and I went home intending to buy a farm and settle down with a wife who knew how to keep house, manage livestock and keep order in the dairy shed, things which the fine ladies of Miklagard do not know how to do."

"And did you ...settle down with a good Norse woman?"

Ragnar shrugged.

"Seems that I have a talent for courting the wrong woman...because of that, I ended up killing a man in a fight, an honest fight I assure you. But the man I slew, as ill luck would have it, was one of the king's men and his life was highly rated, three times the going compensation for the life of a regular freeman. To pay the man-price I had to part with all of my hoarded silver, and I was left without means to buy a farm; so I decided to go a-viking again."

His gaze lingered on her hair.

"Truly amazing…so like your mother..."

"You must've heard," Thora said, "that she died?"

"I learned of her death a while ago when I was spending the winter in Birka; it is a town bustling with traders from everywhere, and news goes around quickly there. I came across a man from Iceland who told me your mother had died. That was more than seven winters ago... you were still a child I gather."

Thora folded her hands in her lap.

"Yes. Every day I seem to remember more about her," she said softly. "I remember the stories she told and the songs she sang... about the farm by the fjord where I was born...about the trolls dressed in ferns, lichens and tree-bark who lived, she said, in caves deep in the forest. I was a very small girl then, and I asked her if we might go see the trolls, and she laughed and said that would be unwise since trolls are known for their short temper and vile habits... and some of them eat children she said... My mother was fond of the trees around the farm and along the fjord, all of them helping to shelter people and animals from cold winds. She so loved the forests, the dark stands of needle trees and the tangled places of oak found in the glens ... and she never appeared to be truly happy again in treeless Iceland."

"I was very fond of your mother," Ragnar said slowly. "I would have courted her, if Thorvinn hadn't pursued her first. He and I were old friends and foster brothers, and so it would not do for me to ask for the hand of the woman he had set his heart on. It wouldn't be proper."

"But you continued to be friends," Thora said.

"Oh, we remained friends, Thorvinn and I. We remained friends and partners in trade until Thorvinn ran afoul of King Harald Greycloak. Dark days followed, and Thorvinn and his entire household were forced to leave his ancestral farm and seek refuge in Iceland."

"And you came to visit us there one time, you said."

Ragnar remained silent, twirling the tips of his moustache.

"I paid a short visit there," he said at last. "I found it hard to be in your mother's presence then, married to Thorvinn; I feared that some day I might forget myself and turn my friend and foster brother against me."

Thora considered his words.

"A wise decision," she said at last. "Many a man is dealt his death blow by a former friend for lesser offense than making sport with his friend's wife."

Ragnar stared at her in silence. Suddenly he rose to his feet with a happy smile and he raised his voice over the din of the livestock stirring in anticipation of feeding time.

"And here I find myself on the same ship as Rannveig's orphaned daughter, a grown young woman and the spouse of our young skipper it turns out...tell me, what became of Thorvinn? I heard he went missing a few years ago."

"It happened two summers ago. He left for Greenland with a shipload of merchandise, and he never returned. The ship was found wrecked at Isafjord. It must be assumed that he perished with all his crew."

A slow smile crept across Ragnar's face. He shook his head.

"It takes more than a regular shipwreck I wager, to send Thorvinn Haraldson off to feast in the great hall of the gods."

He furrowed his brows.

"What if he happened to return belatedly to his home in Iceland, and found no dutiful daughter waiting there to welcome him?"

Thora said, "He has no home to return to in Iceland. He left nothing but debts behind, which I paid for, the hard way."

She explained how the farm was lost.

"And so I decided to come to Greenland, and Gunhild Grimsdottir took me in as her fosterdaughter. I was very fond of her...."

Thora stared at her hands. "Gunnhild died last winter after bearing another child...it was she who insisted I marry Ivar, her son."

"I see," Ragnar said. He sat down again.

"So then, your husband is also your foster brother...a questionable choice some people might say... on the other hand, it would seem that in Greenland young men and women coming of age to be married have few suitable prospects to choose from."

Thora sighed.

"Both my mother and foster mother used to say that a woman forced to make up her mind between a bad choice for a husband, or a worse one, had best settle for the man who has sufficient property to keep his family out of poverty."

She changed the subject.

"I wonder what made you come out here with Thrand. We're not exactly going a-viking, your trade of choice I gather. There's no reason to expect rich pickings in Westland, no treasures of gold, silver or silk that anyone knows of. Bjarni spoke only of trees, no cities or harbours filled with trade ships, nothing to interest a man of your stature and skills. We, Greenland folks on the other hand, consider ourselves rewarded if we should find trees that are free for the cutting, straight enough to use for house roofs and ships, and some tall enough to make a good mast."

Ragnar laughed.

"To tell you the truth, I never meant to come out to Greenland or go on this venture... an ill-advised one perhaps... I intended to sail with Thrand on his spring run to Iceland, no farther. A part of the ship's cargo was mine and we expected to sell the goods in Iceland at a good profit. He and I meant to return to Norway with the silver earned, and outfit a long-ship – thirty two oars we had in mind – to go harassing amongst the southern islands."

He waved his big hands in a gesture of helplessnes.

"Turned out the trading in Iceland was dismal because two of its fire mountains erupted last fall, wrecking pastures and crops and causing the death of uncounted numbers of livestock. 't Was a mistake to bring iron and wine to Iceland when nobody thought to buy luxuries."

Thora nodded.

"It would've been better to carry grain."

"And so," Ragnar went on, "we transfered what was left of our goods to Sigurd's ship – larger than Thrand's — and decided to sail on to Greenland. We did not expect there to be any silver in Greenland either to pay for our goods, but we counted on getting plenty of ivory in return – counted wrongly, again. Turns out Ivar already took a cargo of walrus teeth to Iceland making good trade with skippers from Norway who arrived before us. Now we're taking part in this Westland venture of yours for a last chance to turn a profit this season."

He beamed Thora a crooked-toothed grin.

"I never expected to come across the daughter of my old friends. The Norns of fate, Thora Thorvinnsdottir, arranged that we should meet."

"The maidens of fate most certainly had a hand in this," Thora agreed with a slow nod.

"Although, I also believe it is up to each of us to bend our fate in ways best suited to us. The Norn maidens, seems to me, are so busy arranging the warp of life's weaving for each of us mortals, they'll be happy enough to leave the arrangement of the weft threads to us."

Ragnar was silent, appearing to weigh her words.

"Perhaps...." he said. "I'm not sure that you're right about this, Thora Thovinnsdottir. They say the Norns are fickle maidens, set on following their own minds when they lay out our lives for us; whimsical to a fault they're said to be, apt to amuse themselves by placing us, mortals, in the way of disaster."

From the bow came Thrand's call to his friend to come over, and Ragnar made his way back to the foreship. Thora smiled at the contrast between them — Thrand, an old man unremarkable looking with watery eyes, and Ragnar, his friend and trading partner, powerfully built, a seasoned warrior with a thick, grizzled beard, piercing glance, proud carriage and owner of a splendid sword; Ragnar was unmistakably a man to be reckoned with and no ordinary trader possessed a sword like his, Frankish-made with gold inlay on its ivory hilt.

Pestered by the lads who were curious to see his sword, the burly warrior agreed to pass it around; the exquisite damascened blade went around from hand to hand, appearing alive in the sunlight, its dark centre line wriggling like a freshly hatched adder. Ragnar demonstrated the blade's keen edge by shearing a handful of wool from the nearest sheep; he dropped the small flocks inside the scabbard to add to the lining and slid the blade back inside.

Ragnar now moved to the stern into the shade from the awning, and Thora leaned back against her chest turning her face to the sun and reflecting on the flickers of envy she saw in the eyes of the men passing the sword around; it made her uneasy. Ivar's reckless young *karls* from Greenland tended to be short-tempered. Most of Thrand's Norwegians by contrast were mature men, seasoned warriors, though none of them equalled Ragnar's stature. Her gaze turned to Mord and Auzur — Ragnar's nephews she was told – also sailing with Maelstrom Tamer;

both of them, though still young, looked like experienced fighters with good though not exceptional swords.

Thora cast a sideways glance at her *thrall* who seemed comfortable enough leaned against the shipboard near the mast. Sofar Eidyll appeared not to suffer ill effects from the ship's cavorting with the waves; satisfied that for the time being, he didn't need anyone's help to care for the livestock, Thora closed her eyes.

She listened to the younger *karls* rowdy with boredom slamming the dice harder with each new game. *They're full of themselves; but will they be persistent and hard workers when called upon?* There would be a need for willing and able hands to share the work of building a winter house and felling and hauling timber, all in a short time, steady and arduous work without glory. Ivar had foolishly refused to bring more male slaves. *What makes him so sure we'll find native Westlanders to capture and put to work?*

On the fourth day after they had last sighted land, Ivar recited Bjarni's directions aloud in an effort to silence the doubters; he reminded them of the wooded land, Markland, which Bjarni said they would find if they kept a steady southwesterly course. If they strayed too far north, they would end up in Helluland, a place of barren rocks washed by a frigid sea littered with drift-ice; too far south, and they risked to get caught in the current that had carried Bjarni back home. Or worse, the same current might push them to Ireland and land them all in big trouble. Tales abounded of Norse seafarers shipwrecked in Irish waters, who were captured and sold as slaves.

"Do keep awake!" Ivar yelled at the steersman. "We cannot afford to stray from our course."

After days of almost continuous gambling, the men grew weary of playing dice; they took to telling tales involving mishaps at sea which doomed a band of sea faring men to a wretched death, or granted them a miraculous escape from the terrors that lurked in the sea's cold, black depths. Thora wished they would talk of something other than maelstroms dragging down ships, whole fleets no less, or a giant squid which could pull a *knorr* underwater with ease and suck the men one by one into its cavernous maw studded with sharp bony shears instead of teeth.

Relieved, she opened her eyes when Auzur, Ragnar's nephew, asked his uncle to tell of his travels; after some urging, Ragnar obliged.

"Well then, I will tell you of life in the fabled city of Miklagard as I saw it during the time that I served as an officer in the imperial guard. The emperor's court, you must understand, is rife with conspiracy and betrayal and so, for his personal safety, the emperor depends on his palace guards; Norsemen are favoured over all other men to serve in the emperor's personal guard, since it's well known that a Norseman will not break his oath of loyalty, no matter what."

Thora listened spell-bound to the picture Ragnar painted of life in the imperial capital, that sprawling city in the South located between two seas.

"The living is easy, the weather mellow... too warm at times ... and the emperor's most generous to his loyal guardsmen," Ragnar told them. "I know of no other place on earth quite like the great city of Con-stan-tino-polis."

He let the word roll off his tongue in separate chunks, tasting every morsel.

"The ladies of the court," he went on, "wear jeweled rings around toes and fingers which are linked with delicate gold chains to their ankles and wrists; and they sport flower-patterns on hands and feet painted with a dye the colour of blood."

Ragnar was a good story teller. Thora could almost smell the whiffs of exotic perfumes when the ladies of the palace walked by.

"The fine houses I visited were filled with strange, heady scents," Ragnar said. "Some of them so powerful... taking a deep breath of air saturated with such a scent can knock a plain fighting man to the ground and leave him with a crushing headache."

After Ragnar fell silent, a few lads from Greenland prodded Ivar to tell of the journeys his father took him on to Norway and the Dane lands. Ivar obliged them. He told of the towns he saw where merchants from every known place in the world came to meet and hustle. He described crowded market quarters, narrow alleyways between houses arranged shoulder to shoulder, built of wood without stone, sod or plaster.

"Even the roofs on some house are wood-shingled," he said, "rather than covered with sod, and others are thatched with reed or straw. It's not hard to see why the townspeople never seem to be short of timber; ships loaded with tall straight logs arrive daily from the forest lands around the East Sea, and much of the timber is traded on to the merchants from Friesland, Frankland and beyond who spend the summer living in their own quarters inside the trading towns in the lands of Danes and Swedes. They come to the North with ships carrying goods from the South, glasswork and cloth and fine swords; these they trade for amber and furs, and fish too, shiploads of herring salted and dried."

Thora closed her eyes; she longed to wander through those narrow alleys between closely spaced houses surrounded by the hustle and bustle of foreign folks richly dressed and speaking in strange tongues, trading for furs, ivory, timber and fish from the North and East in exchange for spices, fine goods, and salt brought up from the South. If she only could visit such a place once in her life — not to stay, mind you; who would wish to spend a lifetime in such crowded quarters?

"Wait till the foreign merchants discover what treasures we'll bring in from Westland some day," Ivar said with a grin. "We'll dazzle their eyes with gemstones and slaves of a kind not seen before. Timber we wouldn't bother to trade down there. Any timber from Westland we'll be able to sell in Greenland or in Iceland if needed. And if we find proper ship trees, we'll build us another ship and fill her with timber as well; two ships, twice the profit for all of our crew to share."

"Hear, hear!" the men chanted, slapping their fists on their thighs.

Some Icelanders urged Thora to recite the bloodlines of her father's famous horse stock. Reluctantly, Thora obliged.

They asked her about the origins of the striking white dog, not letting up until she told them all that Thorvinn had told her about the Khazars and their dogs.

When all tales were told — some more than once — Ragnar suggested they pass some time reciting verse, well known poems composed and performed by traveling *skjalds*, or for those who chose to, improvised verse of their own making addressed to someone in the audience and intended to draw a response.

The men joined in eagerly, aware that boredom leads to brooding which in turn has a way of creating unpleasantness — though verse-making could, as everyone knew, create unpleasantness all of its own.

Ragnar took the first turn, reciting an old verse known to all and unlikely to stir up bad feelings.

"Never say, 'it's been a good day,' until sundown.
Never say, 'she's a good wife,' until she's buried.
Never say, 'this is a good sword,' until you've tested it.
Never say, 'she's a good girl,' until she's married off.
Never say, 'the ice is safe,' until you've crossed it.
Never say, 'the beer is good,' until you've drunk the last."

He challenged Ivar to continue. The young skipper, known to have little talent with words, looked uneasy. After a long silence he came up with lines that caused people to stir.

"Never say, 'this is a good ship,' until it has safely brought you home.
Never say, 'this is a good horse,' until it has carried you through deep snow.
Never say, 'this is a good sheep dog,' until
the last ewe is back in the pen."

Then, looking from Thora to the slave girl Achren, he added a last line:

"Never say, 'this is a fine woman, until she carries your child."

He fell silent and gazed at the cluster of slave women who sat huddled in the bow rolling their eyes.

Thora, no more given to wordplay generally than her husband, rose to her feet; stretched tall as a fir seeking sunlight, she scanned the smirking faces around her pretending she didn't hear the giggles from the girls in the foreship.

She cleared her throat and recited in a steady voice,

"Never say, 'this day is bad,' why, we're all alive.
Never say, 'this ship is bad,' why, she is afloat.

Never say, 'this horse is bad,' why, it's on four feet.
Never say, 'this dog is bad,' why, it warns of strangers.
Never say, 'this wife is bad,' why, she keeps to her own bed.
Never say, 'this skipper is bad'...
Until
he ignores the course,,
and shackles his gaze to the foreship."

She leaned back against the chest and closed her eyes, pretending not to notice the chuckles. A quick glance through her eyelashes at Ivar, leaned against the opposite ship board, showed her that he was livid. With jaws firmly clenched, he appeared to be laboring over his lines of response until Ragnar to everyone's relief, jumped in with another well-known verse.

"Loving a woman whose heart is false
is like driving an unshod horse over slippery ice,
a high spirited two-year-old, not quite broken yet,
or like handling a rudderless ship in a fierce storm,
or like a crippled man catching reindeer on the thawing hillside.
But, to be fair, I know both sides ...
Men's minds are equally treacherous to women."

Some men applauded.
"Well said!"
Ivar, biting his lips declined to have another turn at making verse.

*   *   *   *   *   *   *   *   *   *

WESTLAND

...a country which some call Ireland the Great. It lies west in the sea near Vinland the Good.

Irish priests have sailed to the edge of the frozen sea, a day's journey beyond the land where the sun scarcely sank below the horizon

LANDNAMABOK

NINETEEN

....they thought the land fine and well-forested, with white beaches and it was not far between the forest and the sea. There were many islands and wide stretches of shallow sea

GRAENLENDINGA SAGA

They were small, ill favoured men, and they had ugly hair on their heads. They had big eyes and were broad in the cheeks.

EIRIK'S SAGA

Thora looked out across the restless sea; there was perhaps a valid point in all of this seafarer-talk about seeking freedom away from the land. If men came to choose sea over land because it made them feel free – and men unless bonded, were hardly unfree to begin with compared to women – would the sea and the unexplored lands beyond not offer freedom to a woman as well, especially one who had foolishly shackled herself to a husband she resented?

What had made her think that the prospect of once again becoming the mistress of a thriving farm was a good enough reason to marry Ivar Ulfson? Once she had thought two things to be of importance when considering a man for a husband - a *straight gaze and a narrow waist*; now that she was married to a man fulfilling those requirements, she had learned they were mere trifles to consider; there were other, essential things needed between a husband and wife, and neither her mother nor anyone else had cared to mention them — respect and a measure of fondness for one another must be part of a succesfull marriage.

Yesterday's edgy verse-play confirmed to all of those present how things truly stood between the skipper and his wife.

After five days and nights of sailing they lost sight of the other ship for good. Lighter and faster than Maelstorm Tamer, Sigurd's *knorr* had surged way ahead. Men with close friends aboard Aegir's Pride began to grumble.

"We'll meet up with the others no doubt at the first place that is found to be safe for beaching a ship," Ivar said curtly.

The steady weather kept holding and two more days went by with little change. People made the best of their food supplies passing around bits of fish and smoked meat and dried seaweed, chewing slowly to make every bite last and break the monotony of never-ending daylight.

Ragnar, wiping shreds of cod from his beard, sent Thora a grin.

"The older a man becomes," he said, "the less sleep he needs...and the more time he has to remember all that he failed to accomplish in his allotted lifetime in Midgard."

Thora asked, "Is that why you came back from the fabled city, because of things you neglected to do back home?"

Ragnar rubbed his greying beard.

"I told you, I grew homesick for the North and wished to settle down to farm."

"Why?" Thora probed.

Ragnar shrugged like a bear after a swim.

"Why do women always insist on knowing a man's reasons? I wanted to settle down with a good woman…that's all."

Thora chuckled.

"But surely, there must be plenty of good women in the city of Miklagard!"

"Plenty," Ragnar agreed. "Women of breeding, beauty and wealth… and every one of them equipped with a tongue like a filleting knife."

He raised his eyebrows.

"They were too clever for me, a simple-minded fighting man."

"Did you find any woman to your liking in Norway?"

"I thought I did, more than once. But I was no longer the same man as the one bearing my name who left all those summers ago; I didn't fit in any more, and it made the women I fancied ill at ease. Friends I sent out to negotiate over suitable prospects on my behalf, all returned with the same message. *So and so would rather they found her another man for a husband.*

"I asked my friends to keep looking in other places. A man after all would be ill advised to pursue, let alone marry, a woman whose mind is set on discontent. Then one day the fickle maidens of fate decided to turn against me; maliciously they goaded the brother of a woman I fancied into challenging me to a fight. We had a good and honest fight and in the end I dealt my opponent his death blow."

Thora nodded.

"Yes, you told me. This man turned out to be well connected, and they charged you triple the man-price owed for a commoner."

"And so I had to let go of my hopes for a wife and a farm," Ragnar said with a sigh.

Thora nodded.

"And so you went roaming again."

Ragnar rose to his feet, grinning.

"There is no worse way to die for a man than to perish in bed of old age. And there's no better way to find what he seeks for a man who hopes to meet with an honourable death, than by going a-viking."

"Seems to me," Thora said, "that this voyage of ours doesn't hold out much promise for a fighting man such as you who seeks to die with honour...our main purpose on this journey is to find good timber, and a man might sooner find his death getting crushed by a felled tree."

Eidyll continued to keep track of time scratching a few words every few days into the scrap of calfskin he carried in his belt pouch. Thora watched him writing his journal entries in his neat, rounded script; she sighed again with frustration because she couldn't make sense of his writing.

A loud cry from the bow broke the sleepy silence, waking up those who were dozing and causing others to abandon what they were doing. Grim, posted in the bow, ran to the mast and scrambled to the top.

"There!" He pointed southwest. "See the birds? Look at them, clouds of birds skimming low across the water."

Ivar unlatched the wooden crate strapped to his sea chest, hauled out the largest and boldest of his three ravens and threw it up in the air.

The loose-feathered bird circled the ship once or twice squawking before it flew westward. All day long the voyagers scanned the horizon for land or for the black bird returning. At midnight when daylight was as it weakest, the raven re-appeared to settle on the bow looking exhausted. Grim used a puffin net to catch it without getting his fingers jabbed. He put it back in the crate and fed the birds a few chunks of dried fish. Dispirited, people took to their sleeping bags in silence.

By the time the sun gained strength the next day, Ivar freed another raven. It also flew westward, and this time the raven did not return. All through the day Ivar kept steering due west. The sun was at its lowest announcing another twilight night, when another shout from keen-eyed Grim startled everyone.

"Land in sight!"

Once again Grim clambered up to the top of the mast.

"Beware! Cliffs to starboard...and massive surf."

Everyone rushed to starboard, arrested by roars from Ivar.

"Sit down, you fools! Stay where you were or we'll capsize and serve ourselves up to the Midgard Serpent!"

"Get a hold of yourselves!" came Ragnar's thundering voice. He grabbed two youths by their hair and hauled them to port-side.

"Stay right here," he growled, "or I swear you'll find yourselves swimming for those there cliffs."

It wasn't long before they all saw a dark wall of rocky cliffs towering against the red-streaked sky. Ivar ordered the sail furled and the oars manned all night to keep the vessel from drifting to shore. Not until full daylight did he steer closer to examine the coast, frowning at the wave patterns which ran every which way between and over submerged reefs.

"An inhospitable coast, like Bjarni was saying," he muttered and headed back to sea, calling for the sail to be raised again and continuing south without losing sight of the coast. All day they scouted for a possible landing place without finding a single break in the reefs or in the forbidding rows of jagged rocks guarding the shore like giants lined up shoulder to shoulder, feet surrounded by boulders and rock fall.

Auzur spoke for all.

"A fine place this is for seabirds and seals," he grumbled, "and a nightmare for folks in need of fresh water and grazing for livestock half starved."

Another day and a half passed and they were leaving the cliffs behind. The coast changed to low sand dunes and beaches strewn with pebbles and shells; here it seemed safe enough to approach land as long as they dodged the numerous shoals.

They headed for the first welcoming place spotted by Grim — a stretch of shallow water backed by a dark rise of needle-trees rimmed with white beaches riddled with channels, meandering freshets feeling their way out to sea.

Ivar ordered the sail lowered and the oars brought out. Slowly they pushed their way against the withdrawing tide through a wide channel into a lagoon separated from the sea by sandbars.

Jubilant shouts filled the crisp air.

"Look there at the beach!"

People pushed each other around pointing to the dark body of a ship beached on the sands – Aegir's Pride was waiting for them at the tideline.

Dwarfed by the expanse of sky, water and dark forestland beyond, Sigurd's men ran across the sand and splashed into the water waving like madmen. Greeted with cheers and good-humoured taunts, Ivar ran his *knorr* aground next to Aegir's Pride.

"Good of you to bring us fresh mutton to celebrate," Thrand beamed. "We're famished for something to eat other than fish."

They untied three wethers aboard Maelstrom Tamer, trussed them up and slaughtered them on the beach. Reduced to little more than bone and skin after their journey, the sheep provided barely enough meat after roasting to allow everyone a taste.

"Right," Sigurd said after chewing the last bit of flavour from his morsel of mutton.

"Let's explore upstream in the channels for freshwater and food – there ought to be fish to catch."

The land ranged from well-watered to water-logged. They filled their barrels with freshwater and set out to explore. Thora, Eidyll and the older bond-women led the remaining livestock along the shore in search of grazing, turning them loose amidst plenty of saltgrass and seaweed.

"Let's gather up seaweed to take with us in the ship for fodder," Thora said, collecting an armful of rockweed and spreading it out to dry on the beach near the ship.

The sheep seemed to savour the salty forage but the horse, after tentative bites of seaweed and saltgrass, ambled off in search of better fare.

The land beyond the lagoon up to the tree growth consisted of gravel scattered with lichen covered rocks, stunted trees and wind-torn bushes. The creeks teemed with fish waiting to be netted or speared. Three young lads returned from the woods to report they had seen reindeer tracks there.

"Let's go hunting for meat."

Ivar hesitated, but Sigurd and Thrand were firmly opposed.

"We need all hands to catch fish and cut firewood and smoke what we can't eat right away," Sigurd said. "We'd be foolish to waste time and effort chasing after reindeer."

They stayed there for two days catching and preserving fish before they felt ready to leave this peaceful and welcoming shore.

Thora threw a last glance at the sands that sheltered the hidden lagoon which had served them so well. It had been good to set foot on land again surrounded by space to wander about. Above all else, it had felt good to give her eyes a rest from her estranged husband and his bonded bed-woman fussing and fawning over him.

They kept sailing south along a coast which remained low and unchanging, beaches of pebble or sand, shallow bays and lagoons too numerous to count; once they saw the longest stretch of white sand backed by low dunes sparsely covered with grass and scattered bushes. The place offered no firewood close to sea, nor any other reason to go exploring, and after some calls back and forth across the water the skippers decided to steer out to sea.

Suddenly one of the girls aboard Aegir's Pride called out, pointing to shore.

"Look there, what is that dark thing in the surf?"

Grim raised his hands to shade his eyes.

"Those are boats!" he shouted. "I see two of 'em…one rower in each… no… two rowers."

The *knorrs* pushed by a favourable wind were catching up fast with the small boats which lacked sails.

"They look to be made of hide," Ragnar suggested.

"Skin boats…see how they're hugging the water."

By now they could see the vessels clearly – two slim skin boats, each propelled by two people facing forward wielding double-headed oars in a frantic effort to escape. They steered for the mouth of a small stream. The *knorrs* closed in on the fragile crafts, small and narrow like floating spear points — no match for a ship under sail with a following wind.

Aboard the ships men rushed to open their sea chests grabbing helmets, spears, axes and mail shirts – those who had them.

Thora blinked her eyes filled with tears by the cutting wind. She turned to Eidyll.

"I can't right see if those are men or women. Can you make out which?"

Eidyll shaded his eyes.

"They seem to be…men I believe, men out hunting…I see spears and harpoons lashed to the decks of their crafts."

They were bumped aside by eager fighters jostling for the chance to deal the first blow. Ivar pushed his ship ahead of Sigurd's, intending to run Maelstrom Tamer over top of the skin crafts. Thora glanced at his white-knuckled hand grasping the steering oar, and his posture, rigid like that of a dog about to pounce on a bird. *What is it with men that they find such pleasure in hunting down others?*

The fleeing crafts kept side by side closely together.

"We've got them now," Ivar murmured. "We'll hit them both at once."

Grim in the bow let out a sharp whistle.

"Heave to port!" he yelled.

"Reefs ahead to starboard," Ragnar bellowed.

The grizzled warrior slipped his sword back into the scabbard and skipped away from the bow; he turned to Ivar with a ferocious glare.

"By the hammer of Thor, keep off those reefs, man! Hallowed Odin, can't you see those wretches are playing us for the fools we are?"

Ivar groaned and applied his full weight to the steering oar in an effort to jerk it around. People planted their feet to counter the impact, swearing at the cunning quarry who had led them into shallows riddled with reefs.

"Drop the sail!" Ivar cried; the heavy sail came down in a jumble.

The ship shuddered and squealed, almost coming to a halt; the noise of the keel grinding across rocks drowned out screams and the clatter of weapons; the *knorr* kept grating across rock after rock, then came fully afloat again without crippling damage it seemed.

"Man the oars and hoist the sail back up," Ivar commanded, steering his ship out of the shallows toward Sigurd's *knorr* which had veered off in time.

Howls of laughter erupted aboard Aegir's Pride. Sigurd slumped over his steering board choking with mirth.

"The hasty dog gets his teeth knocked out," he jeered.

The talk aboard Maelstrom Tamer was subdued. Ragnar glared at the other ship and its merry crew.

"What's with those fools?" he muttered. "They think this funny? If we'd sprung a leak we'd all be stuck here for days scouting for trees, cutting them down, adzing out boards for repairs. No laughing matter, I say."

He fixed a baleful stare on Ivar.

"Mind you, they have every reason to poke fun at us; a man who takes his father's only *knorr* to the edge of the known world ought to be smarter than giving chase like an eager puppy."

Ivar showed no sign that he had heard.

The skin boats slipped into the creek headed for some low hills crowned with scraggly trees.

Ragnar observed, "Who knows how many fur clad wretches with bows at the ready are waiting for us among those trees."

He looked around the circle of men, resting his glance on Ivar at the steering oar.

Without a word, Ivar turned the bow away from the creek.

TWENTY

He held in his hand the same axe he used to slay Thrain, which
he called the 'ogress of war,' a round buckler, and he wore a silken
band round his brow, and his hair brushed back behind his ears.
He was the most warriorlike of men, and widely known for that,
going in his appointed place, neither before nor behind...

NJAL's SAGA

They sailed a southerly course for two more days and nights until the low shore veered to the east hugging a marshy lagoon separated from the sea by a gravel bank and breached by a half dozen stream channels shining in the sunlight. Behind the lagoon was a spread of green growth, too far to make out with certainty whether they were grass-meadows or lagoons choked with water-weeds.

Beyond the green ribbon were low hills covered with needle-trees etched black against the clear sky, prompting them to go ashore and assess their potential for timber. Only one channel appeared deep enough to allow the ships access. Even so, the keel of the heavier vessel,

Maelstrom Tamer, scraped the bottom; the *knorr* cut a path through armies of silver-scaled salmon fighting their way in along with the ships.

The green belt behind the lagoon turned out to be dry land covered with grass and sedges — proper grazing for livestock including a fussy horse.

After Aegir's Pride and Maelstrom Tamer were safely beached on a gravel bank and their sails rolled and tied neatly, all fanned out across the delta armed with gaffs, clubs, scoop and draw nets, plodding through salt-marsh and running water to the main stream boiling with salmon struggling upstream to spawn.

Thora and Eidyll moved up to their knees into the shallow stream, a draw net stretched between them, sinkers touching the pebble-strewn bottom; they drew a circle around a mass of writhing fish and steered them into a narrowing inlet toward Halla and Akka waiting at the far end with scoop nets, gaffs and clubs.

Alerted by soft growling, Thora looked to the dog; Khagan stood on a small rise overlooking a creek filled with foaming brown run-off from the spruce woods upstream. Hackles raised, the dog scanned the woods beyond the creek, howl-barking a challenge at the spruce trees.

Something was moving between those trees. Thora strained her eyes. Was that a bear standing on its hindlegs? Or could it be ... a man?

She held her breath, waiting for her vision to clear. A man stepped forward from the spruce trees, and another behind him, both carrying spears, both dressed in knee-length fur tunics without sleeves.

Others emerged from the woods and lined up in front of the trees. The dog's barking rose to a frenzied pitch alerting every last Norseman. Some drew together with whatever tools and weapons they had at hand, gaffs, swords and poniards; others rushed back to the ships to retrieve spears, shields, battle axes, bows, helmets and mail coats.

Thora splashed ashore and ran across the beach to retrieve the quiver and bow she had left lying on a log, strung and ready for use. She grabbed her weapons and made her way to a patch of tall sedges followed by Eidyll clutching a fish spear. Down on her knees, Thora notched an arrow, peeked over the sedges and whistled in low tunes to call the dog.

Khagan paid no attention. The white dog, at other times anxious to keep his feet on dry ground, had boldly moved into the middle of the fast running creek and halted, head up, feet firmly planted and hackles raised.

The two natives armed with spears, who had appeared first, moved away from the woods edge walking with slow, deliberate steps to the far side of the stream.

Thora winced at the sight of Khagan out in the open, presenting the perfect target for enemy archers hidden between the trees. *Fool dog!*

Eidyll jumped up. In one fluid move he splashed into the creek, grabbed the dog by the scruff with both hands and dragged him into the sedges.

Thora breathed relief; she clamped an arm around the dog's neck beaming Eidyll a smile.

"I owe you," she whispered. "Khagan does too."

The others refused to crawl on their bellies through the sedges like Thora and Eidyll. Each man stood his ground stretched tall, shouting and brandishing weapons.

Hrut, a young Icelander, yelled, "Come out from those trees, you wimps, afraid to show yourselves! Are you genuine men or mere trolls?"

His friend, Atli, jumped up and down like a berserker banging his poniard on his shield, biting the shield's iron edge and shouting a stream of abuse across the water; the two strangers, short men with broad shoulders, bare legs and muscular calves, began to cross the stream using their spear shafts for balance.

"Men or trolls, which are you?" Atli yelled again. "You're no giants for sure!"

He fell silent.

The strangers, oblivious to verbal abuse, kept on crossing the creek.

Two Greenland brothers, Skeggi and Grim, offered to move ahead and meet the Westlanders at the nearside of the stream, but Ragnar, their most seasoned fighting man, told them to stay back and wait. If these turned out to be hostile folk preparing an attack, he said, it was better to wait till they were within arrow reach.

Khagan rumbled another growl tensing his muscles and Thora placed her hand on his neck, finding no collar to grab. What happened to his collar of braided sealskin? *Worn out.* She tightened her grip on the furry scruff, digging her fingers into the muscle, tearing her fingernails with the effort to hold the dog back. Eidyll reached over and looped his pig-leather belt around the dog's neck.

The short-statured strangers dressed sparsely in skin clothing, stood on the near side of the stream and Thora, keeping her fist around the dog's improvised collar, raised herself on her knees for a closer look. They seemed to be ordinary men, definitely not women and least of all trolls. Well-proportioned, lean and muscular, they seemed to lack beards or any facial hair. One, the taller one, looked to be covered in reddish-brown ointment from top to bottom.

"Look," she said to Eidyll. "Look, how straight they're holding themselves, and did you see the long strides they took wading the stream? Trolls they say are easy to tell apart from men by the way they carry themselves, awkward, bent forward, and by their furtive, shuffling gait. Clearly these are men, though it remains to be seen what kind of men. Did you ever in your homeland come across men like these wearing hides and furs without a scrap of woven cloth?"

Eidyll shook his head.

"They're unlike any folk I ever saw or heard of."

"Maybe they are Lapps," Thora went on, thinking aloud. "Lapp folk are said to be of short stature with no beards and narrow-eyed faces much like these."

"Look!" Eidyll said, pointing. "They have stripes and circles painted all over their faces and arms."

"And their ankles are circled with white paint of a sort," Thora added. "I think those tunics are made of reindeer skin with the fur turned out."

She slapped her forehead.

"Reindeer...The Lapp folk tend reindeer the way other people tend cows, horses or sheep, my father told me. But how could a band of Lapps have traveled here? Lapps are said to have no ships, only small boats that are unable to sail the seas, and besides, Lapps they say will never part with their reindeer, and reindeer couldn't swim across the sea this far; they may look similar but these men must be a different people unknown in our part of the world."

Thora took another long look at the striking features of the approaching men, their prominent cheek bones emphasized by red and black paint stripes. The taller one with the red skin paste wore a bear-claw necklace. A hood-shaped hat covered his head leaving long braids of black hair touching his shoulders. The other man's shiny black hair, unbraided, also reached to his shoulders. Both wore bright blue feathers twined in their hair and pendants of shells and feathers in their earlobes.

Thora gazed at their bare legs, spare with well-defined bone, muscle and tendon – *desirable in men as well as horses*. Below the knees, above the white paint lines circling ankles and lower legs, they wore tightly wound strings with dangling sea shells which produced clacking sounds when they walked.

She squinted at the strangers' spears, long straight shafts tipped with wicked looking points.

"What are those spear points made of, you think?" she whispered to Eidyll. "They don't look like iron points…some kind of glass perhaps?"

"No," Eidyll whispered, "those are not iron I'm sure. Stone perhaps, a glass-like stone…could be flint of a sort."

The two men, spears pointed down, advanced through the sedges to the line of Norsemen waiting on higher ground, hands fisted tight around their weapons; all looked to Ragnar for the signal to attack. But the old imperial guardsman raised his hand, motioning the others to stay put while he and Sigurd stepped forward to meet the strangers.

The Westlanders stood calmly waiting, spear shafts turned down to the ground. Ragnar and Sigurd moved forward with slow, wary steps. Sigurd clutched his axe and Ragnar had slipped the bag from his sword hilt and rested his hand on the ivory grip, fingers playing for luck with the dangling gemstones called 'cats' eyes.'

Thora, her stomach sore with tension, watched the pair of old warriors walking straight into danger; and they carried no shields.

She looked back to the others.

Ale-bellied Thrand gripped his curved Saracen dagger, took a step ahead and turned around; the others standing behind him shuffled their feet in the gravel.

Thrand called out, "You lads who have bows, have y'er arrows ready."

His high voice had a sharp edge and his words carried far.

"Seems to me these troll folk are right handy with spears... throwing spears from the looks of 'em."

Thora turned to look again at Ragnar and Sigurd, now face to face with the strangers; seen up close, the Westlanders' skin clothing appeared less tailored than that of the other men they had pursued in their skin boats. These two however had splendid footwear, well-made and decorated with embroidery of some kind. They wore no trousers or leggings, just a loose, untailored loin cloth of soft, supple skin below the sleeveless tunic of furred reindeer hide. *Easily reversed to hair-side in when cold weather arrives...they seem to be a thoughtful, practical people.*

The older and taller one of the two Westlanders took charge, addressing Ragnar and Sigurd in a language no Norseman seemed able to recognize — long strings of syllables and lilting sounds which none in the Norse party could make any sense of. From time to time the man gestured with his free hand as if stressing a point, and occasionally he used his entire body for emphasis. At last he fell silent, glancing from Ragnar to Sigurd and back.

Ragnar shook his head to indicate he hadn't understood. The younger Westlander stepped forward, gesturing.

For a while the Norsemen failed to comprehend; they continued to stare and shake their heads.

"Ah, fishing!" Ragnar suddenly exclaimed, and his solemn face brightened.

The strangers grinned and both now dragged the imagined net, hauled it ashore, dumped the imagined catch on the beach, pretended to grab each fish by the tail and club it on the head.

"Right," Ragnar concluded. "They must have watched us gathering salmon...or perhaps they also came here to fish."

The Westlander men appeared friendly enough and Ragnar seemed equally eager to keep the peace.

"We ought to think of something to give them," he said, "to show that we have peaceful intentions."

The skin-clad men were a step ahead of them. Each took from under his shirt a small package wrapped in birchbark and placed it at the Norsemen's feet.

Ragnar was first to open his package; he peered at the content, turned it this way and that and held it up to his nose.

"Looks and smells like fat," he said uncertainly, taking another sniff.

"Strong...rancid....something to eat, I wonder... or an ointment of some sort?"

The older Westlander pointed to his own mouth. *Eat!* He and his friend rubbed their stomachs, belching profusely.

Ragnar broke off a piece and put it on his tongue, cautiously. He raised his eyebrows.

"Not bad! Dried berries preserved in tallow of a sort, much like the travel food we use back home on long journeys."

Sigurd tasted his, and agreed.

"Dried berries and rendered fat."

Ragnar called out to the other Norse who remained tense, eager to surge forth at the slightest signal.

"Quickly, we need a fast runner to get us some cheese to give to these folks. Go, go, be quick about it," he urged, pointing his chin to the younger of the two Westlanders.

"Quickly now, before this beardless lad insists I hand him Bone Cleaver."

The young Westlander was pointing a stubby finger at Ragnar's half drawn sword; next he turned his hand palm up. *Can I hold it?* Ragnar hastened to push the sword further into the scabbard.

The lad waved his hand up and down. *Can I have a look?*

Ragnar drew the sword out, spun it around to catch the sunlight and used it to shear off some sedge. The keen edge cut through the tough grass-like stems like a sickle through barley. Both Westlanders hummed with appreciation.

Again the young man held out his hand. Ragnar pretended he hadn't noticed; he turned to Grim, back from the ship with a package wrapped in woolen cloth.

"The last of our cheese...," the lad said, panting. "It's all I could scrape together."

Ragnar unwrapped the cheese and handed some chunks to each of the Westland men. He pointed to his mouth, grinning.

Warily, the natives sniffed at the crumbly pale substance; the older one sneezed.

Ragnar took a piece of cheese and ate it with loud smacking sounds.

The native men exchanged glances; the younger one brought a small chunk of cheese to his mouth, licked it, nodded with seeming delight and swallowed the bit. His companion shrugged, snorted, and followed the other's example. The salty cheese seemed to please them and their faces lightened up in smiles. They seemed eager for more; Ragnar handed them the rest of the cheese as well as the woolen wrapping; the two examined the woven cloth curiously, rubbing it between their fingers. Again they exchanged a quick glance with one another, took their spears and marched back to the stream wading across and heading for the woods.

The Norsemen, frowning, watched their visitors go.

"Perhaps there are others who want to come out and show themselves," Thrand said. "I'd like to have an idea how many more of them are hiding between those trees."

But all remained quiet after the two had disappeared in the woods.

All through the night the Norsemen kept fires burning in case the natives returned with or without hostile intentions. Nothing stirred across the river that night, or the next. The reindeer folk, as the Norse now called them after their clothing, did not return.

All except Ragnar and the two skippers continued to catch and cure fish the next day; Ragnar walked away along the beach. Thora watched him stretching out on the sand wrapped in his cloak for a nap. At noon he stirred awake and she decided to bring him some half-cured salmon.

"You haven't eaten all day."

She sat down beside him.

"And what, old friend of my father, did you make of these men?"

"Intriguing folk," Ragnar said after some thought. "I wasn't sure at first what they looked like under those layers of paint. Later, when we stood face to face, I noticed their features are similar to those of the men from the eastern plains who come to Miklagard each spring to visit the court."

"The Rus, you mean?"

"No. I mean the Khazars and other horse breeding trading folk from the East who journey to Miklagard and also upriver to Holmsgard. At the beginning of each spring the khans of the mounted horse clans living on the eastern grasslands send emissaries to the emperor in Miklagard. Their faces resemble those of these natives of Westland — high-cheeked with dark, narrow eyes; mind you, the people of the grasslands wear clothing of woven cloth, not animal skins like these men. They do have many furs to wear, but the visiting khans and their escort wear furs the way we do, on top of clothing of wool, linen or silk. There's one more thing, come to think of it, which the plains' men have in common with these Wesstlanders, besides the shape of their faces – they do not have a full beard, often no beard at all. Some have faces as smooth as a woman's, and others have a moustache only, long, thin and droopy. Perhaps they and these reindeer folk are distant cousins after all."

"But how could that be?" Thora pondered. "The horse archers you say live east of Miklagard, and we have sailed steadily westward always following the path of the sun."

"And yet," Ragnar said with a shrug, "these men bear more than a vague resemblance to the eastern horsemen of the grasslands."

They continued to smoke-cure salmon for two more days, packing layers of fish between sheets of inner bark torn from spuce trees until they had filled all vacant space in the two ships with fresh food supplies. On the third day Sigurd and Ivar decided to pack up and continue on south.

"It's high time we found us a place to build a lodge for the winter," Sigurd said, "a place with good timber and enough of it to make up two shiploads for the journey home."

TWENTY ONE

*This land must be named for what it has to offer
and we will call it Markland (Forest Land)*

GRAENLENDINGA SAGA

They followed the coast to starboard running east and later south on a fast current into a fog-veiled channel, a strait maybe, or possibly a fjord with no way out. Out of the swirling mist an island took shape, tall vertical cliffs streaked with bird droppings and speckled with nesting gannets. Several lads wanted to set foot on the island to gather fledglings.

Ivar pointed to the churning water racing past the rocks.

"I see no proper anchoring place in this current, and no place either between those rocks to safely land the small boat."

The current carried them quickly past the island; soon the channel was widening to a sound. The fog had lifted and the sunshine revealed a low coastline to port and a rise of high cliffs to starboard.

Ragnar said, "Let's hope we can continue on through the sound we seem to be in, and out on the other side; it'll be hard to turn and go back where we came from against the current and wind combined."

The shores to both sides kept receding and eventually they lost sight of the land to port.

"We must decide which coast to follow," Ivar said, turning to Gorm.

"Go up in the mast and signal the others."

Gorm climbed up with a length of wadmal tied to a stake, waving to signal those in the other ship that Ivar wished to hold council. They lowered the sails on both ships and moved together under oar, close enough to lash the ships side to side.

Ivar spoke loudly to be heard over the wind.

"I suggest we follow the coast to starboard west-southwest rather than going due south along the other coast. We want to winter not far from good walrussing grounds in the spring."

Sigurd disagreed.

"Never mind walrussing," he scoffed. "I say we follow the coast to port, continuing south as far as it takes to find a good wintering place with timber to cut in the fall and winter and enough grazing to keep our last animals alive for awhile."

Ragnar, Thrand and most others agreed with Sigurd.

Thora kept her opinion to herself; she saw no need to set Ivar on edge by expressing her own preference for the southerly course which seemed to offer a chance for a horse to live through the winter without hay.

Overruled, Ivar resigned himself; the sails went back up and a following breeze pushed them south along a coastline with low cliffs. They steered close to land scouting for a place to go ashore and roast a few whethers, though Ivar rejected every landing place the others suggested.

"I'm not risking my ship to ease your growling stomachs," he said, pointing to erratic wave patterns, proof of hidden shoals protecting these narrow, rock-strewn beaches.

"Methinks your appetite has blinded your eye sight!" he added. "A seal couldn't make it safely to land here."

The coast was gradually rising, tall cliffs in a broken line and later one long steep wall of coloured rock, red, green and purple without any plant growth at all. Ragnar, shading his eyes against the sun, stared at the bare rocks with their strange, garish colours.

"This place must be one of poison and death," he said.

Grim snorted, tossing his head.

"There must be a fire breathing dragon roaming around there, scorching all life to death."

Skeggi, his brother, grinned.

"Then please explain, my fanciful brother, why is the earth not burnt black and why are the rocks not covered with soot?"

The ships seemed to sail faster as if they too were eager to leave behind this inhospitable stretch of shore; the evening grew dark, a deeper dark and much earlier than they were used to in the North. They could no longer make out the coast well enough to keep sailing close, and Ivar headed back out to sea to spend the night away from the reefs guarding this inhospitable land.

At daybreak they closed in on the shore once again, hugging the coast and passing more cliffs, made up of grey stone this time, until they reached a wide channel leading into a fjord lined with rocky bluffs and behind them a rise of low hills cloaked in green forest.

"Timber!"

The men clamoured and stamped their feet demanding the steersmen set down the ships on the first sandy beach they saw near the mouth of the fjord.

"We have earned our mutton roast!"

The skippers raced one another to shore and most men had scrambled overboard before the vessels were beached. Everyone staggered to shore wading and swimming, pausing to stretch and limber up, clambering to the top of the wooded brink to gather firewood. Gorm and Auzur lost no time killing and gutting the whethers and preparing the carcasses, skinned and butchered, ready for roasting even before the others had fires blazing on the gravel beach. After days of separation the crews of each ship were eager to mingle around the fires, jesting and teasing, squabbling and making up, waiting for the meat to be done.

Sigurd said, "We could do with some music."

Thora called Eidyll away from tending the fire.

"Why don't you take out your flute and play us a tune."

Before long, Eidyll's merry flute tunes added to the cheer.

A family of grey jays flew down from the trees and dashed back and forth between the fires to snatch wood-dwelling moths that tried to escape the flames. The birds fluttered almost within reach of the fiery tongues, risking singed feathers for a chance to catch another fat moth.

Gellir Sloppy-breeches, a young Greenlander, cried out.

"Hey! Let's place bets on those birds and see how many moths each of them catches in, say, the time it takes the flute player to finish a tune; mind you, those who do the counting cannot themselves place any bets."

It didn't take long before the men were caught up in the gambling game, each yelling encouragement to his chosen bird, applauding or howling over the verdicts issued by Ragnar or Thrand who had volunteered to solve disputes. The game occupied them long enough to allow the roasts to cook properly, and the few mouthfulls of mutton passed out to each were a welcome change after days of subsisting on crudely smoked salmon; it was a fitting way to mark what they hoped was the end of their sea journey for now.

After the meal a number of men coiled up in the sand for a nap ignoring the calls to board ship until the sails were raised and the ships pulled away from the beach, and the stragglers had to swim after the ships and beg to be hauled onboard.

They moved into the fjord under sail and later by oar into the narrowing part upstream and eventually into the river which ran to begin with between low, marshy banks; these gave way to steep, washed out shores of exposed clay and gravel with rocky outcrops and pebbled beaches interrupted by grass-fringed marshy streams seeping into the fjord. The river curved sharply to starboard, and around the bend was a sheltered stretch of water hemmed between gradually lowering banks until they reached a long, narrow gravel beach bordered at each end by a green meadow. At one end the meadow was watered by a brook meandering its way into the fjord; the back lands were thick with needle trees and some stands of spruce grew right to the water's edge. Ivar ordered the lads to rest their oars.

He shouted across to the other ship, "Methinks this could be our wintering spot!"

"Sure looks that way," Sigurd hollered back. "Our wave steeds are ready to rest their weary bellies on the gravel; let's scout out the shore lands here."

Again the men rerfused to wait for the ships to be beached, choosing instead to tumble overboard and splash ashore. Fast-footed Odi was first to return after exploring the marshy meadow.

"Reindeer tracks!" he shouted, pointing to muddy hoof prints between the sedges.

Thora and Ragnar looked at the water-filled tracks, large, two-toed and clearly defined. Thora squatted to examine them closely.

"By the looks of these I would say there were two reindeer here only this morning, a mother and calf perhaps, nibbling on the saltgrass."

She covered the larger track with her hand.

"Look at the size."

Ragnar nodded.

"It's a good house site that has wild meat around."

"And grazing at hand for livestock," Thora added.

Ragnar pointed without comment to more tracks criss-crossing the bare patches of mud and sand between the woods and the meadow.

"So far," Thora said, smiling, "the gods are keeping their part of the bargain in return for the feast we served them in Greenland before setting sail."

Without delay Thrand put together two hunting parties led by Norwegians experienced in tracking and hunting the fleet-footed reindeer. The others fanned out to explore the rivershore and nearby forest. Thora and Eidyll took inventory of the meadow beside the meandering brook.

"We have enough grass and sedges here to keep a few livestock in fodder," Thora said. "We could even cut some for hay...the winter may turn out not as mild as we're hoping."

They returned to Sigurd and Ivar who had remained with the ships.

207

"It seems," Sigurd said, surveying the land, "that we have enough level ground between the tideline and the woods to build a ship-house as well as a lodge large enough for us all with some storage space for winter supplies."

Ivar frowned.

"Thrand will have to keep his woodworkers at home from now on; no reason why they couldn't leave the hunting to others. They're needed here to build us a decent lodge as well as a *naust* for the ships."

Thora reveled in the many trees covering this land like a prickly green bearskin. She imagined the hall they would build here — a low slung lodge sheltered from weather by growths of tall trees, some bearing evergreen needles and other trees draped in seasonal foliage, a place reminiscent of the home of her birth by the fjord. She glanced at Ivar who stood, arms crossed, scanning the woods. *Tallying up how much hardwood, spruce and pine there is to build his new ship.* Ivar's mind was so easy to read. She sighed. If things between them were different, she would be excited with him over the shipbuilding venture.

She closed her eyes trying to picture herself on Ivar's new ship or any other heading back to Greenland. Did she want to? This land, this very place, filled her with joy and a sense of belonging.

TWENTY TWO

We'll divide our company into two groups. One half shall remain by the longhouses and the other half shall explore the land. They are never to go so far away as to be unable to return the same evening and no one will separate from the group.

GRAENLENDINGA SAGA

Early the next day, a day of sunshine, they began cutting trees for the lodge. The sea breeze coming in from the fjord died as soon as it encountered the woods; before long everyone working in the woods was assaulted by biting flies, clouds of them settling on exposed skin around eyes, ears and temples, forcing people to spend equal time working and swatting flies.

Thrand, charged with overseeing the house building, grew impatient over the lack of progress.

"We can't be sure how long the warm weather will last in this place before winter returns. You men had better double your efforts, or we'll have no place to keep out of the cold and no *naust* for our ships either before the earth freezes."

Most men except those from Norway, marveled at the size of the trees. They marked the biggest ones to be cut later, selecting smaller trees split and sectioned to make palisade-walls for the outside of the house.

"It's a good and quick way to build house walls," Thrand said to the Icelanders. "In this land of fine trees we want none of your clammy Icelandic walls of rock and sod to bother ourselves with."

They dug the split poles two feet into the ground enclosing a rectangle large enough to hold thirty people and their possessions. Along the centre line they erected a row of tall posts connected at the top by horizontal beams.

Mord and Auzur, both experienced shipwrights and carpenters, suggested cutting the roof rafters long enough to reach across the palisade walls to the ground.

"That way we could extend the roof cover all the way down and have space to store firewood; it will also help to keep the weather off our house walls," wiry, thin-faced Auzur explained.

They worked hard and ate well with plenty of meat to go around for all; the hunters kept finding more bands of reindeer foraging on the grey lichen that grew in thick pillows all over the upland barrens.

They discovered other things too.

"Today we found the remains of a boat or some kind of small watercraft," Ragnar announced one day, leaving it to his companions to butcher the young reindeer bull they brought home.

"Anyone knows what to make of this?"

He tossed something large on the ground, a piece of birchbark lashed with spruce root to a thin wooden slat.

"We broke off more pieces to show you," Ragnar said.

One by one the other hunters added their pieces, some large, others small, to the pile until it became clear they were fragments of a small boat entirely made of bark lashed to a frame of flexible wood slats.

"We found it on a beach facing the open sea," Ragnar said. "Looks like a discarded vessel, long and slim, broken in two... perhaps it was thrown on the rocks and left behind."

He raised his eyebrows. "Could be it was left there in the spring by people who came to the mouth of the fjord to catch salmon."

"In that case we may get a chance to capture some slaves next spring," Ivar said with a grin. "Slaves with strong arms will be an asset to work the oars of the new ship I intend to build."

Thora noticed that Auzur and Mord exchanged questioning glances.

Ivar had better talk to them first; he'll need expert help to build the ship of his dreams.

"Come," she said to the younger women.

"We'll need to make another visit to the bog."

They went out to collect more of the grey bog moss they used to chink the cracks in the outer walls.

Old Halla looked up from the pile of moss she was sorting.

"In one more day," she said, "we'll have the walls free of drafts."

"How easy it is to build a lodge in this land of plentiful wood," Thora said to the women from Sandurness "Think of the massive amounts of rocks and sod we hauled from the uplands down to the fjord to build our new farm in Greenland!"

The heat of the sun seemed to grow more intense day after day.

"We're ready to put on our first roof cover of birchbark," Thrand said. "It's time we had shelter from sunshine and rain."

Akka nodded. Born and raised in the North of Norway, she was familiar with the ways of the Lapp people and their use of birchbark.

"It's late in the season to cut bark," she said.

"Birchbark is easy to work with in the spring. Now we'll need lots of steam to soften it first."

Once softened, she showed the others how to sew the bark sheets to the rafters with strands of split and soaked spruce root. For roof vents they cut out rectangles which could be lifted and lowered with the help of long poles.

The woodworkers — happy to work under roof in shade and away from biting flies — finished the inside walls fitted with pegs and shelves; they also built benches and tables and platforms for sleeping.

Eidyll took part in the wood work whenever he could steal away from his crude smithy housed under a lean-to, taking short breaks from the endless chore of straightening iron pegs and rivets. In his spare time he fashioned wood working tools for himself and asked the carpenters to show him how to build tables and benches and make smooth round pegs to attach to the center poles for hanging utensils, clothes and weapons.

"I never liked black-smithing," Thora heard him say to Mord.

"It's hot, dirty, and hard on the arms and wrists; my uncle gave me no choice in the matter; he simply sent me to town one day as an apprentice to a blacksmith friend of his."

The men from Iceland and Greenland were ready to collect roofing sod in the upland barrens.

"Not so fast, lads," Thrand said, shaking his head.

"Digging sod is for badgers. We'll use fir boughs on top of the birch-bark roof cover to keep warm inside or cool when needed, and on top of the boughs we'll put another layer of bark weighed down with poles – that way we'll prevent rain and snow from soaking the roof."

"What about wind storms?" asked a man from wind-blown Iceland.

Thrand grinned. "We'll just have to cut enough poles and use them to weigh the roof down properly."

*　　*　　*　　*　　*

Thora counted the barrels of seal oil and sighed – barely enough to see them through winter if used for food, and none to spare for the lamps she had brought. Unless they found a source of lamp fuel soon, they'd have nothing to rely on for light other than the wood fires in the trench along the centre aisle.

"Without any lamp light to see what we're doing," she said to Halla, "it's a good thing that we have no wool this winter to be made into cloth."

A few days later there was a short, violent storm blowing in from the fjord which tested the roof; everyone rushed to pile on more poles, scrambling up on the roof ridge and lashing them on tightly.

The house roof coped with the storm as well as Thrand had predicted, and on the following day the lads rowed out to the mouth of the fjord for some beach combing; toward dark they returned with their small boat full of unexpected bounty.

"We found three stranded *grindevhal* for the taking," laughed Mord staggering ashore loaded down by a big slab of whale blubber. "We'll not be short of fuel oil this winter; roll out the cauldrons and barrels and get some fires going!"

All through the next day the men took turns rowing back and forth to butcher the small whales and bring the chunks home while the others kept the fires and tended the rendering cauldrons. Sigurd ordered a barrel of precious salt brought out to preserve some of the meat. They cut strips of blubber into slabs small enough to submerge into the cauldrons half filled with water, working without pause singing and laughing, smiling with greasy faces, oil-slicked arms glistening in the sunshine.

Thora and Groa, well-matched in height, went off and on with oil barrels carrying a full barrel between them to the house each time, struggling to pull up their shifts heavy with oil and keep them secured under their waist belts. The full barrels found a place safe from bears inside the lodge against the rear wall.

"I believe," said Thora, dumping another slab of blubber into the cauldron for Halla to stir, "the whales are a sign sent by Njord to let us know we are still in his favour."

It was reassuring to think that the Norse gods seemed to have power in this distant corner of the world after all. One of these days they might need to call on their support against an attack by enemies. They had no idea who the people were who left the broken birchbark vessel on the beach; were they akin to the reindeer men they met earlier at the lagoon? Would they turn out to be friend or foe? As much as Ivar might dream of capturing native Westlanders to use and sell as slaves, it could turn out otherwise. *What is to stop an army of Westlanders from raiding us? What if it is we who end up killed or captured and sold as slaves?*

She would set some slabs of blubber aside as offerings to Odin and Tyr later – tonight after the wind died down and the smoke of the burn sacrifice would rise unhindered.

TWENTY THREE

---

*...had a child by his mistress named Nereid, and on the
command of his wife the child was put out to die.*

VATNSDAELA SAGA

Thora woke up before anyone else stirred in the lodge. She lay for a while listening to the snores and sputters and sighs of the sleepers around her; how fortunate that she had her sleep platform in the middle of the longhouse all to herself. Ivar had claimed a spacious place against the back wall to share with Achren, and Thora had made a point of assuring all who would listen that she fully agreed with the arrangement since, "it isn't wise for a woman venturing into lands unknown, to grow unwieldy with child."

It was Halla's task to start the morning fire, but the old woman was still asleep in her narrow bed by the door. Unable to find her own way back to sleep, Thora sat up and yawned. In the faint light spilling through the half-open smoke holes, she scanned the line of platforms along the opposite wall. Thrand and Sigurd — each with a young woman from Iceland by his side — occupied platforms next to each other. Ragnar, two spaces further down the row, seemed thoroughly asleep with Groa by his side. She couldn't see Ivar and Achren in the dark end of the house, though most nights she caught the sounds of what appeared to be rough pleasures.

Thora felt concerned for Ivar's bedmate. Inspite of her proud and defiant bearing, Achren was to be pitied. Yesterday the young bond-woman had beaten her to the wash barrel by the door; she stood pouring cold water over her arms and shoulders and breast when Thora approached. The girl covered herself quickly, though not fast enough to hide the bruises and bite marks on arms and breasts.

"Perhaps you wish to sleep by yourself for a while," Thora suggested. A woman, bonded or free, should not be required against her will to suffer Ivar's rough pleasures.

"Talk to Halla if you like — she knows ways to get a woman's moon blood flowing more often and longer; a sure way to repel a man's attentions."

Achren's green eyes stared back at her with a sulky expression.

"Methinks it an honour to share Ivar Ulfson's bed."

Thora shook her head. *The silly heifer.*

She piled up sticks in the fireplace and allowed her thoughts to roam; the pile of kindling collapsed and she had to re-stack. Why did it bother her so to find that Ivar abused his bed-woman? Was it any concern of hers? Ivar respected her wishes after all. He made no demands on her, and Achren seemed well enough pleased with the arrangement. Still, the girl's bruised arms and battered breasts told another story.

Halla continued to snore.

Thora raked yesterday's ashes aside and turned her mind elsewhere. Though she had tried to make the brown substance she bought from the herb woman, last longer by adding ever smaller pinches to Achren's morning gruel, she ran out of the herb some time ago. What if the slave girl conceived, and what if she bore Ivar a low-born child, a son, while she, Ivar's lawful wife, remained childless by choice? Would Ivar be tempted, for want of legitimate offspring, to elevate the status of Achren's base-born son and pronounce him his heir?

She shook the ashes out of her hair as if that would help to shake off her gloomy thoughts.

Many a man maintained a number of base-born sons for house *karls* – though most wouldn't raise a low-born son for an heir... but Ivar might ...if only to spite her, his resented wife.

The pile of kindling collapsed a second time. Thora took a firm hold of her wandering mind and re-stacked the lot this time with more care into a neat, airy pile; she inserted a crumbled piece of the black tinder fungus Halla cut from the trees behind the house, and blew softly to nurse up the glow in the bits of coal still alive in the ashes; for a while she remained, sitting back on her heels watching little tongues of fire reaching up to play around the sticks, teasing them ablaze.

Thora reached for the water-filled cauldron hooked to the tripod. She lowered the iron pot till it nearly touched the flames and went outside to the latrine, a trench dug in soft sand away from the forest edge and its tree roots.

There were muddy footsteps around the latrine left by visiting men and women as well as other tracks telling tales of four-legged night visitors, fox, weasel, a pair of wolves and...Thora stared at the jagged hole excavated overnight at the far end of the trench. Foot prints the size of her own, ending in short claw marks, criss-crossed the soft ground; whatever it was that passed by, it had churned the loamy sand into mud like a mob of pigs passing by; but pigs didn't leave tracks with claws; these tracks, not as large and long-clawed as a sea bear's, must be made by a land bear of some sort stopping by last night to root around the latrine in search of things that appeal only to dogs, pigs and bears; and that bear by now would have very bad breath.

Thora rushed over to the livestock pen, relieved to find that neither livestock nor the dog left with them inside, had come to harm. She tossed an armful of chopped alder and poplar inside for fodder and was about to leave when something told her to take a closer look at the animals. The sheep and the goats were skin and bone after the hardships at sea, but the mare...Thora blinked her eyes...the mare seemed to have gained weight. Was the horse putting on fat, or was something else going on with her?

217

She rested a hand on the horse's flank and waited, tossing her head with disappointment – no tell-tale movements as she had hoped. She tried the mare's other side, and suddenly she felt her own heartbeat quicken. Yes! There it was again, a faint little jerk, and another one – something in there was stirring, tiny spasms out of pace with the mare's breathing; it could mean only one thing.

She sighted along the mare's flanks to be sure. Fluga was growing wider without gaining any fat on her neck, back or quarters; there could be no doubt….the mare was in foal!

Thora chewed on her lip trying to recall the previous pasturing season; Fluga was briefly turned out with Surtur before they decided to keep the black stud colt penned in, so Eidyll could work with him. The foal could be, no, must be, Surtur's! No other stud had been turned out with her mare. Whether a colt or a filly, this foal would be a keeper, well worth the effort and hardship involved with raising a foal in this land choked with trees.

She released Khagan from the pen, grabbed a bucket and went to the creek to fetch water for the penned animals. The lanky dog bounced ahead, pausing at the latrine to sniff at the bear spoor. He looked about, put his nose back to the ground and, ignoring her calls, lunged into the woods. Thora ran after him, anxious for his safety. A dog brave enough to stand his ground against a bear menacing his flock, might also be fool enough to challenge one for no reason – and not any old bear, to judge by the tracks, no, a big old male quick to anger.

Thora beat her way through dense stands of trees studded with dead-wood spikes placed at eye-level for a woman, though not for a dog following his nose across the moss-covered forest floor.

She scanned the ground ahead – no tracks. And where was the dog?

From up ahead came a woof, then a volley of barks. She scrambled through dead-fall and rotting timber until she stumbled into a clearing. There, at the base of a solitary yellow birch was Khagan hopping up and down in time with his barking, peering up into the tree.

Scraps of bloody fur lay scattered on the ground between torn up blueberry bushes, and there were tufts of coarse black hair around a half-eaten length of greyish intestine, and a gallbladder left untouched.

218

Thora followed the dog's gaze up into the tree and forgot to breathe. Halfway up, wedged between two branches and covered with flies, sat the severed head of a black bear looking grotesque; the tongue, swollen like a fishing float, protruded from the side of the mouth and the eyes were caked shut by a crust of black-brown blood that had oozed from the cleft skull.

TWENTY FOUR

_____

_____

After the first winter passed... they became aware of natives

GRAENLENDINGA SAGA

...when right beside their ship, a walrus rose up. Kormac hurled a spiked pole, striking it, so that it sank again; the men aboard thought they recognized its eyes as those of Thorveig the witch. That walrus came up no more, but Thorveig turned out to have sickened and died.

KORMAC's SAGA

_____

_____

Thora searched the shadows between the trees around her, ready to bolt like a skittish horse. *What am I looking for?* People, unknown people, must have killed the bear and put its head up in the tree. *Why? To put a spell on us?*

She listened to the unfamiliar songs of forest birds – *real bird songs, or signals between unseen people watching me?* What if those who put the bear's head in the tree, were still lurking nearby? Could they be native hunters who, guided by the bear they were tracking, discovered their longhouse lodge last night? The sky had been clear and a half moon enabled keen-sighted hunters to easily track a bear which followed its nose to a place reeking of things any bear would think worthy of scavenging.

She could almost see them now, shadowy hunters creeping up to the lodge; they might have spied through the cracks in the housewall, deciding that the sleepers inside were too numerous to overcome for a small band of hunters. Perhaps they left with the intent to return in large enough numbers to mount an attack.

A chill puckered the skin of her arms, bare under the rolled sleeves of her summer shift. She narrowed her eyes at the shadows. This was no place to linger. Hidden behind the green wall of the forest there might be eyes following every movement she made; though Khagan hadn't warned her of hidden dangers, he seemed too pre-occupied with the smell of bear to be relied on at this time.

"Come, come away with me," Thora hissed, grabbing the dog by his new collar of braided horsehair; she clamped her other hand around his muzzle to silence his growls and dragged him into the woods toward home.

"Fool dog!" she scolded him in a whisper, darting furtive glances behind her.

"Stop making a fuss."

Guided by broken branches and twigs she retraced her steps through thickets and stands of trees back to the lodge, trying not to panic at every shadow or glitter between the dark-needled branches. Images whirled about inside her head, scenes of skin-clad natives creeping around the lodge in the moon-silvered night, peeking in to count the sleepers.

Why had Khagan not sounded alarm last night to warn of the bear and of those guided in by the bear's tracks? Perhaps the dog — shut in with the livestock and unable to patrol the camp — had failed to notice the intruders who might have come in from the other side rather than taking the path by the livestock pen and the ship-house. From now on she would leave the dog roaming free at night, no longer confined with the livestock. The horse could be relied on in his place to take up guard duty inside the pen, awake on her feet all night watching over the sheep and the goats. Fluga would no doubt create uproar over anything she sensed stalking around the pen.

Back at the house Thora found the others in various stages of getting up. Before she was halfway through her story, every man had jumped up, grabbed his arms and rushed off to the woods. By midday they returned in pairs or small groups with nothing to report.

"We followed the tracks you made this morning," Thrand said to Thora, "all the way to the butchered bear, and we failed to see any signs of people...those who killed the bear are perhaps sorcerers skilled in magic, able to turn themselves into whisps of smoke leaving no traces."

Sigurd responded to Thrand's suggestion with a snort.

"Why wouldn't that bear have been killed by regular hunters? Any native of this land familiar with these woods will have ways of moving around without leaving footprints. From now on we'll keep armed sentries in the ship-house at night in case these wretched *skraelings* should try to set fire to our ships. Without our ships we'd be trapped in this place and pretty much at their mercy; they could harass us to no end, so we wouldn't be able to build ourselves a new ship."

Ivar hammered on the hard-packed floor with the butt of his spear to signal his agreement.

"We'd be sitting targets for arrows and javelins launched from the woods by men we can't see. We need to be prepared."

All promised to adhere to the new rules – that no one was to go out without carrying weapons, and that slaves couldn't be ordered to go into the woods to collect kindling or carry out other chores without armed *karls* coming along for protection.

"It would appear after all..." Ragnar said with a wry smile, "that this land is already taken."

*　　*　　*　　*　　*

The first snowfall came and went, and the men sped up the logging in hopes of having enough timber cut and stacked before snow-buildup, to make up two full ship-loads in the spring. They cut mostly trees of moderate size which could be hauled full length to a clearing in the woods where others sectioned them to shipping size; from there the timber was yarded, several sections bunched together, to a flat area near the ship-house to be stacked above the high waterline.

Day in day out the mare struggled to haul trees and sectioned logs with the help of a rough sled, a heavy cross-piece on two runners which kept the butt-ends off the ground to reduce drag. Thora would not have anyone else working with the horse besides herself and Eidyll – the only people who knew the mare was in foal. Little by little she reduced the mare's loads without being obvious; at the same time she wanted to prove the mare's worth, especially to Ivar and others who kept insisting the horse shouldn't have come on this journey in the first place.

By midday Thora took the makeshift harness off the horse to give her a rest. She handed the assembly of straps to Eidyll to hang on the sled; when she reached up to take off the bridle, she saw Ivar approaching with energetic strides.

He paused, frowning, staring at the horse, and walking around her for a closer look.

"Mmm, I see... Freyja has been busy twice working her magic around here."

He nodded at the mare's rounded belly.

"Good to see we'll have a foal out of this mare around the same time my bed woman's due to give birth to my son. We shall have tender foal flesh at hand to be relished by Freyja and Thor on occasion of my son's naming."

Thora blinked; she took a moment to gather her thoughts and make sure her voice wouldn't quiver.

"I trust, husband," she said airily, "the gods will be well pleased to feast on mutton or goat, as much as it would please them to feast on horse flesh. This foal I intend to keep and raise."

Ivar gave her an evil glance.

"At the time of my son's naming we'll have no sheep left for anyone, gods or mortals, to feast on. We're not in Odin's hall, do I need to remind you? Here we have no magic sheep of the kind they're keeping in Valhal, sheep that are butchered, roasted and eaten over and over in never ending bliss. The ewe and the goat are the last we have, and they're spoken for to be roasted at tonight's feast which we promised the men now that they've cut all of the timber to make up two ship loads."

Thora shrugged.

"The ewe and the goat are yours to do with as you like, and the mare and her foal are mine – I decide whether they live or not."

"You, woman, will decide no such thing," Ivar snarled. "But for now, enough of this. I suggest you go to the house and tell those girls and women to begin preparing the roasts...oh, and tell your maids to bring out the last of the flatbread!"

Rattled by the argument, Thora turned to Eidyll who stood waiting beside the horse and the sled.

"You can leave the sled at the log pile and take the horse and the harness home," Thora said. "The logging work is over I understand; you can turn the horse out to graze till dark."

On her way to the house she slowed her step at the livestock pen. Groa and the three bond-girls from Iceland were leaning on the fence talking and laughing with Gorm and Skeggi who had finished skinning the slaughtered ewe.

Thora dug her heels into the dirt, stretching tall.

"Right!" she snapped.

"You girls get your butts over to the house and help the old drudges to sweep away the dirt. We can't put on a feast in a place covered with filth. I want to see the floor and every shelf and platform free of dust and piss and fish bones. And I want every cauldron scrubbed and all of the waste buckets emptied and scoured with sand."

She pointed a finger to each of the girls.

"And, I want you, you, you, and you, to keep things clean, neat, and tidy from now on. We've lived in squalour long enough with you lot loafing about while all of us others as well as the horse worked ourselves to the bone in the logging woods."

Thora took a deep breath.

"From this day on," she declared, "I'll be staying home to remind you girls of your duties. This place is turning into a hog sty and you lot seem to think you've nothing better to do than fooling around with the lads!"

The men began slicing off choice parts of meat long before the cuts were properly roasted. Thora told Halla and Akka to save the gristle and bones; boiled together with the ewe's head, these bits would make a nutritious stew for those who stayed home while the men were off tomorrow to hunt reindeer.

She called Akka and pointed to a leg bone tossed into the ashes.

"Take that and other discarded bones to give to Khagan – and mind that you split them first so he can get at the marrow. And..."

Distracted, Thora watched Achren running off to the latrine.

Again? How often, at a feast without ale, did a woman need to take a piss? *Ahah.* What was it that Gunnhild had said to her one day, when she was close to her time? *With the rate this child is growing, I seem to have no room to spare for my bladder.*

She frowned, feeling some concern for the girl. *She's barely fifteen.* Granted, Achren was no likeable girl, but what else could one expect of a young woman with no control over her life? Then again, wasn't Achren born and raised a Christian like Eidyll? *And aren't Christians taught to accept life's sufferings with humility and patience?*

Thora seated herself on a log bench away from the blazing fires taking her time to chew a piece of fatty tendon that wouldn't soften. The goat and sheep secured in their pen each night after dark had been half-starved for fodder, and their meat was exceedingly tough and hard to chew.

"Well, I am glad to see you taking some time out for yourself."

Startled, Thora looked up, into the ruddy face of Ragnar Bearbladder flushed from the heat of the fire.

"I also needed a cool place to be," she said, "away from the fire."

Ragnar muttered, "I say it's an ill-favoured feast without beer or wine or mead — men don't thrive on naught but water to drink!"

Thora wiped the grease from her chin. She moved aside to make space on the log.

"I disagree with you there," she said. "I think it's a good feast when men are forced to keep their heads as cool as the springwater they must use to relieve their thirst."

"Maybe so," the Norwegian pondered, fingering the grizzled upper half of his neatly plaited beard. "Still, efforts to make merry, I say, are doomed to fail without a drink that's fit to spark some cheer. Why don't you tell your *thrall* to play us some music to liven things up?"

Thora called out to Akka, "Go find Eidyll. Tell him to come and bring his flute."

Akka stayed away for a long while before returning alone.

"No one has seen Eidyll after he came home to put the harness away; Halla sent him out across the brook to gather crowberries for the stew. Seems he's still out there taking his time. Halla says she's tired of waiting."

TWENTY FIVE

─────────────────────────────

─────────────────────────────

Thorhall disappeared and some went searching for him. On the fourth day Karlsefni and Bjarni found him at the edge of a cliff. He was staring at the sky, his mouth, nostrils and eyes opened wide, scratching and pinching himself and mumbling something.

EIRIKS SAGA RAUDA

─────────────────────────────

─────────────────────────────

The morning after the feast Thora was up at first light, worn out after a sleepless night spent fretting over Eidyll's disappearance. *Something bad must have happened to him.*

No one else seemed to share her misgivings.

Mild-mannered Thrand said to her yesterday, "I'm not surprised, Thora Thorvinnsdottir, your *thrall* has run off at last. You're a hard mistress to please."

Ivar said with a dismissive shrug, "Never mind...we'll have one mouth less to feed, and the *thrall* did leave behind a good supply of ironware — we have all the nails and braces needed for my new ship."

227

Nobody offered last night to go out in the dark looking for Eidyll, and now, at first daylight, the men seemed all passed out sprawling on top of their beds, and she couldn't stir anyone into action. With a shrug, Thora grabbed her bow and went out to take a look across the stream in the uplands where Halla had told the *thrall* to pick berries.

The unexpected chill outside took her breath away; she frowned at the grey sky heavy with snow about to be released. It felt good to swing up on the horse's warm furry back; she whistled for Khagan and headed for the creek scanning the partly snowed over footprints in the vicinity of the house until she found the single line of footsteps, presumably Eidyll's, leading from the yard toward the creek.

The mare made her way cautiously across the treacherous footing, hooves probing the fragile ice sheets that covered puddles and waterholes. Thora halted the horse at the partly frozen creek; the single line of footsteps had moved out on the ice, broken through, and continued on the other side to the hill upstream where crowberries grew in abundance. The maids went there in early fall to harvest berries for drying; any left unpicked would now be shriveled with frost, perhaps turned sweet enough for Halla to use in the stew.

Thora turned around. The trees on the other side of the creek formed a dense stand allowing a horse and rider no space to pass through. Rather than leaving Fluga in the meadow alone, without the dog for protection, Thora decided to return the horse to the safety of the pen and resume her search for Eidyll on foot.

Back at the longhouse she found most men out of bed at last, gathering outside to prepare for another hunt now that the fresh sleety snow made for easy tracking.

Sigurd raised his voice.

"Anyone offers to stay here to keep guard?"

His question met with deep silence.

"Is it even wise at all to go out hunting today?" Thora asked.

"For all we know Eidyll may've run into a bunch of *skraelings* yesterday...what if they're still around and waiting for us to separate into groups small enough for them attack? Do I need to remind you of the butchered bear?"

"My wife has little else on her mind these days than making a fuss over invisible *skraelings*," Ivar sneered. "If she had her way, we'd all be cowering at home scurrying between the lodge and the *naust*, quaking with fear on account of some shadowy wretches who dare not show themselves."

He strung his bow and marched off along the shore path.

"I'm going hunting. Those of you wanting to join me had better make up your mind."

Sigurd and most of the younger men decided to go with Ivar, but Ragnar and his nephews remained in the yard, and Thrand chose to stay home as well. Ragnar eyed the men filing into the forest path.

"Methinks," he observed, "that reindeer are few and far apart in these parts, living in small herds foraging in barrens and clearings, mere gaps in the forest. With many hunters and few reindeer in a confined place, arrows could find their way into an unlucky hunter or two."

Thora changed into her shepherd's clothes. Eidyll couldn't have flown away over the treetops after he left clear tracks on both sides of the brook. She collected her bow and quiver, short spear and long horse-hair rope.

"Let's go," she said to the dog.

"Hey, wait!" Ragnar called out. "Where are you going? Nobody and surely no woman should be going into the woods alone at the risk of running into *skraelings* ....If you must go, I'll go with you."

"No, there's no need, really" Thora said. "You must stay here to take charge in case we're attacked."

"Then Auzur will go with you," Ragnar insisted.

"With only four of you here to defend this place," Thora objected, "no man should leave here to help me search for my slave. I am well-armed and my dog counts for two armed men. And I needn't be long; there's enough snow on the ground to move quickly on skies."

She called Khagan, looped the rope around his shoulders and chest for a makeshift harness, tied the free end around her waist and reached under the roof edge for a pair of skies made by Thrand's woodsmen.

Ragnar handed her a long slender pole, shaking his head.

"The daughter's as head-strong as her mother."

With her skies strapped on Thora pushed off with her pole, alerting the dog with a tug on the horsehair rope.

"Go, Khagan, pull."

The dog, with a look of surprise, refused to move; to change his mind Thora jabbed him in the ribs and after a few times of this, Khagan gave in, running ahead at the tap of the pole; it took a few more jabs before he learned to keep the rope taut and not come to a sudden stand-still.

Filled with joy Thora skimmed behind the dog over the thin layer of sleety snow near the brook, calling out Eidyll's name for Khagan's sake to let the dog know they were searching for the *thrall* and not out to hunt wildlife. She paused at the brook urging the reluctant dog to wade across. Khagan sniffed about, undecided; he raised his head, tasted the air and looked across the stream. Thora took off her skies and sloshed her way through the icy creek; at last the dog decided to follow, splashing away in a futile effort to keep his feet dry.

The dog pulled steadily upstream on the other side winding through dense tree stands till they reached the berry patch on the hill. Here was a clearing where they had yarded logs with the horse all through the fall. Ahead of them ran the single set of footprints they had followed, still going one way.

Thora leaned her skies against a tree; she examined the clearing scattered with piles of bark partly covered with wet snow which melted in patches of sunshine, obscuring the footprints. The place seemed to be emptied of any life with feathers or fur except for a flock of snow sparrows marching about like an army of feathered flat-footed dwarfs. Khagan lunged after them, nearly pulling Thora off her feet; she jerked back on the rope and together they watched the birds erupting into the lead-coloured sky, like a cloud of snowflakes fluttering upwards.

Thora walked Khagan around the edge of the clearing; she hoped he might pick up Eidyll's scent trail.

"Eidyll, Eidyll!" she chanted, "go find Eidyll."

The dog forged ahead leading her to an abandoned stack of snow-coated logs. Here the snow was churned up and mingled with mud, criss-crossed by many different footprints *as if a scuffle took place here*. Khagan led her to the other side of the clearing to a shady place with more multiple footprints leading into the woods. Three or four people it appeared had left the clearing together.

She strapped her skies back on, tightened her grip on the dog leash and resumed her tracking. They came to a depression in the snow surrounded by icy footprints – *someone fell down and was hauled back on his feet. Eidyll did not go willingly with his captors.*

They continued up a long hill to forested uplands blanketed by a thicker layer of snow than what was present below at fjord level. Khagan lunged ahead, and Thora edged her skies sideways to brace; should she turn around or continue? What if she ran into Eidyll's captors?

She met Khagan's golden-eyed eager gaze; the dog threw his full weight into the harness and Thora braced again.

"Wait, you ill-mannered brute; wait till I have my bow strung!"

With her bow at the ready and two arrows loosened inside her quiver waiting to be used, Thora let Khagan lead her into the forest. In the dense undergrowth she lost sight of any tracks and resigned herself to be guided by Khagan's sense of smell. The dog continued to follow the scent, slipping under branches, through dense brush, and negotiating with ease all manner of places which posed a challenge to a tall woman on skies.

She shortened the dog's leash to keep him close by her side and squeezed her eyes shut between the spruce trees studded with deadwood spikes.

"Easy...go easy, you nimble-footed rascal."

They emerged from the spruce stands; Thora opened her eyes to look around in the small clearing; there were three or four smudged footprints in the snow only two steps away. Khagan turned to face her, a proud look in his eyes.

"Well done," she laughed.

The place was not, she discovered, a clearing on solid ground; they stood on the frozen and snow-covered surface of a forest pond. Overhead the sun was peeking through the clouds – *already close to mid-day.* A jumbled line of multiple tracks ran across the pond to the opposite shore; they were unusual tracks not made by regular footwear, leaving a channel more than a foot wide in the snow, the steps large and rounded like those of a giant troll; the natives of this land seemed to use a devise other than skies to move on top of snow — some sort of webbed frame judging by the traces of webbing that were faintly visible within the oval outlines. Intertwined with the webbed tracks and sometimes overlapping them, she discovered a single line of regular foot prints poking deep holes in the snow. She could almost feel Eidyll's exhaustion, staggering on through the deep snow without skies or other means to ease his progress.

They followed the tracks across flattened rushes to the other side and up on the bank and paused at the remnants of a fire, charred sticks and bones within a scattering of grouse feathers. From here the tracks wound their way onward between widely spaced knotty spruce trees toward a cedar grove.

Khagan halted at the foot of a lone old spruce to peer into the spreading branches above his head. Thora felt reluctant to follow his glance. Had Khagan found another bear part stuck up in a tree? Cautiously she looked up, relieved to find the dog was pointing to something harmless this time. Up there, underneath the fourth set of branches, sat a bundle of twigs bunched together; could it be one of those clusters of twigs which seemed to sprout naturally out of the inner branches of some spruce trees she had seen behind the lodge?

Thora took off her skies; she hauled herself up into the tree far enough to put her hand on the cluster; they were twigs alright, but they hadn't grown naturally - -somebody had put them there tied together with black twine, or was it? *Could it be horse hair?* But horse hair was coarser than this...and, what was that sitting on top of the twigs... feathers? She ran her fingers over the feathers, no, not just feathers – they were birdwings, two complete wings of a large bird....white, mottled with black, wings of a snowy owl tied on top of the twigs with some sort of black hair... human hair?

Thora tumbled down from the tree stifling a scream. She jerked Khagan away from the tree whispering, "Owl sorcery."

Her stomach tensed. Owl sorcery according to those in the know , was strong-powered magic. Was Eidyll taken by sorcerers?

She whirled around to hurry back home. Only a fool would get mixed up with black arts for no other reason than to recover a *thrall*, regardless of his many talents.

In sight of the lodge back on the icy path by the fjord, Thora spotted Groa jogging toward her. "Thoraaah, you're back! Thank to the lady Freya. Everyone else is gone...Ragnar and his nephews have gone into the woods after all and besides... this is women's work."

She gulped for air.

Thora Thorvinnsdottir, Halla needs your help with Achren. Her child is coming!"

Thora frowned.

"How can it be? It's not even close to her time!"

"Her birth pains have started I tell you, and she's in bad shape Halla says."

They found Achren in Halla's bed; the old woman ran off and on to gather up up pillows and blankets from assorted sleeping platforms to support the young woman in a half-seated birthing position.

"There you are!" Halla shook her mop of grizzled bond-woman hair cropped short.

"It shouldn't be happening now," she muttered. "It shouldn't be coming yet, not for quite some time. Her spasms are weak; we need your slender hands to go in there."

With Thora's help, Achren delivered her son at half term, a child the size of a dog whelp. Halla cradled him in her hand, a reddish chunk of flesh shaped like a dwarf child wrapped in wrinkles; they watched the tiny spark of his life flickering briefly, and fade away.

Thora took a deep breath. Achren seemed to have conceived almost as soon as the brown peaty substance ran out — an uneasy thought. *Could the herb have worked havoc with the girl's ability to carry her child to full term?*

True, the little boy's death put to rest her fear that Ivar might legitimize his first son, raise him up from base born to free born and arrange that the child of a *thrall* would some day be master of Sandurness. Still, it had been wrenching to watch the tiny infant squirming in Halla's calloused hand, and turning blue and lifeless in the next moment.

Achren searched the hall with a haunted look in her green eyes, just as Gunnhild had searched for her newborn daughter. When Unna eased little Halldis into her mother's arms, the haunted look in the mother's eyes was replaced with a tenderness that was painfull to remember, considering the way things had turned out with Gunnhild. And for Achren, there was no such comfort to be had at all.

Thora reached out to brush the sweat-soaked hair from the girl's forehead.

"Rest," she said, "Halla will take care of everything."

Furtively Halla slipped the dead infant slick as a snared rat, into Thora's hands. Thora turned away to spare Achren the unbearable sight. While the old woman busied herself with the exhausted young woman, Thora eased out the door; in passing she grabbed a shovel from under the roof edge. At the edge of the forest behind the lodge she chose a space between spruce roots and there, in a mossy hollow, she dug a tiny grave; she eased the dead infant into the hole and filled the dirt back in, placing some rocks on top and marking the tree with her knife in case Achren should ask for the place later.

Back in the lodge she rummaged in her pigskin pouch for what little she had left of the tea which Thjodhild had given her to stop Gunnhild's bleeding — barely enough for two ladles of brew. Halla went out to collect hemlock needles, returning with her apron full of brown dormant buds.

"These will do, although they're better in the spring when they're greening," said Thjodhild's knowledgeable old bond-woman.

"Still, these serve the purpose almost as well as the leaf tea, my lady used to say."

TWENTY SIX

The snow would never settle on that corner of Thorgrim's burial mound, and frost would never take hold there. People thought that Frey had so enjoyed the sacrifices Thorgrim made to him that he did not wish the ground between them to freeze.

GISLA SURSSON's SAGA

Two days after the stillbirth, Akka, out to fetch water, came rushing home at a fast shuffle without her water pails.

"They're back, our men are back and they're loaded with meat and fowl!

The women and men in the camp ran out to meet the returning hunters by the brook. The men were fording the stream in pairs carrying between them suspended from poles, rolls of uncured hide and choice chunks of reindeer meat. Some carried fat geese tied together by the necks. They dropped their loads at the lodge leaving it to the slaves to pluck the geese and take care of cleaning and curing the reindeer.

Thora took Ragnar aside.

"It would be best if you told them of my search for Eidyll and mentioned the owl sorcery I came across. Men will be sooner inclined to listen to you than to me; Ivar habitually mocks what I say; he suggests that I don't know the difference between the world we can see and touch, and the world where we dwell in our dreams and nightmares; still, I think Sigurd and Thrand will listen to you when you tell him what I found, and I hope they take measures to see to our safety."

Ivar heard Ragnar out, scoffing as expected at the suggestion of *skraelings* coming and going without being seen.

"How could anyone come close to our camp and not be noticed? Besides," he stressed, "we just returned from roaming the forest for nearly three days after a snowfall, and not once did we discover any men's tracks in the snow other than our own."

Thora, though loath to take issue with him in front of the others, said, "This land surely isn't without native people. Think of the men dressed in reindeer hides which we met by the lagoons. If men are able to live in such a place among stunted trees not fit for timber, why should we assume that this land here blessed with timber trees and berries and reindeer wouldn't be home to native people?"

"Not to mention," Ragnar added, "a butchered bear and powerful owl magic....these folks mean to tell us we're not welcome, and they have shown us their power by capturing one of us in clear daylight and taking him to their sorcerers' den."

The men looked uneasily at one another.

"Here's what we'll do," Sigurd said, rubbing his stubbly beard.

"We carry on doing the things we always do but we need to take more precautions. I suggest we double the night guards outside the lodge and assign men to take turns after dark spending the night in the ship-house."

Ivar shrugged. "I go along with that as long as we don't go chasing phantom sorcerers in these cursed woods for the trifling sake of recovering a *thrall*."

*　　*　　*　　*　　*

The frost deepened without let up and most people's energy and time was entirely spent in the rigorous grind of day to day survival. They were dismayed at the thickness of ice in the fjord, astounded how this could be in a place this far south where the sun never failed to climb above the horizon. In the short days around Yule tide, the air seemed to warm up some during daylight and on sunny days all who could, left the dank lodge and seated themselves against the sun-exposed wall of the *naust*. Still the nights remained frigid.

"This place methinks is as far south as Ireland or Frankland," Ragnar pondered, looking up from the mail shirt he was greasing with goose fat.

"It has to be, judging by the arc of Sol's sky road which leaves us plenty of daylight all winter, no less than in Frankland; friends of mine settled downriver from a Frankish town named Paris; there they boasted, the river never froze over and winter snowfall was rare though they had lots of rain they claimed. And yet, our winter here in this place has been much colder than in Frankland. or Ireland.

The creek was frozen solid and it took two *karls* armed with sturdy wood axes to open up water holes twice a day for the sake of people and livestock. Mord rested his axe and wiped his sweaty brow before enlarging the small hole he had just made in the ice. Thora waited patiently with the thirsty horse and the empty pail she had brought to carry water back to the house.

"Don't you think," Mord said, "there is something unusual going on with the sea here? Back home the water of Sognefjord seemed to stay much the same all year; it warmed only slightly in summer. The same goes for Ireland where I spent two summers and winters; we rarely saw any ice along the seashore. Here on the other hand, the water flowing in from the sea is quite sluggish, ready to freeze. And think of this — we sailed between ice bergs last spring not far from the strait Ivar named Straumfjord, only a few days sailing from here."

Thora nodded, casting a sullen glance at the freezing fjord. If things kept going this way, it would be a long time before spring break-up and the beginning of grazing season.

Spring did indeed come late, and the air was still cold during the night and early morning; yet, the ice melted faster than they expected, warmed by sunshine later in day.

"It seems after all that winter in Westland runs out of breath early enough," Ragnar reflected.

Soon the drifting ice was largely gone and the men took to the new rowboats they built during the winter to pursue spring runs of smelt and salmon. Most felt it was time to gather provisions, load up the timber and go home. The more talk there was of going home, the more Ivar grew moody and argumentative.

"We need to explore first what lies south of here," he said. "We might find better timber for shipbuilding in the South, tall and straight pine for a mast – and good oak perhaps for keel-wood."

Thora for once declared herself in agreement with her husband, though for reasons she kept to herself. She was in no hurry to return to here old life at Sandurness and she felt right at home here between the trees; besides, if they journeyed further into Westland instead of rushing home, she might find out what became of Eidyll.

His absence bothered her more than she liked to admit; others said they missed the cheerful tunes Eidyll used to play on his flute. Hroald, a Norwegian in Thrand's party, came forward one day, asking to borrow Eidyll's flute to try playing a tune he remembered.

Thora rummaged in Eidylls' sack with belongings without finding the flute. Eidyll, she remembered, often carried his flute inside his belt pouch and he must have had it with him on the day of his capture. She hoped it would have done him some good; maybe he had played for his captors and maybe because of it, they had spared his life.

"You'll have to craft your own flute," she told Hroald.

"Ask Halla to lay aside a suitable goose bone; we still have some geese left of the ones we smoked, and Halla intends to make a meal of them soon."

Thora lingered over Eidyll's wood carving tools to examine his chisels and draw knives; she had always wished to have her own set of high seat posts to adorn the homestead she hoped to build one day. Ulf and other settlers in Greenland had brought their high seat posts from Iceland, hoping to toss them overboard shortly before landfall and follow their lead; the posts would unfailingly wash ashore, the belief went, in a favourable location for settling. Thora smiled. *A likely location to find driftwood at least.* It turned out that Ulf nor anyone else had needed their posts to guide them to a new home, for all the land in Greenland was already claimed by Jarl Eirik, and he granted allotments to people in any way he chose.

Still, in this land so rich in nice, straight-grained timber, it would be worth her while if she crafted a set of dais posts to add colour and style to a hall of her own some day. Four auspicious posts holding good luck could increase her chances to acquire a farm of her own. In any case, few things felt better than working with wood, always warm and alive to the touch and full of surprises that could be revealed by skillful hands and a sharp chisel. Yes, she would try her hand at wood carving.

The grass had barely started to grow and there was little green to be seen among the brown sod. Still, Fluga grazed in the meadow all day long growing plump and adding sheen to her coat in places already shed out for winterhair. Seen head on, the mare presented an enlarged version of the barrel-bodied toy-horses Thora used to craft as a small child out of turf with twigs for legs. Fluga's approximate time to foal had come and passed. Would this foal never stop growing? It would be so good to have Eidyll around to share her concerns for the mare.

Thora had been sleeping poorly plagued by dreams of a monstrous foal whose dam, a straining mare made of turf, was unable to expel; eventually the poor mare disintegrated to a soft crumbly dust and the foal was able to break free at last; Thora woke up in a sweat. Had it been a mistake to drag herself and the horse to this land?

Filled with anxiety she visited the pasture at every opportunity, gloomily staring at the bulging horse and nursing resentment toward the gods who didn't seem to care. Other than a safe passage, she had received few favours so far in return for the pile of silver she had offered up to both Asa and Vana gods before leaving. These days, if anything, she was off worse than before, having lost her valuable slave of many skills — one of the few valuable possessions the Norns had allowed her to keep. And now, if Fluga's foaling didn't go well, she stood to lose her one remaining Hestardalur horse.

She tore herself away from the pasture and marched back to the house listing the valuables still in her possession and searching for some she could use to buy for her mare a divine favour or two. From the bottom of her chest she pulled out a rarely used bridle with silver clasps — a prize she and Fluga had won in a flying pace competition half a lifetime ago beating every other champion pacer in the district.

She buried the bridle beside a corner post in the horse pen and called for Freyja's blessing on behalf of the horse. For a goddess who catered to birthing women, it wouldn't be much of an effort to extend her favour to a foaling mare.

Thora was late getting up the next day; everyone else had gone outside except Halla who was boiling more tea. She handed Thora a mug of astringent brew made of the leathery fuzz-backed leaves she had the girls collect daily in a nearby tamarack bog. The old slave returned to the fire for more warm water leaving Thora to sip her tea.

"'t Is a good time to pamper yourself, young mistress," Halla said firmly, rubbing her watery eyes. "Time you had a leisurely wash now that we have plenty warm water."

Thora leaned back with a sigh of pleasure. On quiet mornings like this she loved to indulge in a thorough body wash, surrendering her curly hair to Halla's capable hands afterwards; she took her time for a thorough body wash and a rinse of her hair with foaming soapwort, followed by more luxurious warm water rinsing until there was no trace of foam left.

Halla took a towel to her wet hair, patting it nearly dry before combing it out with slow, meticulous care and taming it into four braids; she wound the finished braids around Thora's head, using silver pins to keep them in place. As a concession to her married state, Thora had agreed to wear a bright blue scarf wrapped around her head, folded to a band narrow enough to leave much of her hair exposed to the wind.

Arms crossed, Halla examined the result of her efforts. Thora slipped into the worn shepherd's clothing she resorted to once again for daily wear, so she could move freely in this land of trees where a woman's shift kept catching on branches and shrubs.

The old servant shook her head.

"Such a good looking young woman ... and such an unfortunate way of dressing...your husband could divorce you if he wanted; any husband could, on account of his wife's insistence that she wear men's trousers."

"Good," Thora said.

"I am of a mind myself," she went on, "to call for divorce on account of the insult my husband subjected me to in front of everyone in our household; remember the day he presented his bed woman with a bright blue cloak? I have no doubt everyone else remembers it too. Next, in front of all who journeyed with us in the ship, he chose to mock me in verse! If luck should bring us back safely to Greenland one day, I intend to call witnesses to the doorway of the house at Gronsetur, and declare my wish that I be released from my marriage."

Halla shook her head, muttering.

"The kind of memory you have, my young mistress…it tends to keep things alive for a very long time."

Fondly, Thora glanced at Thjodhild's old slave, bold enough to speak her mind, always busy with her hands and always cheerful – except that at times old Halla talked no sense at all.

"Stop frowning, you old hag," Thora grumbled.

"In this tree-blessed land no woman in her right mind goes about in a shift and kirtle down to her ankles. Any sensible woman should sit down at least and shorten her shift."

She gave Halla a mischievous grin.

"You would do yourself a favour, old woman, if you cut a wide hem off your shift so it reaches just to the knees; that way you keep the bothersome wadmal from snaring your ankles and legs!"

At the sight of Halla's shocked face, Thora burst into uproarious laughter.

She pulled the knot in her scarf flat against the side of her head and went outside, chuckling at Halla's tight-lipped look of disapproval.

Khagan came jogging across the muddy yard to meet her; he seemed in high spirits with a spring to his gait and a bouncy curl to his tail.

Why's he so excited?

Thora followed the tall white dog to the meadow, pleased to find the mare grazing peacefully beside the brook. She lingered for a while, never looking away from the dappled straw-coloured horse, so easy to overlook in the straw-coloured meadow; she raised her hand to shade her eyes;, since when did horses other than Odin's steed, Sleipnir, have more than four legs?

"Fluga!" she screamed. "You secretive witch... foaling all by yourself when nobody's around!"

She raced through the meadow; Fluga greeted her with throaty nickers, at once delighted and concerned, soft eyes gazing at the cream-coloured filly foal which staggered on oversized legs by her side.

Thora fell to her knees amidst the brown winter-grass. She reached out to the foal, waiting for it to take in her scent, whispering, "Fluga, you self-willed old mare... when nobody was watching ... like all of your clan at Hestardalur, independent, strong-minded mares who like to do things their own way."

Rocking back and forth on her heels she recalled the shapes, faces, colours and marks of dozens of mares related to Fluga – her dam, granddams and sisters – reveling in memories though not for long. She turned to the filly to examine her closely. Never again during the horse's lifetime would the placement of her bones be as visible as now right after birth. By tomorrow, after the filly had drunk her fill of the mare's milk during the night, her bones would already be slightly obscured, wrapped in a growing layer of muscle and fat.

Delighted, Thora found the newborn horse to be perfect in shape and proportions – short back, good length of neck, chiseled head with large eyes. Her limbs were straight with well defined tendons and prominent joints, aligned in the proper places to support the body like well-crafted corner posts holding up the high seat canopy of some wealthy *jarl*.

Thora smirked at the shiny white star plastered on the filly's fore-head — the mark of her sire. Though the star looked overly large for the foal's woolly forehead, her head would seem to grow faster than the white mark and in time, before her second winter, the star would seem pleasing and properly sized for the horse's face.

Thora waited till she was sure the foal was sucking well, smacking her lips and flicking her ears and stump of a tail right along with her sucks. Relieved, Thora went to search for the afterbirth, growing anxious again when she found no trace at all. She told herself there was no immediate cause for alarm since Fluga, like many mares, could have eaten it.

She followed Khagan to the edge of the woods, suspecting he had good reason to scamper toward a shady hollow; and there it was, a soiled patch of remnant snow and the dog licking the last patches of blood in the snow.

"You scavenger," Thora grumbled. "You could've waited for me to look at that first before you gobbled it all up."

Now she had no way of telling whether the mare had cleaned out completely.

Khagan, well pleased with himself, flashed his teeth in a grin.

Thora began to stroll home to the lodge, turning to take another look at the foal.

The tiny horse stood on top of a knoll, head high and ears pricked, watching her.

Like a falcon ready to take flight…or a winged horse gathering itself to leap in the air and soar away.

"Arvak, will be your name," Thora whispered. "Early Dawn, after one of the chariot horses which pull Sol's wagon across the daytime sky."

She pulled a silver hairpin from her braid and returned once again to the meadow retracing her steps to the place where she suspected the afterbirth had been. The dog followed eagerly, sniffing for overlooked scraps. Thora scratched the crumbly old snow aside, digging a mouse-sized hollow in the thawing earth underneath. She slipped the spiral-tipped hairpin into the hollow, filled in the dirt and patted it down; Freyja's divine powers proved to be undiminished in this foreign land. 't Was proper and wise to show gratitude for a wish fulfilled, and there could be no harm in asking that her good fortune continue.

She glanced at the sky overhead and lowered her gaze to the fjord's waters, placid on this windless morning — a giant silver mirror for the sky to admire itself.

"Accept this little piece of silver, Freyja, as token of my gratitude. And grant that the new filly named Arvak, grows to be strong, swift-footed and blessed with a falcon's keen eyesight. That she and her dam may prosper and live through many winters in good health and become the foundation of a new herd of Hestardalur horses someday, somewhere. Accept my silver, Freyja, and keep me and my horses in your favour."

TWENTY SEVEN

...from the cape they saw three hillocks on the beach. These it turned out were three hide-covered boats with three men asleep under each. They divided their forces and captured all of them except one, who escaped with his boat. They killed the other eight and went back to the cape.

GRAENLENDINGA SAGA

While sailing north along the shore, they came upon five men sleeping in skin sacks by the shore. They had boxes beside them filled with a blend of reindeer marrow and blood. Convinced they were outlaws they killed them.

EIRIK SAGA RAUDA

The salmon were running up the fjord in huge numbers; they crowded into the river and were met by men on the water with nets and gaffs pulling out fish after fish filling the rowboats they built during the winter. After each haul the women were overwhelmed by the numbers of fish to be cleaned and dried or smoked. Thora never let the girls out of her sight, making sure each did her share of the work. After some days of this, to the women's relief, the men exchanged nets for clubs one morning and set out to collect eggs and fowl instead. They were headed for a stretch of rocky shore and inshore islands where Mord had discovered nesting *geirfugl*, spearbills or oilbirds unable to fly, "more plentiful than all of the *geirfugl* at Akranes," he assured them which sent the others to collect their weapons and clubs in a hurry and crowd into the boats. Everyone knew of Akranes, a place famous in Iceland for its large flightless spearbills visited each spring by people who came to bludgeon them by the boatload for their excellent oil and resilient feathers which were sought after for blankets and pillows.

All men joined in the bird venture except for Thrand and another Norwegian who walked with a limp; the two of them decided to stay and guard the home site.

The slaves continued splitting and cleaning the last loads of salmon and putting them on drying racks set on a windy stretch of beach. Thora took her tools and the carving on which she was working – her first set of high seat posts commissioned by Sigurd — down to the beach and settled in a spot where she was able to keep sight of the fish racks. One-eyed Sigurd had asked her to carve him a set of dais posts from a straight-grained pine log he had set aside, and Thora welcomed the chance to develop her skills before she decided to carve her own posts some day.

The more skill the carver brings to a set of high seat posts, the stronger the magic that finds its way into them, according to accepted wisdom.

Thora rested her chisel and mallet to take a critical look at the spearbill she was trying to carve perched on top of the first post – the webbed feet didn't look right awkwardly cupped around the top of the post, and the whole bird appeared too angular. It needed softening with rounded curves to look convincing. Thora let out a sigh. Curves were the hardest thing to carve with Eidyll's tools. Designed for utility wood-working, Eidyll's straight chisels were poorly suited to shape curves and other intricate details of fine carving. She intended the post to have a slender, elegant look, right from the base all the way up along the sinuous coils of Nidhog — the great serpent of the Netherworld – and on to the spearbill perched on top, about to be caught in the serpent's fanged jaws. Sigurd had expressly demanded she carve a coiled serpent; the rest he had left up to her fancy.

From behind her back came the sound of Thrand's lisping voice.

"Some fine wood carving you're doing there, Thora Thorvinnsdottir."

He rubbed his fleshy hands together.

"The great serpent appears to be truly alive and exactly as he must be these days, having lived since the beginning of time....shabby, run-down, slow and stiff after spending uncounted winters in the Netherworld. Old Nidhog's showing his age, poor fella. Stiffening coils to a serpent must be like stiffening knees to the unlucky warrior who escaped death for too many years."

Thrand, burdened by a considerable paunch, showed surprising agility in avoiding the swipe Thora took at him with her mallet.

Cheeks aflush, she examined the bird and the serpent, chipping away a bit here and a bit there, wondering if there was enough wood left for the serpent to remain robust and convincing after she chipped away the awkward angles of its coils.

Down by the ship-house Thrand chanted a ditty he composed on the spot.

"When snakes stagger and spearbills are lean, men must don armour, make ready for battle, for Ragnarok is a-closing iiiin...tarara rara..., when snakes stagger and spearbills are lean...."

By mid-afternoon shouts from the fjord alerted those left in camp that the men had returned. One small boat lay beached and three more filled with shouting men were approaching the shore. Thrand and the other home guards rushed to the waterside. The slave women dropped their fish knives and ran after them.

Thora sighed and put her mallet down. All hands including her own would be needed to clean birds and render the blubber.

The day's bright sunshine aimed darts of light at her eyes. For those used to the late spring and hesitant summer in Greenland and Iceland, Westland's balmy spring air felt like high summer. She raised her hand to shade her eyes. Down by the beach the commotion continued, growing louder.

Thora placed her chisel on top of the mallet to protect the freshly honed edge and walked down to the water.

A throng of men and women jostling and jeering surrounded the first boat set down on the beach. Thora pushed through the crowd, amazed to see Gorm and Grim headed for the ship-house and between them, a half-naked captive barely able to walk. The man collapsed at every other step, and his captors jerked him up by the arms to force him ahead.

Ivar, his arms full of fur cloaks, brought up the rear wearing a wolfish grin.

The men halted at the ship-house with others around them talking and shouting until Thrand arrived raising his hand to command silence; he turned to Ivar.

"Where did you find the *skraeling?* Are there any more?"

Ivar pointed in the direction of the headland north of the fjord.

"We found a whole bunch of 'em digging for clams in the tidal flats... away from the beach where they'd left their boats – all of them fashioned from bark. They hurled stones at us and ran for their weapons which they had, foolishly, left behind on the beach by their boats."

"Hah! But we were too quick for them," Sigurd said, scratching his empty eye-socket.

"We cut them off and slayed all except for this one. He did get into a boat and pushed off, but he couldn't wield his oar too well because of a sword cut to his arm. Gorm swam after him, capsized the craft and captured the wretch."

Ivar reached out with his knife to cut a double string of green-blue stone beads and pearly shell disks from the Westlander's neck.

"These don't look at all good on a *skraeling!*"

He fingered the greenish blue stones.

"I told you we'd find treasure in this land. We'll have the wretch tell us where we can find more like these."

The captured young man glowered at him with eyes squeezed to slits, black and glittering like shards of obsidian.

Ivar pointed a mud-covered boot at him.

"We'll leave it to my wife to look after those cuts. See if he couldn't live long enough to tell us what we need to know."

He ran the necklace lovingly through his fingers.

"In Kaupang I saw people trading such stones brought in from Sweden the Cold; the merchants of the town rated them highly."

Ragnar rubbed the blunt tips of his fingers across the smooth, polished surface of the blue beads.

"I have seen these same stones," he said, "traded in far away lands and in the markets of Miklagard. The fine ladies of the court value them for earrings and for necklaces, strung together with blue lapis and blood-red coral."

"These wretched clam diggers seem to be rich in furs," Auzur said with a grin, holding up a short cloak of red fox fur.

Ragnar shook his head slowly.

"Funny thing, that. They're not fond of clothing it seems, but they appear to value good furs."

Thora reminded the others, "We shouldn't lose any more time moving the captive to the shelter of the ship-house and attend to his wounds."

She sent two girls back to the house for warm water and scraps of discarded cloth which she kept washed and rolled in her chest to be used for bandages.

"And tell Halla to come down here too."

On her knees beside the injured stranger, she took her time to examine the barefoot captive. A breechcloth of honey-brown hide was his only clothing. He wore armrings of hammered copper just above the elbows and strips of marten fur tied snugly around his wrists. His earlobes held pendants of blue feathers and bleached bone whittled to spirals. Around his legs below the knee he wore multiple strings of little white shells and dangling puffin beaks, red and yellow, which rattled when he stirred.

Gorm stood behind her muttering, "The wretch had a long fur robe in his boat when I capsized it; the robe floated briefly and then it sank, but the water was shallow and I meant to claim the robe for my own after I finished dealing with the *skraeling* — had Ivar not beaten me to it."

A number of men pranced about in fur robes discarded by the clam diggers; others showed off cloaks of feathered goose and swan skins.

Ivar displayed his booty, three feather cloaks besides the prize robe of black-brown lustrous fur that had belonged to the captive.

Ragnar ran his hand over it, shiny and smooth as marten fur.

"Fisher, I reckon — a kind of marten," he explained to some questioning faces from Iceland. "Fishers are larger than a marten and their fur is more valuable still...where I grew up, we used to trap for them in the mountains."

Ragnar handed the spear around which he had found on the beach; afterwards he ran his thumb over the glassy stone point, holding it out for all to see.

"The point's made of chert I believe, a glass-like stone that cuts well, like flint. See how well-crafted it is, shaped with skill and polished to perfection? Their bark boats were loaded with piles of chert, rough-cut chunks, each wrapped in a piece of skin and stored between bark sheets and mats woven of rushes."

He ran his thumb again across the keen edge.

"Looks to me they returned from a journey to mine or trade for the stone — they seem to use it for weapons and tools...they also had tools made of antler and shells, and chisels of beaver teeth. There was nothing made of iron — perhaps they don't know iron working."

The girls returned from the house with pails of warm water and strips of cloth. Behind them limped Halla leaning on her stick.

Thora pointed to the wounded captive.

"Halla, this man needs your help."

"Ohoh, no, young mistress, don't ask me that!"

The old woman appeared horrified, scarcely daring to look at the wounded man.

"Please, do not demand of me that I put my hands on a troll. You know perfectly well yourself, Thora Thorvinnsdottir, how to treat wounds. My old mistress taught you — I was there. Now I am here to give you advice if you need it; but I beg you, don't ask me to touch this abomination."

"Foolish woman," Thora scolded. "Don't you see? He's no troll; he's an ordinary man who looks different from us, that's all."

Thora looked at him more closely; after a long silence she muttered, "Rather good looking too I think underneath the blood and grime."

She bent over to pat the man's hairless chin and cheek.

"Just a man, Halla, a man without a beard, see?"

Halla kept two horse lengths away; Thora shrugged with resignation, kneeling to wash the blood and dirt from the *skraeling's* face and limbs. An axe had grazed his skull leaving an oozing wound behind the ear and both of his arms had received sword cuts. He also had deep, ragged cuts in his left leg both below and above the knee.

Thora cleaned the wounds as gently as she could, glancing occasionally at the unresponsive face of the man who kept his eyes firmly shut.

She straightened up to stretch her back, intrigued by the *skraeling's* flamboyant hair style – a single lock of coarse black hair, shiny with grease and weighted with copper beads rested on his forehead; the rest of his dripping shoulder length hair was gathered at the neck and twisted to a knot which held a pair of sky-blue feathers.

Thora took the wash cloth and began to clean blood from his left thigh and lower leg exposing three deep cuts, one above and two below the knee.

"Here the flesh will need to be stitched back together...Halla, you know how to do that I believe."

The old slave nodded without as much as a glance for the *skraeling*. With a dramatic sigh she untied the cord of her medicine bag and lowered herself stiffly to the ground. She pulled apart the edges of the cuts in the shin below the knee, deeper and more severe than the slash across the thigh muscle. Thora glimpsed something shiny and white deep down in one of the shin wounds.

She whispered, "Is that what I think it is, exposed bone?"

Halla shook her head.

"It's only the sheath protecting the bone. The cut will heal in time... if he's allowed to live that long."

She rummaged through her bag, unable to find what she needed.

"I need to visit the bog on the other side of the little hill to gather fresh bog moss," the old woman said. "It'll take care of the bleeding."

"I'll send one of the girls," Thora said.

Halla snorted, shaking her head emphatically.

"They'll come back with any old moss. It needs to be fresh and light-green to be any good."

"I can find it," Thora said. "I'll go myself; that's better than you spraining an ankle up there."

"No," Halla shouted. "I beg you! Do not make me stay here alone with that...with this...*skraeling!*"

She spit out the words and struggled to her feet.

"I may be old but I can still take care of myself, and I have my walking stick for support."

Left alone with the wounded stranger, Thora sat back on her heels; the shin wound looked clean enough – better not to touch it now. She remembered Thjodhild's words. *Never wash a wound that isn't soiled.*

It took a while for Halla to return with a basket full of the feathery moss growing profusely in the black spruce bog nearby.

"This," Halla said, "will prevent further bleeding and speed up the healing."

She took a fistful of moss, put the thick, springy wad on the wound and held it in place with a bandage. She did the same with the other leg wounds and the cuts on on the man's arms, using the last scrap of cloth to bandage his bleeding head. Thora tightened the knots some more causing the captive to grimace. He opened his eyes and fixed his gaze on her, muttering something incomprehensible. Was it a curse, or a thank you?

"Nothing more I can do," Halla said looking relieved. "I take my leave."

She limped back to the house twice as fast as she had come.

Thora surveyed the result of their combined efforts; her gaze wandered from the Westlander's bandaged head to his strong shoulders, spare torso and lean limbs, sinewy like the legs of a well-bred horse. Perhaps she could persuade Gorm to let his captive live and trade him to her in return for something he liked her to carve for him out of wood — anything he fancied as long as it could be shaped without too much effort using Eidyll's straight chisels.

She looked again at the *skraeling's* muscular shoulders, arms and legs —the makings of a strong *thrall*. He might make a decent replacement for Eidyll.

Once again she ran her fingers over his chin — no trace of a beard, smooth-faced like the reindeer men they ran into last summer. Could it be that Westlander men were unable to grow beards? Or did they remove facial hair as soon as it appeared? Absent-mindedly, she ran her fingertips again over his cheeks when, of a sudden, strong fingers dug into ther shoulders and she was jerked to her feet.

"So!" Ivar snarled. "This is how my wife tends to the wretched captive...administering tender caresses!"

Thora, eyes ablaze, spun around to break free.

"I'm trying to learn more about this man and his kind," she hissed. "It was you who ordered me to take care of him, remember!"

Ivar growled, "Halla can take care of the wretch as long as we need him alive. You will no longer lay hands on him."

Thora, boiling with anger, succeeded in holding her tongue; she watched Ivar marching off to join the others on the sunny side of the lodge before she turned back to the *skraeling*, a man unlike any other she ever set eyes on; a smile crept across her face; those clean features not obscured by any facial hair were strangely pleasing she found, and those glittering eyes filled with mystery prompted her to find out what might lay hidden in there.

She went to Ragnar who sat with his nephews inside the *naust* cleaning filth and dried blood from swords and poniards.

"Tell me again, my far roaming friend," Thora asked, "what did they look like, those emissaries of the horse khans you spoke of? Were all of them beardless like our captive and the reindeer men we met earlier?"

The old warrior nodded.

"It is common for a good many men living east of Sweden the Cold to shave the face, and sometimes the head too."

"And did you see any men wearing feathers in their hair and earlobes in the way of these Westlanders?"

"No," Ragnar said. "The men of the eastern tribes are much like us; they wear feathers in their hats but not in their ears. I recall visiting horse khans and their retainers splendidly dressed in colourful woolens or silks; some of them wear fur-lined cloaks, but always, as I said before, on top of woven clothing."

"They can't be the same people then," Thora concluded.

"No," said Ragnar. "And they couldn't be, we agreed, because we've sailed steadily westward and could never come face to face with men from the eastern plains."

After the evening meal everyone gathered by the empty ship-house preparing to play dice by the light of a lamp freshly filled with oil; the evening was warm enough for mosquitoes to linger, and Thora told Groa to fetch another lamp and set it to burn away from people to reduce the winged nuisance.

Ivar tapped the hilt of his sword for silence.

"Sigurd and I have made our summer sailing plans," he said. "We are each determined to take a different course, and you men need to make up your mind which course you wish to go and whom you wish to join. I and most of my crew are decided to go exploring some more, and we invite some of you shipwrights to stay on and help us to build the new ship. Sigurd will now tell you his plans."

Sigurd took his time scratching his scraggly silver-streaked beard and darting his one-eyed glance around the half circle.

"We," the Icelander said at last, "that is, myself and Thrand, intend to load our timber and set out for home without further delay; myself and most of my crew need to make our way home to Iceland after a short stay at Eiriksfjord where we hope to exchange some of our timber for Greenland goods; our Norwegian friends have an even longer journey sailing home after re-fitting Thrand's ship which was left in Iceland.

None of our men care to spend another winter away from home and family."

"Although," a Norwegian woodworker said, "some of us might change our minds about that. Let's first hear what Ivar and his Greenlanders hope to achieve by staying here longer."

"It's all the same to me," said Ivar. "Little do I care who'll come with us, and who decides to sail back home. We, Greenlanders, are in no mind to leave this land in a hurry without further exploring. We mean to sail south to find treasure other than timber. Most of us from Greenland are young, without a farm of our own, and we stand to gain little from rushing home instead of searching for goods more valuable than timber... things which are easily carried, like furs and ivory, and precious stones. We also need time to cut more timber and build us another ship to fill with the treasures we hope to find...as well as some slaves perhaps."

Gorm kept staring at Ivar's shiny fur cloak.

"I would consider voyaging south with Ivar," he said. "First though, I wish to know how far his party of Greenlanders intends to go, and what makes him think we'll find treasure down there."

Ivar ran his hand over the smooth fisher fur hugging his shoulders.

"I suspect," he said, "there are more of these precious furs to be found in our captive's homeland, and more blue stones as well."

He reached up to finger the blue necklace which Achren had re-strung and attached to his neck-torque of twisted silver.

"We must get the captive to point out the way to his homeland."

After much talk back and forth, more than a dozen men, Greenlanders, a handful of Icelanders, and even a few from Norway including Ragnar and his nephews, agreed to stay on for part of the summer to go roaming with Ivar. The others decided to go home with Thrand and Sigurd aboard Aegir's Pride.

Ragnar paid Ivar a silver armring to allow Groa — Ragnar's bed-woman through the winter — to sail with Sigurd as far as Sandurness; Groa was now with child and begged to be sent home where, she said, she might call on Thjodhild's assistance with the delivery.

Ivar decided to send Achren home also; she had remained sickly and taciturn after her stillbirth ordeal. He traded some of his share in the timber with Sigurd in return for Mari, the youngest of Sigurd's Icelandic bond-women; Thora smirked after taking a close look at Mari; yes, she did have speckled green eyes similar to Achren's, though not as insolent.

"Good to hear you and your nephews are staying with us for the summer," Thora said to Ragnar.

"I'm a man of action," Ragnar said, "and no longer young. Once a man my age decides to go home, he might never go roaming again; chances are he'll die in bed of old age, and there's no honour in that!"

TWENTY EIGHT

*A shadow fell across the doorway and a woman entered, short
in stature and wearing a close-fitting tunic. She had a scarf
over her head and light red-brown hair. She was pale and had
eyes larger than anyone ever had seen in a human head.*

She came to where Gudrid was sitting and said: what is your name?"
"My name is Gudrid. What is yours?"
"My name is Gudrid," the woman said.

GRAENLENDINGA SAGA

The lodge and the home site, bustling with life all through the winter and spring, seemed no longer a place to call home after Sigurd and his crew sailed away. People began to mope about, and Ivar tried to restore their spirits by discussing his plans to find fortune.

"We ought to find out where our captive came from; I suspect the place is worth raiding for booty and slaves. We'll get the wretch to draw us a map in the sand to show where his homeland is."

Ivar's *karls* were ready to take the injured man from the *naust* down to a sandy patch of beach, when Thora objected.

"Moving him could open his wounds again."

Ragnar suggested they bring sand up to the ship-house instead.

"Carry up sand and dump it between those logs, enough for him to draw on."

Ivar took a stick and drew a cross in the sand aligning the cross to point north, south, east and west. Next to it he sketched the lodge facing northwest, and below it the *naust* and the outline of the fjord running down to the sea with the coast running north-south past headlands and reefs all the way up to the cape.

"That's where we found the clam-diggers."

For good measure he added some fishes drawn where the sea was supposed to be.

The surly-faced captive watched from half-closed eyes.

"Now," said Ivar, poking his own breast with the stick.

"Ivar, Ivar Ulfson."

He raised his eyebrows and pointed to the captive who ignored him. Ivar repeated his unspoken question gazing intently at the surly Westlander, as if by a sheer act of will he could force him to respond.

The man opened his eyes wide, returning Ivar's stare with one of his own, dark and unreadable.

Ivar exploded with anger; he spit in the other's face.

"Son of a troll," he growled, "sucker of a she-wolf's teats! You understand me well enough."

He whipped out his knife and kneeled, grabbed the man's left ear and pressed the knife point behind it firmly, drawing blood.

"Your name, and quickly," he demanded, "or I slice off one ear and the other one next."

Thora cringed. How could gentle Gunnhild have birthed a boy who grew into a man so ready and eager to inflict pain on others?

Gorm grabbed Ivar's arm to re-claim his prize captive.

"Let me remind you, Ivar Ulfson, this *skraeling* is my captive and not to be damaged. If you lop off his ears you'll have to pay me compensation."

Thora sat staring at the captive whose gaze hadn't wavered. She raised her hand.

"Let me try to gain his trust."

Ivar wheeled around, eyes dark with anger.

You'll want him to keep both his ears so he can hear your sweet whisperings...changing bandages...hah! I saw the way you were carrying on with your hands all over the wretch!"

Ragnar stepped forward.

"It'll be for the good of us all, Ivar Ulfson, if you allow your wife to try her luck with the *skraeling*. He might confide more easily in the woman who dressed his wounds."

Ivar's eyes narrowed; he sat silently brooding before he took a deep breath and let go of the man's ear; he stood up, fingers playing with the hilt of his sword, stretching tall to face Ragnar.

The old Viking, his own sword partly drawn out, gave Ivar a casual glance.

"Not to worry, lad. The wretched *skraeling* will not, 's long as I'm around, take advantage of any woman, free or slave."

He ran a finger along Bone Cleaver's blade as if searching for blemishes.

Ivar frowned. Once more he tapped the hilt of his sword before he moved his hand away and stomped off after landing another glob of spit on the captive's face.

Thora traced the stick through the sand drawing lines and squiggles without meaning, trying to make up her mind. Did she want to do Ivar's bidding? What if she found out where the *skraeling* came from, where his people lived and where they might find more of those precious blue stones? It would trigger a raid bringing death and disaster to his unsuspecting people.

She sat up straight, dropping the stick.

And what of it? Wasn't raiding a part of life as inescapable as winter? How many men restricted themselves to trading only, to further their fortune and that of their families? Most men, eager for quick gains, would not pass up a chance to venture out on a raid. *Skraelings* were likely doing the same, trading for glassy tool-stone one day and raiding for slaves and valuables the next. This man's party journeyed along the coast in small swift vessels suited for harassing, and they carried plenty of arms to carry out raids.

Lost in thought, Thora played with a lock of hair escaped from her scarf; Thorvinn used to go off every summer harassing in distant lands — a source of pride to his wife and daughter who, after his safe return, would proudly bask in the glory of his adventures.

And Ragnar? He too had spent much of his life away from home in pursuit of fortune; he too was proud of his deeds and respected because of them. Why then would the thought of Ivar wishing to set out on a similar venture in Westland fill her with loathing? Could resentment be clouding her judgment? Why else would the thought of Ivar and his men ransacking a *skraeling* settlement somewhere, seem suddenly wrong to her?

Then again, she had never known any of the people raided by her father and his friends, nor set eyes on the injuries brought by their swords and axes to the flesh of men, women, and children. Now, after looking into the eyes of Gorm's injured captive, she dreaded to think of what her companions would do to him and his people if found.

In the back of her mind lingered Ivar's accusations. *Ridiculous.* Had she not tended the captive's wounds because Ivar told her to? She would gladly have returned to her wood carving, had he assigned someone else to care for the *skraeling.*

After a long session with the captive, Thora learned that his name was "Elkimu."

In return she tried to teach him to say hers, in a fashion.

"Thola," was all he could make of it.

The way he said it shaping the unusual sounds with visible effort, made her smile. Then again, the way she said his name might be just as awkward, although the man kept a straight face when she tried.

After a rest the men began to prepare Maelstrom Tamer for the summer's journey, and Thora returned to the *skraeling*. Ivar's sketch of the coast was still in the sand. Thora picked up the stick and pointed to the place near the cape where the skirmish with the clam diggers took place.

"Elkimu," she stressed, tapping the spot and keeping an eye on his face. He seemed to be watching and listening.

Thora raised the stick and described a wide arc.

"Elkimu?"

The lines around his mouth softened a little. *The face of a beardless man is easily read.*

He reached out for the stick, planted the point firmly on the beach where he was captured, tapped his chest and stressed, "Elkimu." Next he whipped the stick back to the place where Ivar had drawn the lodge.

"Thola!" he said.

She nodded, holding his gaze.

He circled the stick in the air, asking, "Thola?"

She took her turn walking the stick to the north drawing the strait of Straumfjord, through which they had sailed, moved the stick out of the strait up north along the coast where they met the reindeer men. Next, she moved out east, paused to draw more fishes – more sea — before walking the stick out of the sandbox east-northeast across the sea, indicating with sweeping arm gestures that they had come a great distance.

"Thora," she repeated drawing an imaginary line in the dirt beyond the sandbox to indicate a shoreline and pointing to the grass beyond to indicate land.

Elkimu shook his head, eyebrows raised. *Not possible!*

Thora shrugged. She pointed again to the clam-digging spot and to him, circled the stick in the air and raised her eyebrows in a question. *Where is your home?*

He took the stick from her and walked the point southwest across the sea, sketching little fish shapes on the way. At the southwestern edge of the sandbox he sketched the crude outline of what looked like a peninsula but turned out to be an island separated by a narrow channel from a mainland to the South. He moved the stick back to the island and planted it in the middle.

"Elkimu," he said with a wistful smile.

Thora jumped to her feet. Could it be true? Was he a native of this land no more than she or any other Norse? It appeared that Elkimu and his companions had come from somewhere else overseas — to do what, to trade or raid, or fish? How many days sailing would it take to reach his homeland to the West? Should she tell Ivar? If she told him, Ivar was likely to change his mind about sailing south, choosing to go west first and raid Elkimu's homeland.

And, would that be so bad? Like all of the others, she had decided to come on this venture hoping to find fortune and claim her share of what they found. She had also hopes the journey would offer her chances to free herself from Ivar and enable her to return to Iceland with enough wealth to buy her own farm. That way she could marry a man of her own choice, a man to her liking whom she wished to father her children; and nothing short of owning a farm and a thriving horse herd could fulfill that dream.

And remember, a shipload of timber isn't enough to make us all wealthy. Ivar was right claiming they would need to bring home more valuable things than timber; they would need to find slaves, precious stones and furs to make a fortune for everyone; if they failed, she, more than anyone else, would find herself going home defeated with little choice left than to live out her life at Sandurness as Ivar's wife, taking orders from the sisters who with Ulf's blessing were running the household.

Thora dropped the stick and jumped to her feet, determined to tell the others what she had learned from the *skraeling*.

TWENTY NINE

_____

_____

He asked her to show the woman respect and said he wanted her
to live with them in their home. Jorunn replied, I've no intention
of wrangling with some slave-woman you have brought home...

LAXDAELA SAGA

I am Njal's wife, she said, and I have as
much to say to our housefolk as he.

NJAL'S SAGA

_____

_____

The thought of yet another land to the West, new and unknown, caused a stir among the fortune seekers; only Ivar expressed doubt.

"A woman's sweet whisperings do not induce men to speak the truth. It is pain, suffering and the fear of more suffering which causes men to reveal secrets. Why would we cross another unknown sea to chase after smoke when we're just as likely to find fortune going south along this coast which has sheltered us all winter? The living is easier in southern lands and the people tend to be numerous and wealthy, rewarding to raid. Besides, if we go south we needn't hold on to the *skraeling*; it's high time we disposed of him."

Thora was no longer in doubt which course to support, now that Elkimu's life was at stake; she raised her hand to speak.

"I was asked," she said, "to find out from the captive where he came from, and I think he told me the truth; he came across the sea from a land to the West, not all that far away."

Ivar scoffed. "The beardless misfit tries to mislead by pointing us to nowhere."

Ragnar spoke up.

"I suggest we decide on a compromise; we sail westward for two days, no more. If by then we haven't found land that looks promising, we turn around and sail south. Let's have a show of hands."

"That way we have little to loose it would seem," Atli said raising a hand.

One or two others followed, and all at once many more hands went up; Ivar shrugged.

"If that's what y'all want...alright, two days it is, not a day more."

No man it turned out was prepared to stay behind and guard the house and the stacked timber, and so they entrusted the lodge to the care of the two old slaves, Akka and Halla. Mari, Ivar's new bedwoman, also begged to stay ashore to be spared another sea journey.

"I've been unwell lately and I fear the dreaded sea sickness will kill me."

She glanced at Ivar, a slight smile on her face.

"There could be a special reason I've been feeling unwell."

Ivar seemed undecided.

"Three women together without men to see they keep peace between themselves," he said, "will end in disaster. Who's to keep them from squabbling, or running away? I gave up a good deal of timber in exchange for Mari."

Mord burst out laughing.

"Why would they leave this place, with nowhere to go? The land's the same everywhere, water and trees, more water, more trees."

"We'll take the oars away," Auzur said. "That way, they can't go far in the boats; I say, let Mari stay here... by Thor's beard we don't want a sea-sick woman retching aboard ship."

Thora kept her thoughts to herself. *As if it makes any difference to take the oars away.* Nothing could be easier than using the firewood tools to fashion crude oars. Still, as Mord pointed out, where would they go?

All agreed to the suggested compromise and they gathered at the ship-house converted to summer kitchen to enjoy a hearty reindeer stew, the last cooked meal they were likely to have for a while.

Ivar wiped his lips; he took a long draft of water and slammed his wooden mug on the ground.

"There's something useful these women can do during our absence," he said.

"When we're ready to fill our ship with valuable cargo for the home run, we can't afford horses taking up cargo space...we had better be sure to leave the women an axe large enough for knocking down a horse. While we're away they'll have time to butcher both horses and put the cuts in the smokehouse to add to our food supply on the home voyage."

Everyone stopped eating and all stared at the skipper's wife.

Thora spooned up another mouthful of soup before resting her spoon.

"The horses," she said looking around, "go where I go. I don't intend to leave them here with the slaves and I don't see why they couldn't sail west on the ship with us."

Ivar, eyebrows raised, looked around the circle.

"My clever wife has lost her reason! We all know it is foolish to bring horses on a sea-roving venture. It's established practice for raiding men to gather up local nags at landfall and use them to quickly ride in, and quickly pack out the booty."

Thora gave him a wan smile. "Methinks, husband, you won't find any horses in this land to use for a quick raid."

She raised her chin. "And besides, and I said this before, these horses are mine and not yours to do with as you please."

"And Maelstrom Tamer is my ship," Ivar stated; he looked around the circle daring anyone to disagree.

"Wrong again," Thora said in an even voice. "You are commanding the ship, Maelstrom Tamer, but it is your father who owns her. The ship will not be yours until Ulf is dead and buried, and then, as your wife, I will own one half of our property including the *knorr*. Have your forgotten the conditions Jarl Eirik stated at our marriage? As husband and wife we each share equally in common property unless exempted as personal possessions at the time of our marriage; both of us claimed only our weapons, horses and slaves as I remember, and there are witnesses to that."

She met his eyes without blinking.

"As for slaves," she continued, "those not exempted at the time of our marriage became our shared property and the same goes for those acquired during our marriage; therefore, any slave you care to use as your bedwoman, is my property as much as yours."

Thora took a deep breath.

"If you wish to keep your sleeping arrangements without my objection, then you shouldn't interfere with my horses. You need my help to ask the captive for directions and I'm willing to come along on tomorrow's venture. I do not trust the care of my horses to a pair of old women and one sickly girl, none of them able to provide proper horse care; the mare and the filly are coming on the ship with us, if I am to go, and you will need me to engage with the captive."

Warned by the flicker in Ivar's eyes, she ducked in time to escape the blow.

On a signal from Ragnar, Mord and Auzur grabbed Ivar by the shoulders and held him in place long enough to regain his composure; he sat down, surrounded by silence.

Ragnar said, "Methinks the proper place for berserkers is on the battle field."

Early next morning they made ready to depart. Here and there men were grumbling over the skipper's wife sailing with them on a raiding venture.

"Never mind her ability to deal with the *skraeling*. Everyone knows women bring bad luck to a ship, especially on a sea-roving journey."

Others objected to taking the captive Westlander onboard. Gorm, trying to march the limping *skraeling* to the ship, was mobbed by half a dozen men pushing and shouting.

"The clam-eater will lead us to our doom," howled the Icelander, Hrut.

"The wretch will find a way to warn his friends and lure us to our death," whined young Odi from Greenland.

"Whether or not he deceives us," stated quick-minded Atli, "now is the time to do away with the wretch before he brings us misfortune."

Ivar stalked from the ship-house toward the commotion. He raised his hand.

"I feel the same way you do about Gorm's captive," he declared, "and about my wife coming with us. However, since you all insisted to go raiding the *skraeling's* homeland for slaves and treasure, he needs to come with us as a guide, and so must my wife like it or not. Our little venture would be pointless without proper sailing directions...and it's up to my clever wife to see that the wretch doesn't deceive us. Besides, we could use him as a hostage in case we find his kin and it turns out that we're badly outnumbered. To save his skin he'll try talking sense into them and convince them to give us what we come for."

"Talk to his fellow *skraelings?*" Skeggi shouted. "Precisely what we're afraid of! Who can tell what he'll say? And why should we put trust into anyone's words, least of all those of a double-tongued captive? Let's rely on our axes and swords to do the talking I say."

Ivar cautioned, "'t all depends on how many we find ourselves up against."

"We don't even know where to find what we're looking for," Ragnar Bearbladder reminded everyone. I suggest we keep the *skraeling* at hand and watch him closely for signs that we're in proximity of his home and people."

"My guess," said Skeggi, "is that he'll lead us astray on a merry chase right from the outset."

Ivar shrugged. "We'll give it a try for two days as I said, and no more."

*   *   *   *   *

The captive directed them southwest into open sea. They sailed all day with no land in sight, though birds were flying everywhere — land couldn't be far away.

The men took turns glaring at the captive slumped against the side of the ship; now and again, someone reached out to tighten the lashings which strapped his wrists to an oar hole.

Ivar sat at the steering oar with a grin on his face, tossing his wind-blown mane.

"We'll find out soon enough if the misfit leads us astray," he declared. "In another day we agreed to turn around and head south and I look forward to making the vermin pay for the time we lost on his account."

The weather turned dark and unsettled. The sea ran ever higher building into erratic, heaving swells which had an uncanny way of battering down on the ship when she was least ready, sliding into the depth of a watery trough. People, horses, even the dog were tossed about and Thora felt seasick for the first time in her life.

During the night the wind increased to a storm. Ivar ordered the oars manned and the sail reefed to the smallest strip needed to steady and steer the *knorr*. Maelstrom Tamer seemed a mere play-thing for the thrashing snake, Midgard Orm, or its local equivalent knocking the ship about. Massive waves stacked up to looming towers of water, each one capable of swamping the *knorr* should it crash down full force on the ship.

All through the night the oarsmen struggled to keep the ship upright and facing the waves while others, on their knees with buckets and scoops, bailed all they could. Everyone knew that the ageing *knorr*'s battered hull couldn't hold out much longer against the onslaught.

A grey morning broke, and still the storm showed no sign of mellowing. Atli, in a fit of nervous laughter, suggested they take out wagers on the outcome; the others gave him cold stares and he fell silent. First one, then a second oarsman ceased to row, slumped over with exhaustion and compelling the others to increase their efforts. Ivar, straining to control the steering board, was forced to call rowers back to the oars before they had a chance to regain their breath. Over the roar of the tempest came a cry from Gorm, the lookout, lodged in the bow on hands and knees. He pointed across the turbulence.

"Land ahead, beware, sandbank to starboard!"

Thora crawled to the horses and cut the ropes tying them to the picket line. Ivar convulsed into action; he clung with all his might to the steering oar, barking at the oarsmen and attempting to pull the *knorr* about before she hit the shallows. Ragnar jumped to his aid — too late. Maelstrom Tamer bumped to a creaking, grinding halt on the sandbank.

The sudden jolt nearly capsized the ship sending people and animals scrambling. Another jolt brought men and beasts to their knees. The ship groaned and rocked under the might of the waves, each next one working her deeper into the sand. Suddenly, hammered by pounding breakers, the *knorr* keeled over to starboard and men, woman and beasts became a wave of thrashing limbs spilling into the salty cauldron.

Thora grabbed hold of Fluga's tail before the breaking surf pushed her underwater. She held on grimly, loosing all sense of up or down, trusting in the horse to drag her ashore. The water grew shallow, and sooner than expected she found her feet. All around her others were staggering to their feet on the sandbank, destructive and life saving at once. On the other side of the bank the sandy bottom descended abruptly into a deep channel separating them from the beach. Men battled their way to shore tripping and floundering after they fought their way across the channel too deep even for horses to make it through without swimming.

Thora collapsed on the beach at the waterline among others sprawled on wet sand, ridges of washed up seaweed and wads of quivering foam.

She opened her eyes, flinching under the evil-eyed stares of gulls gliding just overhead on wings tilting slightly this way and that to adjust to wind gusts. She raised her head and stared at the beaked faces, yellow eyes scanning the prone shapes of the shipwrecked. The birds uttered scornful calls and moved on as soon as they saw someone stirring,

One by one, they found the strength to get up from the beach and search for others; everyone it turned out had made it to shore alive though not without injuries.

Thora examined the mare and foal; both horses and even the water-wary Khazar dog had reached the shore uninjured not counting scratches and minor scrapes.

Ivar, pale-faced and tight-jawed, sat in the sand holding his left arm, frowning at the broken bones piercing the skin.

Ragnar raised himself to his knees and crawled over to Ivar, abruptly forcing the ragged-edged bones back into place with a single firm pull.

Thora took the small axe from her belt and began splitting driftwood. She handed Ragnar a few pieces for splints and stacked the others into a pile, enough to build a small cook fire.

Many men had bleeding wounds; Thora took out her knife, cut the hem off her tunic and tore the cloth into strips for bandages handing a few to Gorm to replace the bandages lost in the ordeal by his wounded captive. She offered to bandage a gash in Ragnar's left arm but he waved her away.

"First things first."

He walked to the waterline and called the others together.

"You and you," he said, pointing to the tallest and strongest of those with only light injuries, "follow me. Before the tide rises we must take out of the ship as much as we can to lighten the vessel. Once the storm eases, we'll wait for the tide to turn until it is high enough to move the ship off the sands, yet low enough for the horse to stay on her feet and help us dragging the *knorr* afloat."

By mid-day the wind was down though the surf was still running high. They rested in the shelter of the sand dunes among their scattered possessions waiting for the tide to rise. Ivar lay curled up in the sand, his splinted arm supported by a sling.

Thora broke off a branch from a washed up tree and took it to the *skraeling* who was lying on his side with his good leg folded underneath him and his bad one stretched out at an awkward angle. Gorm hovered over him frowning at the injured leg. Thora kneeled beside him.

"It looks worse than before."

She looked closely at Elkimu's face; his bronzed skin seemed paler than she remembered. She dipped a rag in seawater and washed out the wound as well as she could.

"Do go ahead," Gorm said, after she finished tending the wound.

"Ask him where we are."

Thora circled the stick in the air, eyebrows raised in unspoken question.

Elkimu glowered, refusing to take the stick.

Gorm left in disgust.

Thora took off the fresh bandages blood-soaked already, rinsed them out, squeezed them dry and put them back on.

"Better?"

She made a few more attempts to draw a response; Elkimu's stony eyes seemed to mellow; he reached for the stick, checked the sun for bearings and traced a narrow, oblong shape in the sand running northeast-southwest; at the eastern end was a hook-shaped tongue of land jutting into the sea. All around the drawing Elkimu dotted the sand with little sketches of fish — they were on an island.

Thora looked for someone to tell; she found everyone at rest, eyes closed, cradled in the sand. She turned away; later would be soon enough to share what she had learned.

Among the items salvaged from the ship were an iron cook pot, several watertight leather bags with drinking water and a few bundles of dried salmon and cod soaked with seawater.

Thora took her axe to a piece of driftwood to fashion more kindling and bigger sticks of firewood. Her knife and flint were still safely tucked inside her pouch, but the tinder was soaked and she put it aside. After a few failed attempts the kindling caught fire, and by the time the others stirred awake she had a blaze going.

Two lads from Greenland grabbed the salvaged cauldron, filled it with water and hung it from a sturdy driftwood tripod over the flames.

Thora dropped in chunks of salmon and cod and sat down to stir waiting for the soup to come to a boil. The lads, alone or in small groups, drifted off to explore the beach.

By the time the soup was boiling and ready to eat, there was no one around besides Ivar and a few others with broken bones. Thora received no response inspite of her calls down the beach where she could see the others in the distance. At last a few of them waved their arms and came running toward her.

Atli and Hrut were first to arrive and collapse on the sand. Atli said between gasps, "We found a whale!...the gods are smiling on us ...there's a young sei whale... on the beach... freshly dead ...no flies."

They scrambled back to their feet, grabbed some salvaged rope to lash their knives to pieces of driftwood for flensing tools and jogged down the beach back to the whale. Soon the others came back as well looking for rope to turn their knives into tools to cut whale blubber.

Thora looked at the bubbling cauldron; even those too weak to help with the whale butchery would not eat of her fish soup, preferring to wait till they could have their fill of whale stew. Already some were returning with slabs of whitish pink blubber and purplish blood-dripping flesh which needed to be cut into smaller chunks to fit into the pot.

"Wait just a little till I've had my soup," Thora said. "Whale meat isn't for me."

Not fond of stringy whale meat, she quickly filled two bowls with fish soup — one for herself, and the other for Elkimu — before she surrendered the pot and her place by the fire to the men eager to boil up their oily brew.

THIRTY

Shortly afterwards they found a beached whale and
flocked to the site to carve it up...The cooks boiled the
meat and they ate it, but it made everyone ill.

ISLENDINGA SAGA

.....brother Leif beat one of Steinn's men to
death with a rib of the whale.

The following verse was composed on these doings:

'Hard were the blows which were dealt at Rifsker;
no weapons they had but steaks of the whale.
They belaboured each other with rotten blubber.
Unseemly methinks is such warfare for men.'

KORMAC'S SAGA

After all had their fill of the stew, the men curled up to rest in sandy hollows between patches of dune grass. Khagan, drowsy after gorging on whale meat, lay sprawled among them.

Thora wondered how the horses were faring. They had wandered out of sight behind the dunes, picking there way through the tough grass nibbling a mouthful here and another one there.

She climbed the first row of dunes – no horses. From here she could see far and she took her time looking in all directions. An unbroken row of dunes stretched to the South to what seemed to be open sea judging by the paler sky which could be the reflection of water touched by sunshine; on the opposite side to the North the dunes ran on a little while until they reached the sea; to the East was a low lying lagoon and beyond it low hills and more shimmering sea. *Elkimu told the truth.* They had washed up on an island, one of some size but an island nevertheless.

She went down the first row of dunes and climbed up on the next – still no horses; only one more row left to go before the land sloped down to the large, marshy lagoon. No horses here either; but there were plenty of hoof tracks, all of them leading south along the lagoon. How far had they strayed? To a foraging horse the lagoon's salty cordgrass must seem way more inviting than the tough marram grasses growing in the sand dunes.

Thora peered across the lagoon, not sure what she was seeing there out on the water in the far distance — something flashing to and fro in sunshine, tilting like…oars. Her heart was hammering. Those had to be oars, dozens of oars flashing in the sunlight way to the South.

She rushed back to the beach and found the others all slumped in the sand, green-faced, moaning and retching, clutching their stomachs. With an effort of will Ragnar climbed to his feet.

"The whale be cursed! Must've been dead a good long time….no flies huh? …storm swept 'em away I gather!"

Elkimu seemed to be resting comfortably away from the others with his eyes closed and no vomit nearby. *Why's he not sick?* Maybe he only ate the fish stew she brought him and none of the boiled whale.

She turned to Ivar, shaking him by his uninjured shoulder.

"Ivar Ulfson, husband, wake up!"

He opened his eyes.

"There's a lagoon behind those dunes and out on the water are many people in small boats. They're a long way off yet and they don't seem to be headed toward us, but we should be prepared in case they come here."

Glassy-eyed Ivar looked to the empty sea.

"What water? Lagoon? Can you talk sense, woman?"

Thora pointed inland.

"Other way.... Behind the sand dunes," she repeated, "is a lagoon filled with brackish water... by the looks of the grasses that grow there. Far out on the water there are people in boats and we're in no shape to do battle. I think we should leave rather than wait for the tide to rise further. With luck and some effort we might be able to rock the ship off the sands."

Twice more she repeated her warning before Ivar appeared to be listening. He dragged himself on his knees first to Ragnar, then Gorm. The four of them rallied the others until all were gathered at the water-line. The tide had turned and waves were washing over the sandbanks; unsteadily, the men splashed their way to the ship. Maelstrom Tamer lay keeled over to starboard resembling a beached whale. Though still lodged in the sand, she shifted a little with each new wave.

Ragnar said, "The tide rises fast; it won't be much longer. Where are the horses? With the help of that mare we could have the ship afloat in no time."

Ivar scowled; he turned to Thora.

"I gather you couldn't find the beasts. Your horses aren't even here when we need them; I wish we had feasted on horse roast rather than leave them for a bunch of cursed *skraelings* to eat"

Maelstrom Tamer seemed eager enough to straighten up without the help of a horse. Between bouts of retching the men bumped the ship across the sand, inch by inch, into deeper water until she came afloat. They left her secured with two anchors and hurried back to the beach to gather up their belongings.

Ivar sank to his knees. "I need to rest for a moment," he said, clutching his arm. The others flopped down in the sand as well. Ivar pointed to Gorm, still on his feet...

"You, get up on those dunes and keep an eye out for boats full of *skraelings*. With some luck we'll have everything loaded and ourselves safely aboard before they're here...everyone who feels strong enough had better start carrying things onboard."

Thora whirled around to face Ivar.

"We can't forget about the horses!"

Ivar didn't respond.

Thora raised her voice.

"We can't leave without them! I'll go find the horses while you go on loading and row out to sea if you must; out there it's safe to anchor and wait for me."

Ivar opened his eyes.

"We'll leave when we're ready to go," he said matter of factly. "I intend to leave this wretched place as soon as we can."

"But..." Thora fell silent.

"And I'm in no mood for arguments," Ivar added. "I won't have men killed to salvage a pair of useless beasts."

Thora took a deep breath, persisting, "Those boats aren't likely to be here for a while, if at all; I'll have enough time to find the horses and bring them back."

Ragnar interfered.

"Your husband is right," he said putting a heavy hand on Thora's arm.

"We can't risk men's lives for the sake of horses. When the ship is fully loaded and afloat, it'll be time to leave."

Ivar smirked.

"That won't take long, I assure you. Men grow wings when enemies are near."

"A woman and a pair of horses can also grow wings, you'll see," Thora said with more confidence than she felt. She rummaged in the wet contents of her sea chest, less damaged than the others sitting helter skelter on the beach spilling weapons and tools on the sand.

Ragnar called out, "I'll come with you... but you must promise to return with me to the ship when I say so."

Thora regarded his ashen face.

"Thank you, dear friend, but you look like the ghost of a dead man left unburied."

She put on her old, ragged cloak wrung out and nearly dry, took out her bow and quiver as well as the long rope of braided horsehair. Khagan, the only one not to fall ill after gorging on whale meat, came bouncing at her call.

Thora jogged across the dunes and turned south along the green-fringed lagoon following the double line of hoof tracks. From time to time she surveyed the water, relieved she could no longer see vessels anywhere. Perhaps they had pulled out at the opposite shore.

There was no sign of the horses either. Thora scanned the empty land. Left to themselves, the mare and her foal would be doomed. If the past winter by the fjord was anything to go by, no horse in this land of deep snows would survive without help to see the next spring. She took a deep breath and hurried to catch up with Khagan who was following scent with his nose to the ground, moving at a relentless ground covering trot.

Out of breath, Thora slowed down. She looked to the sun, large, fiery red, suspended low in the sky; the day was growing old, and the size of their shadows, woman's and dog's, had doubled since they set out. The *knorr*, fully loaded, would be anchored well away from the shore, her deck crowded with men keeping a lookout and wondering what had become of her.

The horses appeared to have trekked south along the lagoon without detours, hugging the shore till they rounded the end and continued north along the opposite shore until, abruptly, they had veered inland winding their way between bushes and trees. Thora watched Khagan; he had halted and was testing the air; she looped her rope around his neck.

"Don't run out on me. Seek, seek the horses."

The dog pulled toward a row of eroded red hills topped with dark-needled spruce like trolls wearing winter hats. They went up a small but steep ridge and Thora halted to scan the narrow strip of land in front of her, and behind it, the sea. Here on the other side, the coast was made up of green hills instead of sand dunes, and ending in cliffs of red sandstone looming over a narrow beach. In places where breaks in the cliff allowed the evening sunshine to touch the beach, its red sand glowed brightly as if painted with blood.

Thora looked to the grassy hills dotted with scattered spruce stands – horse country; no wonder her horses had found it...but where were they hiding?

The dog tugged on the leash, ready to barrel down the boulder-strewn slope. Thora slipped the rope off his neck.

"Go on then, kill yourself if you must."

She picked her way downhill slowly winding between sandstone boulders. This was no time to sprain an ankle.

Down below she discovered what Khagan had known all this time – a pair of horses, one large and one small, looking up at her from their lush pasture near the edge of a cliff.

Thora forgot all caution; she rushed down the hill and buried her face in Fluga's matted mane, savouring the warmth trapped between mane and furry neck and inhaling the horse's sweet scent; though not for long – they had no time to spare.

She took the rope, tied a slip-knot around the mare's lower jaw, hurriedly wiped the horse's sand-covered back – both horses seemed to have had a good roll in the sand — and swung up on the horse, tapping her flanks.

"Go mare, fly."

They came out of the hills at a flying pace, racing against time. On the flats by the lagoon, Thora pushed the horse into a gallop along the grassy shore all the way north and around the end of the lagoon back south; the filly ran along close by the side of her dam like a very large clinging burr. At the place where she had come across the sand dunes to begin her quest for the horses, she guided the mare back through the dunes halting on top of the last one to survey the beach while the horses were catching their breath.

The tide was pulling out once again and the beach stretched wide, glowing in the last rays of sunshine. The sea rippled gently in the still evening air, its surface empty as far as her eyes could see.

Thora breathed with quick, shallow gasps searching for the anchored ship in the approaching twilight – sea and beach lay before her seemingly empty of life; nothing moved on the water to disturb the glowing surface.

She slumped over on the horse's neck and closed her eyes, fighting down panic. She straightened up and opened her eyes. *Perhaps this isn't the place, not where we crossed through the dunes to begin with.*

But she could see the remains of her cook fire, now high above the tideline and beside it were the pieces of someone's sea chest smashed to splinters. There was nothing left on the beach besides ashes and bits of charred wood — every man and every salvaged thing was gone; even her own sea chest was no longer there.

Up here, on the back of a horse perched on top of a dune, she should be able to see the tall-masted *knorr* out at sea. Her gaze, sweeping across the evening-still water, met with nothing to dwell on except for a raft of seaducks settling in for the night.

In a daze Thora heeled the horse down to the beach and along the tide line, examining the sand. There were marks of a scuffle in the sand around the fire place; she dismounted to sort through rotting seaweed kicked up by hasty feet, revealing pieces of worked wood freshly broken and remainders of a splintered wooden shield, its round shape and iron braces indicating a Norse origin. Thora stared at the smashed wood and churned sand – scant traces left by the people she had lived with for so long; tonight they would all be washed away by the tide.

The sand told a tale of many feet scrambling in panic...a surprise attack, perhaps resulting in bloodshed; confusion and panic had prompted one Norseman to toss away his splintered shield.

Thora looked again to the sea trying to convince herself they were still out there somewhere, too far to be seen, waiting to return for her by daylight. Ivar would have no qualms leaving her behind but she trusted the others would overrule him...unless...*they're all too sick, or injured, to argue.*

For now she must face the truth – there was no ship waiting out there to take her and Khagan and the horses back on board.

The mare was growing impatient and fidgety. Gulls circled overhead — *why so many?*... all seemed focused on a certain place behind the first row of sand dunes, casting sideways stares at the woman and the horses on the beach and sparing an occasional glance for the dog poking around in the marram grass halfway up the first dune.

The horses faced with flaring nostril into the evening breeze from the land which carried the sweet scent of marsh grass. Thora had also turned her back to the sea, closing out the great emptiness; she let her gaze and her mind roam inland, determined to think only of tasks at hand banishing all other thoughts. She untied Fluga's jaw rope and hobbled the horse's left hind.

"No more roaming for you, my friend."

She paused to look at the footsteps leading in and out of the dunes, and at the gulls banking back and forth behind the first dune ridge. She looked to Khagan, rigid as a wood carving, pointing to the place circled by gulls. Suddenly he bounced away, up and over the first dune. Thora followed, wary of what she might find.

She halted on top of the dune between clumps of marram grass, staring at the ground; someone, right in front of her feet, had emptied his bowels in the sand; there was a trail of blood leading away, a thin line of crimson spatters clinging to the marram's leathery leaf spears. The dog stood halfway up the next dune, baying without pause.

Thora moved on, pushing her feet through the sand and trying to turn her mind away from the pictures whirling inside her head – her Norse friends retreating to the ship fending off a horde of attackers coming out of the sand dunes. Did every last Norseman make it to safety? Whose blood was this, spilled all over the grass?

The dog was waiting for her in the hollow between two dunes. He gave her a quick glance and a woof before he lowered his head to touch something he found in the sand. Thora took a slow step, and another, craning her neck — something dark was lying on top of the sand, an elongated shape not moving; *a log,* she tried to convince herself although she already knew the truth; here was a man lying in the sand, and he was dead.

She lunged forward, grabbed Khagan's collar and jerked him aside before he could lick the blood-soaked head of Kari Steggison; Kari, the boy from Brattalid who joined the Westland venture last summer against the will of his mother, Ragnhild, one of Thjodhild's dairy maids.

THIRTY ONE

Thorgrim ....said, 'It is a custom to tie Hel-shoes to a dead man that he may wear them on his journey to Valhalla, and I will do that for Vestein.'

GISLI SURSSON's SAGA

Oblivious to the chilly wind blowing up at sundown, Thora stared at Kari Steggison's lifeless body. The boy lay flat on his back, naked except for a thin cover of windblown sand; he faced the sky with empty eye-sockets – the gulls had seen to that.

A string of memories surged through Thora's mind – Kari, teased by the older men, squirming with embarrassment, looking away to hide the flush on his beardless face. Eager to prove his valour, the boy had insisted on further exploring the new land with Ivar rather than boarding Aegir's Pride to sail back to his mother in Greenland.

Did the others escape? Were any taken captive? Why must it be Kari who met his end here?

The boy, surely, had seemed no more unlucky than other young lads. And yet, some cloud of ill luck must have followed young Kari across the sea, stalking, waiting, catching up in these remote dunes to pounce on him. Perhaps Kari, or his mother, had failed to honour some god or goddess; some immortal could have whispered to the Norns that Kari Steggison had to die before he could become a man.

She tried to unravel how it happened. Perhaps the boy had left the others and entered the dunes to relieve himself, unaware of stalking enemies.

Thora kneeled in the sand to examine the body, throat slashed, skull shattered, blond curly hair sticky with blood and soiled with sand and brain matter. Someone seemed to have cut his throat from behind and the boy had stumbled a few more steps before they finished him off with a club to the back of his head, stripped the body and kicked it into the hollow below.

His killers had taken his clothes, knife, iron arm-ring and even his shoes.

Thora, trying to keep her teeth from clattering, looked up to scan the dunes; perhaps the enemy was still here and watching. She looked to Khagan, but the dog looked around calmly showing no signs of alarm.

Determined to pull herself together, Thora made up her mind. It would be wrong to leave the body lying here exposed to scavengers with or without wings. Kari's spirit wouldn't be able to move on if she failed to bury the lad; he needed to leave Midgard, the world of people, properly before descending to Hela where dead people received their judgment.

And what would be the outcome of Kari's judgment? Clearly, he had been struck from behind...something which could be held against him. Any man failing to meet the enemy face to face would be considered unworthy, forbidden to enter Valhal in Asgard. Then again, Kari was still beardless; one so young ought not to be judged the same as a full-grown man.

Khagan helped to excavate the grave, clawing sand back and using powerful kicks to clear it away.

They made a long row of closely spaced holes in the sand; next they removed the sand between the holes to create a trench both long and wide enough to receive the youth's slender body. Instead of the usual pebbles to cover the eyes, Thora chose two flat stones large enough to cover the body's gaping eye-sockets; she cut some good-luck runes into a strip of bark torn from a bush, rolled it up tightly and wedged it under the boy's swollen tongue. The runes would enable him to speak with eloquence when questioned at his judgment.

She rolled the body into the trench, pausing to catch her breath and trying to think of anything else she could do for Kari's sake. *Of course!* She took her hunting knife — large and awkward for the purpose — and pared the nails of his fingers and toes; any dead arriving with un-pared nails would be counted among the wicked and whipped with thorny switches aboard the sinister ship, *Naglefar*, to be carried off to the realm of doom.

She caught sight of Kari's bare feet sticking out of the sand and remembered that a man needed Hel-shoes to make his way to Valhal; with no shoes to spare, she decided to wrap his feet with dune grass, the closest she could think of to take the place of proper Hel-shoes.

There was nothing more she could do to secure a happy afterlife for Kari Steggison.

Thora piled up more sand and a few stones on top of the grave to protect the boy's remains from scavengers. Stones were not numerous on the beach, but clam shells as large as her hand were plentiful; by the time she had gathered and piled up enough shells to protect Kari's remains against greedy beaks, claws and jaws, the sun had slipped over the edge of the world.

She climbed to the top of a tall dune facing the sea and called on the maids of Urd that they might carry the boy to Valhal.

"It's true that Kari Steggison was slain from behind…still, he died a brave warrior and does not deserve to be drowned in the pool of foulness. Kari Steggison would have faced his enemies with courage if only these *skraelings* had been honourable fighters who attacked him head-on. It can happen to anyone to be ambushed from behind and dealt an inglorious death."

Surely, the gods would see reason.

Eager to move away from this place of bloodshed, Thora hurried back to the horses still not fully convinced that Maelstrom Tamer wouldn't return. Granted, the crew had been too few in number to win a battle against dozens of water-born warriors sneaking up from the lagoon, and once aboard ship, Ivar would have argued against a return to the beach for her sake. She could almost hear his voice. *I will not return to that unlucky beach risking my ship and all of our lives for the sake of my wilful wife.*

But there were others onboard who did not share Ivar's feelings, enough of them surely to make Ivar see reason.

And Elkimu? What had happened to him? Did Gorm succeed to hold on to his captive in the midst of confusion and take him back to the ship? Or could Elkimu in spite of his bad leg, have made his escape in the scuffle? Did he know these warriors? Were they his people perhaps?

Common sense told her to find a safer place for the night than here on the beach. In the deepening dusk she could still make out tracks of men moving single file across the dunes to the lagoon; she continued south along the lagoon, cautiously, to find where these tracks would lead. Perhaps the *skraelings* were camped on this side of the lagoon, or perhaps with luck, they had crossed the water at some point to camp on the opposite shore where they seemed to be coming from when she first saw them; in that case she could spend the night on this shore in relative safety.

She traveled slowly, relying on the mare and the dog to warn her of enemies. The dog...but where was he?

She gave a soft whistle, fearful to draw unwanted attention. Immediately a woofed response came from across the sand dunes. Had the dog gone back to the beach? Thora hobbled the horses and crept through the dunes toward the sea side. Before she went far enough to see the beach, her nose told her what was going on. She walked to the dunetop and looked down at Khagan, greyish white in the fading twilight, gorging on the putrified remains of the sei whale.

Thora whistled her two-toned signal to call him. The dog looked up, tore away one more time at the whale and came trotting up oblivious of the reek he brought with him; Thora told him to stay behind the horses rather than run ahead of them, and her.

The tracks of many feet along the lagoon ended abruptly in a patch of wet loamy sand gouged by drag marks — evidence of boats, a dozen or so, hauled ashore and dragged back into the water.

For now it appeared safe enough for her to explore the base of the dunes for a source of drinking water. Thora searched in vain until dark for a freshwater pond or even a trickle to relieve her and her animals' thirst. She gave up for now; it was time to find a place to sleep and continue her search tomorrow. She turned the mare out to graze, hobbled this time to prevent further wandering.

Thora collapsed on the sand, exhausted, almost nauseous with thirst. Too tired to stop the dog from excavating a sleeping spot behind her back showering sand on her, she allowed him, reeking breath and all, to snuggle against her back.

"Lie still. And do not burp!"

She was tickled awake by the full moon suspended low in the sky like a golden fruit of the Southlands; confused, it took her a moment to recall where she was. She looked over the shimmering lagoon across to the low hills on the other side, dark folds edged by moonlight. Khagan lay stretched out flat, snoring softly, occasionally kicking his legs and yelping in his dreams.

Thora sat up savouring the night air, oblivious to the mosquitoes drifting in on the gentle breeze from the salt-marsh. Small bats flitted by, barely visible against the dark velvet sky. There were shrieks and whistles of rodents and night birds in the sand dunes, and once the call of a small owl.

She shivered, recalling the owl magic of the *skraelings* who captured Eidyll. Was he still alive, Eidyll, her *thrall* of many skills? How easy it was in this world to lose someone, and easier yet to be lost oneself.

*   *   *   *   *

The next time she woke up Thora blinked at the night sky splashed with stars. The moon, suspended high above her head by now, had changed colour from warm gold to frigid silver and Thora shivered under the cold white stare of the round unearthly eye. Strange to think that somewhere in the familiar world across the water, life as she knew it continued much as it had for the people she used to know and had liked, or disliked. Life carried on without her for men like Ragnar and his nephews, quiet, confident, considerate, and for unsavoury men such as Ivar and others of his ilk, and for the women slaves who, some at least, would have taken to loafing off now that she wasn't there to set them straight.

She wondered about the fate of Eidyll; could he still be alive somewhere in this vast land? She wished he could have found Greater Ireland before the sorcerers captured him. For all she knew, her lost slave might be awake tonight looking up to this same sky and hearing these same sounds, the cries of night-hunting birds, the twitter of bats… wondering as she did about all things stalking, creeping and slithering in the shadows.

Thora was fighting her tears. Here she was, stranded without friends on a speck of land washed by the sea and infested with hostile *skraelings*. Only a woman cursed with exceedingly bad luck would find herself in such straits…and to think of all the offerings she had made to the gods in the not so distant past!

THIRTY TWO

_____

_____

There was a woman, long, long ago
.......When she walked among the dry leaves
Her feet were so covered
The feet were invisible
She walked through the woods,
Singing all the time,
"I want company; I'm lonesome!"

ANONYMOUS MIK'MAH WOMAN, 1880's *)

*) from The Old Man Told Us, by Ruth Holmes
Whitehead, publ. Nimbus Ltd., Halifax

_____

_____

The tears had run their course; clear-eyed, Thora looked up to the night sky picturing Maelstrom Tamer caught in moonlight, cradled on the swells of a silvered sea. Men lay asleep surrounded by the *knorr's* fragile timbers, sore, exhausted, unable to revel in the splendor of the night sky. She sighed at the thought of the familiar ship out at sea, or perhaps back already in the fjord they had left only yesterday... it seemed much longer.

She called to mind another ship, Aegir's Pride, carrying the men and women who had put their trust in Sigurd to return them home safely. By now they might be approaching Greenland, closing in on Eirik's Fjord with some luck. Aboard the ship would be people looking forward to seeing friends and family in Greenland, and others eager to sail on and be re-united with people and places in Iceland or even beyond.

Had she ever felt this lonely before? Or felt such a deep a sense of dread? The thought of roaming around this island, fearful of meeting hostile *skraelings*, with no one to share her worries, relief and occasional laughter, was terrifying.

Who could bear such a life? Men and women, without the company of others, tended to lose their reason and once the mind fell apart, shattered into meaningless fragments, nothing could piece the shards back together. It had happened to Narfi, the young son of Thorvinn's bed woman, Gudfinna. Almost from birth the boy had wandered inside his own head, around and around in a world of unreason. Narfi, the Unkempt, went about blabbering without sense and one day he disappeared and was never seen again. Some said he had stepped off a cliff. Others thought he must have slipped into a rock crevice and turned into a troll.

Thora wrapped her cloak tighter and rolled over against the snoring dog; Khagan stirred and stopped snoring.

*　　*　　*　　*　　*

Shortly before dawn Thora woke up once again, stiff, cold, with a parched mouth, and not at all pleased to find that Khagan had deserted her. She had counted on the dog's sense of smell, hearing and eyesight to keep her safe through the night. He might have gone off to find something to eat or drink. If she followed his tracks he might lead her to water.

The mare was antsy, refusing to stand still and wait to have her hobbles undone. Thora yelled at the horse and yanked the strap. They were all the same, dogs, horses, and men to come to think of, most of them, always thinking of food. What kind of guardian dog hungry or not, left his charges unprotected?

She couldn't make sense of the dog tracks which didn't seem to lead in any particular direction, winding in and out of the dunes; she might as well return to the beached whale and see if the dog had gone there for his breakfast. Perhaps she would find drinking water on the way down.

The mare didn't need prodding to slip into an easy canter egged on by the rambunctious filly who was leading the way bucking and snorting.

Thora's mood lifted. Arvak would grow up to be a splendid, spirited horse. The filly's antics brought tears to her eyes, first of joy, then of sadness. Caught on this island where horses weren't likely to live through the winter without forage or hay, the filly would never grow up to become the horse she could be. And if by some stroke of luck the horses survived this winter and maybe more, where would she be herself? *Will I be alive and able to see and enjoy?*

On top of the last dune she pulled the mare up and sat squinting against the morning light trying to find the dog. She rubbed her eyes. Her eyesight seemed to carry no farther than the reach of her arrows these days — not far enough to determine whether the distant white splotch between dunes and dead whale was a dog or a gull. She narrowed her eyes; too large for a gull and possessed of four legs, the white spot had to be Khagan, but what was the thing, dark and not moving, beside him? Again Thora rubbed her eyes. The dog seemed to be sniffing the dark thing; it seemed quite large — a seal perhaps. Or, a dead man... another corpse that needed to be buried?

She blinked. The thing in the sand seemed to stir – it must be a seal! No, it couldn't be. A seal would raise its head and flash its teeth at the dog.

Incredulous, Thora watched the shape taking form — the form of a man, unmistakably, a man sitting up on the sand waving his arms.

He cannot get up because of his leg!

Elkimu! She kicked the horse into a gallop, barreling down the dune like a crazed woman, screaming at the top of her voice, "Elkimuuuu!"

Thora slid off the horse and fell to her knees, speechless, staring into his glittering eyes, reveling in the presence of somebody else — someone alive.

His face contorted with pain, and she looked at his swollen leg stretched out on the sand giving off a cloying stench. She tried to make sense of Elkimu's presence, now, in this place.

Ivar and the others must have fled in a great hurry or they wouldn't have left the captive behind. And how could the *skraelings* have overlooked a wounded man lying on the beach? Did they think he was dead?

Lost for answers Thora gazed at the sea, empty beyond the white-crested surf as before. There were no sea ducks or gulls out on the water today, and no plovers or gulls on the beach; a relentless wind chased a rustling ribbon of sand along the base of the dunes.

And yet, the world so bleak and forlorn this morning, now seemed a smiling place full of promise; she was after all not alone in this place; they were two now, a man and a woman marooned on a patch of land lost in an unfamiliar sea, for ever perhaps; whatever terrors or delights awaited them in this place, they would face them together.

The gods had kept their side of the bargain and the further outcome depended on her, on her efforts to nurse this man back to health.

THIRTY THREE

For sorrow my brows drooped over my eyelids
Now I have found one who smoothed
the wrinkles on my forehead

EGIL's SAGA

A dizzying multitude of questions churned inside her head. Thora decided for now to ignore them all. She examined Elkimu's injured leg — swollen worse than she remembered.

She sat back to think. The wound had gone foul. If allowed to keep festering it could lead to his death. On this dry and sandy coast she couldn't expect to find the moss Halla had shown her, the moss that was able to draw out foulness from a wound. There had to be something she could do, something to reverse the poison waiting to spread from Elkimu's injured leg to the whole of his body. If only she had someone at hand to ask for advice. If only the two of them had enough words in common to discuss what to do next.

They faced each other in silence, each trying to read the other's thoughts.

Thora felt close to tears; in his eyes she saw the mirror image of her own desire to speak and be understood. She felt sure that they could, given time, improve their skill in using gestures but it would take effort and time, and for now they must resign themselves to the barest of mutual understanding.

Like an impatient colt Elkimu shook his long hair, unkempt and no longer braided; he asked in gestures that she hand him a stick washed up in the seaweed, and drew the outline of an island in the sand with a sprawling lagoon running north-south. He used parallel scratches to indicate the sea around it, adding for good measure little sketches of fish in the sea. Next he traced the shape of a *knorr* beached by the shore, and not far from it on the beach he pictured a large fish with a small, lacklustre spout over its head – *whale soon to be dead.*

"Elkimu," he said, pointing to himself. "Elkimu, here!"

He planted the stick in the belly of the whale sketch.

Incredulous, Thora searched his face.

Did he mean to tell her that he remained hidden inside the whale? Had he been there the whole time during the skirmish and afterwards, waiting for Norsemen as well as *skraelings* to leave? Was that why the dog had run off to the whale yesterday, and again this morning? Khagan had been thinking of more than an easy meal it turned out, and she had failed to understand what he tried to tell her.

And what of this foul odour? It might have more to do with the whale than with the injured leg; still, wouldn't a man who spent all night inside a rotting carcass, be covered in slime and filth? Perhaps he had dragged himself to the sea for a wash. *So many questions, and no way of finding the answers.*

Perhaps...

She dismissed the thought as quickly as it surfaced.

How foolish to think that he chose to stay hidden from Norsemen and *skraelings* alike for no other reason than to wait for her return; the thought was...well, laughable.

She bent down for a fresh look at the injured leg. The wounds in his thigh had almost healed, but the cuts in his lower legs were surrounded by angry looking red skin; they had been close to the bone and both appeared to be festering, oozing yellow puss.

Thora rested her head on her knees. *Elkimu needs the help of a skilled healer.*

What, if anything, did she know about curing wounds? The maiden Norns were playing a wicked joke on them placing two people unable to talk together, on a deserted beach — one of them slowly dying of a festering wound and the other without adequate knowledge of healing craft. Why had she not when she could, spent more time with the lady Thjodhild? Jarl Eirik's wife had seemed eager enough to share her knowledge of herbs and healing with anyone wanting to learn.

Thora sat up straight shaking her head vigorously to banish the image of Elkimu dead in the sand like Kari Steggison, and of herself and Khagan side by side scooping out sand at the foot of the dunes for Elkimu's grave.

No! She decided. *He will not die!*

She needed him to live, to be her companion, to keep her from losing her mind.

If Elkimu died and left her alone on this island, her own will to live would die with him.

She lifted his injured leg ignoring his grimace of pain, placed it into her lap, and un-wrapped the dirty rag which served as a bandage.

A good wash in salt water might turn the infection around. A good wash and nothing else had been enough long ago, to cure a deep wound on Fluga's left fore after a sharp rock cut the mare's cannon right up to the bone sheath.

Same injury, same part of leg — man or horse, how different could they be?

She washed the dirty bandage in sea water, squeezed it as dry as she could and put it back the same way she did with the injured horse. She tightened the knot and gently rested the leg on a pillow of pushed up sand.

She needed to find drinking water without further delay.

"I have to leave you for a while."

She brought an imaginary cup to her mouth and swallowed.

"I must find drinking water."

Mounted on the horse and ready to leave, she turned for a last look at Elkimu and the sea, scanning one more time for the mast of a ship and frowning in sudden alarm at a new unsettling thought.

What if after all this time the *knorr* did return and found Elkimu here? What if Ivar persuaded Gorm to give up his claim to the captive by offering some valuable gift in return, perhaps the cloak of fisher fur on which Gorm seemed to have his heart set? The *karl* would be happy enough to exchange his prized though irksome captive for another prize, one that couldn't run away and didn't need to be fed or protected from further injury. And vengeful Ivar would pay any price for the pleasure of dispatching the hated captive, taking his time to think up the worst death imaginable for the *skraeling* he so despised.

Thora slid off the horse. Water to drink, desperately needed, had to wait once again. First they must move away from the sea and find a safe place to hide from *skraelings*, and Norsemen both.

"We have to get away from the beach."

She took off her tunic and laid it out on the beach; if she cut off the lower part and cut it lengthwise once more, the strap would be long enough to make a sling for Elkimu's leg; once mounted she would attach the sling to the horse's neck for support.

Thora frowned in surprise, her hand with the knife suspended over the tunic which seemed to be covered with dried blood; *of course;* she looked to the horses noting the red smears on the mare's flanks after yesterday's sand bath — the same red as the ointment slathered on the skin of the tall reindeer man.

She smiled and put her knife to the dirty red cloth.

"You, wicked horse, how dare you use me and my tunic for a rubbing post?"

Elkimu stared at her with questioning eyes.

She pointed from him to the horse, indicating with arm gestures, *Up, up on the horse's back.*

"Leave it to me," she said. "You don't have to walk…we'll get you up there for an easy ride."

Elkimu looked back and forth between her and the horse with wide-open eyes filled with disbelief.

"What?" she asked. "What's the matter? Think we can't get you up on the mare's back?"

She pulled him up on his one good leg. He leaned heavily on her shoulder, pushing himself away from the horse's flank.

Exasperated, Thora urged, "Come on now; why are you making this so hard for us both?"

She laughed.

"The horse doesn't bite, I assure you!"

With her hands around the knee of his good leg, ignoring his groans, she heaved him up on Fluga's back. He slumped forward, biting his lips; Thora tied the points of the sling around he mare's neck and lead the way up through the dunes and along the lagoon at a slow walk toward the dark hills beckoning in the South.

She marched on briskly, glowing with hope and trusting they would find safety and shelter in those hills cloaked in needle trees; already she could see the spiked tops of spruce trees promising a place to hide as well as find shelter. Secured against enemies and winter weather, Elkimu stood a chance to get well; but to make that happen, it was crucial that she keep her mind clear and quick, and never allow herself to let her thoughts go astray like Narfi's.

She laughed aloud.

The maidens of fate in their whimsical way had relieved her of the husband she despised. To be abandoned might turn out not to be bad luck at all. She now had a chance, in a way she had never expected, to settle on a man of her own choice.

Struck by a sudden thought, she stopped the horse. *The red cloak!*

It was still in her sea chest, out of her reach before she had a chance to wear it.

Red colours, if the tall reindeer man covered in red body paste was anything to go by, seemed to be favoured in Westland as much as back home. Or could it be that the colour red was supposed to be worn only by the men of this land? Did Westlander men regard red colours not becoming for women? It would be the first question she wanted to ask Elkimu after they learned to talk with each other.

She turned around with a half smile, freshly embarrassed by the gap in her teeth. Elkimu smiled back at her, at ease on horseback at last.

Thora tugged on the leadrope facing the hills again.

"Come on mare, walk on, we have a way to go."

They walked on together with long confident strides, Fluga nickering at the foal and Thora humming a tune which Eidyll used to play on his flute.

LOOK FOR THE SEQUEL

Unamakik

CPSIA information can be obtained
at www.ICGtesting.com
Printed in the USA
LVHW030802211220
674731LV00001B/73

9 781460 233559